AN ETERNITY OF ROSES

THE VALTHREANS
BOOK ONE

NATALIE G. OWENS

ROSE OF ATLANTIS PRESS

COPYRIGHT

To Zee Monodee, my soul sister, the first to meet the Valthreans and root for them all the way.
This one's for you.

ABOUT THIS BOOK

Two lovers separated by an evil curse.
   A desperate quest through time.
   A love that wants to beat all odds.
   And all the while, deadly danger brews around a two-thousand-year-old
secret society and the enemy that lives to decimate it.

"...'Til the end of my life, I shall belong to you as your husband."

That was the promise Adrian made to Emmaline. And then, he was gone forever...

Adrian Segrave, Viscount Bournemouthe, and Lady Emmaline Deramore are about to wed on a much anticipated December day in 1807. But Madeleine de Brandeville, a mysterious Frenchwoman, has her lustful and ambitious sights on the groom. When she sets her cruel plan in motion, she leaves devastation in her path.

Heartbroken, Emmaline embarks on an adventure she'd never imagined having. As the world changes and chaos brews, her fate becomes linked with the Valthreans, a group of immortals who faces a deadly enemy that threatens their place in the human world. But all the while, there is one thing she wants more than any other: to have Adrian back.

When she finally finds her prize and the intense blue flame of desire burns once more, her worst nightmares are far from over and the toughest battle is yet to begin. Will love win in the end?

Indian mythology meets Highlander with Shakespearean twists. Paranormal Romance for fans of star-crossed lovers.

BE AN INSIDER!

Do you want to be the first to hear about Natalie's special events, campaigns, promotions, and new releases?
Go to:
(http://eepurl.com/povjf)

IN SILENCE

You left the lines blank for me, love
And again you ask why I wrote my plaint
When you are in front of me I am lost
In the beauty of your hair, your lips
In the gazelle eyes and the music
From the tongue that licks honey
When I open my mouth for my words
You place your finger on your lips
Enter the silence of my love else
I leave you in the oblivions vast

Like a flute from the reed in silence
Wail I long, as separated from beloved
You make my silence in colours float
When in the bloom of spring I enter
The garden where the nightingale sings
In silence, sitting by the rose
In silence, my love, I live in thee

From "Chaos of Being"

by
Sadiqullah Khan
Wana, South Waziristan, Pakistan
Author of
"The Voices"
A collection of poems

PROLOGUE

"We have scotch'd the snake, not kill'd it..."
[William Shakespeare, Macbeth, Act 3, Scene 2]

300 B.C.
  The Valley of the Sun, Kashmir, India.

He was a dead man.

Guilt, and the bitterness of shame, consumed him. His actions were punishable by death, his fate sealed; but because of him, the lives of his loved ones hung by a thread. For this, he deserved to die a thousand cruel deaths.

He should have listened to his blood brother, Nila, who had warned him this would happen. He should have stopped his selfish quest and left the Chalice where he had found it. Life would have gone on as normal. But obstinately, he had placed his thirst for knowledge above all else. What a thoughtless fool he had been!

Plagued by these remorseful thoughts, Valther crouched on his knees some distance from the foot of the seven steps that led to the Naga King Aravala's throne, his head bowed. He chanced a peek at the irate king through the light curtain of his silver blond hair. Aravala eyed him with disdain, before his gaze pithily scanned the congregation of people who had been summoned there to witness.

A dark cloud of terror hovered above Valther. Its evil shadow had him in a stranglehold. A few hundred pairs of eyes burned into his sides, back, and neck. He knew the hell that faced him, so he summoned the courage to shut out the emotion that crushed his heart.

And then, he prayed. He prayed the others would live, that his sacrifice would count for something.

As if he could read Valther's mind, the king's face darkened with rage. The regent held his imposing frame with confidence—much like the massive Chinar trees Valther loved for the cool shade they offered from branches laden with thousands of five-lobed brown leaves.

Surrounded by seven snake hoods embossed on the throne in an arch above his head, Aravala regarded him like a fearless tiger scoping a doomed bison. Ruthless to the core, his air of stolid savagery competed with that of the deadpan stone statues that flanked the entrance to his summer palace in the Valley of the Sun. Yet, Valther knew the king was no statue but a living, breathing, dangerous threat to anyone who dared cross him.

Aravala curled his talon-like fingers around the bullion edges of the massive chair arms and tapped them impatiently on the intricate carving. Valther kept still as a tense hum flittered through the assembly of cheerless Naga folk. A muffled cry carried across the room on the heavy air.

"You have forfeited your place of honor as Guardian of the Temple. Now, what have you to say for yourself?" the king said.

Valther tried to speak but all that came out was a strangled sound.

"You have betrayed me. Why? Do you wish to rule these people?" Aravala motioned to those standing there behind Valther.

"No!" Valther cried with the tone of a helpless child vehemently

2

denying his mischief to his parents but knowing that their harsh discipline was inevitable.

"The Nagas have shared their wisdom with the world. Now, our enemy Asoka is sending Majjhantika to destroy us, and you want to reap the rewards."

Word had reached the Naga camp that King Asoka, Aravala's sworn enemy and ruler of neighboring territories, conspired to destroy the rubric of Naga beliefs that had survived for centuries. Under his rule, the Cult of the Snake would be annihilated.

"That is not my intent, Sire. I studied the powers of the dragon lake and its surroundings only for our people."

He would never confess to treason. Many moons ago, when his travels brought him here, far from his birth home, the inhabitants of the village had welcomed him with jubilant affection and instilled in him the desire to stay and plant new roots. Nila and his younger brother, Candaka, both hungry to learn and hailing from a hard-working family of agrarians and fishermen, had shown him unconditional kindness and friendship. They made him one of their own.

"I should have known you would use the alchemical knowledge of our ancestors to advance your interests. You are not one of us and I should never have made you Guardian of the Temple."

Valther shook his head fiercely. "I could never betray the Nagas! They sheltered me, became my family and taught me about the valley. This is my home, my life," he said with anguish deeper than the waters of the Jhelum River.

At first sight of this land, blessed as it was with surrounding water and cradled in the bosom of high mountains, his breath had caught in his lungs. He loved this country, with its smiling, copper-skinned people, snow-capped mountains, dense forests, and wide open spaces. To walk amidst the spruce trees or through the yellow corn-fields by the river bank gave him a sense of peace and belonging. In this lush paradise, while observing the majestic wings of the Great Egret that soared freely in these skies, he would reflect on how kind his life had been to him. He had thrived here. His interest in the arcane and natural adeptness in the science of healing had given him the reputation of learned scholar and garnered him the revered position of Guardian of the Temple of the Sun. He had the utmost respect for his title. It meant he was doing what he loved in a place he called home.

But recently, things had taken a curious turn when he made a discovery in an unexplored cave some distance along the river—a group of mystical objects that, according to legend, would allow him to cross the threshold of the known world into a state of immortality. How could such blessing fall on him? Rather than simply pass the information to the king to do with as he wished, he had plainly defied authority.

The king glanced at the said article that had been put at Valther's feet—one of the legendary Cups of Life, the lost seven Chalices of the River Demon. Although sovereigns and peasants alike had sought for centuries to find this treasure, the secret to life eternal, it had until then proved elusive.

"Tell me about your pact with Jalodbhava," the king growled.

Jalodbhava, the water demon that dwelled inside the river, allowed humans to inhabit the Kashmir in return for their worship and respect. In the process, Naga kings were entrusted with the strength and privilege to rule under the demon's patronage. Aravala had thus received his powers and used them to reign with an iron fist. He could control the seasons and the weather, create hail storms and cause untold destruction among the crops. The land was his dominion and he decided who lived and who died.

Immortal himself, he had existed for thousands of years and would live for many more.

"I do not know what you speak of, Sire," Valther answered.

"You lie! You will not confess to being a traitor, then?"

"That, Sire, I am not."

"The legend speaks of seven cups, and you only have one. Where are the others?"

"I have carved this cup myself, that is all I know."

"More lies! Who else shares your power of immortality?"

Valther bit on his lip as pain knifed through his right side. Three days of torture had taken their toll but he did not speak then, and he would not speak now.

"You mock me with your insolence, *foreigner*."

Valther flinched. With that last dreaded word, Aravala had ruthlessly severed his connection to this community. Disowned him in front of everyone who listened.

"I only want to live in peace, Sire. My loyalty is with my people."

The king stood, his lips curled down in scorn. "If you speak of your *friends*, they are as dead as you."

Valther knew what that meant—mortal danger for those he held dear. He hoped Nila and Candaka had a good plan. His pact with them was that if the king captured him, they were to protect themselves and their relatives by leaving everything they'd ever known. With Aravala's oppressive ways, they could never be free. For it would be their death, too, if they failed to escape.

Dread crept under his skin. He took a deep breath and let his mind soar above the despair that gnawed at him, in the same way Nila's late father had once taught him to do when he was distressed or in pain. A form of meditation, with it he took himself to another plane of existence, a place where Aravala could do nothing to hurt him. The ability to control and redirect his mental energies had taken him through the last horrific days and given him the strength to face extreme physical pain.

He braced himself and gingerly got off his knees. Boldly forcing his broken body to stand up, he looked straight into the king's eyes—a sign of disrespect. His arm hung swollen and ached, his shoulders burned, but if one had to die, one might as well die with dignity and principle. The Nagas deserved no less from him.

Showing his rage at Valther's audacity, Aravala pointed his thick-nailed index finger at him. The large ruby ring that adorned it sparkled in its gold setting. "You have sealed your fate. You see, I *know* what can destroy you," he spat.

His narrowed gaze reached out colder than winter on the crests of the mountains that shielded the dale. "I am the Supreme King of the Nagas, lest you have forgotten that," the king derided. His laugh echoed throughout the hall with an ugly pitch. "And beware the snake. It shall be your downfall, *immortal*."

He turned his scouring gaze to the crowd. "If any of the prisoner's cohorts are present, know that the power of everlasting life is mine, and will be granted only to the loyal lieges of my choosing."

When Aravala's arm stretched out like the long branch of a tree, the ground started to quake. With horrifying speed, his hand metamorphosed into the expanding hood of a living, breathing cobra.

While the morphing limb glided toward him, Valther closed his eyes. A tear trailed down his cheek, a crack in his armor.

Be brave just a little longer, Valther. It will soon be over.

He tapped into his memories to beckon visions of the rambling fields in springtime when vibrant flowers burst forth in a carpet of color. He summoned the faces of those he loved to the forefront of his mind, and in the final moments, he even spared a thought for his faraway childhood home in the untamed glades and mountainous regions of Germania. His mind's eye acknowledged everything he had seen, learned, and done for one last time.

It should have been painful, but he was so engrossed in his fantasy that he barely felt the sting of the cobra fangs as they speared through the skin of his throat to inject into the pulsing vein. The poison worked swift and lethal... and if he had the strength to speak as he slipped to the floor and the night engulfed him, he would have remarked, with no little surprise, just how easy death could be.

———

FROM THE FAR end of the hall, Nila and Candaka watched helplessly as Aravala took their friend's—no, their brother's—life. They had risked their lives by showing up at the palace but they could not bring themselves to leave without seeing him one last time.

Nila turned to his younger brother as anger and grief threatened to choke him. "Aravala's men will be looking for us. We must leave and join the others in the cave by nightfall, before Asoka's men attack." He wished he could take every person in the village away but he was not sure who could be trusted. Some of these people feared the king, but they still admired him. He hoped his decision would not come to haunt him.

"What shall we tell everyone? What will happen now?" Candaka asked. His voice cracked at the second question.

Nila could tell by the stricken look in his eyes that his heart was breaking in tiny little pieces. "We shall tell them to be strong and prepare for the worst. It is our duty to help our families cross the gorges to the Arabian Sea and settle in a new land." He placed a hand on his brother's shoulder. "We have the remaining Cups of Life, and we know what to do. It is our fate, and we must fight for it. Our people have braved harsh challenges; they will brave this one, too. Are you with me?"

They would find new roots, create new lives, and most of all, they would honor the gift given to them by Valther. There could be no other way.

The usually light-hearted Candaka gave a somber nod. "Forever," he whispered.

Nila tightened his grip. "Forever," he echoed. "From this day forward, we will use this gift to protect our own from those who will do us harm."

He threw one last look at their despicable monarch and said, "The cobra is now our worst enemy," before he steered them both outside.

"Will we ever return home?"

"Mayhap one day is all I can say. But never forget, brother, home is in here," Nila replied, pointing to his brow, "and in here," he finished, placing a closed fist on his pounding heart.

PART I

Loss

CHAPTER 1

"Stars, hid your fires!
Let not light see my black and deep desires."
[Macbeth, Act I, Scene IV]

DECEMBER *15, 1807.*
  A darkened private parlor in the heart of a cold, country mansion...

"EVERYTHING IS ARRANGED ACCORDING to your instructions, my lady."

Lady Madeleine de Brandeville kept the door to her parlor barely ajar to discourage her butler's prying. "I trust you are right, Roth, or there'll be hell to pay for you. The least for intruding upon my privacy."

Everybody knew they weren't supposed to disturb her when she was in this room. Her mouth curled in vitriolic contempt as she pulled the door back and slammed it fast against the man's panicked expression and startled gasp. Before the wood clicked into place, the air woke the fiery red curls that had broken free from the loose knot at her nape, and made her skin tingle there.

A muted laugh escaped her lips. She liked to keep her staff on their toes, for fear was a most loyal servant. Whenever she addressed Roth —she only had to touch him with her immuring green gaze—his sallow cheeks paled to ghostly white and his withered, gangly frame shook like Norfolk reed in a windstorm. Yet, he chose to remain in her employ rather than be cast into the streets without a scrap of food, coin, or reference to his name. After all, who would want a former thief in their household?

She walked to the table and surveyed the objects laid on it. The crystal felt cool against her hand as she lifted the glass from the table to her mouth. Although one and the same, the rich liquor inside it seemed less dense than the fluid substance at the bottom of the large bowl she looked upon with reverence. It slid down her throat like liquid fire, quenched her thirst with its fiery strength—and the powers that lurked within.

At this late hour, she couldn't hear a sound. No echo of lowered voices. Not even the faintest creak of a door or distant footfall. With most of the servants gone, she wanted to relish the quiet before the storm, and finish her work without interruptions.

After she was done, she'd wait for the perfect chance to make her move. But first, she had to *see*, and to open the gate to her mind's eye she needed one more ingredient. The most crucial one.

After draining the glass to the last drop, she set it down and walked toward the squirming, moaning shape in a corner. A faint strip of light struggled through the sliver of space between the drawn curtains over the windows across the room and reached to the feminine form huddled on a chair. Enough for Madeline to see the raw terror in the pleading, innocent eyes that looked up at her—eyes so young they'd likely never seen the bounty of a man's body or the beautiful strain of his pleasure. The greater the innocence, the more intense the energy that would carry Madeleine's visions.

Her gaze glossed over the captive. The girl's breasts were already full and round, adding value to a fair face and hale skin. It wouldn't be long before she caught some stablehand's eye. This was the right time.

Bound and gagged, her captive let out a muffled scream as Madeleine stopped in front of her. She continued to struggle, attempting in vain to break free from the twisted rope that bit into the milky white flesh of her wrists. Then, when Madeleine drew the dagger from her skirt pocket and let it glint against the drift of light, the begging started.

They always begged, which made her long to silence them forever.

She remembered how once the guilt would make her hesitate. How their fear and agony tugged at her heart.

That was a long, long time ago ... when she still had a heart.

Madeleine ignored the whimpers. She pressed the sharp tip against the frantic pulse of the girl's neck, drawing a thin trickle of blood and a trail of desperate tears that slid to the blade.

"So, where were we?"

———

DECEMBER *21, 1807.*
Belvoir Hall, Annual Christmas Ball.

LADY EMMALINE DERAMORE swallowed hard and tried to calm her racing heart. She stood frozen in the crowded ballroom at Belvoir Hall—three days before her wedding to the dashing Adrian Segrave, Viscount Bournemouthe—feeling like a trapped fox. A powerful pang of unease stung the hairs on her nape and sliced through her lungs.

Something was dreadfully wrong. She darted her eyes around until they settled on the figure of a tall, breathtakingly beautiful woman with crimson hair and an emerald gown that matched her eyes and showcased ample cleavage. Her blood froze.

That woman again.

Lady Madeleine de Brandeville's gaze pierced her, as soulless and frightening as the crater of a dormant volcano. The woman's brazen infatuation with Adrian, the way Emmaline sometimes caught her looking at him with avid hunger, may have been a reason for that focused hatred. But there was something more … something infinitely more sinister about her.

Suddenly, fear the likes of which Emmaline had never felt before scuttled like a parasite up her spine.

Everyone around her was in high spirits. Her cousin and his wife sat close by, in deep conversation with the vicar. A few distinguished gentlemen had imbibed too much of Cook's fiery punch and gathered, ruddy-cheeked, in various spots, away from their wives' accusing gazes. Intricate coiffures, dazzling jewels, and fine coutures molded and buffed the bodies that packed the large space in her soon-to-be home, while fresh young couples danced a lively quadrille under their matrons' eagle eyes. But to Emmaline, nothing existed but the cloud of ill-boding that formed a tight knot around her, cut welts into her, squeezed, crushed.

God above, the woman *smirked* at her. That twisted smile felt like a warning. No, more than that; like an omen. A wicked chill wracked her as if she were standing outside in the frosty December air, clothed in only her shift.

Run and hide!

Emmaline forced herself to turn around and walk away. As she let the guests swarm around her in a thickening buffer, she followed a narrow, veined path toward the exit. An alcove in the adjoining salon secured a bit of solace, away from the crowd. Her only companion now remained a potted fern—profuse, concealing and blessedly mute.

She pressed her back against the cool wall and reached into the side pocket of her gown for her monogrammed handkerchief. Her fingers met with nothing. *Must have left it behind in the retiring room.* She breathed fitfully, hand on her heart, and willed the wild beating to subside.

Then, she summoned Adrian's face in her mind. His smile, his body, his touch. Adrian lazily swirling his thumb on her palm. Adrian trailing his fingertips over her cheeks and jaw, around to that sensitive spot down her nape to the top of her spine. Adrian kissing her, plundering her mouth. Adrian brushing his lips on that delicate juncture between her neck and shoulders, tasting her skin, giving her shivers. Adrian telling her how much he wanted her.

She thought about it until she really felt it, like a warm, tingling breeze on her bare skin. She pondered it until the hunger for the real thing took over. Until fine tendrils of desire chipped at that cold fear and started to slake its debris from her heart.

The hum of voices, the clatter of glasses, the sound of laughter, the music, and the footsteps started to fade from her hearing.

Adrian's words of desire that were burned in her very soul killed all those sounds.

She stood there in her silent cocoon, and waited for the love of her life to come save her.

––––––

THE POTTED PLANT stirred when Adrian walked by it. A hand reached out to grab his coat sleeve and unceremoniously dragged him behind the greenery.

He cursed out loud.

"Hush! It is I."

His jaw slacked in surprise. "Emma, what are you doing here? I was looking for you—" he stopped abruptly when he realized her face had drained of color. He gathered her hands in his to still their visible trembling. "My love, what is the matter? Are you unwell?"

Emma worried her bottom lip. "I just saw Lady de Brandeville in the ballroom. She was staring at me very . . . well . . . there is *something* about that woman. We don't know much about her, do we?"

Adrian's protective instincts roared. He drew her closer to him, rubbed her back in a soothing up-down motion, and pressed brief kisses on her hair until he felt the tension ease.

"Lady de Brandeville is an insignificant nuisance. Why do you fear her?"

"I hate being such a ninny," she groaned.

"Tring, Wing, and Ivinghoe. Three churches all in a row," he quoted as he pressed his cheek in the softness of her hair and inhaled the scent of the fresh red rose—his daily bequest to her for the past two years—nestled atop her head. "Do not be ashamed to turn to me when you feel this way."

He held her quietly for a few moments, wanting nothing more than to take away what ailed her. To touch her. "Have you forgotten that just last week you and your mount almost won a breakneck race on the plain? Few would hope to measure up to such daring," he remarked with the hope that his light tone would diffuse her anxiety.

She cuffed him lightly on the chest and lifted dancing eyes to his. "*Almost* won the race? I clearly arrived first, you scoundrel, and you know it."

He slid his fingers to Emma's nape and massaged her scalp. She bit her lip, as if holding back a moan, then her full, sensuous mouth widened in a thankful smile.

"You know what you need?" he murmured, arousal fanning through him. He guiltily tamped it down.

She pressed her cheek in his black evening coat. "Hmmm?"

"A refreshing swig of St. Albans' Kinder brew. It solves all problems."

Emma chuckled. "If the local brew had all the medicinal properties you claim it does, we'd have no need at all for doctors, only more inns and taverns." She released a contented sigh as his fingers continued to knead into her skin.

What had Lady de Brandeville done to drive Emma to tears? In all his life, he had never met a woman as resilient and devoid of nonsense as his Emma—a woman who loved the outdoors as much as he, and preferred to walk or ride for hours than have tea with other society misses.

The blasted Frenchwoman did take every opportunity to corner him into meaningless conversation at every society event. Although he did not welcome her attentions, he mostly dismissed them as the actions of a lonely widow. He'd always made it clear in his reserved demeanor that he had no interest in a liaison.

A prickling of self-doubt insinuated itself in his mind. Could the older woman harbor genuine hate toward Emma? The thought was absurd when she had the reputation of never wanting for male company. Emma was only a little overexcited about the wedding.

He hooked a wayward lock of hair behind her ear and brushed his mouth across her brow. An awkward laugh escaped her lips. When she drew her head back, her eyes gleamed with moisture.

If humor couldn't banish her doldrums, this was bad.

Powerlessness ploughed into him, but he quickly yanked away the invisible ropes that threatened to pull him down with her. He hooked a finger under her chin. "No one can hurt you. I shall always be with you. Always," he reassured with a searching gaze.

What she needed now was a champion to pull her back up and surround her with strength, not commiseration.

"Don't ever leave me again," she said, blinking back tears.

Like I left you once before. "Never, I swear on my father's grave." Could he ever erase his foolish past actions that could have destroyed both their lives? "I want to see you carefree and happy." *The way you fill me with joy and excitement each day.*

He was here, in her arms, as close as a man's and woman's souls could be, joined, linked. One.

"Oh, but I am! Can you not see? I never thought you to be blind," she made light.

He ran a finger over her dimple. "I assure you I am not blind," he rasped. His hungry eyes traveled over her face to her neck and exposed shoulders. "I'm not blind at all."

"Show me, then," she invited, and brought her seductive lips to his. "Show me how much you can see."

He caught her head between his hands and kissed her, demanded that she part her lips and allow him to explore the moist inside. Reward came when she threw her head back in abandon, and lured him with soft whimpers of pleasure. He pressed forward until Emma's back was plastered to the wall.

If only he could keep her that way always. But no. He loved her free spirit too much.

Yet, he also loved her this way. His prisoner. Trapped between a wall and him. All of her possessed by him.

Her palms dug into the snug fabric that covered his shoulders and trailed a burning path down his back. The tips of her fingers dug into the superfine fabric as she frantically pushed her body against his. She clutched on to him with her mouth, her tongue, her kiss, her whole being.

With one hand, he traced the goose bumps on her upper arms, the delicate curve of her waist, and the full contours of her hips and bottom. After a thorough exploration, he retraced his steps and slid his hand up to her breasts, wishing all the time he could make her corset disappear with just the power of his thoughts.

He imagined a scene like this when Emma would forgo such fripperies so he could touch her the way he wanted...

His hand closed over a breast and kneaded. Driven by impulse, he left her lips and found the exposed skin above her plunging neckline and tasted its sweetness.

Her sigh ended in a whimper, a wanton sound that turned him rock hard.

"Yes, touch me like that ... please ..."

Her words drove him insane, and for one wild moment he considered laying her down, ripping off her dress and taking her there, on the marble floor.

He groaned and kissed her again, deeply. Primal need pulled at its weakened chains. He wanted to swallow her whole, to become one flesh with her. His body screamed for it. But not here.

With a heart full of regret, he forced himself to stop kissing her ... but he couldn't stop touching her. He pressed his lips briefly to the side of her swollen mouth and let them trail downward.

"Mine," he murmured into her neck. Her warm breath brushed his temple when he pulled back a little so he could dive in the deep pools of her doe eyes. They were glossed over.

"I love you, Emma," he rasped.

She rested her head on his chest. "And I *adore* you. I cannot imagine my life without you."

If he closed his ears to the clamor from the ballroom, he fancied he could hear the steady rhythm of her heart. He caught a stray tendril of her hair and twisted it around his finger.

She finally lifted her flushed face to his and gently pulled on his coat. "We must go back," she said without enthusiasm.

"Hmmm," Adrian replied, not budging an inch.

She rose on tip-toes and planted a quick peck on the bridge of his nose. "I would rather stay here, alone with you, but we need to go back before we are missed."

A movement on her head caught his eye. "I think we need to see to your hair first. It seems to have a mind of its own."

She muttered an expletive, and drew a soft laugh from him as she swerved around so her back faced his chest. "You must fix it then."

He raised a brow and surveyed the damage. "At your service, my lady, if I can understand how this works, and if you promise not to curse in public," he said with a wink.

She grinned at him over her shoulders as he lifted uncertain hands to her soft ebony locks. Then she leaned back, and kissed him soundly on the lips. "I promise to be ladylike this evening. So do your best, my love. I have absolute faith in your abilities."

The sparkle had returned to her eyes. When she smiled at him like that, everything fell into place. Emma was his fate, his destiny. There was nothing that anyone, including Lady de Brandeville, could do about it.

―――――――

When they returned to the ballroom, Emmaline was still gathering her wits. She glanced sideways at Adrian's sun-kissed profile that held a strongly chiseled jaw and chin, full lower lip, and straight nose, and she pressed her fingers into his arm. Her gaze lingered on the scar that made his right jawline just a tad imperfect, the keepsake of a reckless act of childhood when he jumped from the branch of a tree and tripped over the jagged face of a rock.

I love you, you make me whole.

The orchestra started to expel the hypnotic strains of a smooth melody.

"I believe this is my waltz," he said, as the lights from the sconces flickered in his blue, blue eyes.

They circled around the animated expanse of the ballroom, oblivious to the other waltzing couples, oblivious to the hushed whispers and the fickle curiosity marked on a few faces. This dance, an import from the Continent where it had been popular for quite a while, was animated and intimate—yet still not widely known in England. But nothing pleased him more than sharing these moments with the woman he loved more than anything.

He tightened his grip on her hand, and discreetly caressed the inside of her thumb with the tip of his. The touch sent a gaggle of wild geese through her belly and caused her to barely miss his foot in a faux pas.

"I should have paid more attention when Mr. Berthing gravely imparted the intricacies of the sacred waltz," she said with an apologetic look.

"I believe you were too busy quoting Shakespeare in your head while he showed you the steps."

Emmaline cocked an eyebrow. "I'll have you know that Shakespeare is infinitely more interesting than any dance in the world, um, except this one, of course."

"Frailty, thy name is *not* Emma," he teased with words dipped in clover. He considered her with unmitigated fondness. "Three days and alas, you shall be my lifelong captive."

The image of her father, the late Baron Kentmore, entered her mind. She remembered him telling her how she looked so much like her mother, who had died giving birth to her, their only daughter. He would sternly reprimand her on her stubbornness and free-spirited nature; then he'd insist that she better think of making a good match than spend hours on end with her nose buried in books.

Now he was gone, forever. Both their fathers were gone. Hers had died during her sixteenth year when he suffered an apoplexy at

White's. Adrian's father and older brother had fallen victims to a tragic carriage accident in October of last year.

They had survived their fathers' objections to their blossoming love because of the bad blood the two men had obdurately tried to trigger between their families. What had started the enmity may have been an incident from their later days at Eton. Grandmamma had once hinted that her father, a rather impulsive young chap, had intended to offer for Adrian's mother before the then dashing Viscount knowingly beat him to it. Perhaps there was some truth to that. Love had a way of making one do unexplainable things.

One thing was certain—when their fathers passed on, all the weary antagonism died with them. Even the new Baron Kentmore, a distant cousin who inherited the Trenwith estate following the absence of male heirs, was indifferent to past rivalries, engrossed as he was in his botanical research. With Adrian's mother's blessing, none of it mattered, but it would not matter, anyway. For Emmaline's heart wanted Adrian, and only Adrian.

True, she hadn't always been besotted with him. In the very beginning, she'd seen Adrian through her father's eyes, and let herself be influenced by his empty words plaited with the ties of old jealousy and contention. But that perception eroded the more she spent time with Adrian.

She instinctively held tighter to her betrothed. With a heated gaze, he pulled her closer so his thighs flirted scandalously with the undulating claret folds of her gown and his chest brushed with the delicate lace of her neckline. So close she was instantly reminded of that moment they'd just shared by the potted plant. Warmth rose up her chest to spread in hot tingles across her face when he brought his mouth to her hair and she felt his breath hitch.

Her cheek rasped against his chin. He smelled of musk and fresh air. Once more, she missed a step, but he held her tight and led their moves with fluid ease. Giddy from the energetic dance and his closeness, she wanted to scream her joy from the steeple tower of the chapel nearby. The chapel where she and Adrian would be wed in a quiet country ceremony.

When the music stopped, he gave her one final twirl and led her into the crowd, his hand possessively on her back before he searched for her arm and curled her fingers around his coat sleeve. While they inched their way toward the refreshments stand, they passed a group of gentlemen who seemed to be absorbed in a serious discussion.

"It appears everyone's busy discussing America and this business with Boney," he told her.

This very day, under Jefferson's sway, the House in America was supposed to have passed the Embargo Act with the intent—or so it appeared—to compel peace between England and France. It was felt that the threat posed by Napoleon and his allies in attacking Britain's economy was too great and the dangers far-reaching. People speculated about the issue and debated it to no end.

"Quite. What do you make of the debacle?"

He shrugged. "It is anyone's guess who will benefit from this heavy-handed diplomacy. I do not believe there is an easy answer to such a question."

"You think these tactics will work? Or, perhaps, this war will never end." She could not keep the melancholy from her tone.

Adrian's large palm covered her hand as he turned to her. "Please know that my life is here, with you. I will not let you forget that." His tone was grave, firm.

"Thank you," she said shakily. "Occasionally, I need to hear you say those words."

His eyes crinkled at the corners. "Do you remember the day we met?" he asked as they continued to negotiate the crowded ballroom side by side.

"How could I forget? You were completely disheveled." She shook her head. "And I had to investigate, of course. I had to see my enemy for myself, especially after my father warned me to stay away from you and your property."

Barely fifteen, she'd been on one of her daily exploits into the countryside, complaining to herself about why women couldn't dress like the more sensible male species, when she saw a young man standing in the water. His dripping wet shirt clung to a lanky chest while he engaged in a rather undignified struggle with a goat. The silly animal stood stranded in the middle of the river that ran just beyond the border to her father's adjoining land. While the nineteen-year-old Adrian pulled and prodded with all his might, it stubbornly refused to budge.

He'd shot her a withering glance. Obviously, he'd got himself in a pickle, but had a hard time admitting to it.

"Are you coming in?" he'd finally growled. The words, *I need help,* seemed to be stuck on the roof of his mouth, never to see the light of day.

"Of course not," she'd said with a raised eyebrow and crossed arms. "I'd get my gown wet. And I shouldn't be here, anyway. My father doesn't want me to talk to you."

"You say? You don't even know who I am!"

"Oh, I *know* who you are."

He'd grunted, and gotten back to his task, ignoring her from then on, while she continued to watch him and scold herself for not turning around and walking away.

Silly, silly girl. Sillier than that silly goat.

She hadn't even been able to stop herself from staring, and the more she'd seen him struggling, the more she'd felt shame for not helping.

Muttering to herself that she was in for a good tongue-lashing from her father, she'd waded in the river, gown and all, and helped him push the hapless beast toward the river bank.

"You made me squirm." Adrian grinned, drawing her from her reverie. "You were as determined as that goat to be the bane of my existence," he teased, and drew an indignant huff from her. "*But,*" he added, his gaze burning, "you were quite magnificent. From that moment, I knew you would one day belong to me."

Emmaline had barely started to respond when a groom came upon them, carrying a silver salver.

"My lord, a gentleman is waiting in your study. He insists upon meeting with you."

"Who is it?"

"Mr. George Canning." A crisp, white card with neat lettering lay in the center of the tray.

Emmaline's head shot up. "The Foreign Secretary?" she asked in surprise.

Adrian picked up the card. He read the name printed on it and scowled. "What the devil," he muttered. "The man himself."

He had often communicated his mixed feelings for the gruff but hard-working politician responsible for gathering intelligence to protect British interests. He said the man would stop at nothing, even condone the sacrifice of civilian lives, to attain his goals.

"I'll see him now, then." He dismissed the servant and turned to Emmaline. "Canning has a way of requesting people's attention at the most inopportune times. I shan't be long. Wherever you are, I'll find you." He clasped her hand and planted a solid kiss over her knuckles before he turned on his heel and left the ballroom.

What did Canning want with Adrian?

Adrian had told her that before he traveled to France, Canning would send trusted agents or missives to Belvoir and never personally attended to such matters. The man rarely left London. After his work on the field, Adrian had continued to assist Lord Hawkesbury and the Foreign Secretary, albeit in a strictly consultory capacity.

But the last time they had asked for help, Adrian left her after agreeing to take an assignment on impulse, prompted by his sense of duty and a desperate request from a friend who worked for the British government. It had been madness, but he later told her that they desperately needed someone who looked like a young peer on a tour of the Continent. He'd returned near death, his body slave to a raging fever, yanked back by his father and brother's tragic loss. Besides, his mission had failed because the man he was sent to bring back to England had been shot dead. A fate that could have easily been Adrian's.

She'd fallen headfirst into a crater of burning despair before his recovery sent her scratching her way to the surface. In that time, she'd rarely left his side. Her reputation had meant nothing when faced with the alternative of losing him.

She stared down to realize her hands were clasped too tightly, and unlocked them; underneath the gloves, her skin felt clammy and cold.

An empty chair beckoned. She walked over and sank down on it. First Lady de Brandeville, now Canning. Was fate playing tricks on her? She reached inside her and sought the spirit to banish these absurd thoughts. She was a strong, sensible woman, and would not stop being so now.

From the corner of her eye, she saw Lady Philippa Segrave, Adrian's mother, make a beeline toward her. Emma pasted a smile on her lips. She grabbed a thread of resolve, and forced the tight, heavy shackles around her lungs to ease.

MADELEINE KEPT her rage in check while she watched the viscount dance with the Deramore chit, who now sat in the company of Lady Segrave. She thought back to that moment when she had briefly locked eyes with the younger woman. She'd sensed the panic that had gripped Lady Deramore and made her escape somewhere before she returned some time later, once more a chirpy little sparrow, clutched to the viscount's arm. Her cheeks had been flushed and her eyes had sparkled.

Madeleine knew that look. The afterglow of passion.

We shall see who laughs last, you worthless trollop!

Forcing an amiable expression, Madeleine wandered into the mêlée of distinguished guests, and stayed out of Lady Deramore's line of vision. All the forced smiles and society prattle had given her a headache. Time to make an exit. She had everything she needed to proceed and there was no reason to linger.

The sight of the lovebirds engaged in intimate gestures had strengthened her determination to see her plan to completion. Soon, Adrian would be sampling Madeleine's exclusive sensual favors. And when the time was right, she would have his title, wealth, and powerful connections to take advantage of as she wished.

Above all, she would have *him*. All of him.

She licked her lips as wicked images of their glistening bodies engaged in passion filled her head. Images that had fueled her obsession since she first laid eyes on Adrian at the Havershams' summer picnic August last. That day, she'd wheedled her way to an introduction. Attraction had flashed through her like a poisoned arrow, and her desire festered to a point where she had to sate it.

He was a peer and to his advantage, a virile man—all lean muscle and golden skin, his face angular, yet with a soft edge to it. The short puckered scar that licked the base of his right cheek gave him an air of subtle menace that she found difficult to resist. He was every woman's dream, a man handsomer than sin. And a very rich one. The death of his father and older brother had landed him a pot of gold on a platter. By reputation resourceful and competent, his already considerable wealth was said to be increasing by the day. He had a large townhouse in Mayfair and entrée to events in Prinny's social calendar, as well as close friendships among the most influential people in London. Precisely what she needed to gain a higher foothold in the ton.

A long time ago, the Duc d'Orleans had informed her of the Prince of Wales' penchant for Parisian life in his earlier years. Even with the strained situation between England and France and Prinny's change of attitude toward the French, she would revive that dormant appetite once she entered his intimate circle of friendships. His love of the fairer sex would work in her favor.

She would also find the best candidates for membership in the brotherhood among the cream of society. The Cult of the Snake needed more blue blood in their ranks and coin in their coffers to counter the scourge of the Valthreans. When the latter were completely destroyed, her people would have absolute power over the aristocracy, and control the wheels of commerce and society.

Arrangements for the move were finalized and all her trunks were packed. She had discharged her servants and hired a skeleton staff, a few fresh faces from remote villages, to take with her on the impending journey north.

And most importantly, she'd taken care of the young orphan maid who'd fueled her power of sight the previous night. She'd been one of the best subjects Madeleine had ever used, with virgin blood so pure, dense, and strong that the visions could last for over a month.

Madeleine caught a glimpse of her upper body in the large gilded mirror that hung on the south-facing wall of the ballroom. For a woman in her thirty-sixth year when she was turned into her powers, she had striking looks. Adrian would have no complaint with her insatiable appetites that would without question make the notorious Messalina blush.

In London society, she was touted as a *deliciously foreign eccentric*. In the demi-monde circles, talk abounded about her infamous soirées. She took full advantage of a certain degree of freedom attributed by her assumed state of widowhood, carved out the life she desired for herself. What she wanted, she took.

She had tasted the fruits of a dissolute life. And now she wanted respectability and wealth, to do with as she pleased. Adrian would give her all of this. Eventually, she would reward him by sharing her secrets and powers with him, but only when he was ready. One day, he would thank her for taking him away from the prospect of a miserable, lackluster marriage.

Before that time came, she knew she would have to rally all her skills as a seductress to make him fully hers. Adrian was not like the others. He did not grovel. He did not *look* at her. He completely ignored her and drove her mad with jealousy. He reminded her of … Massimiliano.

But that was a closed book, a distant memory. Now, Adrian filled her thoughts. He would come to want her as she wanted him. He was still a man, after all.

She wound her way past cloying perfumes and insipid conversation and peeled herself from the stifling ballroom. After she retrieved her cloak, she called for her carriage but did not have the patience to wait inside. She slithered out, braced for the cold, and let the huge oak door shut behind her. Her senses sharp like a perfectly tuned violin, she could distinguish Adrian and Emmaline's mingled smell as she carefully descended the slippery front steps. Their lingering scent hung on the brittle night air.

The delicate satin of her gloves did nothing to prevent her fingers from turning numb, and the jeweled pins in her hair jabbed at her freezing scalp. She ground her teeth against the cold, while treading where the round and resplendent Frost Moon, along with the light from the windows, showered her path with subdued illumination. The frigid white stone groaned under her delicate evening slippers, like stepping on crumbed gingerbread biscuits topped with sugar, the sound fresh and crisp.

She mumbled a foul curse, pulled the cloak tighter around her, and bit on her lower lip until the taste of copper seeped into her mouth. Her vehicle approached at a snail's pace until finally, the coachman reined in the horses. A groom jumped down and opened the door to the carriage, offering her a hand in assistance.

She grabbed his wrist and exerted as much pressure as she could through the gloves. "What took you so bloody long? Get on with it. I have no time to waste."

The youth's lips thinned and his jaw clenched, as if he'd just swallowed a curse. His lips were blue from the cold and probably poor circulation.

When she stepped inside, she released him and let herself sink in the plush, warm cushions of the seat. Despite the fact that the chill had entered her pores to settle deep inside her wintry heart, the beginnings of a smile formed on her cracking lips. A harsh laugh gurgled in her throat.

Relish these final moments, Lady Deramore, for soon, your prince will be forever mine.

The carriage wheels moaned and rolled as they left behind the sound of laughter and merriment at Belvoir.

CHAPTER 2

"Fair is foul, and foul is fair:
Hover through the fog and filthy air."
[Macbeth, Act 1, Scene 1]

DECEMBER *22, 1807.*
Trenwith.

"MORNING, mam. We 'ave a glorious day outside meltin' the cold. Look!"

Hattie moved briskly about the room but Emmaline couldn't bring herself to unglue the lids of her eyes, let alone *look*.

"Hmmm."

As soon as the curtains were drawn, a burst of sun rushed inside and licked her face like a faithful hound waking its master with balmy kisses. She turned around to face away from the windows. *Just a little more sleep....*

"Last year this time 'twas freezing me bones off and half the village drowned in floodwater. Here, I 'ave brought you some hot chocolate and lemon scones, just as you like it. Your bath be ready soon, cushty and warm like."

Her lady's maid's familiar, Cockney accent rattled on in cheerful notes. Emmaline dove under the thick blankets, with the hope of claiming a few more winks, but the strong natural light that invaded her chamber pierced mercilessly through the bedsheets. The warmth feathered her closed eyelids, told her it was long past her usual waking time.

"Eat your breakfast, mum. You need your wits and strength about you, 'specially now. Be back shortly with your bath."

"Umm . . . uh." She grunted. *Bossy woman.*

"Ah, silly me, almost forgot. Lord and Lady Kentmore are gone to the village to deliver a food basket to ol' Millie and her sister."

The door opened and closed behind a chirping Hattie and Emmaline savored the silence. She turned on her side, smiled into the pillow, and stretched before she surfaced from the sheath of blankets. When she gingerly opened one eye, her first view was the plain white marble fireplace that sat placidly at an angle with the windows. She opened the other eye and blinked. A ceramic jug filled with red roses from Adrian—some fresh, others in various stages of wilting—sat on the mantle. She did not have the heart to throw any away until the petals withered and died.

Turning back the crumpled bedclothes, she slid to the edge of the bed where she sat still for a moment, let joy flood her like the spry brightness of the light that now bled abundantly in her room.

Soon, she would not be spending the night in an empty bed. She'd be in Belvoir, with its understated Georgian stateliness nestled amid worked land that bordered fertile patches of beech woodland, waterways, and, to the north, the unmatched drift of the Chilterns. She'd be home, where she'd wake up snuggled to Adrian's warmth amid crumpled sheets, her body flush against him and a leg wedged securely between his muscular thighs.

A smile tugged at the corners of her lips as her thoughts drifted to the previous night.

The ball. The excitement.

Adrian's touch.

Madeleine de Brandeville.

A prickly chill rushed through her, making her jolt with a reluctant awareness that defied all rationality.

I'm getting married to the man I love. What is there to worry about?

The aroma of lemon and chocolate intruded upon her thoughts. Her stomach growled. She slid her feet into a pair of slippers and walked toward the uncovered tray laid out on the small table that doubled as a writing desk. A fresh rose stood in a fluted vase on the silver tray. She grabbed an oversized wool weft twill shawl from the back of the chair. The Chinese design wrapped around her like albatross wings as she hugged it to her and rubbed her cool palms against the soft material. Welcome warmth seeped into her through the thin night rail.

She lifted the cup of hot chocolate and took her first sip of decadence. The hot liquid poured down her throat to her stomach and brought the blood rushing to her skin.

"Manna from the gods," she sighed.

Eating was a quick affair. She wiped off the scone crumbs from her lips and downed the last of her hot chocolate. As if on cue, Hattie arrived, trailed by two footmen who carried in a bath tub, towels, and pitchers filled with water. Moments later, while her head rested on the copper rim and rose-scented steam permeated the air, she thought of the afternoon rendezvous she and Adrian had planned at the little spot by the river where they had first met. She could hardly wait to run her fingers through his gold-streaked hair. To steal an hour alone, away from relatives, bustling servants and wedding guests.

As the water turned lukewarm, reality set in. Reluctantly, she sat up and gave herself a vigorous soap scrubbing and rinsed herself thoroughly, then got out of the tub and toweled herself dry.

Before she left, she would look through her correspondence—a task she always preferred to perform in the comfort of the library. Providentially, most of the wedding guests, including members of her family, were given refuge at the much larger Belvoir Hall, a testament to her future mother-in-law's generosity and understanding.

Her day gown was fashioned from plum velvet and meant to be worn over a modest high-necked chemisette. Forgoing stays meant she could dress herself without a maid's help. Setting aside the thought of Hattie's disapproval at her continued denial for assistance, she made quick work of arranging her thick long hair in a simple style, tied in a ponytail at the nape with a length of deep purple silk ribbon. The bath had energized her. She walked briskly to the door and started to turn the knob, but stopped first to glance back at today's rose in its long vase that basked in a runnel of sunlight.

Hattie was right. This augured to be a wonderful day, and she shouldn't waste a minute of it.

She blew the rose a kiss. "See you soon, my love."

———

MIDDAY IN LADY Madeleine de Brandeville's private parlor...

MADELEINE WALKED to the large table in the center of her work room. She reached out with willowy, pale fingers to reverently caress the object that lay still, so still, on the tabletop. Her beloved chalice. Inside it laid a man's leather glove and a neatly folded, lace-trimmed handkerchief with the monogram *E. E. D.* She picked the glove and buried her face in it, breathed in Adrian's male scent, then, placed it next to the chalice.

"Beauty is transitional, power is eternal," she chanted over and over. In her trance-like state, she gave thanks for the glory of her gift. *Power is all things*—this singular thought drove her.

Willow bark, chickweed, the injurious extract of evergreen plants imported from the East. The heat from the Demon's Chalice intensified with the addition of each iniquitous ingredient. Overcome by ecstasy, she stood over the ancient roughly hewn basin and welcomed the supreme energy that had lived through centuries and witnessed countless events.

When the waves of delirium subsided, she opened her eyes and looked inside the chalice. The handkerchief was mutilated, reduced to shreds. Reaching in with a wooden stick, she removed what remained of it from the bowl and threw the pieces aside.

Then she took a long lock of red hair, her own, moistened with jasmine oil and sprinkled with sugar. She carefully wound the hair around the glove and placed them inside the sacred chalice. Finally, she added blood to complete the circle.

Virgin blood.

Six drops, the perfect number.

She placed her hands above the objects as if blessing them and recited her spell.

COME to thee who owns you, my love
When next you lie down, surrender
To all others you'll be immune
I make this vow
When next you touch feminine lips
Thine you shall become
Be gone your old life
A wall erect that stands through time
Night and day
Be bound, unfree
Thy lover's caress
It conjures you, it seizes you
Heed this plea
May you never have release from her
Until thy breathes thine last breath

EVERY WORD STOKED the fire inside her, from red to blue to incinerating white. The chalice responded by creating the perfect

33

storm inside and above it, a contained squall rising in a pillar from basin to ceiling. The eye of the tempest—the hair-bound glove—lay at the bottom, as if gaining a secret strength with each dizzying churn of the hot air surrounding it.

An unbreakable spell for Adrian's heart, mind, and soul. A spell he couldn't escape.

He would be hers until she died.

Hers forever.

When the storm ended, she looked around her. This chamber was her kingdom, one of the few places in the world where she allowed her true self to escape from the gilded cage of the *ton*. It was where she plotted and designed, where she decided what direction Fate's wheel should turn and on which spoke it should stop. She vowed to have a similar refuge in Scotland.

The furnishings were simple and sparse, perfect backdrop for her muse. Heavy black curtains shielded pointed arch windows and a large carpet weaved hues of dark cherry, black, and gray. On it sat a few scattered chairs, a chaise upholstered in jet black silk, a stone hearth, and three walnut tables with carved friezes and sturdy columns for legs. The tables' surfaces were weighed down with all manner of bottles, bowls, and vials, the patina of the wood scratched and worn with overuse.

Leagues apart from the understated elegance that graced the rest of her home, this room remained nonetheless her favorite. And the smell of it—to the average person, it would seem like the bizarre, unpalatable bouquet of a combined kitchen and apothecary. But to Madeleine, it was the scent of victory. Of success. Of *control*.

"Thank you, Claude, for giving me this," she whispered to the shadows in the room as she ran a finger around the jagged base of the chalice. It still glowed and sprayed the room with a spell of dazzling light a thousand times brighter than the dreary British weather could ever provide. Her fingers tapped the gold locket nestled between her breasts, then wrapped firmly around it. "And this, too," she added sadly. "Despite everything...."

Then she pulled her hand away quickly, as though the metal had burned her, and banished the sad thoughts.

Instead, she thought of her long ago lover, in pre-revolutionary France, who yearned for the pleasure that came with pain and shared his love for the Black Arts with her. He was partial to humiliation, and had become so infatuated that one night he had sought to impress her by disclosing the secret of the chalice.

Drink had a way of making one careless, and pleasure made one blind. Both, administered at the same time, made one reckless.

"So you have this chalice, my darling? Where do you keep it? Tell me, I beg you. I swear to never tell. You know I love you so..."

To her eternal fortune, Claude's tongue was loose that evening. Loose enough to tell her about his kind—their powers, and most importantly, their weaknesses. For, it turned out, he was no mere human. She listened keenly with vast excitement and marvel. He told her of his most prized possession, the Demon's Chalice, which he kept cleverly hidden in a secret chamber accessible from his private rooms at his Château du Sart in northern France. She convinced him that making her immortal, like him, would allow them to always be together. He could not deny her. He wanted to marry her.

But, he was not rich enough, not powerful enough, not attractive enough for her. Furthermore, his modest estate was leagues in splendor from the homes of the prestigious Loire Valley.

Finally, the chalice wasn't even his! His brother, a more influential peer, had placed his misguided trust in him and asked that he keep it in his vaults for a year or more while the man spent time on his plantation in the Americas.

Still, he served his purpose for a short while.

After his muddled confession, Madeleine developed a sudden love of reptiles, mostly exotic snakes. Even knowing the danger to her new self, she decided it was worth the risk. Her plan was simple, like all the best plans are.

"Please, Claude, will you not humor me? I will make it worth your indulgence, and I promise to be careful," she had coyly offered.

And Claude, her smitten subject, did humor her. "Certainly, dear, but only harmless ones."

"Mais oui, bien sûr, mon amour," she assured. *Of course, my love.*

Tragic, though, that one of the cages was defective, the very one with the coral snake in it, the cobra that had the sole power to destroy one of Claude's immortal kind. One clear summer night, the reptile broke free and found its way to the bedchamber. Claude died alone in her bed, barely shocked to wakefulness when the venom took his last breath. It had been ruled a scandalous but ill-fated accident.

During the inquiry, she demonstrated proper aplomb when describing how lucky she considered herself to be alive, and how glad she felt that nobody else had been bitten by the horrible creature. *Sacre Dieu*, it certainly did not look like those deadly cobras from India in her picture book. How could she know? The servants assured her they had secured the cage after feeding. *Quelle horreur!* she had exclaimed with tears streaking her face. She would never keep another snake again. Her heart was not in it anymore. It was broken with grief.

Since she'd appropriated the chalice shortly after Claude's demise —he had conveniently left it in her home—her life had been paradise. She would be forever grateful for his gift to her, involuntary though it may have been. Its power was the catalyst that granted her all she desired.

What had carried her to this new phase of her life.

She relentlessly plied her craft in the feeble light of the still room and meticulously prepared the requirements for the morrow. Opening a valise she had placed by the table, she carefully packed her herbs and potions. Then, she reverently wrapped the chalice in a length of velvet and placed it in a separate trunk, cushioned by her clothing.

She could not, *would not*, fail. Not this time. The cosmic barrier she had created with her ritual over the chalice would allow her to live freely with Adrian—just the two of them and no one else in the world between them. Its strength had been sealed with virgin blood.

Doused with numb satisfaction, she stretched her arms and

rotated her head to release the fatigue. She'd never forget this night. The blood from her slave had proved pure and wholesome, the perfect vehicle to heighten her rapture. She deserved a few hours' rest.

Her body tingled at the prospect of what was to come.

"Hmm, yes," she sighed as her breasts scoured the stiff baleen of her corset.

She walked to the door and twisted the knob with one flick of her trim wrist. In the dim corridor, a red candle flickered from a sconce within arm's reach, leaving shadows on the walls.

After she stepped out the room, she gave the door a slight push to close while she retrieved a key from her side pocket. She inserted it in the lock, turned it, and pocketed it again with a pat. Her fingers reached for the candle and grabbed it. Her long shadow preceded her as she walked into the tombal darkness toward her bedchamber. A drop of blood-hued wax stung her and trickled in a thin rivulet down to her ring finger, settling there.

A sign of commitment.

She thought of the spell she'd just cast. Her strongest one yet. Irreversible.

Adrian's will was out of his hands.

The next woman he bed would be bound to him forever. He'd never be free until she breathed her last.

Madeleine had staked her claim. The bed they'd lie in would be hers. Without her in his world, he'd lose the will to live. Wither away like dust in the wind.

That, of course, was no concern because death would never knock on her door.

Yes, she smiled to herself in wicked self-assurance, *tomorrow*.

———

THAT SAME AFTERNOON...

. . .

INVIGORATED from the fast ride through the country paths west of St. Albans and its bustling Market Place, Emmaline lifted her skirts out of the way, swung her leg over the saddle, and slid smoothly from the horse. She readjusted her wide forest green skirt to conceal the convenient man's breeches she liked to wear for riding astride—even though she wouldn't act so scandalously unladylike around other people, it gave her comfort to wear it—tethered her mount to a tree, and observed her surroundings.

The chalk hills here sloped gently into the valleys below them, a world apart from the craggier surfaces and steep inclines of the bluff in Buckinghamshire. Nonetheless, these chalk formations offered breathtaking views from any vantage point along the escarpment.

Adrian sat a little farther down the slope with his head against a tree trunk, his crossed legs stretched out on the grass. He contemplated the water of the River Ver, which looked more like a stream rambling in the shadow of the anomalous osier, the water sandwiched between a profusion of overgrown watercress on either bank. As narrow and inconsequential as the Ver looked now, it was hard to imagine it as the Roman navigators had originally seen it when they built the city of Verulamium alongside its then traversable waters. Yet, the river continued to live, a constant in their lives. Draining from the chalk hills so characteristic of this region, it connected this land to the ocean through the Thames.

The water lived in them, too, because it fed their lands. It nourished the soil they walked on, and it had brought Adrian and her together. With this water as witness, they'd woven the first fibers of their love.

Emmaline sighed with contentment while she thanked the heavens for the fortuitous turn of the weather. It was considerably warmer than last night and nowhere near as cold as it should be this time of year. The Ver should be frosted over by now, or, at least, by January, but it clung on to this sudden bizarre bent toward a spring-like climate.

The sun's rays zigzagged on the calm water and reflected from the scattered rocks nestled in the shrubbery on its banks. The deep gold in Adrian's hair caught a spark of sunlight when he moved and casually raised a booted leg. His hand rested on his knee while he idly rolled a blade of grass between his fingers. She removed her gloves and placed them in the side pocket of her skirt.

For a while, she drank in the sight of him. His thick black overcoat stretched over broad shoulders and a powerful back; its folds slipped to the grass to reveal muscular, buckskin-clad thighs and polished Hessians. A light breeze stroked the tips of his hair, making the golden tones flicker, the same breeze that nipped at her face while she studied his profile. He looked so serene. This was a place where responsibilities, fears, and reservations did not exist—exactly where she had first set eyes on him, where she had finally found home.

"Come sit with me," he called to her without looking back.

Yearning to get close to him, she removed her hat and walked to him. His cheeks were flushed from the open air. A half-day old stubble cast the faintest of shadows on the sharp angles of his chin and jaw, and gave him a roguish air. With a lopsided smile, he offered her his hand. She reached out to him, letting her gaze roam from the depths of his eyes to his exposed throat where he had untied his cravat. A light smattering of hairs peeked from the top of the shirt.

"You are late," he taunted in a silky tenor voice.

"I am sorry. I—"

Before she had a chance to finish, he pulled her to the ground and settled her against him, with her back to his chest. His thighs held her prisoner while his arms came around her, making her shudder.

Keep me close, always.

"Are you cold?"

She turned her head to look into his face, and swallowed hard. "Not at all. I feel splendid."

"As do I." He deposited a light kiss on the tip of her nose. "Now."

She admired the prettiness of the water and the rolling hills beyond it, then turned and burrowed her head in the crook of his neck. "Cook detained me a little longer than planned with the *carte du jour* for the wedding," she explained.

He tightened his embrace, entwined his fingers with hers. Etched with little nicks and bruises, his were the hands of a man no stranger to physical work.

"I miss your grandmother," he said suddenly, surprising her. "She would have been happy for us."

Lady Amelia Penhurst, Emmaline's Italian maternal great-grandmother, had bequeathed Emmaline her exotic Mediterranean looks—olive skin and big brown eyes—and her staunch loyalty to those she loved. The woman had been their most ardent champion and loved Adrian like a son. Fiery and outspoken, she protected the secret of her true age with dogged determination.

Adrian once teased her, "Lady Penhurst, you have probably negotiated the Triple Alliance of 1788 but are too shy to admit it."

She'd waved him off and pinched his cheek, responding that *that* would have been impossible as she had no interest whatsoever in politics. Her death shortly before Adrian's departure to the Continent devastated them both. Especially Emmaline, who regarded her like her own mother and had always secretly wondered if the headstrong lady would outlive them all.

"Wherever she is right now, she is probably telling everyone what to do and how to accomplish it," he chortled.

"Grandmamma should be here," she said softly. "But—"

"But?"

She shook her head, instantly regretting the impulse to speak of the past. "Nothing . . . " Her voice trailed off.

"Say it," he insisted, squeezing her fingers a tad harder.

"I was just thinking of your brother and your father. I—" She stopped when she felt him stiffen.

He buried his face in her hair, while her heart sank, felled by the depth of unspoken emotion that poured from him. "You know that even if Father were still here, I would still have married you."

"I know."

The breeze stilled along with their voices, as though nature acknowledged the raw emotion that gripped Adrian at the mention of his father and brother. But, no one more than Emmaline knew how, for a time after he'd assumed Arthur's responsibilities, he was like a shored fish that had lost its shoal. Although the tragedy wasn't his fault, he had still not completely shaken the sense that he was merely a usurper who'd slipped in shoes that were too big, too *wrong*, for him.

"Belvoir has not been the same without them," he brooded.

Emmaline cursed herself for bringing up the subject, and shook her head. "Do not say that. Belvoir is safe and thriving because of *you*, Adrian. What about all you have done in the past year, the knowledge you have accumulated by sheer will and determination? All you need to do is ride through the estate and see it with your eyes. The tenants could not be more fortunate to have you."

She had no doubt – Adrian was made for Belvoir, and Belvoir was made for him. His daily strolls to the corn fields and the wheat fields dotted with haystacks, the backbreaking tilling of earth pregnant with promise, was as much a part of him as she was. Adrian was not the kind of idle aristocrat to manage his property from the comfort of his study. The tenants loved him, not least for his advanced notions on soil improvement, animal husbandry, and estate management. Even his dutiful father could not have matched Adrian's common sense and perseverance.

She turned her head sideways to look up into his eyes and waited for him to say something, anything. The shadows of regret, anger and guilt played on his face but quickly they ebbed, and the crease between his brows vanished, as though he'd finally decided to lift that weight from him.

He drew deeply into his lungs as he drew lazy circles with his thumb around the back of her hand. "The voice of common sense and reason. You see why I can never let you go."

This was her Adrian, never one to agonize too long over things, even when he had good reason to. Relieved, she let loose a brilliant smile and returned her gaze to the quiet scene before them.

A crisp breeze picked up to torment the cress leaves and their hollow stems, making them quiver and bow to the water. However, the spate of cool air was short-lived, chased away by the steadfast sunshine.

"It is so beautiful and peaceful out here. Perhaps it is no coincidence that William the Conqueror received his title in Hertfordshire. What other place better glorifies the unique beauty of the British countryside?" she sighed.

"It is more than that to me."

It is more than that to me, too. She caressed his fingers, one by one, with her free hand. "Those memories, the times we spent here, shall always be ours. And, very soon, we shall make new ones to relate to our children."

"Yet, many of those tales would not be fit for young ears," he drawled as he ran a blade of grass gently around the shell of her ear and neck, shooting sensation straight to her brain and all her female senses.

"You're not playing fair," she croaked, stifling a moan.

"Most know me to be a reputable man."

"They do not know you as well as I do."

"So you, my minx, think me a rogue."

She hid a smile and lifted their linked hands to her lips to drop feather-light kisses on his knuckles. "Only because a *minx* such as I needs a match. Although, they say married life changes people."

"Does it now?"

"Be forewarned. I may become shrewish and unmanageable."

"I may become grumpy and churlish."

"Grumpy? You? Impossible. I would sooner lose all my teeth and hair."

"No, I shall take care of you. I shall make you happy," he said against her temple, his tone suddenly serious.

"I have no doubts." The air around them brimmed with the masculine scent of him. "But please, tell me, anyway... tell me that we shall always be like this. That nothing will ever change us or drive us apart. Perhaps some would think we are too privileged and marriages of love exist only in books."

"I could tell you whatever you wish, but words mean nothing if they are not supported with actions."

Was that old guilt and helplessness in his voice? "What's past is past. We can only look ahead. All that matters is what we are doing now."

The backs of his fingers brushed against her cheek as he lowered his lips to her ear. "Look at the water," he said with quiet conviction. "Look at the slopes of the hills, the trees, and the vast lands in front of us. So delicate yet so raw, so real. So strong. They have been this way for centuries, and will be so for many more. They just *are*. This is how I feel about you, Emma. This is how I love you, in the purest and most natural of ways. You are meant to be mine. You are in my blood."

The impassioned words hummed a ballad inside her chest. She shifted her body around and lifted herself in a kneeling position, her chest flush against his, and took his handsome face between her hands. "I love you, Adrian Segrave, with all my heart, body, and soul. I am proud to become your wife. You'll never have to prove to me how utterly good you are."

His arms circled her and pulled her tighter against him, until their lips were a mere inch apart. "No, *you* are the one who has been good to me, against all odds."

As his warm breaths mingled with hers, she ran a finger over his full bottom lip. "I have only followed my heart. Adrian, you are my anchor." She gave a laugh. "Without you, I am not half as wise as you believe—"

His hand flew to her mouth to silence her. With a gentle caress, his fingers trailed down to her chin and around her jaw. He reached for the ribbon that restrained her hair and loosened it to bury his hand beneath her freed tresses.

"I just want—"

"Enough," he cut her again before taking her mouth in a searing kiss.

Her hands crept under his coat and settled over his shirt. Living, breathing, taut flesh stretched beneath the thin fabric.

Angling her head to the side, he deepened the kiss and explored her, ran his free hand down her back, around her ribcage, and skimmed his thumbs under her breasts.

43

At her moan, he broke the kiss. Breathless and trembling, she gave him a shaky smile and let her forehead touch his.

"I think we should go," he said brusquely, and pushed her slightly away. But there was something in his eyes that told her it pained him very much to do so.

"So soon? I thought we had more time."

"We do, but it is getting cold out here. Come with me."

Disappointed that he had ended their romantic interlude so quickly, she stood and watched him take an unsteady breath before he followed suit and took her hand. Without a word, she let him lead her to her mount, where he untied the reins and pulled the beast with them.

"Where is your horse?" she asked, suddenly realizing she had not seen it earlier.

"Already where we need to be," he said cryptically.

They walked up the slight incline and turned right onto a narrow path. In less than a quarter hour, they stood inside the hunting lodge that Adrian's father had built and for which Adrian had commissioned repairs. The old viscount had loved this place and after his death, Adrian did not have the heart to see it crumble. Inside, the restored furnishings were unpretentious but comfortable.

He got behind her, placed a handkerchief over her eyes and tied it at the back of her head, then guided her forward. "Walk straight on… now a few steps to the right…and here we are."

The blindfold fell from her eyes to reveal that a padded settee with fluted armrests had been pushed back to make space for a blanket laid out with a feast of her favorite foods atop it. Crusty bread and cheese, roasted chicken, beef pies, fruit cake, plum pudding, Devonshire cream, sugarplum jam, and a jug of beer. Leaves of holly strewn among the plates added a touch of earthy cheer, and a single rose stood in a small vase in the center. A heaped-up fire crackled in the fireplace and a vase of more roses decorated the dark wood mantelpiece.

"A picnic!" she exclaimed.

She rushed to the display and sank down on one of the scattered green cushions, then stretched her arms to the fire. "I just realize how hungry I am. It has been a while since breakfast."

"In spring, we will be able to do this by the river."

Like a child let loose in a roomful of toffee and sweetmeats, she took it all in. "It doesn't matter. This is perfect."

Picking a small slice of cake, she then spread it with a dollop of jam and bit into it. Adrian shrugged off his coat and sat beside her, legs crossed. "Here, taste this," she said, and slipped the last bite in his mouth. "Is it not divine?"

"Divine, indeed," he replied.

He caught her finger between his teeth and took his time to let it go. The look in his eyes put the blazing fire to shame. How could she not launch herself into his arms and hold him tightly?

"Adrian," she kissed his cheeks, eyes, temples, and lips, "you are so good to me."

"You may not want me the way I feel right now. I may scare you away," he replied huskily, his eyes spangled with a dangerous light.

He looked at her like a wolf looked at a rabbit.

She couldn't help a shiver. "Whatever do you mean?" she asked breathlessly, drawn by the movement of a muscle that twitched at his jaw.

"This."

His mouth swooped down to hungrily capture hers and his tongue delved deep inside to taste her, to tangle with hers. As the heady scents of sandalwood, soap, and man assailed her, she held on tight, like a ship in a sea storm; if she let go, she would be lost to the turbulent waters. Her hands eagerly explored his hard chest and the rippling muscles on his shoulders and arms. Every touch, every caress, ignited her body into a mass of heated energy that licked at her most sensitive spots, stoking the blaze.

"Wait," he murmured, pulling back and making her knees buckle. "Are you sure of this?"

Yes, you silly man!

"We are to marry tomorrow, and I need you," she panted, her mind muddled by the kiss.

She thought of that terrible, wordless encounter with Lady de Brandeville, that sense of premonition that sent her into a spiral of doubt and confusion until Adrian had come to chase the fears away. But she knew, felt it deep in her soul—she never wanted to waste another minute of their life together.

"Adrian, please love me," she added when all he did was stare at her. "I do not wish to wait a moment longer. I do not want to be good."

"Emma," Adrian whispered against her cheek. "Emma."

———

AS HE HELD his beloved close to his heart, Adrian floundered on the high ropes, about to fall off a huge precipice. He kept her there as his mind reeled with so many thoughts. Emma floored him with her bubbly innocence, her passionate enthusiasm. She drove him wild and his head needed clearing. Someone had to keep two feet on the ground, and he needed to be man enough to do it...but God above, tilling fields all day was much harder than this!

Expert at acting the perfect gentleman, he had so far attempted, sometimes poorly, to manage his passion with self-discipline; to behave in all the good, acceptable ways so as not to dishonor her. He had done her sufficient harm without adding to it unnecessarily. What if he took her virginity and something happened to him before they married? Life was a capricious mistress. She could come and go at any moment, without notice.

Emma was right, he had tried too hard to prove himself but in truth, he never had to. Not with her. He could just be himself, ask anything of her, and she would give it to him.

Adrian Segrave, you are such a fool. A mad fool.

Honoring the memory of his father and brother had been his principal goal this past year. If he allowed himself to set aside his guilt, he would have had to face the turning of a new page, to step into the uncertainty of the future. To admit to himself that he was every bit as diligent as his brother would have been.

Words mean nothing if they are not supported with actions. He had said that himself. But it also depends *what* actions one takes. He was man enough to make his own choices. Had he deluded himself all this time, especially with Emma, in striving to follow the rules and play safe rather than let their feelings take their course? Had he neglected what meant most to chase his own demons? The thought was too painful to process, so he pushed it back and filled his mind with the sweet scent of woman and roses.

Roses. How could a mere bloom ever replace the joy of her in his arms? It was nothing but a shield. It allowed him to feel that he could bury himself blamelessly in his work, to spend countless hours, sometimes days, away from Emma. After the experience in France, he had done his utmost to eschew a questionable reputation. He was so damned reliable, never taking unnecessary risks, always in control.

Above all else, the rose had become a replacement for his real presence in her life. Yet, he had to do what was right, did he?

Damn it. Damn it. Damn it all to Hell!

The knot around his chest loosened a little as he realized this was his opportunity to make amends. He smoothed his hand down her back.

"My love, you know that if I do as you ask, you can never undo it," he said in what felt like a cork-brained attempt to explain himself.

She pulled back and observed him, the fire in her still burning for him and showing in her face.

"Why ever should I want to?" she replied without hesitation.

After seeing the stark determination in her eyes, he simply nodded. He would do this right.

After kissing her gently on the cheek, he spread another thick blanket on the soft carpet then reached between them to unbutton her jacket and remove it. He then lowered her slowly on her back. His gaze never strayed from hers.

"Adrian—"

"Trust me, love. Trust yourself."

He lifted her lower body and slid off the rest of her clothing, leaving her only in her shift.

"You are exquisite," he said with reverence as he discarded his waistcoat and shirt and lowered himself gently on top of her. "I want to taste you."

His mouth journeyed over her neck and shoulders, fed on her warm, supple skin before returning to her lips. While his tongue delved in her sweetness, he let his fingers caress her face and jaw, then cradle her nape and splay in her glorious hair, spreading out the long, silky locks.

"Don't ever cut it off," he commanded, eliciting a shy smile. "The way a woman should be..." he murmured when he slid the shift down off of her, past her rounded hips. She had a breathtaking woman's body—curved and supple, one she ought to be proud of.

His hand moved to her breast and found a dusky nipple. He closed it between thumb and forefinger. At that first contact, she gasped and threw her head back. He kneaded until it pebbled to a tight, inviting peak then filled his hands with her soft breasts.

Her smooth olive skin had gone a shade darker and her face glowed with the wonder of self-discovery. Unable to resist the temptation, he replaced his hand with his mouth. He swirled his tongue around her swollen nub, tasting the saltiness of the plump flesh. The headiness of her scent pulled him in, made him close his lips over it and nip the hardened tip until she was a woman aflame in his arms.

"Please, Adrian," she begged.

Her voice, filled with urgency, was the most arousing thing he'd ever heard. Tamping down his need, he feasted on her. This was her first time; he needed to make it as pleasant as possible for her. He suddenly wished he were more experienced, more worldly. He'd had his fair share of lovers, but none who'd commandeered his heart.

Besides, his interest in other women ended three years ago when his feelings for Emma changed from innocent infatuation to passionate devotion, when she walked right into his heart and locked herself in.

"Please," she repeated with glistening eyes.

His hand found her moist core. "Open to me." He gently stroked, worked that area of throbbing flesh with light, circular strokes until her eyes glossed over. "That's right, love, feel it," he breathed against her cheek.

He took her to the edge of the precipice but didn't want her to fall just yet, so he suddenly stopped. The look on her face as he did so was something he wished he could immortalize. Leaving her, he stood briefly to remove his breeches then covered her with his warm weight.

Meanwhile, he tried to calm his raging pulse—to put his needs aside and think only of her.

With a sly grin, he dove straight between her legs to dip his mouth onto her honeyed center. Her surprised gasp tugged at the long strings of his desire and toyed with his imagination. All he could think of was what he wanted to do to her, in how many ways he wished to take her.

He flicked his tongue around the swollen clitoris—a taut bundle of nerves that yearned for release—and occasionally up and down in a concerted assault on her senses. Intuition took over as he found the perfect tempo to take her to that special place where ecstasy put roots and built its palace in a faraway land. He wanted to take her there and cover her in gold and flowers, to see her eyes up close as they lost focus and she loosened her grip on the real world.

Slowly, he inserted a finger inside her, then another. She quickly adjusted to him so he started to slide in and out in a mimicking of the act of love. Her walls cocooned him, gripped his fingers greedily as she bucked against him, clearly wanting more. She moaned, twisting her body and turning her head from side to side, as if in the throes of a fever. It wouldn't be long.

Drawing on her flesh, drunk on that feeling, he immersed himself in that intoxicating scent—in the taste of her flesh—the most erotic act he'd ever done in his life. Her body shuddered with the first waves of fulfillment, so he closed his mouth around her and drew harder, while increasing the pace of his finger thrusts. Suddenly, she bucked hard against him and screamed, her back arched, her body tense.

As she floated back, he kissed his way up her body and settled on top of her. He carefully pushed against her entrance, but froze when she flinched. He ran a gentle hand over her full hip and hooked it under her leg, putting pressure upward to lift it slightly.

Then her expression eased when instinct took over. She wrapped her legs around him, and crossed her calves at the small of his back. On a moan, she scraped her teeth and tongue against his jaw and raked her nails down his back.

"God," he groaned. *Keep that up and this won't last long...*

Roughly, he grabbed her hands and pushed them up above her head, pinning them there with one of his own. He braced himself on the other arm.

His gaze fixed on the rise and fall of her full breasts, the erect nipples dark and tempting. He drew on them both, hard and fast, moistening the tips. Heat rose from her skin, flaring him up and rushing to his groin. Her irresistible chin lifted as she threw her head back and cried out. He bit gently into it and tasted again the delicious skin there. His entire body burned for her.

The feeling was one he wanted to hold on to but he was finding it harder and harder to keep it in check.

"Ah!" She trembled in his arms—too much to bear. "Mmmmm."

Her eagerness, the alluring sound of her pleasure, drove him head-first into a bottomless ocean of lust and heat, a spiral of desire that tugged him closer to ecstasy and urged him to seal their union.

His body trembled with seismic shock as he relinquished himself to the inevitable and felt the beat of his woman's heart. He closed his eyes and surged forward to enter her with one mighty thrust, while he swallowed her cry of pain in sweet kisses.

Her walls throbbed around him, pulled him farther inside her, welcomed him in the heat of intimacy as she opened up more and more.

Mine, Emma. You're mine and no one else's. I'm marking you now.
Mine.

———

"Oh!" Emmaline bit her lip and dug her nails into Adrian's shoulders. The sharp sting of him inside her quickly ebbed, followed by a feeling she had never felt before.

She abandoned herself to the sweet sensation because she was at the place she was meant to be, with the man she loved more than anything in the world.

Adrian allowed her some time to adjust through the initial discomfort. "Look at me," he said, concern in his voice. "Emma, are you alright?"

His broad back muscles flexed under ironwood hard skin and the touch of her hands. "I want ... I can't ... this feels..." He hesitated, which exasperated her. "For heaven's sake, don't stop now!"

When he started to move in a leisurely, steady rhythm, her body was once more swept away into a different world where something immensely powerful and all-consuming loomed just above her, beyond her reach. Her inner muscles flirted with his flesh as she climbed to her bliss, feeling so alive and pulsing around him.

He groaned, feeling it, too—her desire matching his, ounce for ounce. Frantic, she urged him to forget all delicacy, to speed up his thrusts and sweep her up in a fierce pace. He relented quickly, as though he couldn't wait for the moment to let the beast in him roar.

And it started again then. That wonderful thrill deep in her gut, overwhelming with amassed intensity as she neared the edge. Her head fell back when ecstasy crashed through her. She clutched on to him, and let herself go over with a keening moan.

Immediately, he tensed inside her and released a groan.

"God, Emma," he gasped as his mouth pressed against the sensitive juncture between her shoulder and neck. He rolled to the side and pulled her with him so they would lie facing each other. His hand caressed her face, and her bare back soaked up the heat from the fire.

"There is no turning back now, minx."

She smiled into his eyes. "You always say I'm meant to be yours." This spontaneity, this union, felt right. It *was* right.

Then a thought struck her. "Let us marry today, right now. It shall be our pledge like Loki and Odin who became blood brothers in that version I read of the early Norse myths." Steeped in renewed excitement, she sat up gingerly, pushing the soreness to the back of her mind. She lifted the rose from the vase behind her and turned to Adrian expectantly. "What say you?"

Adrian took the rose from her hand and motioned for her to place her hand on his, palm upward. Usually iridescent gems of an intense ocean blue, his eyes had turned to near obsidian. He gently pierced her tender flesh of her palm with the thorn, drawing a tiny drop of blood.

"More," she urged at his hesitation. "You must cut all the way across."

She helped by placing pressure on his hand. Within moments, blood oozed from her skin.

"My turn."

He made an incision across his hand and set the rose between them. Their palms joined directly above it so that their blood dripped in its downy petals. The rose then seemed to radiate more beauty, more vitality.

Adrian spoke first. "Emmaline Elizabeth, my Lady Deramore, from this day forward, as the Universe is my witness, I pledge my heart, body, and soul in eternal love to you. 'Til the end of my life, I shall belong to you as your husband."

She made the same promise to him. A pledge, sealed by blood.

"I love you, Adrian," she said over the lump in her throat.

"And I love you."

Tears of joy brimmed in her eyes as they huddled back on their makeshift bed.

"We must return home soon," she said sleepily.

"Soon, but not just yet . . ." Adrian murmured. He looked sated and buoyant, adrift toward slumber.

She planted a quick kiss on the bridge of his nose and snuggled against him. The fire had shrunk but still burnt quite strong, and his body kept her warm. As did the thought that she was now Adrian's woman, in the true sense of the word. This was the closest to perfection she would ever get.

But through the fog of her dulling senses, Emmaline started to wonder. Despite the numbing happiness of this moment, the rose beside them a testament to their union, she could not stop an uncomfortable feeling of foreboding from creeping up inside her—much like the one of the previous night upon seeing Lady de Brandeville—to insidiously erode her inner harmony. It was almost as if they were being...watched. Yet, they were completely alone and the door to the cottage was locked. Angry at herself for once again thinking such thoughts, Emmaline did not speak of them to Adrian and secretly calmed her fears by listening to the steady rhythm of her lover's heart.

———

MADELEINE WATCHED the image of the two lovers as they lay naked, limbs entwined, before a fire. She lapped up the scene like a masochist in the throes of inflicting self-torture. She'd screamed, cried, and worn a path in her rug as she paced back and forth like a wounded tiger. Then, she'd returned to the chalice and forced herself to see.

Her mind was still grappling with what had just happened. What was *never* supposed to happen.

How could she not have considered the possibility that Adrian and his future bride would be intimate?

She'd stupidly assumed they would follow all the rules. Instead, they had rutted like animals.

And *bonded*.

They'd shared blood. It wouldn't nullify her spell, but would likely weaken it. She didn't like this, because damn if it didn't throw her impermeable magic headlong into a vat of uncertain contents.

Emmaline would have him until she took her last breath, and he would follow soon after. Let himself go. The all-consuming power of Madeleine's spell would make this happen.

Without the mortal Emmaline in his life, he'd wither away. How long it would take, she didn't know, but happen it would. They were one flesh now...and two souls joined together as one. How could she counter such a force? It would be her greatest challenge yet.

Madeleine realized her fatal error.

She suddenly wished she hadn't unlocked her mind to sight today, although she had to know. Sight into the future wasn't yet possible for her. If it were, she'd have stopped the damage before it was too late.

But the past and the present couldn't be undone. Once she'd started her visions, she couldn't stop watching. She couldn't stop *them*.

The fluid in the chalice and in her body teemed with energy that begged for an outlet. The visions came without the choice to control which secrets to learn and which to hide from.

Today, the sight gave her images of Adrian, gloriously naked, his muscles taut and glistening with exertion as he claimed another woman.

Not something she wanted to witness.

Jealousy was too puny a word to describe what she felt. If she tried to convince herself he'd come around when she showed him how a real woman treated a man, it would be nothing but a delusion. The spell wouldn't be denied.

She had created it—a faultless charm—and now it would work. With the wrong woman.

What would she do now? How long would it take for Adrian to self-destruct from living without Lady Emmaline Deramore in his life? A year? A century?

Change of plans—her rival could not die...ever...or Adrian would be lost. Lady Emmaline Deramore would live.

She'd clean up this mess. Take Adrian for herself. Make sure he lived as long as she wanted him to.

An ingénue like Emmaline was undeserving of such power, but Madeleine's hands were tied.

Madeleine hurled a crystal glass at the wall. She walked to the spot and stared down at the broken shards of glass. Removing the locket from her neck, she set it with trembling hands on a nearby table. The bare skin where it had rested prickled with the awareness of its absence.

Men.

She'd learned about their proclivities at a very tender age. If she'd known then what she knew now, she would have been able to control her father and his disgusting habits. Instead, she allowed the beast to violate her in ways no father ever should before she had the good sense to leave that prison and seek a nobleman's protection. Another debaucher's protection.

Eight years of abuse had served well to shatter any romantic notion she may have ever entertained about the male gender. If she'd learned one thing, it was that a woman should only grant the illusion of control to a man.

Never her heart. Never herself.

So why was she this angry? Adrian had no power over her. He was a man. He may be bound to Emmaline, but he couldn't deny his nature.

She needed to vent her rage on something. On someone.

Picking up a pointed piece of glass, she rushed to the chair in the corner. Her slave was unconscious, barely breathing. Patches of blood had dried around the gushes on her forearms. It had spilled on the armrests where her hands were tied, and stained the rich grain of the walnut with gruesome marks.

Summoning the sight was a ritual she performed sparsely, or when Mr. Anthony, the accommodating Master of the workhouse in Bishop's Stortford, was able to supply a particularly attractive specimen without familial ties or strong friendships. The coin she sent him through Jones fed his ill-managed gambling habit and kept him out of debtors' prison.

This one girl would satisfy her enough. The alternative would have been a long night in Mrs. Kilworth's pleasure den, and she preferred to stay in today.

A frisson of excitement leapt up Madeleine's chest as she ran a sharp edge of the glass up the girl's arm and then below the rope across her wrist, careful to only produce a long, superficial scratch along the way. For now.

The girl's eyes shot open, the large blue orbs terrified and guileless. Despite a body that had crossed the periphery to womanhood, her spirit still clung to the innocence of youth. Madeleine watched the pretty plump face twist in a macabre mask of pain.

"At last, you are awake, poppet," she purred. "I am not finished with you yet and I am positively dying to play."

A game to be followed by an unforeseen visit to the woman she hated most in the world.

CHAPTER 3

"By the pricking of my thumbs,
Something wicked this way comes."
[Macbeth, Act IV, Scene I]

DECEMBER *23, 1807.*
Belvoir Hall.

ADRIAN ENTERED the dining room early to find that it already had one occupant at the table. He pulled a chair back and sat down, whistling a tune.

"Aren't we chipper this morning."

Adrian offered the older woman across from him an affectionate smile. "Good morning, Mother. Dare say I am. Did you sleep well?"

"As well as could be expected, my lord. There is still so much to do and only one day to accomplish it. Yesterday, my scatterbrained sister addled my mind with her incessant gossip and as usual, Cousin

Imelda has predicted all kinds of doom to befall us by year end. My poor head feels like a merry-go-round."

She sighed and chewed on a dainty morsel of shirred egg.

"I trust our wedding guests are all settled, then?"

"A few are expected today but for the most part we have a full house. Thank heavens, most keep London hours even in winter and they are still sleeping the sleep of babes. My guess is they shall not be making an appearance for a few hours more."

"By the by," she added after a short pause, "Smith delivered a message from the Jenners. It said their roof is leaking again." She tore a bite-sized morsel from a Bath bun and ate it.

"Yes, I have been apprised. I shall see to it after breakfast." Adrian made a mental note to notify his steward but he always liked to see to things personally first. After all, the tenants' industry was what made the estate profitable.

He ignored the array of dishes on display and accepted a covered plate from the footman. The silver dome, when lifted, revealed an enormous beefsteak.

Lady Philippa Segrave eyed her son with weary incredulity. "I cannot understand how you can consume that monstrosity this early in the day. I say, your constitution must be made of steel."

"But, Mother, there is nothing like a succulent cut of beef to revive one's spirits at the start of day. You should try it."

She shot him a look of exaggerated affront. "Not upon my life. The sight of so much meat on one plate makes me ill."

"It is a pity then, although this particular one is not quite as tasty as the usual," he sighed as he chewed the first forkful with a bit of difficulty. "Cook must be experimenting with her spices again."

She smiled fondly. "Perhaps the unpleasant taste will induce you to amend your preference to more acceptable breakfast fare."

"Not likely. I need my strength, especially now that I am about to be *leg-shackled*," he ribbed. He winked at her as he sliced into the hearty fillet and popped a large bite into his mouth.

The dowager threw her head back in a mock gesture of exasperation. "Ah, you're impossible! But, I trust our dearest Emmaline will set you to rights," she finished in a triumphant tone.

"Did you not hear, she already has."

His mother's tiny frame shook with laughter. Her angelic blue eyes danced and in that moment, Adrian thought, despite the graying hair and deep grooves around her mouth and eyes, she looked so young and beautiful—a perfect English rose.

"How I wish…" she started, but her voice faltered.

"I know. So do I."

Their eyes met. As much as he had lost a father and brother, she had been deprived of a devoted husband and son. They shared this unspoken connection, a sense of unity in loss. He admitted to himself that for her, it must have been near unbearable. What loving parent wants to survive their children?

They sipped their coffee and enjoyed a few moments of silence until Adrian finally stood. "I cannot leave the Jenners waiting with a cracked roof so I have to bid you leave. I will see you at dinner and please, do not overextend yourself," he said, wrinkling his eyebrows.

"You know I cannot make such assurances, silly man. The wedding's in the morning! My *son*'s wedding."

He approached her and laid a hand on her slender shoulder. "I suppose I should have known better than to ask you that."

"You must be riding today," she remarked, patting his hand and looking up at him with undisguised affection. "I see you are dressed for it."

He gave her a lopsided smile. "Yes, Mother, and I promise to be careful." As he often did, he had anticipated her question.

"Make sure you do, then. I daresay you look rather dashing in blue superfine. Gives you a dignified air. You look *every inch* the viscount."

He chuckled and bent down to whisper so only she could hear. "Must you embarrass me in front of the footmen?"

She offered him her cheek and squeezed his hand. "Always," she replied just as softly, her face beaming as he planted a soft kiss on her weathered skin. "I shall look forward to seeing you at supper, my son."

———

MEANWHILE, at Trenwith...

EMMALINE LOUNGED in the library with a book on her lap. Breakfast remnants of hot chocolate and lemon scones lingered on her taste buds. Huddled in an oversized leather wingback chair with stockinged feet tucked under her, she indulged her fancy without guilt. She had pored through so many lists and trudged through so many tasks that her head still spun. Reading her novels was a much more enjoyable pastime, but today was different.

While she immersed herself in thoughts of her encounter with Adrian the day before, she couldn't get past the first page as her mind kept summoning images of his heavy body moving above hers, his hands setting her on fire, and his gaze running over her in undisguised desire.

Lewis' croaky bass forced her attention away from her shameless reverie.

"What, uh, can you repeat that please?"

"You have a visitor, my lady."

Lewis stood just inside the door to the library holding a small silver tray. His old frame bent like the spine of a crossbow, and his protruding ears brought to mind times long past. Times that involved her as a little girl playing piggy back with the butler and pulling on the fleshy lobes for purchase. A paragon of patience, he never rebuked her for it.

Only once did she remember him losing his usual cool composure – when she had suggested he retire and enjoy the rest of his life in a lovely cottage on her father's estate. He would have none of that, he had insisted. His place was in the household performing his duties, or nowhere at all. And that was that. She never again brought up the subject.

Emmaline landed back on Earth and blinked at the butler.

"A visitor?" Who could it possibly be? She was not expecting anyone to call.

"It is a lady. Red hair and rather tall. Quite … extravagant, if I may say so."

"Does the lady have a name?"

"Yes, Lady Deramore. Here is her card."

He presented the tray whereupon sat a rectangular piece of high-grade ivory stock. She uncurled her legs and lowered them to the floor as she picked it up to read.

The bold letters slammed into her head with a loud bang. The open book slipped off her lap as she clutched the card with both hands so she could re-read the printed script one, two, three times.

"What could *she* want with me?" she whispered in disbelief.

Lewis looked uncharacteristically flustered. "Pardon me, my lady. I can tell her you are not accepting calls—"

"No, no, Lewis, it is perfectly fine," she interrupted. "I shall see her in the drawing room. Could you please have Lily bring some tea over there? I can only hope the woman does not intend to stay long." The last sentence was spoken in a low grumble, but she was sure it was loud enough to reach Lewis' still sharp ears.

Emmaline thought she imagined the butler's lips twitch.

"Certainly, my lady."

Left alone in the library, she frowned and mentally prepared herself for the encounter. What was Madeleine de Brandeville doing here? They were not friends, or even well acquainted, for that matter. She had been invited to the wedding only because of neighborly courtesy. The rumors said the Frenchwoman was a rather reclusive sort who preferred the delights of the city and her own mysterious set of friends.

"Bloody hell, I suppose I better get this over with," she muttered, wiggling her toes. Swearing was something a lady would never do but sometimes the circumstances warranted it, even if she could only do it in private.

If she had a choice, she'd rather have a visit with the Devil's witch Mother Haggy, the feared ghost of St. Albans, than see this woman.

She found the slippers and slipped her feet into them. She stood, shrugged her shoulders, straightened her skirt with clammy palms, and tucked a stray lock of hair behind her ear. "There, there . . ."

Taking a long, steady breath, she left the room.

"Lady Deramore, you look lovely. Thank you so much for receiving me this early. I feared I would not be able to see you before my departure," her visitor greeted when she joined her.

"Your departure?" Emmaline said, confused.

Oh, joy! But why bother to come here and tell me?

"Yes, *très chère*. My wandering blood yearns for warmer climes. I have been planning a trip to Italy for a while and finally, the time has come."

The epitome of elegance, Lady de Brandeville sat straight on a French style Hepplewhite chair with gold upholstery and a serpentine back. Thankfully, this allowed Emmaline to find a seat in the matching chair across from her, rather than share the settee at more proximity than she could bear.

"I have ordered some tea," she said hesitantly. "It should be here soon."

"Thank you. You are too kind."

An uncomfortable silence ensued. Emmaline's gaze fleeted from the huge claret plume adorning the gentlewoman's bonnet to the deep burgundy carriage dress that perfectly matched her magnificent red hair.

She searched her brain for a question to ask. "So, when shall you leave?" she finally spouted, praying she did not sound too eager.

"Today, I am on my way south. I decided to pay you a visit to offer *félicitations* for your wedding and let you know that regrettably, I shall not be able to attend." A wistful smile tugged at the Frenchwoman's lips.

"I am indeed sorry to hear that," Emmaline lied. "We would have loved you to join us at the breakfast." She prayed she would not get struck by lightning as she picked at an invisible piece of thread on her skirt.

Footsteps patted inside the room when she was pondering what else to say. She could not have chosen a better time for Lily to make an appearance.

"Tea and scones, my lady."

"Just lay the tray on the table, thank you. I shall pour." Lily curtsied and left. "How do you like your tea, Lady de Brandeville?"

"Call me Madeleine, please. And I hope you'll allow me to call you Emmaline. I feel as though we are friends," she cooed.

Her tone came across as fairly...what in God's name was the word? *Rehearsed.*

"Uh, certainly." Emmaline gritted her teeth. She was trying hard to be gracious but it was such a chore. All she wanted to do was to make *Madeleine* disappear. To say that the woman put her on edge was an understatement.

"I admit there is another reason for my calling on you. Would you consider me too forward if I asked you to offer some advice in regards to a book on travel describing the cities of Italy? I am in dire need of a guide and I have heard about your immeasurable love of reading. It is silly of me to leave this until the last moment but..." she sighed, letting her voice trail away.

What an exceedingly odd request. "Uh, I am sure there is something of the sort in the library."

Wonderful. Now she was starting every sentence with an "uh." The woman will think her an idiot.

"Oh, I would never impose on you in such a manner. It would be preposterous of me. I did not mean to imply that I want to you *loan* me a book. I would simply like a title to a good tome which I could purchase *en route* if I am lucky to find it."

"That is quite all right. It is no trouble." She would shave all her hair off and ride through Hyde Park bare-headed at the height of the London Season if it meant getting Madeleine out of the house as quickly as possible. "If you care to wait a moment, I'll go and look through our collection. I think I have just the book in mind for you."

Madeleine gave her a direct look that sent chills down her spine. "I must say, Lord Bournemouthe is *so* lucky to have as devoted a woman as you for a bride."

"Please pay no mind. I shall return shortly," Emmaline said, purposely eluding the reference to Adrian.

"Before you leave, kindly tell me how you like your tea. I shall pour."

"You must not disturb yourself. I shall do the honors upon my return."

"I am not inclined to take no for an answer," Madeleine insisted, "after you have showed me such kindness."

"Fine, then. Two teaspoons of sugar and cream."

"Of course."

Emmaline needed to get out of there as fast as polite manners allowed. She had made it all the way to the library before noticing she was holding her breath. Letting it out in a *whoosh,* she started to pace around the room, willing her heart to stop racing.

"Calm down. Calm down," she mumbled against her thumb as she sank her teeth into it. "Ouch!" she cried out when she bit a trifle too hard. She blew on the offended digit, waved it about to ease the throb.

If she attempted to describe in words how Madeleine made her feel, everyone would think that a collacine of maggots had taken up residence in her God-given mind. But how could she deny her intuition? It seemed to issue a loud warning whenever she laid eyes on the woman.

Suddenly, she remembered what she was there for and walked to the leftmost shelves of the wall adjacent to the door. Her practiced eye searched for a name and found it printed on the second book from the right on the bottom shelf. She pulled it out and read the cover.

Bartolommeo Borroni, the author, had it fresh off the Veladini printing press in Italy – a sophisticated traveler's guide from Milan to all major Italian cities, including maps, etchings, and all sorts of interesting historical and geographical information. A precious gift from a widowed aunt who had recently returned from a jaunt on the Continent, Emmaline was happy to part with it now. She could eventually replace the book, but she did not ever want to feel this way again.

"Good, let us drink tea and be done with it, then," she said to herself, and dragged her feet back to the drawing room.

Madeleine had finished pouring the tea and sat with her hands on her lap, clutching a pair of fine kid leather gloves. She greeted Emmaline with a grateful smile.

"I hope I did not put you through too much trouble. You must think me terribly rude."

"Not at all." *Yes, I do. Rude, forward, and double-faced.* "I found something for you."

Emmaline extended her hand and showed her the book, making sure Madeleine's fingers did not come in contact with her skin when she reached for it.

Madeleine leafed through the book and shook her head. "I cannot take this. It is too lovely."

"Of course you shall. Call it a gift meant to wish you a wonderful voyage." *And to send you off posthaste.*

"Then I give you my sincere thanks, Emmaline. Why do you not drink your tea and tell me if there is enough sugar in it?"

Emmaline frowned. "You shouldn't have…"

Madeleine waved her off. "Ah, never mind propriety. It is a pleasure."

Emmaline sipped heavily from her cup, keen to finish this charade. Whatever Madeleine was up to, a show of friendship was the last thing on her mind.

The brew had a bizarre taste to it. Something stuck in her throat and made her cough. Loose tea leaves? Not like Cook to be so careless.

"Are you all right, *très chère?*"

"Perfectly fine, thank you." Emmaline took another large sip. "Although it is rather hot in here, is it not?" She ran the back of her hand over her temple and pulled at the collar of her chemisette.

"Hot? I feel just right. This room is very welcoming."

Sweat beaded on Emmaline's brow and her hands became one with the porcelain cup handle. The sitting area rivaled the bowels of Hell, and not just because of the company. If she were alone, she would seriously consider stripping naked.

She could now see the bottom of the empty cup. Deep and dark, enough to get lost in. She placed it carefully back on the saucer. Pain whipped her, once, twice. She pressed a hand to her stomach and doubled up. When it subsided, she could barely sit back properly, let alone apologize for her behavior. Why was it so hard to move?

"Wha … I … arrrghk…" Her tongue stuck to the roof of her mouth and her breaths came short.

"*Très chère*, you look rather pale. Shall I ring for some water?"

Bloody hell.

"Y…" Madeleine had two heads. And four arms. They … *she* was still drinking tea.

"I cannot make out what you are trying to say, Emmaline. Perhaps it is best to lean back and settle down. You must not overexert yourself. The feeling shall pass, I am sure."

She could hear everything, every single sound and movement. The tapping of Madeleine's fingers on the chair rests. The random swish of wind hitting the windowpanes. Every swing of the fretted brass pendulum from the ormolu clock on the mantelpiece. But still, she could not speak a coherent word, or control any part of her body.

Tick. Tock.

Tick. Tock.

Madeleine's narrowed gaze slid down her form. After what seemed like an interminable silence, she waved her hand in the air and sighed. "Oh, all right. I can tell you now," she said in a bored tone. "It is chickweed, in addition to a special recipe of mine to take care of other irksome things, such as memory."

"Ah … waaa…"

"You will become paralyzed for a brief period, Emmaline. When it is past, you will somewhat remember my visit but not the details, of course, at least not for a good while. I cannot have you on my heels so soon. Let us just say that for some time your brain will be, how to say it? *Muddled*, yes, but eventually, clarity will return."

Tick. Tock.

Madeleine was standing now. She was tall, *so* tall. The gloves were on the table. She walked toward her. The motion was too fast. It dizzied Emmaline.

Why was the lady wiping her teacup? How strange, a lady cleaning teacups.

Tick. Tock.

"Cannot have them snoop around and finding the leaves. Sit back, I will only take a moment. Oh, I forgot … you *cannot* move, *oui?*"

Madeleine's shrill laugh tore through her wits. She wished she could shut her eyes and ears to the ghastly sound.

Madeleine rummaged through her reticule. "Where is the blasted thing? Ah, here it is." She lifted a small glistening object to the light of the window.

A knife?

Run! She wants to kill me.

Emmaline tried to sit up.

Cannot move...damn her!

Tick. Tock.

"Did you really think I would let you have him?"

The blade approached.

God, no.

Tick. Tock.

"I want him and he shall be mine. He shall *always* be mine. And you shall suffer the pain of losing him forever. You will never find him."

Madeleine lifted Emmaline's hand, palm upwards. She could not feel that contact. Trying to pull her arm away was impossible, pointless. Her body was useless. Her legs, her arms, her face—everything had gone numb.

Tick. Tock.

Madeleine pointed the knife toward her palm.

No, stop! What was she doing to her?

"Do not fret, *très chère*. I see you already have a cut on your hand. This will not hurt at all; you must thank me for that," she sneered.

Stop calling me 'my dear', you fiend.

The sharp edge cut into her palm, but if she did not happen to see a line of blood gushing out she would never have noticed.

Madeleine made a similar incision in her left palm, too. Her face remained impassive at first, no hint of pain. She rather looked as though she enjoyed the feeling. The woman was well and truly touched in the upper works.

What if madness ran in her family? As the twig is bent, so is the tree inclined. It was exceedingly dangerous for someone like that to roam freely in society. She had to warn Adrian, somehow. The instant she managed to get out of this pile of trouble, she would.

Adrian.

Tick. Tock.

"Get ready. How lucky for you not to feel this. It was not so pleasant when it was done to me. It is a nuisance now, but a necessary one."

Madeleine placed her bloodied palm on hers and held on. Her fingers seemed to spread out and curl around hers like tiny snakes stretching from Medusa's head. Like many of the Gorgon's victims in the myths, Emmaline longed to avert her eyes from the evil image but could not. She could tell something was happening by the look of Madeleine's twisted features but it was like being in another universe and seeing herself from far, far away. Madeleine did not scream; her lips were sealed in a thin white line. Her eyes misted, as if she was bracing through waves of extreme physical pain.

Tick. Tock.

Then, the woman's expression returned to its beautiful perfection. Whatever had just happened, it was over.

"We are done, Emmaline. I have given you the most unique of gifts. What do you English say? Give and take is fair play, *oui*? I take Adrian, and give you eternal life in return."

Madeleine prodded her so she plopped back into an undignified position on the settee. Her fingers traveled over Emmaline's face in a Judas caress.

"You will be fine in less than a half hour," Madeleine continued matter-of-factly. "Not quite enough time for the doctor to arrive, I promise. For all intents and purposes, we only had some tea together and a nice little chat. Look at that." She pointed at Emmaline's hand. "Your wound is already healing."

Madeleine donned her gloves and picked up her reticule. She tucked the knife inside it.

Tick. Tock.

"I suppose I can alert a footman to your *malaise*. I vow, all the preparations for the wedding must be taking such a toll on you. Unfortunately, I cannot tarry. After all, I have a fine man to go to. I feel quite like the expectant bride!"

No!

She looked outside the window and made a face. "Indeed, I better rush before rain starts to pour. Really, one never knows with this English weather," she said dryly. "I bid you a good life, Emmaline. If you have a care, it shall be a long one."

She turned to Emmaline with down-turned lips and spite in her eyes. "I have no notion why you and Adrian foolishly decided to consummate your union before the wedding. It displeased me greatly, but Adrian will be well taken care of. I give you my word. *Adieu.*"

She made to leave then thought better of it and turned to face her again. "It may be long before all your memories return. But should you get any silly ideas, I assure you that the only way the shield between you and Adrian can be destroyed is through death. I made certain of that. Adrian shall *never* be yours for as long as you breathe," she spat before marching away.

Tick. Tock.

Shield. Dies. Destroyed. Never be reunited with Adrian.

What did she mean?

Tick. Tock.

Tick. Tock.

Gong. The half hour had struck.

The click of the door a moment later signaled Madeleine's departure and Emmaline's only thought before she fainted was, *Adrian, please, I need you. Adrian, where are you?*

———

BELVOIR HALL, *the Master's bedchamber.*

.   .   .

SMITH MOVED inside the Viscount's bedchamber with the quiet agility of a cat. After he'd spent days trying to think of a way to get Bournemouthe out of the house, an unforeseen blessing fell on his lap. The damage to the Jenners' roof was as good an excuse as any other to achieve his purpose, and it happened with perfect timing.

Satisfied with the fortuitous turn of events, this morning he had seen to the Viscount's breakfast. His prey had specific culinary tastes and forwent the customary buffet, which made his job significantly easier. Serving the meal was part of his duties as footman in the Bournemouthe household. With the vial sent by Lady de Brandeville safely in his pocket, lacing the beefsteak had proved to be child's play. Cook never left the kitchen but she was too distracted with chopping up vegetables for dinner to pay him any mind.

With calculated movements, he carefully picked several items—shirts, breeches, underclothes, cravats, stockings, footwear, a couple of waistcoats and coats, and other miscellaneous things, as much as necessary for an extended trip—and tossed them in two burlap sacks he had managed to slip into the room with him.

At last, after having to pose in the paltry position of footman for three months, things were starting to pay off. He ached to return to his old life as an artist but Madeleine had him by the bollocks with the promise of opium and sex. If he performed this task properly, she would be very happy. And when she was happy, he was a *very* satisfied man. His cock stirred at the thought.

"Must get on with this," he muttered to himself. He could not wait to join the others at the inn and be rid of this place for good, but he had to stick around for some time to avoid raising any suspicion of wrongdoing. Too risky for him to go to Madeleine, so all instructions came through the middleman, Jones, when they met in a neutral location such as a tavern or market.

He was going to see this through. Madeleine would reward him for his diligence. Compensation in coin would be just the thing, but the pot would be so much sweeter if she allowed him into her bed again. A woman like Madeleine could wake the dead with her sensual tricks. She was his muse, and he pined for her—so much that he was prepared to share her with the bastard aristocrat if need be.

He hoped she wouldn't take long to send for him.

He finally concluded the sacks were full enough and proceeded to rope both necks with lengths of thick twine, secured in tight knots. Then, he dragged them to the window and made sure nobody was about before opening it. The Viscount's room was on the second floor. It faced a tranquil area in the garden of sprawling lawn hemmed with trees and shrubbery.

The crisp morning air whipped at his face. Only the stable-hands would be outdoors at this time, and by now he was used to everyone's timetable. The gardener was not likely to show up on this side of the mansion for at least an hour.

He held on tight to the end of rope, lifted the laden gunny bags on the ledge and pushed them out a little too quickly. The fast forward momentum and the heavy bundle caused him to tip too far over the ledge.

"Sodding rags!" he ground out through clenched teeth. After regaining his balance, he slowly lowered them to the ground below. The three foot high clipped holly hedge that lined the wall beneath Bournemouthe's window allowed enough space between the hedgerow and the wall to serve as adequate concealment for the two bags until Jones and his slow-witted nephew came to retrieve them.

When the sacks reached solid ground, he let go of the ropes and hastily closed the window. He paused to take a deep breath before he tip-toed to the door and cautiously turned the knob. Pulling it ajar, he stuck his head out. Nobody around. He eased out of the room with padded feet and reached the servants' stairway without incident.

He patted his chest as he negotiated the stairs. The letter was still there, hidden in the inside pocket of his uniform. It bore Bournemouthe's seal—a task he had the opportunity to perform earlier in the day. When the time was right, he would figure out a way to enter the Viscount's study and place the note somewhere conspicuous. He had taken a peek at the forger's job. Jones claimed the man was the best in the business and he had to admit, Jones was right. If he were one of *his master's* close relatives or associates, he would have no doubt Bournemouthe's hand that penned those words.

"Smooth as oil," he said to the empty walls as he made his way down to the kitchen. The wheels were in motion and there was no stopping them. "Now all I need is a good tumble."

All the excitement gave him a ravenous appetite. Lettie would do nicely. She was sweet on him, and he had tried her once, a week earlier, when he caught her dusting her mistress's private parlor. She was all alone and begging for a good swiving. As he remembered that day, his manhood swelled and rubbed against his breeches.

But, as he stepped into the kitchen, all he found waiting for him was a small army of household staff. A quick look at the suspicious faces gave him pause. For one, Mrs. Fornsby, the big-boned house-keeper, looked about ready to pounce. Three footmen stood ramrod straight behind her wearing unsympathetic expressions. Two of them carried each a burlap sack; they were the selfsame ones he had just deposited behind the hedge below the Viscount's window.

Fuckin' hell.

Mr. Merriam, the butler, stepped forward. "Smith, do you care to explain what you were doing just nonce in the master's chambers?" he asked in an accusatory tone.

He moved to the side and let the other footmen surround him.

"Please follow me," Merriam added before Smith could answer the question. "I believe you should say your piece in front of the mistress."

CHAPTER 4

"Come, thick night,
And pall thee in the dunnest smoke of hell,
That my keen knife see not the wound it makes,
Nor heaven peep through the blanket of the dark,
To cry 'Hold, hold!'"

Back at Trenwith...

"Lady Deramore, please wake up."

The pungent odor of hartshorn tempered with hints of jasmine and thyme burst through Emmaline's senses. Her stomach flipped.

"The salts are not working, Lewis. Look at 'er, she's still as a broomstick. We must send for the doctor and Lord and Lady Kentmore!"

Hattie's alarmed, squeaky voice ricocheted back and forth inside her head. The pounding turned atrocious.

"Let me try a few more times. If she does not come to, we shall do as you say."

Lewis had an innate mistrust for doctors. She must look an awful sight if he was considering sending for one.

"Do you think Milady's visitor had anything to do with this? Perhaps she upset her some way, and she was in an awful hurry, weren't she?"

"Calm down, Hattie. Were it not for the lady in question, we may not have been alerted to Lady Deramore's state. Now, allow me to concentrate and stop the chattering."

A grunt then ... silence. *Thank you, Lewis!*

Emmaline's head continued to throb and spin as if a gale wind blew through her, but without her maid's prattling, it resembled Purgatory more than Hell.

Someone—she guessed Lewis—passed the smelling salts back and forth under her nose. The strong fumes crept through her nostrils to her lungs. Short and fast breaths rallied inside her chest and a strong tickly sensation rose to her tonsils. What resulted felt and sounded like an asphyxiated half-cough.

"That's better. Hattie, hand me that, will you?"

Soft steps walked away from her, the sound of liquid poured, and glass clinked with glass.

The steps hurried back.

"Mum, 'tis Hattie. Lewis 'as some water for you. Take a sip."

Thirsty. The cool rim of glass pressed against her sealed mouth and a few drops of moisture made it through her parched lips. The water soothed her tongue that felt distended like a lizard's dewlap. She tried to open her mouth and eyes at the same time and managed the former, at least in small measure. A bit more liquid poured in.

Little by little, life returned to her stiff muscles and joints. Her eyes fluttered open and her rescuers came into focus. Hattie stood in front of her wringing her hands and wearing a troubled expression, and Lewis knelt on one knee with the goblet extended half-way to her lips, one arm keeping her in a sitting position.

Sweet God above. How could she faint on her couch, while seeing a visitor? She could not remember a thing that happened after she gave Madeleine the book and sat with her for a short while.

"What, uh, what happened to me?"

"You be passed out, mum," Hattie offered, stating the obvious. "Cow's bells, ye got me terrified as a sweet angel in Hell. Now, ye must go upstairs and rest."

Emmaline raised her head and somewhat found her speech. "I c-cannot. I m-must … get … Adrian."

Lewis handed her the goblet and rose to his feet. Although weak, her fingers curled easily around the stem. He let go after making sure she could hold it. She took another sip of water.

"Lewis, you tell 'er she needs sleep. Fainting must've addled her wits."

Emmaline gave an undignified gasp and cleared her throat. "Hattie, I—I have no idea why I … let you speak so."

She let her because Hattie knew her more than she knew herself, practically raising her.

"Because I make sense, is why. We shall send a note to Lord Bournemouthe telling 'im you are sick and not to get his feathers ruffled. Ye'll 'ave ample time to snuggle up to 'im tomorro'."

Emmaline's face heated. She was sitting up straighter now, her feet flat on the carpet.

"I should let you go without a reference," she griped.

"Harrumph, nuthin' but empty threats."

"Insolent harpy."

Lewis looked from one woman to the other and witnessed the irregular exchange between mistress and servant with the characteristic blank expression on his face. Never mind his calm demeanor; he must think them both mad. Yet, although Hattie's straight tongue drove her to the door of insanity at times, her concern for her well-being was touching. The woman loved her like a mother.

"All right, I will rest for a while but I shall write a note first. See that it gets delivered to Belvoir Hall." Emmaline attempted to lift her body from the couch but her head reeled and she sank back down as if pulled by gravity. "Damn it," she mumbled.

Lewis gave her a quizzical look. "Excuse me, my lady?"

"Never mind. Just talking to myself."

"Quite right."

Another attempt to rise failed miserably. It elicited a helpless moan and this time, also an unvoiced curse.

Lewis bent down. "May I help you to the desk, Lady Deramore?" he asked, but did not wait for her answer. He curled his hand around her upper arm. "Hattie, you take the other side."

Together, they helped her up and walked baby steps to the escritoire at the far end of the room. They lowered her on the chair and waited patiently while she scribbled a message. It seemed to take forever with her fingers feeling cramped and cold. Finally, she was done with it and handed it to Lewis.

"I shall take care of this shortly, Lady Deramore, but allow us first to assist you up the stairs to your bedchamber."

She nodded, too tired to complain. After her feet made the laborious climb to her room, she let Hattie attend to the removal of her clothing. It was so easy to submit to slumber the instant her head lowered onto the pillow.

Same time, at Belvoir...

"John, old chap, what a shiny specimen we have here."

"Always a pleasure, m'lord. He's a fine 'un. All saddled and ready. My Tom 'elped with the brushing this mornin'. Methinks one day 'e'll make a fine stable master, jist like 'is dad." John unveiled a buck-toothed grin.

Adrian returned the smile. "I am sure I'll agree."

John had been at the Bournemouthe estate since he was a mere child, when his father took care of the stables for the preceding viscount. From an early age, working with horses was all he wanted to do. And he was mighty good at it, too.

Adrian offered Thunder an apple and patted the animal between the eyes. "Feel up to a ride, my boy?"

The horse snorted in gratitude and John made an echoing sound. "Weather's tak'n a bad turn today, sir. Rain 'n sleet be comin' down any minute. Kin feel it in me bones."

Adrian turned to look at the overcast sky outside the stable door. "Maybe," he agreed. "Best if we run, then. I think Thunder is rearing to go."

"So he is, m'lord. 'ave a good ride and watch the ground or ye'll find yerself in a peck of troubles. Be frozen in some parts." John tipped his cap in salute and walked off as a young groom ran toward him.

"M'lord!" he gasped. "Sumthn' 'appened ... about Smith ... the footman ..." He stopped in front of him to catch his breath.

"I need to get to the Jenners early. Can Merriam handle it?"

"I dunno, sir. They be holdin' 'im now and Milady's talkin' ta him. He stole sumthn' from ye."

Adrian nodded gravely. Smith was the new groom who'd served him breakfast that morning. He seemed a quiet enough sort.

"Shouldn't be much longer than a half hour. When my mother's done, tell them I want Smith held in his room and his door guarded until I get back. Keep all other staff from entering except for Merriam and Fornsby."

"Will do, sir." The boy ran back to the house.

Adrian guided the horse out of the stall and hoisted himself on the saddle. As abrupt as towering ocean waves in a storm, a dizzy spell rolled into him. He shook his head and willed his stomach to settle. Could he be coming down with the ague? Two of their maids had fallen sick last week, what with the weather being more changeable than a thorny debate in the House of Lords.

"Bollocks," he objected to his thoughts. A good shot of brandy upon his return would set him to rights. He banished the thought as he eased Thunder into a trot.

"Let us take it easy for a while then we will set you free."

In minutes, he reached one of his favorite riding spots—dozens of acres of open grassland, which led to some of the tenant farms. He urged the horse into a gallop.

"There you go. Good boy!"

He loved the freedom of riding hard against the wind. A passion he shared with Emma, and another reason for loving her. On the worst days, he was careful to avoid slippery roads but in large spaces such as this, he let his senses rule. He became one with the beast beneath him and the nature around him; an experience far more exhilarating than a reeling Season among the London *haute monde*.

Another wave of giddiness riffed through him. Soon, he would be upon the path that eventually forked westward to the Roman ruins and north to Beech Bottom Dyke. Usually unencumbered by traffic, this was the most efficient route to the Jenners' cottage so he pulled at the reins to slow Thunder down and gather his wits.

The horse obeyed but his body did not. The ground and trees ahead seemed like brown and green smears on an amateur artist's canvas. No matter how hard he tried, he was unable to blot them out. He shut his eyes and opened them again and again, hoping to clear the haze. It failed to work.

Once more, he drew in the reins to lull the horse into a slow canter. Sweat beaded his brow. Finally, a blurred shape resembling a dirt road started to materialize but the strip of land oscillated in front of him, see-saw fashion. He felt like a child on a swing but it did not make sense. Thunder was moving at a snail's pace.

"Hell and damnation." He grunted.

Pain sliced through his belly with a butcher's knife. His torso doubled over until his face was buried in Thunder's mane. He let out a muffled cry.

What is wrong with me? he wanted to say.

His body shook so violently that he feared the horse would panic and set off in a wild gallop. Suddenly, it seemed too much of an effort to hold on to the reins and his thighs weighed him down like heavy sacks of flour. His arms became two poles of gelatin, nerveless. There was no part of him that he could control. The ache persisted, but he felt detached from his body—a respite he somewhat welcomed.

He was slipping, slipping down, lower, into some subterranean world. Dots of light in a spiraling vortex paraded behind his eyelids. A storm of color burst into the picture and pulled him deeper into the abyss. He was barely aware of losing his grip on the saddle and dropping to the ground.

No pain flooded him now, only a universe of nothing, and the awareness of his muscles gone stiff. He sank into a soft pillow of mud and muck, but it did not smell like much of anything. He now faced the darkening clouds above, puffs of gray swansdown with radiant linings, and he floated on air, just like them. The feather-soft clouds seemed to make his bed, comfort he could sink in. He needed to let go; he felt so, so tired. Tiny drops of water fell on his dry mouth and face. Something like rain; it teased him but he was too numb to bother.

Nothing bothered him, so he kept his eyes closed. A beautiful vision with silk black hair, doe eyes, and glowing olive skin burst through the mad haze.

Emma.

In the absolute silence and the swirling fog that claimed him, that vision stayed with him.

Emma, I love you. No, I mustn't die now. Not now. Let me see you again.

Then he simply drifted. He drifted and swayed in this giddy world of color and light, and went to sleep.

———

FROM HIS HIDING place behind a poplar, Jones watched Bournemouthe sink to the ground like a puppet severed from its string. His employer's recipe was taking effect sooner than he thought but something was amiss. He had paid a visit to Belvoir Hall and Smith had not left the bags with the viscount's things as agreed.

After he and Billy checked more potential hiding places in the vicinity, they returned to the carriage empty handed but unseen. Billy did speak to one of the scullery maids who was sweet on him and found out quickly what was going on. At least, his shallow pate of a nephew was good for something.

It seemed that Smith had been caught coming out of the viscount's room. The maid said that he was being questioned but did not know much more, except that she heard he may be guilty of thievery.

Most likely, Smith would blow the whistle about the mistress' involvement. Jones groaned. The last few days he had been a bunch of nerves, mainly for fear of what the mistress would do to him if they failed, whether through some fault of his or otherwise. Lady de Brandeville demanded results; how he got them did not matter one whit to her as long as he *did* get her what she wanted. Sweat burst through the clammy skin of his brow and his stomach knotted up as he thought that he needed to inform the mistress about this unexpected pickle. She wouldn't tolerate a botched job.

He had high hopes for Lady de Brandeville's plans, and he admired her cautious thinking and intelligence. She was a right one, despite the fact that she was a woman. In his mind, he had been hoping that this ship would sail easily and everything would turn out like a charm. Now, they were in a serious predicament. Smith could destroy them all.

But first, he needed to deposit Bournemouthe in the carriage and see to the horse. He had to make sure to avoid all major roads as the viscount was well known around these parts. The plan was to ride at breakneck speed, or as fast as a two horse carriage would allow, for five hours north. Then, they would stop a half mile away from The Crown Inn, where they were instructed to meet Lady de Brandeville and stop for the night. The next day, they would continue their journey with both carriages.

Clearly, there would be some changes to the plan. Bournemouthe needed clothes and they had better steer clear of major roads. Lady de Brandeville should not attract attention, and with her streak of vanity that could be a problem. Fortunately for them all, she had the foresight to hire modest transportation.

Jones sighed. The mistress had told him that Bournemouthe should be unconscious for the better part of a day. He hoped she was right as he stepped down from the carriage and walked toward the gent's limp body. Billy trailed behind him.

Jones looked up at the sky. "Make yerself useful and 'elp me get 'im inside. We must hurry up and be gone before the storm blows over."

———

December 24, 1807.
   Trenwith.

STREAKS OF LIGHT ran in relay to dispatch the gloom through the partially drawn curtains. Emmaline woke to the concerned face of Adrian's mother who pressed a cool palm to her temple.

"Lady Segrave," she said hoarsely. "This is unexpected."

Thoughts of Madeleine's visit rushed to the front of her mind and she remembered being helped upstairs by Lewis and Hattie. They had told her how Madeleine had sought help when she lost consciousness. How utterly peculiar that she could not evoke most of their conversation. The woman must be well on her way toward her Italian vacation by now.

She stretched her body underneath the blankets. "What time is it? It is kind of you to visit but you should not have troubled yourself. How long have I been asleep?"

A distraught pair of blue eyes—they were Adrian's eyes, limpid, alive—looked straight into hers. Lady Segrave sat on the edge of the bed and curled her aging hands around Emmaline's.

"My dear girl, how are you feeling today? When I was summoned yesterday and found Hattie in a fit, I did not know what to think. The doctor is of the idea that all you need is rest. You have spread yourself thin with the wedding preparations."

Emmaline pressed her hands into the mattress and abruptly lifted herself up against the pillows. She pulled her hand from the other woman's gentle grasp to fly to her aching head. She clenched her eyes tight when an arrow of pain shot through her eyes. It took some time for Lady Segrave's words to sink in.

"Wait a moment, did you just say *yesterday?*"

The dowager's face softened in sadness. "Yes, my dear. You slept all day yesterday and through the night."

"What time is it?"

A pregnant pause. "It is well past noon now."

Emmaline felt the blood rise to her head. "*What?* And the wedding? Why has nobody come to wake me up?"

The questions gushed from her lips faster than pouring wine at the village fair. Bile rose to her throat. She needed answers. *Now.*

"Emmaline, please calm down. I wanted to be here when you woke, to give you the news."

Lady Segrave looked stricken. Dread tainted every inch of the room and squeezed the air from her lungs.

"News?" Emmaline asked lamely.

Her visitor sighed and pulled a folded sheet of paper from the side pocket of her dress. She passed it to her with shaking hands then she got up and walked to the window to look out with absent eyes into the garden.

"That letter was found in a footman's pocket at Belvoir yesterday afternoon. Smith—that is the footman's name—he told us..." Turning around, she briefly rubbed two fingers against her temple. "Well, he told us the most incredible story." She linked her hands tight and raised them to her lips. "Dear God, Emmaline, something awful has happened!"

She rushed back toward Emmaline and sat back on the bed where she broke down in tears. Her breathing became short as she poured out her sorrow. Then she placed a palm on her heaving chest and the other across her mouth as if to still the unbearable emotion. She dried her eyes with the back of her hand. Stunned, Emmaline hadn't even thought to offer her a handkerchief, she suddenly realized.

As their gazes met, Emmaline saw the pure anguish in Adrian's mother's eyes. Panic replaced the haze, but this was soon knocked over by sheer terror. Blood drained from her face and coursed down her body.

"Lady Segrave, please tell me what happened. Is Adrian alright?" she asked, while grasping the other woman's arm.

"No, he is not. Well, I do not know. Emmaline, Adrian has been kidnapped."

"Kidnapped? How? By who?" she asked blankly.

If the situation were not so serious she would have laughed. How could such a thing be possible? Adrian had no enemies that she knew of. Aside from his trip to France where he acted for his country, he had never engaged in gratuitous confrontations or allowed himself to get in trouble. Other men his age gambled and lived dissolute lives. Adrian was a paragon of restraint and responsible manhood. She would never doubt him.

"You shan't believe this, but it appears that Lady de Brandeville, that horrible Frenchwoman who attended the ball at Belvoir, has been planning this for months. According to what Smith told me, he was in her employ and doing her bidding."

Lady Segrave related how Smith was caught.

"Those sacks with Adrian's possessions were to be picked up by some other accomplice who works for her. It did not take much to get Smith to tell us everything he knew once informed of the legal ramifications of his actions. Plainly, courage and loyalty are not his strongest qualities."

"But, where can she possibly take Adrian? Nobody could get away with such a thing."

"Men have kidnapped women for centuries, dear. In this circumstance, the roles have been reversed but the concept is the same. We still do not know where they are headed, or why she's doing this. For some reason, perhaps fear or ignorance, Smith has not been forthcoming with that information. My son never made it back home yesterday and I was forced to summon the judge who is holding him in a cell until he comes to his senses and decides to speak."

Emmaline digested Lady Segrave's words. She stared at the broken seal of the note that she still held in her hand. For a long moment, she simply stared at it, then, she pulled her legs up and opened the paper flat on her raised thighs.

In the oppressive silence, she read it over and over.

MOTHER,

I have just been apprised that an Englishman's life is in danger and I have been charged with returning to France to negotiate his release. I understand this is a most inopportune time but I have been given no choice in the matter. Kindly give Lord and Lady Kentmore, as well as my dear betrothed, my sincerest regrets. I shall endeavor to redeem myself upon my return.

Respectfully yours,

Adrian

HER FISTED HANDS tensed as they held the paper in place, crumpling the sides. Her nails dug into her skin.

Perhaps this was what Canning's meeting was about. But no, that was not possible. Adrian told her the man had merely sought advice and she believed him. The calligraphy was unmistakably Adrian's, but the words, the coldness of them, were certainly not.

And then there was Smith, the footman, who had confessed to foul play.

Lady de Brandeville was the key to all of this.

Her future mother-in-law placed a palm over her hands. "Emmaline—"

"I assume you know this note was forged. This did not come from Adrian," she said with absolute certainty. "Adrian is a viscount now, not a second son without responsibilities or something to prove to make him act in such a foolhardy manner."

Lady Philippa gave a long, ragged sigh. "Smith could have easily stolen some of the paper from Adrian's desk and passed it to a forger. Adrian was only supposed to go visit one of his tenants to ascertain the requirements for some repairs. This," she motioned to the note, "is shocking and illogical."

Emmaline nodded, glad that she and the older woman saw eye to eye. "Adrian would never do this to me or you. I would never have believed it. How could she do such a thing!"

Enraged, she shrugged Lady Segrave's hand off of her like she would a fly. Then she balled the letter and discarded it on the bed.

Lady Segrave's face was drawn and pale. She must not have had much sleep last night.

"We have organized extensive searches and your cousin has kindly offered all the help he can. But it is not an easy task with this weather. It rained most of the day yesterday and it is hard to make out any tracks in these conditions. Lady de Brandeville's residence is empty and the staff has been let off. We have located a few, the cook and a couple of maids, but none could be of help."

Emmaline shook her head. "No, it can't be."

She wanted to curl up into a ball and forget the world but instead, she buried her face in her knees and pounded at her shinbones with clamped fists. She was cursed, but it made no sense. The worst thing was the ambiguity of it all.

Was this to be her fate, then? Was Adrian never to be hers?

Was he in danger?

"My darling girl, I am so sorry. We must think what to do..."

Her heart cracked, her mind overcast with tar-like bleakness. "Please, leave me alone," Emmaline cried, uncaring of her manners.

"I shall do as you ask, but promise me you will eat something. I had the maid bring up a cold lunch earlier."

Emmaline gave a slight nod, if only to humor her visitor. The brief touch of a hand settled on the top of her head and then, the mattress rose.

Left to herself, she let despair pour from her gut. Since Madeleine's visit, things went haywire. Between heaving sobs, she wondered if the woman had given her something to harm her. Poison? But again, it was a ridiculous thought, and she did not want to think such things or waste more time.

She cried until there were no more tears left, until a sense of emptiness settled over her. It was as though she had left her body to observe her life from somewhere far, far away. The void was so much better than the unnecessary cruelty of raw, bruising pain. She wished she could stay this way and simply drift through life, without having to think or feel.

But that wasn't possible.

She ran the back of her hand over her eyes, washed away the tears. This was not the time to cry. Not now. Not ever. Tears would not return Adrian to her, safe and sound. She had to act.

She was dressed with speed and left her room, resolved to find out what happened. Madeleine had mentioned a trip to Italy; that was one detail she remembered. She'd start by sharing that information so no stone would be left unturned.

She'd get Adrian back. For no woman or man, nothing in the whole wide world, could take him away from her.

———

THE SUDDEN ROCKING motion jolted him from a dark, dreamless world. Through shut eyes, he realized he was lying on something soft but narrow, and his head had just thumped against a hard surface.

He was in some sort of vehicle, a carriage perhaps, and it must have hit a small rut in the road. The bumpy movement continued as he swayed in time with the wheels, but the ride felt a little smoother now. Almost lyrical—the repeated motion of back and forth, side to side, up and down, like when the sea washes its detritus onto the shoreline at the beach. The water then retreats and returns with more gifts for the receiving land.

Somewhere in the back of his mind, he thought he might enjoy the rhythmic sensation if his entire body did not feel like stiff tree bark. Or if his head were not seeking purchase, like a juggler's balls vying for a catch in a warm palm. He felt dazed and confused and most of all, he was wary of the situation.

Where was he?

But more importantly, *who was he?*

He opened his eyes. A giant scarlet feather attached to a small black hat was the first thing that greeted him. It clashed with the profusion of red curls beneath it. The woman wearing it wore a tightlipped, rankled expression that quickly turned to one of distress when she realized he was watching her. She immediately reached for his hands and clasped them firmly.

"Darling Adam! *Mon Dieu*, you are awake! I have been at wit's end, worrying about you."

The lady had an accent. Keeping his hands limp underneath her gloved ones, he sat up slowly and winced in pain.

She had called him Adam and she was touching him with a certain intimacy. Damn it all, what was going on here? Why was his mind blank?

If his muscles could make themselves heard, they would creak louder than rusted hinges. He must have been lying in the same position for a very long time. But despite the aches and pains that jabbed at him, only one thought nagged.

"Who..." He felt odd. He moved his jaw and mouth in a chewing motion. "Who am I?" he asked in a staccato voice.

To speak those first words was a Herculean effort. He licked his dehydrated lips and attempted to stretch his back and, to the extent that space would allow, his arms. Even with the pain that caused, he felt slightly better.

"What do you mean, my love?" she replied.

My love? "Excuse me, if you pardon my ... speaking plainly, what I mean to ask is, what am I doing here and ... and who are you?"

Shock replaced the semblance of concern. The woman's eyes widened to the point where he could see the whites above the green irises. One hand flew to her mouth to stifle a gasp. She made a rather theatrical picture.

"*Dieu du ciel!* You do not recognize me, do you? What shall I do now?" she cried.

Adam—he supposed that was his name—refrained from answering that question. The circumstances were too strange for words.

"You must have hit your head harder than I thought," she added, as though an afterthought. Her extended hand squeezed his tighter.

"Hit my head? What in the devil is going on?"

It seemed that in his anxiety to know the truth he had forgotten his manners, along with everything else.

"You fell from your horse on your way here yesterday. Something must have scared the animal. When you did not arrive at our meeting place, I sent someone to trace the route back to London. You were found early last evening lying face down in the filth. Your ride was grazing some distance away. There is no need to tell you how upset I was—"

"And who am I supposed to be?" he interrupted.

"Why, darling, your name is Adam Alvar. We just eloped. We are on our way to Scotland to get married."

The woman's words tumbled hard and fast into his brain, yet, he never felt a *thump* of recognition. Words failed him. He swallowed and waited for her to offer more information.

"Your father, Francis, never accepted the idea of you wedding a Frenchwoman. Alas, he died not long ago. For years, he had been suffering from the gout. Terrible indeed." She shook her head sadly. "Life is so short, *n'est-ce pas*? It is why we are taking hold of our own destinies, *mon amour*. Rushing to Scotland, it is all *très romantique!*" she said dreamily. She clasped her hands together on a heartfelt sigh and gave him a brilliant smile.

For a wild moment, he wondered if he had sneaked into somebody else's dream.

Or nightmare.

But the carriage was real. This woman was real. Her voice was real when she said, "But we can discuss all of that later. My name is Marie Colette Marchand, do I not look at all familiar? Does your head hurt?"

"No, ah, a little." He grimaced as he gingerly touched his temple. "I am sorry but I cannot … remember a thing. How can I reach my family?"

"As I said, your parents are dead, but I can tell you a little bit about them. Your father joined the church at an early age and you pursued a career in law. You are an only child, and so was your mother, who passed away a decade ago. Anything you have comes from my side of the family. I was widowed when I met you. You can say that I am your *only* family."

Her tone was curt and impatient. Then, her eyes softened. "I can still remember the day we met, my dear, as if it were only yesterday," she added quickly, as though regretting her behavior.

She reached out and touched his knee. Acting on reflex, he pulled back. "Why Scotland? Usually those kinds of elopements involve chits fresh from the schoolroom and furious relatives." Odd how he still knew general details about life in England but none about his own.

She removed her hand and shifted uncomfortably on her seat. He steepled his hands on his lap and looked down at them, hoping she was not about to engage in hysterics.

"As I said, it is *très romantique*. If you remembered everything, you would approve," she countered in a composed tone.

Touché. "Where am I from?"

Was that a hint of hesitation he sensed from her?

"Surrey."

"Wherefrom in Surrey?" he insisted.

"*Mon amour*, please do not exert yourself. I promise to answer your questions later but for now, I only want you to get better."

He would not be deterred. "I understand but kindly tell me, where are we going once we leave Scotland?"

She sighed. "To be frank, I—we—possess a charming little property in Scotland. London can only satisfy so long. And you know that as my husband, all that is mine becomes yours," she said with an indulgent smile.

A tear formed at the corner of her eye and started a downward slide. "*Mon Dieu*, I am so happy you are safe. I had a doctor visit you when you were unconscious." She sniffled, and raised a white handkerchief to her face to dab delicately at the dampness. "He gave me some medicine for you to take each morning and taught me how to prepare it. If you let me take care of you, we shall make sure you become well again in no time."

Adam kept silent. He turned his full gaze on her and tried to conjure a memory. She was undoubtedly beautiful, but he felt no connection with her. He felt no connection with anything around him. Least of all, to himself.

He could not hide his puzzlement. Marie moved to the edge of her seat, leaned over, and poised her hand on his cheek. Her lips hovered near his for a moment, then, pressed down on his mouth. Stunned, he kept his lips closed when her perfume made him recoil at some deep, elemental level.He did not want to offend her with an open rejection but he did not want to give her the impression that he wanted this, either.

Marie did not strike him as a stupid woman. In fact, he could tell she fast discerned his lack of responsiveness by the way she stiffened. Her mouth trailed to his cheek in a light caress before she sat back on the black velvet seat and crossed her hands primly on her lap. Her lips tightened to a thin line.

"But of course," she said with a shuttered expression. "How inconsiderate of me. I should give you time to get used to my affections. You will learn to love me again, I vow, and our marriage shall be a happy one."

Love. Marriage. All too much to take in, but offering a weak 'thank you' was all he could muster.

"Where are we now?" he finally asked.

"Not quite sure. Somewhere in Hertfordshire, I presume," she said noncommittally.

He returned his attention to the bucolic scenery outside the carriage window and forgot about garnering any more information. They would have to stop within a few hours, and he could ask the innkeeper a few questions if need be.

Rain drizzled down, so light it barely made a sound as it fell against the carriage window. Adam watched the drops hit the glass and slide in thin, trembling streams across it, pushed away from him by the north-facing wind. The slender rivulets would briefly meet, slide over the pane together and then separate, branch out in different directions, like a complex system of interconnected veins.

The landscape beyond the perfect chaos of the rain-spattered window also had a calming effect. The fields, trees, hills, and worked land in the distance called to him as they passed. The thought struck him that this might be an important clue to his past life.

Or was he grasping at straws? If he had to be honest, nothing bespoke of his past which hid somewhere behind the blank pages of his consciousness.

He would not have guessed his name had it not been told to him. He could not remember his family or his home. He could not recall who he loved and how he lived his days. It did not matter that he had no family, as Marie had told him. He was a shell of a body with no attachments, no memories to speak of. It gave him straight away a bleak feeling, and he wanted himself back.

He was spent. His body continued to throb from lack of exercise but if he had the option to move, he doubted he could even stand on his feet and walk without help. He wondered how long he had been sitting in this carriage. It seemed to be going too fast.

Why such a hurry?

He could not shirk the nagging voice in the back of his mind urging caution. There was something contrived about the way his companion behaved that didn't sit too well with him.

But, it was only a gut feeling with no solid basis to it. In truth, what other choice did he have? If he left this situation to continue alone, where would he go? It would be insensible of him to get away from the person who was the key to his past.

Marie drew him out of his introspection. "Adam, darling, you must take this now. I did not have the heart to wake you this morning so I decided to wait."

As she spoke, she searched in her reticule and produced a small flask. She extended her arm toward him and he accepted it. Her fingers brushed his fleetingly, sending a trickle of caginess to shimmy down his spine.

"Drink it. It will help you get a little more sleep."

Sleep. Despite the uncertainty he felt, that was all he needed to hear. He wanted nothing than to go back to oblivion and wake up to a different world. One he felt a tie to.

He tilted the flagon and let the liquid course into his mouth. At the first bitter swallow, his throat constricted.

"What is this?" he growled between coughs. "It is … abominable!"

"I understand but please, it is for your own good. I can give you some wine if you wish to wash out the taste."

Adam tapped his fist several times on his chest. "No need. I shall be fine."

She had asked him to repose his trust in her. Fair enough. But right now, he did not want to have to talk to this woman. He did not want her to touch him. Most of all, he did not want to think about the present or what he should do.

He raised his hand and toasted, "To life." *And, the irony of it all.*

Bracing himself, he tilted the flask again and downed the rest of its contents in one gulp.

Once he got over the taste, the effect spread immediate and wonderful. He let his head drop back and savored the sense of peace and numbness that filled him.

As he closed his eyes, he caught Marie's smile.

"I shall have some more prepared for the morn. We will be stopping somewhere tonight but in the meantime, please have a rest."

A part of him heard Marie's run-on spiel, but not for long.

She had told him his parents were dead. She said he had no family. But even as he let go, he wondered if anyone at all was feeling his absence, right at this moment, in some place within the whole breadth and length of England.

CHAPTER 5

"False face must hide what the false heart doth know."
[Macbeth, Act I, Scene VII]

DECEMBER 24, 1807.
Northbound to Scotland.

ONE MORE HOUR OF TEDIOUS, wet countryside and they would find shelter at an inn. Madeleine's sore bottom and rigid bones complained, but it was all worth the sacrifice. In a few days, they would be settled in their new home.

She thought over the events of the past few days since the Belvoir Annual Ball. Despite the setback that forced her to deal swiftly with Lady Deramore, this affair proceeded to her satisfaction.

Until yesterday, when Jones' alarming report threw her into a vile rage. It was all she could do not to wring his neck on the spot while he stuttered his version of events.

Inclined to believe Smith untrustworthy, she was forced to think fast. There was no time to deal with Smith the way she'd have liked. She had to leave the lion's cage behind and never look back.

First, she had Jones arrange to change horses and purchase food and refreshments at the White Horse in Baldock, but they did not stop there. She instructed that they leave immediately, veer off the Great Northern Road, and travel a few hours longer at the fastest possible speed. She had wisely decided not to hire a lady's maid for the journey. The less people involved in her scheme, the better. She would make use of the help at the various inns if need be, then she would hire new servants in Scotland.

The thought of dyeing her hair sickened her, and not like redheads were an anomaly in England. Wise use of veiled hats and turbans would give her sufficient concealment for the time being. Even if Smith talked, he had no idea where they were going. The only thing he knew was that he had to await her further instructions. He also had no knowledge of her new identity.

Lady Madeleine de Brandeville did not exist anymore, all traces of her gone and replaced with Mrs. Marie Colette Alvar.

Today, they would push forward until dark and continue at the first crack of dawn. When they stopped to rest tonight, she would give *Adam* another dose of her potion so he would go right back to sleep. In the meantime, Jones would pass him off as one of her servants, out for the count from too much drink.

The hounds from Belvoir would be looking for a man and a woman and if she gave the impression of traveling alone, despite potential dangers to a female in such circumstances, no one would ever think her involved in a foul act such as a kidnapping. Jones could get her the room and order the food so her French accent wouldn't give her away. Despite the magical barrier that protected her and separated Adam from his old life, she was not prepared to take any chances until the dust settled. If they pressed on, they would make it to the border in less than a sennight.

After Jones told her about the problem, an idea had formed in her head. When they reached Shap, in Cumbria, she would hire every single horse available at all stopping points so in case anyone pursued them, they would not be able to catch up. The route from there to Scotland was a rather difficult one, and with all the resources firmly in her grasp, she would have the winning edge.

They would marry in Paxton Toll, a village close to the border. As in Gretna Green, a special license was not needed there; a small pile of sovereigns would do the trick. She would use their assumed names at first. In her mind, he was already *Adam*. His new self was her creation, hers to mold as she pleased, including his name. But, the man was still under shock, trying to come to grips with his new situation. Therefore, as of yet, nothing mattered except that he believed them to be man and wife in the legitimate sense.

She would have to decide what to do with Jones when they arrived. Nothing she hated more than leaving loose ends. To keep him in her employ may be the likely solution; Jones was accustomed to her odd requests and never asked questions.

In a way, things may turn out for the best. If at Belvoir and Trenwith they thought Adam to have been kidnapped by her, it would be easier later to return with him and convince them that everything had happened with his approval. That he had wanted her, not Emmaline, all along.

She let her gaze fall on the object of her affections. The immediate problem would be to get him to feel the same way about her. There was also the not insignificant matter of his real identity, which she would eventually have to reveal to him if she wanted to give her long term plan any chance of working. Fortunately, her experience maintained that a besotted man would do anything for the one he desired. Adam was a man—a slightly more complicated one perhaps, but a man nonetheless.

However, there was one, bigger issue she would have to contend with.

Time.

Immortals had only so long before their unblemished appearance would start to make tongues wag. When eventually she gave Adam the gift, she would put him in the same position. Together, they had to become masters of adaptation, learn to take opportunities as they come and make the most of them.

Molding his way of thinking was going to test her strength of mind. A bridge she would have to cross in due time. The rewards promised to be many. Above all, with his connections as the Viscount Bournemouthe, she would accomplish her goal to imbue the brotherhood with fresh, aristocratic mettle. Once that mission completed, she would welcome a change of scene. She was not entirely alone; the brotherhood's support was available if and when she needed it.

All these thoughts made her head pound. She stifled a yawn. It had been a long two days and she'd barely slept last night. She knew she should take a short nap but she was too overcome with excitement. Her body still thrummed with remnants of the rush she'd felt during her encounter with Emmaline. It had been most exhilarating to take Adrian right from under the chit's nose.

Madeleine's eyes feasted on her prize. "So beautiful," she whispered.

His full, sensuous mouth slightly ajar, the dark circles underneath his eyes had softened in slumber. Two-day-old stubble stretched across his strong, square jaw, the tips like tiny golden needles when sunlight beamed on his face. He made a small sound and turned his head to an angle that threw his angular profile into relief. His tongue darted out to moisten his lips.

She could not wait to place her mouth on him, to taste him, touch the most forbidden places of his body.

But she had to be patient. He needed time to get used to the idea that she had a right to be intimate with him. In his weakened state, he could do nothing but trust in her word. Her medicine would keep him docile until she became sure of his devotion, yet, if the dosage was restrained, he would not be hindered from performing his husbandly duties. It was only a matter of time.

Smiling, she removed her gloves and gave in to the temptation. She leaned closer and placed her hand on his thighs, felt the firm flesh beneath the material of his clothing. He wore an old shirt and breeches that Jones had provided beneath his mud-stained coat. The drab, cheap material hung over him. He'd been so flustered when he regained consciousness that he had not even noticed or asked for a bath. When they arrived in Scotland, she would see to replenishing his wardrobe.

She continued the massaging motion of her fingers. His legs were so powerful and masculine, his hips narrow and well-formed.

"*Mon amour*, you are exquisite."

She explored a little higher and edged her fingers closer to his groin.

Just a little more...

The carriage hit another rut, and the resulting jolt brought her to her senses.

Merde! Better stop before she lost all self-control. Reluctantly, she settled back on the opposite side of the carriage. Adam had not stirred a jot but she could not afford to make any mistakes. It would cost her too much.

But for now, they had all the time in the world.

———

1811.
South Bridge Vaults, Edinburgh.

THE SOUND of crushed oyster shells under Madeleine's feet ricocheted off the moldy stone walls. More empty, discarded, whole shells trailed on both sides of her, remnants of meal staples for the slum inhabitants. A meager succession of lanterns showed her the path past long corridors, archways, and a web of narrow tunnels flanked by tiny damp rooms. No windows or outlets were present to afford natural light, although the rain, muck, and sewage always found a way inside through the porous stone—it had done so for over twenty years, since South Bridge had been built.

Here, the splendid palaces and castles above ground were mere trophies of another world, another way of life. Even the dingy tenements of Cowgate were a luxury compared to this.

But what really mattered was that above, on the surface, the most respectable members of society played by the rules.

This place down below was where they came to break them—their biggest, most guarded secret.

The experience was rumored to be so thrilling, so depraved, that people of quality would haunt these secret dens of pleasure despite exposure to poisoned air, slum dwellers, criminals, and the filthiest scum of Scotland.

A series of nine slippery steps led Madeleine farther from the inhabited portion of the vaults, down into a deeper level. The noxious stench so characteristic of Edinburgh hit her as if multiplied by a hundred in this stale underworld, and it pitilessly stayed with her, stuck to her clothing and skin, along with the bone-aching humidity. Despite the dregs of human activity scattered about, what thrived most of all was the funereal silence because she'd learned how to avoid the inhabited tunnel ways. But she knew she'd hear the hum of voices soon.

Every step brought her closer to them, to those who proved the gossipmongers true.

The good citizens who whispered of the goings on below their city with bated breaths and horrified gasps would never contemplate setting foot in these bowels of hell. They could only speculate about the nefarious deeds and devilish pacts that happened in the dark, in godless places such as this, where no one but a villain and his abettor could witness an unspeakable act.

She turned a sharp corner. A cloaked, masked figure stepped before her from an archway to her right.

"Good evening, Madeleine."

"Is it you, St. Giles?"

"You are fortunate it is I and not someone who has no business recognizing you."

He motioned toward the mask in her hand. Although his face was concealed from her, Madeleine knew it well. His sharp eyes missed nothing.

"Forgive me," she said tremulously. She hastily put on her black and gold mask and readjusted her hood.

"Mistakes are the prerogative of commoners, not ours, Madeleine. The Snake Cult is not in the business of losing."

The quiet tone with which he spoke chilled her more than overt anger. St. Giles was a man of calculated words and controlled passions. For this reason, one never knew where they stood while in his presence, also because he made sure his eyes—those mirrors to the soul—were well shuttered. As they were now, aided by the shadows that loomed larger with him here.

She should feel privileged that she'd been one of the few allowed to ever gaze into their cold depths with an awareness of the power he wielded.

"I shall be more careful in the future."

He nodded and turned. "Follow me."

She stepped in line behind him and followed the dark sweep of his cloak, her heart in her throat. This was her sixth encounter with the man in many, many years—she'd counted them. While she'd sought him out the first few times, this meeting was at his request.

It wasn't a good sign. When St. Giles summoned you, it meant that someone in the Cult leadership hierarchy had expressed deep displeasure with a situation. The Cult trusted him blindly. He had clout among the highest echelons—the only ones who knew his real name. Even she was not privy to it, or to them.

She'd learned about his influence a long time ago, when she first met him in a convent, in France. He had been the Cult's answer to her cry for help.

That day, she'd handed him what should have been her most precious gift. A gift she wanted to keep secret, a burden she could not afford.

Or keep.

She found out too late of the Cult's policy that only members of their choosing were allowed to breed—and with prior, specific permission. Their rank in the hierarchy played a huge role. In the upper ranks, marriages were arranged and children produced for a cleaner, ennobled bloodline. Madeleine would have to give up her child so it would be raised by a more distinguished member, St. Giles told her, while she would owe a favor to him, and consequently, the Cult, for disregarding one of its cardinal laws. A harsher punishment was not meted out only because of the Cult's ignorance of her transgression.

Indeed, what other choice had she had? She could not afford to be outed ... or worse.

In truth, the thought of immortals having children hadn't even occurred to her—that a woman turned during her fertile years remained in that state of fecundity—let alone the concept of the Snake Cult having specific rules about it. The power of immortality granted by the Demon's Chalice thwarted only death, and held no purview over other aspects of life.

Claude was gone, and her new life was just starting. She was finding her purpose, and St. Giles had lit a pathway for her. She'd known he'd be the one to turn to since Claude had taken her to a public Cult gathering one night, and St. Giles had been there, presiding over the event.

Lean, square-jawed, and grey-haired, he was a man of reserved authority. Her perceptiveness did not miss the dark energy that charged the air around him. Clearly, he didn't need to speak a word to get people to play his tune. He was capable of anything and everything. His advanced age did nothing to diminish his charisma and appeal.

He never danced, he told her, so she stood with him that night, away from the crowd, and they conversed. She thus neglected Claude for a far more thrilling experience. St. Giles' eyes had gleamed when he looked at her, but his gaze didn't burn with physical desire. A spark of kinship quickly formed between them; an inexplicable, intimate alliance. They both recognized a kindred soul—magic and mayhem come together.

So, to summon him at the convent when she needed him had seemed to her the wisest choice. Her only choice.

Rather than report her, St. Giles had offered his assistance. She never understood why. Perhaps he saw in her a reflection of himself as a younger man.

Or perhaps somewhere deep down, in the cavernous space in the left side of his chest, something still existed there, beating a faint rhythm. But she doubted it. Most likely he thought she'd become useful to him in the future. He humored her to his advantage, for his own ends. Something she would do, after all, were she in his shoes.

On her part, she was forced to trust him.

"Make sure the child has a good life," she'd told St. Giles, "wherever you take it. Make sure they care for it."

"You have my word," had been his answer.

She'd given birth the next day to a baby girl.

They took the little body away from her, immediately. It had been her wish—she didn't want to look at her flesh and blood, didn't want to love her. But it would have been pointless, even if she did. The baby didn't survive, they told her.

She never saw her dead daughter. St. Giles took care of everything. He was the only man who knew her secret, and he'd kept it all these years.

This secret and his link to her past had spun their bond with the tenuousness of fine silk. Yet silk was beautiful, luxurious, and desirable.

Madeleine suppressed a desire to draw comfort from the precious locket that hung from her neck and that, right now, felt heavier than lead. She wanted to touch the cool gold case that she'd kept close to her skin—to her heart—for a quarter century, but she was sure St. Giles wouldn't miss that gesture of weakness.

St. Giles was a riddle to her and most others in the brotherhood but one thing she knew—the Cult relied heavily on his views and wisdom. Mystery swirled around him like seemingly harmless flies, yet, could easily be a carrier to something deadly or at least, far from innocuous.

Madeleine was well aware that her fate lay in his hands. If he stopped trusting her, so would the Cult.

Since she'd married Adam, they had been expecting her to deliver. More money, more connections, more power. Yet, she'd done nothing except chase after Adam's heart like a lovesick puppy for all these years.

And now here she was, St. Giles' presence, reminding her once again who laid down the rules.

A short walk led them to a large, oval-shaped space occupied by a crowd of masked revelers. A large tapestry hung on the wall across her, woven with the words, *Fais ce que tu voudras ...* Do what thou wilt, the motto of the infamous Hellfire Club.

St. Giles stopped at the entrance and allowed her to survey the scene. "A harmless version of Dashwood's idea. Simply an excuse for the privileged set to philander and drink to excess in a secret location. No satanic rites here, no sacrifices, no bloodshed. This is what they want, and this is what I provide in exchange for their favors when needed. Some of the most deserving ones have already been promised Cult membership."

Several cots were set up to flank the walls while low tables laden with bread, ham, cheese, fruit, and wine stretched, side by side, down the middle.

The overpowering scents of cinnamon and grains of paradise permeated the room. The aroma came from the jugs of spiced wine that flowed freely among the attendees.

Hippocras. A stimulant to the senses.

A number of naked women strutted their wares in provocative poses, competing to catch a gentleman's attention. All of them wore similar red masks trimmed with gold. A buxom woman with a fixed smile on her sagging face, possibly the madam, stood away from the action in a corner, and assessed the girls' performance by the intensity of the patrons' responsiveness to such bounteous temptation.

To one side, a scrawny man sat cross-legged between two full-figured females who took turns licking his neck and exposed, sunken chest. The man, whose mask did not disguise his advanced age, giggled like a schoolboy at their shameless teasing.

St. Giles followed her gaze. "The Duke of Queensbury is a fool with a foot in the grave. He ran his estates to the ground, starting with the family seat at Drumlanrig, and spent his inheritance on women, gambling, and racing. Fortunately, the Cult has benefited from his reckless behavior and much of his wealth came to us in some form."

"I have heard about the Duke. His reputation has preceded him. Still, I suppose you know about every single person in this room, even their least known proclivities."

"This would have been the kind of activity you would have favored during your stay in London. These girls are highly trained to please members of both sexes. But, I suppose Edinburgh does not appeal to you as much," St. Giles said in an ambiguous tone.

He never looked toward her as he spoke, but his mere presence confounded her. This was not a man to cross. A man who was said to find great pleasure in taking lives…

"My husband is very demanding, sir," she responded in what she hoped was a wicked lilt.

"It is not what I hear, Madeleine."

"What is it that you hear, St. Giles?" she asked in mock defiance. Many emotions played havoc inside her, but audacity was not sensible, she reprimanded herself.

"Do you really want me to say it? Or, would you like to attempt to feed me more lies? I pray you decide wisely."

He'd turned to look at her now, no doubt sizing her up, but she could not bring herself to look back at him. She merely focused a blank gaze at a half-naked man lounging on one of the cots. A masked woman, garbed in a blasphemous representation of a nun's robe, straddled him and moved in a sexual dance that was old as time itself. The man's mouth opened in ecstasy and his head fell back as she increased her rhythm.

Madeleine tore her gaze away from the pair, not in the least aroused. The winning emotion was now fear. Fear that St. Giles would deem her useless, because that would mean only one thing. Her end. The Cult wanted only the best, richest, strongest, brightest—and most ruthless—in the brotherhood.

"My husband is a little reticent."

"Reticent?"

"He does not love or trust me, and I think it premature to turn him just yet…"

"I never thought you to be a *fool*, Madeleine," he hissed. Irritation coated his words like slick toffee on a child's tongue. "What does love have to do with anything?"

The only way around this conversation was to turn the tables on him. "But you said I couldn't make mistakes, did you not?"

"Watch your words, Madeleine. I only enjoy games of my choosing. You promised to deliver the Viscount Bournemouthe, and I expect no less. The sooner, the better."

One of the prostitutes approached Madeleine and brushed her breasts against her cloak. Her full lips, painted red, arched in a teasing smile as she slid a hand under Madeleine's cloak around her waist. Madeleine was glad for the interruption, although she knew it was only a short reprieve.

The woman whispered in her ear. "My lady, why don't you come with me and let us be friends? If you desire privacy, I can arrange that. Your wish is my command."

"Leave us now," St. Giles ordered. His clipped voice made the girl jump and scuttle away, swallowing her moue of complaint. "Now, Madeleine, I want Bournemouthe. When do you expect to deliver him?"

"I need more time."

"You've had years. How much longer?"

"A … another year at the most. But I need that much. Please," she entreated.

"I will regret this but I give in for the last time. You have been an asset to the Cult in the past when you were still in France. At least that buffoon Claude had good judgment in women and you had better sense in getting rid of him."

"Then you know I'm to be trusted. Many noblemen gave up a

portion of their wealth to the Cult in exchange for help in escaping the guillotine. My connections to Robespierre's people allowed me to pass on invaluable information that you used to your advantage."

"True, but what happened in the past cannot save you forever, Madeleine. Only because Bournemouthe would be a gain to you and I wish you to be happy, for now, I agree to your proposal even though we are at a historic time. It happens that we still could avail ourselves of your ... talents. The Prince Regent is a man who understands human nature and is open to new ideas, like his grandfather, Frederick, who was once a member of a faction of this club. We have the advantage as long as he keeps his status."

"I am aware of that, and thank you, St. Giles. My promise stands true. You shall not regret this."

"I trust I shan't. You have wasted enough of my time. After all, you are not indispensable."

He was right. There were many like her who tried to curry the Cult's favor with big promises.

"Just do your part," he added. "If he's thick-headed about it, make sure to inform me immediately and I'll take care of the problem."

Madeleine nodded. "I understand."

"No more excuses, Madeleine. One year, no more. Next time I want to see you, I shan't notify you beforehand."

"Thank you, St. Giles," she said evenly, although inside, she trembled like a leaf.

"Now, feel free to partake in these many pleasures on offer today."

"I—I think I better go." Madeleine hoped that her preference to leave would not come across as weakness.

A slight pause. "Go, then. Do what you *must*," he said with sarcasm, his words twisting the adage that hung so prominently on the wall to convince the dissolute hedonists that a short life was worth living without regrets.

Madeleine did not wait to be told twice to turn around and leave the strangling hold of the vaults, and of St. Giles, behind.

CHAPTER 6

"Present fears
Are less than horrible imaginings."
[Macbeth, Act I, Scene III]

1814, SCOTLAND.

MADELEINE SAT on the edge of the bed and stared at Adam's palm. Outside, the moon was full and the sky was clear. An auspicious night.

He slept so deeply, he didn't feel the knife slip into his skin and score the flesh. She'd discarded the bloodied knife on the bedside table after slicing open her own palm. A bonding ritual coming seven years too late, and even now as she went through the motions, insecurity ate at her.

The blood flowed out, dark and rich. It waited for her to give it the power of new life.

Last night might have been a breakthrough. She and Adam sat down to dinner together, something they'd not done in a long time as he often avoided mealtimes with her. After a short silence, she asked him if he'd like to take care of some land that came with the cottage. It needed tending, and Mr. Flett knew a couple of strong lads who were looking for work.

This was a conversation she could have had much earlier, but she'd been afraid that the idea would spark a memory in his head. That he'd start to remember.

She should have had more faith.

His eyes had come alive with budding excitement as she spoke to him, asked him what he desired. Then he bowed his head and looked down at his plate, the fire gone. He responded that he didn't know much about working land, that he wouldn't have a clue what to do with it.

She countered that he could learn. The Agricultural Society organized occasional talks and she could take him there. In fact, she had enquired and found out there was one the following Saturday. Also, the members would surely enjoy the opportunity of teaching a novice.

The spark snuck in his eyes again, spread a film of contentment on his face. His lips curled slightly upward, and the look he gave her then seemed like one of gratitude. She was sure he couldn't remember his past, but her words gave him comfort somewhere deep inside him.

Was this what she had to do to get him to warm up to her? She knew some of his past habits. He loved riding and the country, and he was a man who made things happen. If she helped him build something new with the abilities she knew he had, he'd come to see her as his savior.

Why hadn't she thought of this before?

Six months after meeting St. Giles in the underground vaults, she'd requested another meeting. She knew that Adam wouldn't cave any time soon, so she had to play her last card.

St. Giles had a weakness for virgins. Young, untainted women— and men—who could be taught to pleasure him in all the ways he wished. Evil ways that would always involve their submission to pain or even death.

Her chance encounter with William Burke, an Irish transplant who worked as a manual laborer at the Union Canal, proved to be a stroke of luck. A young man who couldn't have been older than twenty-five, he recognized the value of peddling bodies—mostly live ones—to the highest bidder. Burke all but said he'd do for her what Mr. Anthony from the workhouse at Bishop's Stortford had done for her in England.

Madeleine therefore offered St. Giles what he wanted and needed, in exchange for freedom to deal with Adam how she deemed fit.

It had been a gamble. If St. Giles' soul was as black as she'd heard it was, he would not resist her offer.

He accepted and since then, she held the ace. For how long, she had no idea. Although a long time had passed, she would not be surprised if St. Giles was simply playing a long drawn-out cat and mouse game with her, so, in a sense, she remained under his thumb. Any day, he could decide to end their bargain and change the course of their association.

Yet, if she had thought earlier of this solution to bring Adrian to his knees, hers forever, she might have avoided all or most of the challenges she'd had to face with St. Giles and the Cult at her heels, screaming for her to deliver Bournemouthe. Sure, she'd pacified St. Giles by offering the means to appease to his darkest desires, but the fear that he'd turn on her was always there … hovering above her like a black leaden cloud.

That fear dispersed when she thought of her husband and how differently he'd looked at her that evening, simply for mentioning what he loved. He had no idea, but that passion for the land remained in the depths of his mind. Passion that with this new strategy could soon be directed toward her…

When dinner was over, he rose from his chair and said, "I shall go to the study and drink some port. Thank you," while holding her gaze and then pressing a lingering kiss on her hand.

A flutter of hope … the merest hint…

Such hope filled her to the point that she regretted lacing his beef and potatoes with the potion to help him sleep. Perhaps it was time to make a bigger gamble, she'd thought. If she gave him the gift, with which would come renewed strength to start afresh, wouldn't he be even more grateful?

His weakness came not only from the potion, but she also saw the bleakness in him caused by his separation from Emmaline. If she made him immortal, his strength would return, and perhaps his moods would improve. Short of confessing the truth about him, she'd explain to him how she'd applied the only way she knew to heal him. His honorable nature would compel him to be thankful to her for making him better.

She made her decision then. This would be the night when the change would happen.

Her gaze re-focused on his serene face that half-sunk into the pillow as he slept sideways. So peaceful, so at ease. She hoped that the process wouldn't stir him, and that she'd be able to tell him about it at an appropriate time, when he felt stronger, more able—and closer to her than he'd ever been.

She took a deep breath, then joined their palms, cut to cut, and prepared for the painful flow of energy.

It came as it usually did, hard and heavy, like a blow to the chest with an iron bar. Madeleine held on for dear life and watched as the tranquil expression on Adam's face dissipated. He grimaced before emerging from the comfort of sleep. The light from the candle that flickered by the side of the bed allowed him to adjust his vision swiftly, but the pain from his palm must have hit him so hard that his head fell back and a hoarse growl escaped his mouth.

When it ended, he snatched his hand away and stared at his palm, then lifted his angry gaze to her. His eyes had darkened, and burning embers of emotion flew from them to singe her face.

Her heart broke into a wild gallop. This was not the way it was supposed to happen.

"What the devil is this about?" He grabbed her wrist in a throttle-hold before she had a chance to stand and back away. "Tell me now, woman, what did you just do to me?"

A YEAR LATER.

A cottage on the outskirts of Redbourn, England.

EMMALINE LOOKED AT HER SURROUNDINGS. The old woman's abode was clean and in decent repair, with utilitarian furnishings. Drying herbs hung freely from every square foot of ceiling in the first room to the left of the front door, and the hallway brimmed with the musky scent of the earth. But, the cottage itself was not by any means unwelcoming.

The witch. That is how the villagers, sporting cautious expressions, referred to Agnes Pool after Emmaline took the liberty to ask for directions to the cottage located an hour's carriage drive from Trenwith.

Miss Pool led her to a cozy back parlor. A silver striped tabby cat lounged lazily on a rug placed by the fireplace for its comfort. An oriental carpet with faded jewel hues captured the light from the wide window and prettily reflected iridescent color around them. It had seen better days, but that didn't detract from its fine crafts-manship.

"Would you like some tea?"

"No, thank you. Please do not trouble yourself."

Miss Pool looked at her curiously, her acute gaze full of hidden knowledge. "I hope you do not mind Oliver. He is a quiet sort." She gestured to the cat.

"Not at all. I hope I have not come at an inconvenient time."

"Any time is as good as any. Me old bones welcome a bit of excite-ment any day," she said lightly. "I appreciate your coming, Lady Deramore. Have a seat, if you please."

Unusual that the woman's accent sounded both cultured and common at the same time. Despite her lower class rank, she must have acquired some level of education.

Emmaline sat in a chair across from Miss Pool and went straight to the point. "When I read your letter yesterday, I was led to believe that you know something about what has happened to me. It mentioned you were a housekeeper in Lady de Brandeville's household for a time. I need to find out all you know about this."

"I can guess what has been ailing you these past years. Lord knows I have suffered enough guilt for keeping silent so long."

"So why did you?" Emmaline asked bluntly. She was not in the mood to be kind.

"Because I was afraid. That woman, she's a bad piece of work. You must be careful."

Emmaline nodded and softened a little, while trying to think past the beginnings of a headache. "I see, but it is too late to go back for me. I need to find what I have lost."

She could not keep the desperation from her voice. The old woman's eyes, filled with pity, seemed to read through her very soul.

"It may be too late for you, little one."

It felt wrong, and not a bit ironic, to be called *little one*. "It cannot be."

"How do you know? Time is not our friend and people change," Miss Pool said sadly.

Emmaline got up and started to pace the room. "Can you guess how old I am?"

"Why?"

Emmaline stopped in front of Miss Pool. "Just give me a guess."

"Of course, you cannot be a day over twenty. But I know that cannot be if you were betrothed—"

"I am seven and twenty," Emmaline interrupted. "Take a good look at me." She waited until the witch's face showed a spark of comprehension. "I look exactly the same as I did eight years ago. Not a crease more. Not even a blemish. Perhaps it is not impossible for some to remain so youthful looking but I know she did something to me. What that could have been eludes me. She called it a gift, *eternal life*. Those were her words to me as I lay paralyzed on my sofa. I can't believe anything she said but what should I believe? The thought has tormented me..."

Adrian shall never *be yours for as long as you breathe.*

"So you are one of them."

"One of them? I do not know what you mean but whatever it is, I am listening. So many questions have plagued me for so long that I do not have a notion where to start."

"Tell me what happened first and start from the beginning. Then I will help you."

Emmaline went on to relate in detail the events that led up to Madeleine's visit and Adrian's disappearance. She mentioned how at first, no matter how long she racked her brain, many details remained a blank. Nonetheless, she was not able to shirk the suspicion that something more had happened. Then, in recent months, out of the blue, the harsh memories of that long past morning rushed to her, providing clarity. She remembered the drugged tea and the knife slicing open her palm. She remembered Madeleine telling her she would never be able to reunite with Adrian.

And the pain of his loss washed over her again with such force, she feared she would not survive the guilt. The guilt of letting him go without a struggle. The guilt of not telling anyone about it, for who would believe such an outlandish tale?

As if she was not already pale enough, Miss Pool blanched. "She turned you."

"What on earth do you mean?"

Her host ignored the question. She was lost in thought, her eyes half closed in a faraway look. "I overheard a conversation between Madeleine and Jones, her lackey, one evening. They spoke about a journey to Edinburgh. I was so afraid of 'er that I never mentioned it to anyone." She clasped her hands tightly in her lap. "You see, I did my best to be invisible, not to attract attention. I kept to myself." She sighed.

"Did Madeleine not inquire about your past? Your interest in herbs and such? From what I learned about her, she was nothing if not thorough."

"I started late, working with my herbs and spells. Ten years ago, I was more of an interested observer. Besides, I did not talk much and did me chores without complaint."

Emmaline nodded. "Go on."

"She never allowed us in or even near her private stillroom, but I managed to sneak in when she was away. It laid a ways from the stairs at the back end of the house and Jones watched it like a hawk, but he couldn't always be there. Then one day, I was paid a nice sum to leave the house and never return. I suppose I must thank me old mistress for this modest home, for everythin' I have."

Emmaline's eyes followed the woman's sweeping hand gesture. "So did you hear her talk about a certain Adrian Segrave or Lord Bournemouthe?"

"There was mention of a man, yes, some sort of kidnapping plan. I never heard a name and the details were no' very clear, but certain parts … your story seems to fit and I have been thinking about this for a long time. Word of your loss and your family's search have not escaped my ears."

Emmaline swallowed and pursed her lips. Miss Pool was being kind to look away, while she said nothing for fear of breaking down in sobs like a babe. *Knowing* had made things harder—it was certainly more difficult to accept things as they were. Most importantly, now that she knew, she could never forget. Her memories would haunt her forever.

She had resumed a discreet investigation but looking into a decade-long case was much like trying to find a watering hole that did not serve ale. In addition, she could not be forthcoming with her intentions as she feared her cousin, the baron, would think her mad if he found out what she was up to. He might even have her committed for it.

After a short pause, Miss Pool continued. "My employer, secretive as she was, would cover her tracks. A new life, a new name. There are also many ways to separate people using magic. I will tell you what I know, but after that, yer on your own."

"She cut my hand and hers in some sort of ritual. She also mentioned a shield."

Miss Pool's face fell. "That is the worst kind of spell, tough to break. I have never heard of anyone to defeat it."

This was not what Emmaline wanted to hear. "I must do this. No, I *need* to do this. Please do not tell me what I cannot do," she pleaded.

Miss Pool nodded although the sadness never left her eyes. "Then it is imperative that you find the Demon's Chalice." She softened. "Madeleine did not need it to turn you but this is different. I cannot guarantee you will be successful."

"The Demon's Chalice?"

"Have patience and I shall explain. First of all, what else did she do when she cut you?"

"She ... uh, pressed her scar to mine. Palm to palm."

"That's what I feared. You should know then, you are part of a group who call themselves Valthreans."

Emmaline's mind grappled with this new information that teetered with the ridiculous and tried to make heads and tails of it. "I'm confused, how can I be part of this group if I never heard of it?"

Agnes Pool explained that with her ritual, Madeleine had mixed her blood with Emmaline's, thus, turning her into one of the undying —an immortal like her. Shocked and incredulous, she listened and interjected with questions.

"Forgive me, child. I have endured much regret for it but today, I trust I can bring you some hope. Before you leave, I want you to promise to come back tomorrow."

Emmaline looked at her quizzically but allowed her to continue speaking.

"I am going to prepare something for you and I want you to pick it up in the morning. I will also provide you with a recipe to memorize so you can make it yourself when you run out. It is imperative that you always have some of it on you."

"Why so?"

"There is little love lost between members of the Cult of the Snake, to which Madeleine has allegiance, and the Valthreans. It is a struggle for power. This could pose a danger to you and others like you— perhaps not an immediate one, but things threaten to boil over. My brew will sharpen your sense of smell, mask your scent, and give you time to identify your surroundings and seek shelter from the undesirable, should you wish to do so. You'll have a bit of an edge in certain situations."

Emmaline's head felt like a heavy brick filled with lead. "My scent? But exactly who are these people?" Overwhelmed, she walked to the window and looked outside.

Miss Pool shuffled to her and grasped her hand between both of hers. "I think you ought to sit back down, Lady Deramore. There is much more I wish to tell you."

"All right."

They both took back their seats.

"The Cult of the Snake wishes to destroy the Valthreans and their code of ethics. They do not believe the two groups can coexist peacefully. They are evil, ambitious, and utterly ruthless."

The witch related the legend of Valther and his followers, the Naga people who left their home bearing six chalices, the Cups of Life gifted by the River Demon of the Jhelum River in East India; and how they traveled far and wide to seek peace and shelter. She also told her more extraordinary things like how dangerous it was for her people to come in contact with the cobra snake.

As she spoke, Oliver left his bed to curl on her lap. He purred when she started to run her fingers absently through his fur. His slitted green eyes closed in contentment.

"I understand the Cult of the Snake is composed of the descendants of King Aravala's offspring and his supporters, and are sworn enemies of the Valthreans?"

Miss Pool nodded. "You are a quick study, dear."

"But if Madeleine's allegiance is with the Cult of the Snake, how come was I not made one of her own when she turned me, as you say? Why am I a Valthrean?"

"Because all immortals with good intentions start out being Valthreans. It is when these turn rogue, or are raised in that preying culture, that they join the enemy. It is not always what you are, it is what you believe." She regarded Emmaline with an intense gaze then gave a slow nod. "It is time," she murmured, as if she had come to some sort of important decision.

"Come with me," she instructed. She stood and shocked the cat into wakefulness. The creature let out a resentful hiss. "Oliver, behave yourself. We have company. If you wish to be difficult, mind you shall not get that delicious fish I have stewed for dinner."

As if understanding her words, the cat bowed its head and meowed halfheartedly before pattering back to its rug, its bushy tail twitching in indignation.

Meanwhile, one word pealed in Emmaline's head with shrieking brutality—*immortal*.

Bemused, she followed Agnes Pool to a room at the back of the cottage. It was much smaller, darker, and sparsely decorated with a small cabinet, a couple of chairs on each side and in one corner, a dressing table with a large mirror. She grabbed one of the chairs and placed it in front of the mirror.

"What is this?"

"Sit down, please, and look into the mirror."

Miss Pool seemed dead serious. Although skeptical, Emmaline obeyed. Mere moments passed before her reflection grew hazy, replaced by a moving image.

"Goodness gracious!" Emmaline exclaimed as she leapt out of the chair.

"Do not be afraid. Please, sit back down. The scenes you see will tell you about your people. As I already told you, the legend starts in India, thousands of years ago."

In the picture, Emmaline saw a river and vast lands cradled in the bosom of high, snow-capped mountains. It was all breathtakingly beautiful with green forests and wide open spaces. A tall, fair-haired man walked through a thicket of spruce trees and into a yellow corn-field that ran along the river bank. He stared into the deep waters, seeming lost in thought. After a while, he turned around and continued to walk by the edge of the water.

He stopped when he spotted something. An entrance to a cave, mostly hidden by wild vegetation. He approached and entered. Inside, the rock was nourished by water, and a cornucopia of lumi-nescent red pearls that studded it made the dark space look like a bright starry sky. They filled the cavern with an atmosphere of mystery.

The man reached out to touch the walls. Excitement marked his strong-featured face, as though he knew he had stumbled upon something of great import. On the uneven ground were scattered a series of strange objects. Upon closer inspection, they looked like cups or chalices that seemed to be hewn from the rock. The bases were broken from the source in a clean cut and they glowed, as if feeding off of each other's energy. The man sat down and stared at the objects for a long time.

The image faded out, and another one filled the mirror's surface. It showed the same man squatting by one of the cups. As he ran his hand around its circumference, he cut his palm over a jagged area on the inside, just below the rim. Blood oozed in a bubble and dripped on the humid rock. Suddenly, the ground beneath him trembled and the contents of the cave wavered in front of him. Things seemed to displace, like when one is spinning too fast and suddenly stops.

In an instant, Emmaline was transported inside his mind. She felt what he felt. Shards of bright light struck his eyeballs, blinding him, and the shock that consumed his body felt like thousands of hot needles being stuck into every inch of his skin. His heart and lungs trashed against his ribs, like he was being taken apart and put back together. Through it all, though, he never lost consciousness.

Emmaline heard a scream and realized it was not only Valther's, but also her own. A cool hand covered hers, comforting. Miss Pool's.

Two men rushed inside the cave when they heard the man's screams. Tall and copper-skinned with flawless features and lean muscle, they were both exceedingly handsome and looked alike in many ways. They must have been related.

"Valther, what is ailing you, brother?" asked one of the men in a foreign tongue that, oddly, Emmaline could understand. *Magic.*

"Candaka, Nila," Valther grimaced, and looked at each of them as he said their respective names. "The blood ... my hand."

Still connected in some elemental way to his thoughts and feelings, she was aware that his pain was atrocious, like a knife being thrust inside his gut and twisted in all directions, but it did not last long. When the strange phenomenon was past, something had changed. He had experienced something vital.

"Brother, we saw a light inside the cup, like a thousand suns shining within it! What happened?" The man called Candaka's voice brimmed with enthusiasm.

Valther stared at his palm and watched his skin mend unnaturally fast.

"No blood…" he muttered.

"Can you explain?" asked Nila.

Valther looked inside the cup. "My blood runs fresh. It has not dried."

Comprehension dawned and his eyes widened in disbelief. "I think we have found the Cups of Life, the lost seven chalices of the River Demon!" he said with incredulity. "We must be careful," he warned, his expression now sober. "If the king catches wind of this, he will kill us all. I must take one of these to my home and study it. If I get caught, promise me that you will save yourselves and the others. Swear to me you will not try to defend my honor. You must come back to this cave for the remaining cups and leave with them."

"But—" Nila started to protest.

"Nila, why are you always so stubborn? Promise me. Both of you," Valther said with vehemence. "I could not bear it if my brothers and sisters perished for my deeds."

Candaka swallowed. "This pains me, but I give you my word."

Valther nodded and turned to Nila. "What say you?"

"Your word is all I ask," he added when no response was forthcoming.

Nila's face was a mask of inscrutability.

Valther gave a sigh of exasperation. "You surprise me, brother. Speechlessness is not one of your problems, especially when you are describing your fishing exploits and how the barbells always gravitate to you while everyone else returns home empty-handed."

Nila's jaw tensed and his mouth tightened in a grim line, but still he said nothing. The conflict within him was tangible.

"Are you going to answer me?" Valther's tone escalated with impatience.

"Why, Valther? How could we allow you to die without doing anything about it?" Nila blurted out.

"For the love of the gods, because you must let me do what is right!" Valther snapped, but immediately threw him an apologetic look. "Forgive my harshness, but I need you to do this one thing for me."

Nila swallowed hard and looked away. "I have no fondness for your request but I vow to obey your wishes, if you insist."

Valther's face softened in relief. "Then let this cup seal our word, but first, another promise." He stared into their youthful eyes, eyes filled with both love and sorrow. "I want you to vow, on your honor as Naga, that you will only use the Chalice's power for the good of the people. Do you want this gift? Shall you use it righteously?"

There was no hesitation this time as they expressed their readiness and declared in unison, "On our honor, brother."

The three men circled the cup and performed a blood bonding ritual while their image faded into the smoky screen.

Emmaline felt Miss Pool's fingers curl over her shoulder. "Valther continued to study the powers of the Demon's Chalice. He became something of a recluse, spent days making notes for the Book of Magic," Miss Pool explained.

"The Book of Magic?"

"Valther transcribed his experiments and kept them in a journal." She pointed at the mirror. "Look."

Valther sat at a table inside some sort of hut. Candaka and Nila joined him and he grunted to acknowledge their presence but never looked up from the focus of his attention.

"It must be the cobra pearls. I see no other explanation. I could find nothing in the rock that would explain the alchemy of the chalice."

"Valther, you must stop this. People are noticing your strange behavior."

"I have indulged in study before and my behavior was no different," he retorted but, from their expressions, he failed to delude them. "I do not see why you are so concerned."

Nila changed the subject. "I think you need some sport. I say we go fishing today so I can beat you again," he jested, unable to hide how truly worried he was.

"I am not sure I have the time."

"But you do, brother. Without you, fishing is not the same. Besides, you may just get the chance to heal your pride and bring home a full meal."

"I will join you tomorrow," he suggested with reluctance.

The mirror returned to its natural state.

"The king already knew about Valther's passions for esoteric subjects and suspected that something was afoot," Miss Pool said. "While Valther went fishing with his brothers the next day, the king's men searched his home. They found the incriminating evidence, which they delivered to the king. Aravala went blind with fury. He knew the power of the chalice which granted immortal life, and he also knew that that power, through the Naga king's pact with the water demon, should belong only to him. The rest you now know."

"So Valther died…"

The older woman nodded. "A snake was the only thing that could kill him. Not just any snake, but one from the cobra family. Just as it was dangerous for Valther, it is also lethal for any of his kind."

"Why does the Cult of the Snake wish to destroy the Valthreans?"

"King Aravala was a pitiless sovereign. He was, after all, the Snake King. The people were terrified of him and all he cared for were his power and the wealth he had acquired through years of war and bloodshed. His followers believe in the same things. They do not want to share the world with the Valthreans who seek to live peacefully. Clever as Aravala was, it did not take him long to unlock the secret of the chalice after killing Valther. Even the king's enemies proved no match to his personal powers, although they did destroy his rule because, at that time, he had few allies."

"How did Lady de Brandeville get her hands on the Demon's Chalice?"

"That I cannot say. She must have become close with a very influential member in the Cult hierarchy. No one else would have access to something so powerful and dangerous."

Emmaline bit pensively on her bottom lip. "What happened to Nila and Candaka?"

"I can give you one more peek if you want to know."

Fascinated, Emmaline turned quickly to the mirror. "Yes, if you please."

What appeared was a gathering of about thirty odd men, women and children of all ages in a cave. Nila and Candaka stood in their midst.

"What about the Snake King?" someone asked.

Nila rose to his full height. "When Asoka's men attack the land of the Naga, Aravala will be finished," he spat out. "The water demon must keep the balance, so the land stays alive."

"Nila, what about us? What shall we do?"

Emmaline remembered once reading about a prince who shared Nila's name. Indeed, this man's bearing was also proud and regal. He appeared to care for his people. Clearly, they looked up to him as their leader.

"We must have faith. Our travels will be difficult, and it will be long before we can settle in a new land for we must cross the gorges to the Arabian Sea. My brother, Candaka, and I swear on all that is holy that we will protect you with our lives."

Nila paused. You could hear a pin drop.

"When our blood touches the Cup of Life, Valther's name will become our name. We shall find new roots, new lives, and we will raise our children as we always have. We will not let Valther's death be in vain."

A little boy of not more than six years slid his tiny head and toothless smile through two grown-up bodies, his tyke's face awash in innocent awe.

"Will we have to fight?" His voice brimmed with childlike vigor and some trepidation.

"We may, young man. But you will not be afraid." The boy shook his head solemnly. "You are a brave one."

Nila looked up to address the boy's parents and the other adults. "We have these six cups to pass to our descendants on one condition. We must let our children become men and women and they must prove their worth before they're given the gift."

"But—" came one protest from the midst of the pack.

"Do you want your children to remain thus forever in age and wisdom?" Nila offered. After some hesitation, a "no" echoed through the cave. He scanned the crowd. "So we will also protect our young with our lives if need be."

The little boy took a step and stuck out a trembling lower lip. "Will we come back home?" he asked, his tone desolate.

Nila reached out to ruffle the boy's hair. "Someone else asked me that very question today, young man." He looked meaningfully at his younger brother. "And I shall give you the same answer. Mayhap one day, my boy. But home is in your heart and mind. It is wherever you want it to be…"

Once again, the mirror darkened and produced Emmaline's reflection.

"Miss Pool, are these people still alive?"

"I cannot say."

Emmaline nodded, her heart flying out to that young man who was faced with such responsibility.

"You must find your own way, my dear. The most important thing to know is that you are part of this legend now, and, I'm certain, so is your beloved. But if you wish to find more information about yourself, your kind, and how they live now, you must seek it out on your own. I do not live in their world. I never wanted to."

Adrian…immortal. "Where do I find it?"

"That I cannot help you with, I'm afraid."

Emmaline needed time to let it all sink in. She could not possibly be what this woman was saying. This … this *Valthrean.*

Yet, she was.

"You will believe it soon enough, dear. You have no choice."

Could the witch read her mind?

No choice. What horrible words.

"I have no notion of how I am going to succeed in retrieving the chalice."

"You must believe or you never will. Use the potion; it is my special blend and no one knows about it. May I also recommend that you learn how to defend yourself? This is very important."

"A long time ago, Adrian taught me how to use the sword and the pistol."

"Just be prepared. Your life may depend on it one day," Miss Pool said grimly.

"Why are you helping me? Again, I must ask—why now? And, what is the nature of your interest in the Valthreans? I do not wish to be disrespectful, but please understand it is rather alarming for me to find that a stranger knows more about me than I know about myself."

Sadness pervaded the witch's intelligent eyes, faded remnants of a once vivid green. "After my life in Lady de Brandeville's household, I sought out knowledge of the Dark Arts and met a small circle of people who understood my desire to learn. I once was given a choice to make the change, but I knew that such a life was not for me. I had to let go and take my own path, and I have never been without … resources." She gave the mirror a pointed look. "I am getting on in years now and I cannot die with such guilt over my head. That is simply why I have asked you to come."

Of all people, Emmaline could understand human shortcomings. She had lost everyone she'd ever loved, first to tragedy, then to malice and eventually, to time. Her parents, her beloved grandmother, her only love, then Lady Philippa six years later. A charitable and compassionate spirit exposed the dowager to unimaginable disease and suffering. After Adrian's disappearance she threw herself in her life's mission to help others. In the end, the scarlet fever destroyed her frail body. Emmaline was convinced it had been the woman's secret wish to go that way.

Hattie had married a footman and moved with her husband to his new position in Wales, and Lewis finally admitted he was getting old.

He'd decided to join his grandchildren in Yorkshire and spend his last years there, near his beloved moors.

She was all alone now.

Emmaline spoke while holding back the sudden well of tears that threatened to overflow. "Adrian and I were not given a choice."

"Yes, you do have a choice in this, Lady Deramore. Not a choice in being but a choice in *doing*. You can choose to find him. It is not too late."

"We sent men half way to Scotland, but there was not so much as a faint trail."

By the end of January after it happened, the search parties had dispersed and dwindled to nothing. By February, the investigations stopped. To appease her, the baron engaged some people to go on searching but decided to call it off when no progress was made. Also, there was no record of his dispatch on a special mission.

Madeleine's prior household staff knew nothing about her scheme, and Smith, the footman, had nothing more to say except a vague statement that Madeleine would have traveled north. Men were sent to different inns to inquire about a red-headed woman traveling with a man but nobody offered any clues. They saw no point in going beyond Derbyshire, and came to the conclusion that Madeleine must have taken a different route. The idea that she may have gone to the Continent as she'd claimed also went up in smoke when the trail went cold in all directions.

"Your rival has many weapons at her disposal, weapons she has used to keep you apart. Were I you, I'd start in Scotland. Shall you throw down the gauntlet or are you content to let her keep him?"

She never even intimated that Adrian could be dead.

Therefore, if Miss Pool believed he could be alive and well, why should Emmaline doubt that it was so? Her greatest regret was to have become too quiescent about Adrian's disappearance. In the absence of answers, people simply stopped asking. They took the situation at face value and told her to be patient and move on. She had never felt as powerless as when Adrian disappeared into thin air like steam from a bubbling pot. She ignored her instincts to fight, to dig into the matter, and meekly listened to the voices of the majority.

She had been patient.

She had waited.

And after all of that waiting and all of that patience, Adrian never returned, as well as the hope that he ever would. In everyone's mind, including hers, the idea that something tragic had happened to him, or that he had left of his own volition, became the only feasible solution to the conundrum—nonsensical as it may have been. By this time, she had forgotten her early reservations and joined them to the string of unfulfilled promises that she had made to herself, topmost of which was the promise to find him, to never give up.

But she *had* given up, and what greater shame was there than that?

"No," Emmaline replied vehemently. "She cannot win."

"Then do what you must."

"If you were Madeleine, where would you go? Where do I start in Scotland?"

"I cannot say for sure but if she wanted your fellow as much as you say she did, the first thing I'd have done would be to make him mine, above all in name."

Marriage. A thought she couldn't bear thinking, but she couldn't discount anything at this point.

"Thank you, Miss Pool. I appreciate everything you've done."

Emmaline left the cottage after bidding her host goodbye.

Was this a lost cause, she wondered? Miss Pool had implied so when she stated the shield erected by Madeleine could not be easily destroyed. Yet, this time, Emmaline wouldn't be deterred. Come morning, she would talk to her cousin about her desire to do a bit of traveling. Her father had already settled a yearly sum on her, a sufficient amount to keep her comfortable, and she could afford to hire a companion. She'd never known the baron to be unreasonable, and he knew better than to think her interested in marriage at her age. He'll probably be relieved that she decided to set out to enjoy life a little.

Depending on how her trip to Scotland went, she intended to convince him to let her look for a cottage in Somerset. She'd enjoy the rustic, serene surroundings, as well as the theatre in Bristol and the waters of Bath.

She hoped it wouldn't come to that, but she had to prepare for the worst. If she returned from Scotland empty-handed, her search for Adrian would involve a lot of traveling but once she was settled in Somerset—which was far enough from St. Albans to prevent her homebody cousins from visiting much—she'd be her own woman with free reign to make decisions. At worst, people would think her a trifle eccentric.

Her head reeled with a million thoughts. *Don't get ahead of yourself. First things first. What matters is that you know your path now.*

Upon a loud exhale, she winced and rubbed her temples with gloved fingers. The ache in her head intensified now that she had no distractions from her thoughts.

Although she never looked back, Emmaline felt the old woman's soulful gaze bore into her through the wood and damask of the carriage as it gathered dust in the twilight.

Despite the apparent odds, that intuitive pull told her not to give up. That it was time to follow her instincts.

It was time to fight.

CHAPTER 7

"Is this a dagger which I see before me,
The handle toward my hand? Come, let me clutch thee.
I have thee not, and yet I see thee still.
Art thou not, fatal vision, sensible
To feeling as to sight? or art thou but
A dagger of the mind, a false creation,
Proceeding from the heat-oppressed brain?
I see thee yet, in form as palpable
As this which now I draw.
Thou marshall'st me the way that I was going;
And such an instrument I was to use."
[Macbeth, Act II, Scene I]

MEANWHILE, IN SCOTLAND.

ADAM WAS glad that this day, like most days before it, was finally over.
He sat in an armchair with an ankle cocked on a knee, and grimly

contemplated the gray Scottish dusk. The coppery glaze that infused the hoary clouds had reduced to emaciated, broken threads. Weak filaments, overpowered by an indifferent sky that went blacker by the minute, they reminded him too much of himself.

Always a transitory visitor, it was difficult to see much sun in Scotland, although the rugged face of Arthur's Seat on an odd summer day, when the seldom seen sunbeams bounced off the rocky face of the hill and brushed the sloping carpets of grass, was one of the most magnificent things he had ever seen. During much of the year, however, it was cold as a witch's tit out here in the damned Scottish backwoods.

The door behind him cracked open and light footsteps entered the room. He stifled a groan and braced himself for an unpleasant exchange. Marie came in his line of vision when she walked to the fireplace and set two lit candles on the mantelpiece.

"Adam, dear, why are you sitting in the dark and cold? I'll have Flett light a fire for you or you'll catch your death."

He got up and walked away from her. "What a thing to say. You know full well that can't happen," he said with artificial calm.

"I thought you'd be content. I wanted our lives together to mean something to you."

He turned to face her, barely able to hold back an urge to choke her. "Are you referring to your deception? To the fact that you've kept your outlandish secret for years before springing it on me in my sleep, before I had the chance to refuse your so-called *gift*?"

Ending his rant with a snarl, Adam felt his face go wooden, as though a twisted, macabre mask had been molded onto his skin. His eyes burned as he stared angrily at her. If they were the trigger of a pistol and she a mere mortal, she'd probably be fit for burying.

He was so incensed that he only just noticed she had stepped right up to him. He flinched when she touched his shoulder.

She looked up at him with big round eyes, green orbs filled with sham innocence and, to her credit, a hint of what seemed to be genuine discomfiture. "But Adam, I've done my best to make you happy. Why do you push me away? It's been a year! I want to be with you forever. Don't you want that, too?"

Adam bit back a retort, and sidestepped the bait her question offered by saying nothing. If she was looking for an admission of devotion, she wasn't going to get it.

He'd tried, God had he tried to love her. He'd acclimated to her petty deceptions and manipulations, especially in those times when she accepted his need for solitude and took a lover to her bed. What he wanted to tell her now was that he did not care a whit and she could do whatever she pleased, as long as she left him alone with his nightmares.

Because he doubted he was even capable of falling in love with any woman. His heart was too burdened to carry something so light and pure within it.

Marie's hand slid from his shoulder to his chest. While attempting to think coherently, he grabbed her hand and shook it off him, not missing the hurt on her face as he moved away from her.

"Please, talk to me," she pleaded. "I can't stand it when you behave this way. So … distant."

"There is nothing to talk about." Her exasperated breath chafed him. "I know I've been saying this but I must decide what to do."

"Whatever do you mean by that?"

"You cannot deny that things have never been good between us. There are things I've never come to terms with." That was the truth. What Marie had done redefined all traditional notions and beliefs about life itself. It defied all logic.

"What do you want to do?" she asked bluntly, despondency plating her tone.

"First, I must think."

She pressed her lips in a thin line and her expression turned ugly.

"I won't let you leave me! I forbid you. You cannot get away from me ever. You are mine … mine!" she shrieked, her hands fisted at her sides.

Her fits of wrath were like swift, wind-driven ocean currents. These moods and whims set the delicate climate in their household because it was just like Marie to turn from cold to hot in a matter of seconds. God help anyone who got in her way when she was in a temper.

From experience, he'd decided that the best way to deal with an enraged Marie was not to deal with her at all. He pressed a thumb and forefinger to the bridge of his nose and injected a note of threat in his tone. "Not now, Marie."

"But I—"

"I'm tired," he interrupted. "Leave now."

"*Faux-cul!* You are alive and well because of me. I have always taken care of you. I gave you everything. What more do you want?"

Calling him a two-faced bastard didn't do much by way of denting his pride, of which he felt he didn't have much left. He gave her his back to look out the window. He'd never wanted her so much to disappear from his life as he did now. What was a man without direction worth?

The door opened and slammed shut so forcefully that the air shifted audibly around his ears.

The sound of relief. *Blessed solitude.*

How foolish he'd been to place his trust in Marie. Why doubt a person if one has no reason to? But he had been proven entirely wrong. First off, she'd told him the medicine she gave him for several years had been prescribed by the doctor, yet, he rarely saw a medic in their household.

Then she'd deceived him again, and turned him into some sort of monster like her, without his knowledge or approval until the act was done.

He'd given her chances, driven perhaps by some strange sense of honor to do right by the woman who was his wife.

Or was he a masochist?

When that one morning, just short of a year ago, she'd revealed with pride that he would live forever, he finally saw her for the selfish stranger she was. What were her words supposed to mean? He could hardly believe her, despite the fact that her unaltered looks over the years may have corroborated her fantastic tale.

He wondered if he'd have to live with the sickly pallor of his skin and the paltry excuse he had for a body. The truth was that for years he lived within the four walls of this house, rarely setting foot outside to inhale the outdoor air. He'd stopped taking Marie's concoctions but that didn't make things better. He felt just as fragile and miserable.

Would an immortal be this weak?

He could not fathom why Marie still held on to him. To be fair to her, he gave her no reason to desire him because he felt nothing for her. Perhaps she deserved more as a woman, but he was not able to give it to her. To compensate for his failure as a husband, he always turned a blind eye if she wanted to seek her pleasures elsewhere and indeed, he always hoped she would.

Not that his situation was all her fault. It was his punishment for sleepwalking through life, for accepting its poorly dealt cards without any sort of grievance. He'd acted as only half a man by marrying a woman he barely knew based on her word alone, and never questioning her assertions that she was his only family. He had discovered that an empty heart was a sure way to keep all the regrets, horror, and despair at arm's length. By not feeling anything, he could accept everything.

But then he discovered her true nature. Marie was not who she appeared to be, and after all this time, the uncertainties plagued him.

He took a few edgy paces, released a labored breath, and sank back in his chair. His head leaned backward, he let his gaze wander into space. Marie's presence was his worst prison. Now that she was gone until the morrow, he could let himself dream. He had come to respect the listlessness he sometimes felt; the more severe, the more he slept. He relished that, wanted it. Some men drank themselves into a stupor to get to this state. He had it naturally.

At times, he hoped it would kill him—that he'd go to sleep and never wake up.

The coppery shreds of sunlight were almost gone now. Night was his special friend. The few hours of darkness were what he looked forward to the most because sometimes when he slept, he glimpsed the most wondrous thing he'd ever seen.

His angel.

A dark-haired woman, a goddess of unparalleled beauty, who called to him and reached out to him in his dreams. She only haunted him occasionally but often, these days, he willed her to. Her face never came fully into view, often blurred by the veil through which the dream sequence unfolded, but still, he knew it well. Especially when she gave him glimpses of her soft, dark eyes, and lush mouth telling him she loved him.

That apparition felt more real to him than anything else he laid his eyes on in the light of day. It was a sign, as if she'd meant something to him in a life long past.

Two nights ago confirmed this theory like never before. In his dream, she came to him dressed in a long, flowing dress the color of rubies. She smiled a little tentatively.

"Why did you leave me again, Adrian?" she asked. "I thought you would stay."

She then turned around and walked away. After a few steps, she stopped and looked back with such utter sadness that he wanted to hold and comfort her. That look of resignation—of old, renewed pain —jerked him out of his sleep, shaking and sweating under soaked sheets.

He wanted to try to summon her later tonight as he did most nights. Ask her why she addressed him with a different name than Adam. The thought that her brown-eyed gaze, full of love and long-ing, could be meant for another man was too much to bear. He wanted her to be his, and his alone.

And right now he needed her. His beautiful dream was his savior. The shield that kept him from the claws of self-destruction, from giving in to melancholy and the temptation to end it all.

But could he admit defeat? He had to break free, to take what he should have taken years ago.

His life in his hands.

He may not have a past, but he could have a future.

As the moon stared at him through the large windowpanes, he saw one of the candles flicker from the corner of his eye. Tonight, he hoped his dark beauty would come and give him the light to guide him.

———

A FEW DAYS LATER.

A dark alley in Old Town Edinburgh.

MADELEINE DESCENDED the coach just a short way up the road to the agreed meeting place and walked briskly over damp ground. After telling the man to wait there, she walked on. The streets were deserted in this part of nighttime Edinburgh. Her boots rapped fast along the pavement as if they, too, eagerly anticipated what was to come.

She clasped her cloak to protect herself from the cold, and fumed over her and Adam's argument of the past week. They'd had many confrontations in the past, but this was different. She could sense he was on the verge of a monumental decision.

He wanted to leave her after all she had done for him. She'd settled for a modest home, few servants, and a much less privileged existence far away from the thrills of London because of him.

The bastard.

He was starting to get stronger as his Valthrean senses adjusted and molded within him. For the past year, she could control him with magic, but it wouldn't be long before the drugging potion would have a short-lived effect on him, over-ruled by the strength of Valthrean blood. She would either have to drastically increase the dose or think of something else. As he refused his medicine—another sign of his loss of trust in her—she had to resort to lacing his food with it, while making sure that the herbs and seasonings Mrs. Flett used would mask the flavor. This morning, she had mixed a potent dose in the decanter of whiskey in his study. This way, she could be certain he'd drink it as having a glass of Scotch was part of his daily routine before retiring.

Had she been out of her mind to turn him? Why did she ever think it would finally make him love her? It only drove him farther from her.

He barely noticed her. His fractious resistance to a true union of lovers—one that encompassed not only the physical, but his thoughts and emotions—infuriated her. All her efforts to beat the binding spell had failed. Invisible strings kept him securely tied to Emmaline. Without her, his emotions were fragile.

And to think of everything she'd risked to give him time.

Time she didn't reckon she had, despite her arrangement with St. Giles. Her position could be described as precarious at best.

Madeleine had never felt so trapped. Never had to admit defeat, especially because of a man she wanted, a man who despised her.

Desire had brought her to her knees—a bilious curse. Since she'd hatched her scheme in England, her plans had gone up in smoke.

In the first years, she had done her utmost to win Adam. But no matter how often she attempted to get closer to him, she knew now he would never love her. No matter how many times she offered him physical pleasure, he persisted in rebuffing her declared devotion.

Her own magic was her undoing.

With each passing day, her resentment grew along with the bruising humiliation of that knowledge.

More recently, Adam's pointed rejections felt like a constant punch in the gut. He had always insisted upon separate bedrooms, but now he had no qualms in keeping her out of his, in all senses of the phrase, stating that he needed rest and solitude.

A pox on him!

What was most dreadful and humiliating was that the more he treated her with icy indifference, the more she wanted to own that very part of him he denied her. She'd lost interest in her previous, degenerate lifestyle. All she wanted was to own the elusive Adam—the magnificent Adrian Segrave, Viscount Bournemouthe—all of him, including his mind, heart, and soul.

She had to put an end to this absurdity before it continued to whittle away at her good sense.

Last night, she had her first blood slave in years. This time, it had been a male, a young vagrant from the north who'd asked Jones for work. She'd have preferred the maiden blood that Burke could have provided but she'd needed to *see*.

The young man was already unconscious when he was brought to her. Jones had done his part by sneaking him into the sleeping household, even though he wasn't officially her servant anymore. He had found employment as stable master to a wealthy landowner, but he still ran certain errands for her if she paid well. Later, before dawn, he would collect the man's body and leave just as inconspicuously as the way he had come.

Madeleine had a few hours to take her pleasure. She worked quickly, mechanically. She drew her knife and placed a bowl on the floor to catch the flow from his wrists, never pausing to feel the rush, the intense excitement she normally derived from this process.

When she was done, she asked the chalice to connect with the source of her powers, the one entity that knew the answer to every question. In her vision, a heavily cloaked, ghostly figure told her that as long as Emmaline was alive, her link to Adam would survive. Yet, before she'd made Adam immortal, Madeleine had had no choice but to turn the girl because if she died, their invisible bond would have caused the mortal Adam to die soon after.

Either way, the problem was still there. With the shadow of his past, he would not be able to move on and welcome a different life.

Madeleine knew he could see Emmaline in his dreams. She would hear him cry out in his sleep and when she entered his room to check on him, he'd mumble revealing words, words that proved to her the threat that the other woman still presented. He never talked about it but she was no fool. With each passing day, he was slipping from her grasp like dry grains of sand.

There was only one way to change things and make Adam completely hers. She had to get rid of Lady Deramore once and for all —now that she wouldn't be risking Adam's life by doing so.

A clean cut.

After she'd dropped a few discreet questions in the right ears that milled about the underbelly of Edinburgh, she learned of a man who would do anything for the right price. Tonight, she would set the wheels in motion.

Why the man had insisted on meeting in this godforsaken side of town—and close to a cemetery, to boot—she did not comprehend. Greyfriars Kirk made her skin crawl. He did not want breathing witnesses to their conversation, he stated in his missive. Only the dead would listen here.

Poppycock. The woods a few miles beyond her home would have served equally well and they would surely have been safer than this hellhole. But she scarce had a choice. She would meet her mystery man. On his terms.

She turned into a dark alley that led to the church and graveyard, and halted. The mephitic stench of human and animal waste and the stale air were so intense that she almost cast up her accounts then and there. This was worse than the vaults. She held her breath and wrapped her cloak tighter around her. It was so dark that she could barely see beyond her nose.

Suddenly, approaching footsteps scissored through the silence in steady paces. A tall, sleek figure holding a lantern appeared at the other end of the narrow lane. He stopped and placed the lantern on the ground. Feeling him watching her with an odd acuteness, she frowned in consternation. She wanted to get on with this business and return home as soon as possible.

Finally, he moved. A beam of light hit his face briefly but as he stepped forward, it was gone. She could not see much except that he was a big man, with broad shoulders and unfashionably long hair left to fall freely, unrestrained by a queue. There was an aura about him that exuded menace and masculinity. Strangely, it both scared and excited her, awakened long-dormant, sinful desires to frolic with an attractive male. Since Adam had come into her life it was something she only occasionally considered, but this man seemed worth her interest.

Her body responded with a sharp pang of want. While she savored the startling feeling, a faint moan escaped her lips.

Perhaps she would be able to use her charm to finagle some

company tonight. Kill two birds with one stone, so to speak. It had been too long. She needed a man's touch, and this might be just the thing...

Then she smelled him ... that unmistakable scent.

He was *like* her, an immortal.

He stood barely three feet away and, with his back to the light, she was still unable to make out his features. After conquering her initial shock, her mind settled on something more pleasant. Somehow, she had no doubt he was exceedingly handsome. Her excitement grew.

"You are..."

She wanted to ask him many questions, but he spoke before her. "Lady de Brandeville, it is a pleasure to make your acquaintance."

The mention of her real name, which she hadn't heard in years, threw her off balance. Her stomach flipped unpleasantly upon the shocking revelation that she had not been as thorough in covering up her past as she'd thought. Her mind worked fast to think up a quick strategy.

She mustered a firm tone. "You are wrong. That is not my name."

"My lady, I am never wrong," he countered with confidence. "I make it a point to know who all my associates are."

Her hands gripped her cloak until the skin of her knuckles stretched to paper thin. "I am not your associate. Before we settle this business, I want to know who you hold allegiance to—the Valthreans, who abide by the dictates of the Council, or their enemies?"

"I owe allegiance only to paying customers."

His voice was smooth as glass. He also had a faint accent. Italian perhaps, or even French. It was strangely familiar. She searched her memory for a clue.

"Italian and French," he stated simply after her hesitation, picking up on her curious expression. Obviously, among his talents, the gentleman could also count reading minds.

"Charming," she bit out. "But I cannot afford to hire someone I mistrust. This is a very delicate and important task."

"I am your only hope."

"I am not sure I like your impertinence."

He moved closer.

"I think you do, and I also think you'd like to have more than my professional services. Your desire to mate is stronger than this fetid air."

"You are delusional," she gasped without much conviction. His crude language was a titillating, dangerous aphrodisiac.

"I could debate that quite effortlessly, but first, would you like to see what I look like?"

"As you wish," she croaked, suddenly forgetful of her purpose for this encounter. It took supreme effort to sound indifferent when there was nothing she wanted more than to feast her eyes on him.

She watched him reach into his cloak and at the same time, he slowly stepped closer to her, then circled her like a vulture homing on its prey. The path was so narrow that his breath teased her face and his clothing stirred hers as he moved. He stopped when he faced the light and she turned around to bring her back to the lantern.

When the rigid lines of his extraordinarily beautiful face came into view, recognition flared and terror replaced yearning in an instant, clutched her insides and crushed them in its vise—because the murderous look in his eyes left her no doubt as to how much this man loathed her.

She always thought he'd forgotten. Despite what she'd put him through, she never saw him as a threat to her, or entertained the thought he'd one day become one. He'd been still unexperienced back then, and she'd made him a man. The gift of her body, the pleasure of her attentions, would have helped him move on. They ought to have made up for everything.

But they hadn't.

His left hand flew to her throat before she was able to move a hair. He pressed slightly as paralysis overtook her. Her feet were glued to the spot and her mouth dropped open, gagging. He had her firmly caught in his net, and she was forced to yield like a trapped dory.

"I thought..." she wheezed as he kept tightening his hold.

"That I had vanished into thin air, my lady? No, as you can clearly see. My visit is long overdue."

"Did ... all I could."

"I remember what you did, and I've had to live with it all these years. In fact, I'm here to offer my thanks," he scoffed.

"I ... h-helped ... you. After they ... died ... I h-helped. I'll ... give you ... anything. You ... wanted m-m-me ... once ... agh."

His nostrils flared above his thinned lips as he tightened his hold. While her throat constricted, closing up access to her lungs that were now ready to implode.

"Don't think for a second that I ever wanted you," he spat. Then, quicker than the crack of a bullwhip, the ire in his eyes quelled to an arctic gaze. "But I appreciate that you want to accommodate me so. There is one thing I do still want from you."

"Anythi..." she rasped.

"How about your life? I will take your life in retribution for your past deeds."

If she could, she would have scoffed at him. "You ... can't ... kill me like th..."

"You are perfectly correct. My bare hands cannot. But this can."

He chose that moment to lift his right hand to the light and show her the object he held.

It was a sort of vial with an intricate design in brass over the glass case, and a rod with a loop at the end on one side, also made of brass. His thumb pushed some hidden button on the body of the vial and a grating sound ensued, like the scraping of a blade on iron. A wicked looking syringe emerged from the base. That was when she smelled a very distinctive odor. Her kind knew it well.

Snake poison.

He hooked his thumb into the brass loop and pressed downward. A few drops spat out of the needle.

"Ssss..."

"Quite right, my dear. Cobras are a singular nuisance for people like us but personally, I think they have their uses."

Moisture started to slither down her thighs when her bowels loosened. She was disgracing herself, and she couldn't stop it.

"Can you smell your fear, my lady? I can, and it is sweet indeed, like my revenge."

To utter any word was impossible as he roughly pinned her to the wall. He raised his hand and pointed the sharp instrument toward her heart. Her body slumped; it instinctively realized there was no use in fighting. *It's over,* she thought.

Until the voices of a number of men closed in, singing a ditty. Their eyes turned to the mouth of the alley where at least eight figures entered, one with a swaying gait, the others seeming perfectly sober. One of them tripped over himself as his voice slurred over the notes. He leaned into the wall and breathed fitfully. The others spotted them and took on a menacing aura.

"Who's there?" the drunk one wheezed.

His companions started to laugh. If this man didn't kill her, those others would—or do worse. Footpads or murderers? She didn't want to find out...

Her attacker's hold loosened. Surely, he had the good sense to get away from here.

Run!

Madeleine took the opportunity to break free and pull away.

She ran for her life without looking back. Without stopping until she reached her coach and let the horses gallop into the night.

———

MASSIMILIANO STARED at his weapon that he never had the chance to use. One minor adjustment, a little push, and the needle disappeared in its safe case deep inside the length of the carved snake head.

You can't run forever, Madeline.

He turned around and walked toward the light, away from the drunk. He left the lantern behind, walked to his horse, and rode away as quietly as he had come. The biting air collided with his cold face as he rode at breakneck speed. He gripped the reins with painful tension, and held back the cascade of anguish that threatened to eat him up until nothing worth saving was left of him.

Elise's sweet, innocent face outlined itself in the firmament above him. It looked down on him with adoration. With trust. She had thought him a hero, but not knowing that it was not in him to be one had been her undoing. Because of her misplaced reliance on him, he'd lost her forever.

The minute details of her face had long faded from his memory; a source of constant torment to him. He never wanted to forget her, especially the feel of her small, lifeless body in his arms. The guileless look in those big eyes of hers, still untainted by the ways of the world.

Those eyes, if nothing else, would always stay with him. Large, round, and blue in a fine-boned, oval face so like their mother's. Eyes that had turned to him one night during that fateful journey from France to England...

"Have a little more patience, moppet. All we have is each other now and I promise to take care of you always."

Words that lived with him, haunted him, killed him inside. A slow torture and anguish that never ended.

He would give up everything he had, everything he was and could be, for another chance to keep that promise. His jaw tightened and his mouth clamped down on a curse.

He had just told Madeleine that his revenge felt sweet. For most of his life, this had been his foremost thought, and he'd almost achieved his goal.

But as he turned onto a deserted street, he wondered why he didn't come anywhere close to feeling relief. Not even when he had her in his grasp, sure she was about to die.

And finally he understood.

Perhaps he did not deserve to ever be free of his torment.

CHAPTER 8

"Double, double toil and trouble;
Fire burn, and cauldron bubble."
[Macbeth, Act IV, Scene I]

THE NEXT MORNING...

ADAM WAS JUST WAKING from a fitful sleep when Mrs. Flett poked her frizzy head around his bedchamber door, her eyes wild with panic, and informed him that the mistress was gone. She'd posted a note in the solicitor's office. When he saw it was addressed to Adam, he'd had a boy deliver it. Mrs. Flett handed him the piece of paper.

"No telling where she is or what she's up to and ye know there's na arguing with 'er."

"Perhaps she had an engagement for a few days," he suggested, rummaging in his mind for anything she might have told him about taking a trip.

"Dunno, sir."

No matter how flighty Marie was, Adam had to admit she had never spent an entire night away from her home without giving notice first. Something was wrong.

He lifted himself off of the bed. "Let's wait a little longer. If she doesn't return by afternoon, send your husband into town to see if he runs into Mrs. Boyle. If anyone is bound to know anything, it will be Scotland's most accomplished blabbermouth." And the one person Madeleine sometimes kept company with, especially when she wanted to find out something about someone.

"Yes, sir."

Adam's head fell back on the pillow. Mrs. Flett must think him mad to accept Marie's scandalous comings and goings but she never said a word about it. He appreciated her and her husband's discretion as they were the only permanent servants. Among their duties, they saw to the employment of a long string of chambermaids who rarely stayed long after Marie made them take the brunt of her temper tantrums.

He picked up the unfolded sheet and sat on the chair. His wife's scrawled handwriting stared up at him.

MY DEAR ADAM,

LAST NIGHT, I was forced to leave the house in urgency. It is regretful that I am not allowed to share the details. As much as it pains me, I must say goodbye. Quite possibly, I shall never return. Please do not be concerned for I am safe and in good hands. You must make your own way, but know that I do love you, and always have. If it pleases my protectors, one day I will find you. I left sufficient coin in a hidden drawer behind the mirror in my bedchamber. Slide it sideways on the right side. I shall send more in a few months.

Forever yours,
Marie

. . .

MORE SECRETS. Hastily written in a letter Mr. Brown and any of his associates could easily have read.

Adam laid the note on the counterpane and watched it with an odd detachment for long moments, until he decided to get up and go to his study. It would be pointless to write to Judge Rutherford about his wife's disappearance. What was he to do, then?

Unable to bear any intrusions until later that evening, he locked himself in the study. Daylight left and he was still there, trying to mull over things but barely able to think. For the sixth time in an hour, he made his way to the sideboard and poured himself a double measure of whisky.

Marie was gone, but as far down as he reached into his heart—or in his glass—he couldn't canvass a grain of grief, the tiniest sense of loss. Had she been so despicable as to warrant no affection, or was he to blame for having a hole where his heart should be?

Only a week ago, he'd been seriously contemplating his departure from this place, from his sham of a marriage. Now she'd obligingly released him; he should be toasting his thanks to her. But no, she'd cheated him and he couldn't erase that.

A beastly growl rose from the pit of his stomach. Swamped by anger and defeat, he slammed his fist into the solid desk. Once. Twice. Three times.

He ran bloodied knuckles through his hair, welcomed the red-hot pain, and half-sat on the desk. Sweat broke through his skin while his body ached with intense exhaustion. He went hot and cold from one moment to the next, as though he were going through some sort of deprivation or withdrawal.

Dragging himself to the window, he rested his head against the cool panes, while his heart felt the weight of an elephant pummeling his chest. An invisible hand wrung the air from his lungs, drew from him a series of urgent, stilted breaths.

"What ... damn..."

Rapier-sharp stabs of pain sliced through his chest, neck, arm, and jaw, and knocked him to his knees. He clutched one hand to his chest and the other to the wood frame of the window. The whisky glass dropped to the floor to shatter in a hundred little pieces that danced in front of his squinting eyes. A wave of dizziness rolled over him as a strangling vise imprisoned his upper body.

While he scrambled to keep the agony at bay, his head drooped between his tense shoulders. Then, the door opened and someone walked in the room. He opened his mouth around a muffled scream.

A pair of hands caught him under the arms and lifted him into a chair.

"Quick, send for the doctor. Tell 'im to hurry! Master's in a bad way."

Mr. Flett's voice. A shadow crossed Adam's closed eyelids when the man leaned over him and placed his hand across his forehead.

"I'll get you some water, sir."

A few moments later, Flett put a glass to his lips. The pressure eased slightly, and Adam was able to pull some air into his body. However, the discomfort was still there, and he braced himself for more pain.

That's when he knew without a shred of doubt what he needed to do.

If God let him live, if He gave him another chance, he would leave this hell for good. He would sail away and see the world.

———

SAME TIME, at Trenwith, England.

WRENCHED FROM SLEEP, Emmaline shot up to a seated position on her bed. Her heart beat frantically and her night rail stuck to her damp skin. An invisible hand had snaked around her chest as she slept and squeezed hard, making her gasp for air.

A bolt slid open in her mind and opened a door to reveal nothing but blackness, the emptiness that should normally come with death.

The only way the shield between you and Adrian can be destroyed is through death. ... Adrian shall never be yours for as long as you breathe.

145

Madeleine's last words to her rang loudly in her head and filled her with fresh desperation.

She lifted her eyes to the ceiling and let her body fall back on the pillows. Her breaths still came out heavy, erratic. Strangled.

What was this? Why was she thinking of Madeleine now, as she lay alone in her bed? Downstairs, the servants slept in their tidy rooms inside her comfortable cottage. She, on the other hand, would stay awake for the rest of the night, trying to make sense of the crushing weight that compressed her chest with each attempted breath.

It couldn't be her imagination. The ache was sharp, physical. Perhaps she should ring for the housekeeper.

Madeleine's words flashed again and this time she said them out aloud, as though reading from a ghostly script.

Was Adrian in danger? Had something happened to him?

Was the shield Madeleine had mentioned in some way dented, cracked ... broken?

No.

She must be going mad. Madeleine wanted her to stay away from Adrian, so she had used fear to keep Emmaline at bay. She couldn't make herself believe that Madeleine's magic was so strong as to trigger the cycles of life and death. If she did, she would be forced to stop hoping.

A sharp pain cleaved into her chest. Once, twice, three times, the last stronger than the first two. With a strained groan, she pressed a hand to the sore spot and held it there until the pain simply left.

Then, the blackness settled over her again, drained into her butchered heart, along with the sinking feeling that something was horribly wrong.

———

1817, Edinburgh, Scotland.

. . .

THE *AULD REEKIE* was a city that truly lived up to its Scottish moniker, but the new additions of the last century had gone a long way toward changing Edinburgh's reputation from an odiferous, smoke-filled city to one worthy of its place on the map. Superlative architecture produced by the likes of Robert Adam and James Craig—the latter a wet-behind-the-ears but visionary eighteenth-century architect—contributed in great degree toward advancing the expansion and modernization of this Scottish gem.

Emmaline spurred her alacritous mount through streets flanked by multi-story tenements and proud Georgian beauties, until they slowly reduced to a mere speck in the horizon. A woman riding unaccompanied attracted a fair share of attention, so to avoid any speculative looks, she wore her breeches and coat, and pinned her mane of hair under an old fashioned sharp-crowned, flat brimmed man's hat. Her blood pumped hard and resonated through her veins in a feverish tattoo, being that she parlayed all her hopes into this mission.

She pressed on and finally, the stifling city air was pulverized by the coaxing scents of heather, wood, and green as the civilized streets gave way to ever craggier, feral surroundings of virgin beauty.

A score miles beyond the city limits, she took a side path and slowed the horse's galloping pace while sifting through a thicket of hulking tree trunks, contorted branches, and leaves so fulsome they blocked out the already weak sunlight. Finally, she could make out the copse's boundary beyond which appeared a modest clearing.

A medieval-style structure stood in the center of that clearing. The home had certainly seen better days. Broken shutters and cracked stone peeked through the lichen-covered façade.

Her heart took a jolt. She'd searched months … for this?

Inspired by Miss Pool's last words, she'd pursued her only option —a trip to Scotland. When she reached Gretna Green and found nothing, her heart sank, but she didn't give up.

Fruitless enquiries at Chain Bridge and Mordington added to her disappointment. After these towns, she proceeded to Paxton Toll and visited the toll-house where the keeper, Mr. Hume, referred her to the Rev. Mr. Bolt, who performed weddings at the Chapel. The reverend didn't recognize the names she gave him, as she'd expected. Madeleine would have used fictitious names to destroy her trail.

But, when Emma described the couple, it produced a reflective look on Rev. Bolt's face.

He rubbed his chin. "Wait here, Lady Deramore," he said, and left her alone in his office for a few minutes.

He returned with a book so huge he needed both hands to carry it.

"This is where we keep records of the marriages that took place here," he explained as he placed the tome on his orderly desk and opened it. "The names didn't ring a bell, but I remember a flamboyant woman with red hair who came in with a rather reserved gentleman. It struck a chord because she was very clear on what she wanted, while the man barely said a word. It was highly unusual for a couple in love..."

He showed Emmaline their names and signatures. *Adam Alvar and Marie Colette Marchand*. An uncertain clue, but the only one she had. The woman had a French name, which was telling.

From there on, it proved much easier to search for a Mr. and Mrs. Alvar. Someone like Madeleine would plant roots somewhere close to Edinburgh.

Having taken a maid for the journey, she took up lodgings at the George Hotel, thanks to her cousin's generous allowance. In the city, she hired a man, Mr. Haliburton, who specialized in private enquiries, to follow this trace. Further investigation would prove her right, or terribly wrong.

Emmaline stared at the house. This was not quite what she had expected but Haliburton told her that a distinguished French lady by the name of Marie Alvar took up residence here with her husband almost ten years earlier. From the descriptions of the pair, it had to be Madeleine.

A heavy wooden door creaked open and a gaunt, lanthorn-jawed woman with cotton-white hair hobbled out, pail in hand. Emmaline urged her horse to a slow trot toward the nearest tree while the woman reached the well, located sufficiently far from the house. She did not want to scare her quarry away before getting a chance to talk to her.

Emmaline dismounted, tethered her horse to a jutting tree branch, and walked toward the hunched figure. She removed her hat, and a few pins fell off her hair.

"Good morning."

"Morning, lass. What ye be needin'?" she asked without a hint of shock.

Relieved at the welcome reception, Emmaline went straight to the point. "Does ... Mrs. Alvar hold residence here?"

The woman gave a toothless laugh and eyed her as if she were out of her mind.

"Ye're months too late. The mistress left an' never came back. Thank God fer that, if ye ask me," she burred.

Emmaline worked hard to keep her face impassive.

"What about the gentleman who accompanied her to this house?" she asked, doing her utmost to keep her tone neutral?

"Her husband, don't ye mean? The gaffer's been gone a verra long time, too. He left soon after her. Would no stay and kinna say I blame him. Can't imagine why he married her, no love lost between them. But we wasn't paid to think, just did as was told. Mr. Alvar, he be a decent sort."

"Mr. Alvar?" she prodded.

"As I said, 'twas Mr. Alvar, Adam Alvar."

Emmaline felt the blood drain from her face while a chill shimmied through her. She'd already known but to hear it like this drove the nail of finality in her heart.

Adrian—Adam—was Madeleine's husband.

The old woman pursed her lips as if a thought had just occurred to her.

"More'n a wee bit strange that he was always weak and sick, could barely move. But without her here, he got back on his two feet quick as lightning. A fine one he was, but still couldna remember a thing. Perhaps I'd be out of me wits too if I had to deal with the likes of her.

Gave me the creeps, she did. Wouldna allow anyone in her private chambers. Not to say I'd 'ave wanted to..."

"Did he say where he was going?" Emmaline interjected.

"No, lass. But he did mention something about ships and sailing and such. Maybe someone in Leith will know something."

"Do you mind if I take a look around in Mrs. Alvar's rooms?" she asked, her pulse pounding in her head.

"Look your fill. Go in and turn left. Third room was the gent's room. Across the hall was her special one, next to her bedchamber. Have no' touched anything for two years and I still canna go in, the devil's chamber we call it. She was vicious as the fires of Hell, but seeing as Mr. Alvar gave us this house, at least me and my Mr. Flett have a place to sleep and someth'n to put on our table..."

"Thank you," replied Emmaline.

Emma dropped a few coins in her gnarled hands, but then let the woman's excited chatter drift past her as she walked inside.

Following directions, she turned left from the oversized hall and reached out to open the third door in a long, dim corridor. A dank odor did not quite manage to overpower the accompanying aroma of old grime and mold that clung to the walls and floors like a blood-sucking leech.

Seconds later found her inside a dark room. The half-hearted light from the tiny hewn window hardly provided adequate illumination. She could make out a long table, some assorted pottery and a long line of dust-coated jars with mysterious contents.

In the center of it all, swathed in cobwebs and layers of dust, the Demon's Chalice had pride of place. She walked to it and ran the tips of her fingers around the smooth rim, destroying many a spider's home in her trail.

She cupped her fingers around it, and lifted the magnificently carved piece of rock.

It was heavy, but she could manage. Her fencing training had already given her strength she would never imagine she had. The instructor had somewhat lost his composure when he realized he'd have to teach a woman, but money solved many problems and in the end, he accepted the chore.

While holding the chalice under one arm like a treasure to be protected, she allowed her legs to take her where they willed ... right across the hall.

Adrian's room.

She opened the door and swept inside. A larger window, framed by once vibrant curtains in gold and green hues, graced the north facing wall. A huge canopied bed swallowed half the space and a matching carpet covered the stone floor. It was a sophisticated yet unassuming room. It would have suited Adrian's temperament.

She walked to the bed and, remiss of the dust covering it, reclined her body on the counterpane.

For years, Adrian had slept here. Suffered here. Lived his life, ate, and drank here.

More than likely, made love to another woman here. To Madeleine. To *his wife!* Madeleine had truly stolen him from her.

Pain cut through her like a surgeon's trephine. While he lay in this very spot, she had not figured in his thoughts and memories, while her troubled mind sagged with the weight of his ever present image and the memory of their shared moments.

She let herself drift in time for a while, lost herself in the search for an anchor.

"Sweetheart, you know you can't get away from me, don't you? Might as well surrender now."

Emmaline stopped running and swiveled her body around to look at her pursuer. The swift action made her lightheaded. The long, wide corridors of the sprawling Belvoir country mansion echoed her breathless giggles and the light from the tall window to her right painted a wide luminous stripe on her dark crimson dress.

Adrian's favorite color, the color of his roses.

"Why don't you make me?" she dared.

"Just wait 'til I catch you, minx."

Adrian closed in on her in big strides, while she stood immobile with her hands linked behind her back, wearing an impish grin. Without pause, he threw her an equally devilish smile, intent on distracting her with his masculine wiles. But, she wasn't through with their afternoon diversion. She'd make him chase her to the second floor study which, she knew, was presently unoccupied.

Perfect for an afternoon kiss.

"Hmmm ... does the gentleman think I'm an easy catch, then?" she teased.

He laughed at her humor but kept on stalking her like prey, showed her his eagerness for the prize. Only a few feet separated them. But in anticipation of his forward lunge to grab her, she turned agilely and resumed her playful escape.

She realized too late that she had approached a set of two steps about ten feet from the archway ahead. She stumbled and her arms flailed in a wild, propelling motion to keep herself from plummeting to the floor. In a flash, two strong arms circled her and stayed her fall. Those muscular arms pulled her back and enclosed her in warmth.

She could feel the hardness of him as he pressed his body against her back. The fabric of his superfine black morning coat felt soft and comforting to the touch. Her head fell back into his shoulder, where she grasped the opportunity to smell and feel him. She didn't want to run any more. She was done with playing.

Slowly, she turned her body in the circle of his embrace and let her arms wind around his neck. She explored the base of his hairline with the tips of her fingers while she looked up into his beloved face. He was so close that she could taste his breath.

"Thank you for saving me," she said breathlessly.

He looked into her eyes and lifted his hand to first cradle her warm cheeks, then, to tenderly trace the sensitive flesh behind her ears with the tip of a single digit.

"Oh."

His fingers splayed on her skin and slid in the curtain of her loosely bound hair.

"As long as I have breath in me, I'll always keep you safe," he replied fiercely.

His hands, which seemed to ache with need, were now completely buried *in her hair, held her scalp prisoner. But even if she could, she wouldn't have looked away.*

As if pulled by invisible strings, her body drew closer to his, their embrace grew tighter, and their hungry lips met in an intense kiss...

Right now, she wanted Adrian to kiss her like he had then. She wanted to feel his warm lips on hers, exploring and loving her.

She wanted him back.

This was Fate's cruel ploy. The witch had told her that with the chalice, she could make anything happen, anything she wanted. But, right now she didn't feel that way at all. She felt helpless, desperate.

A flood of tears carved a steady trail down her cheeks. For two hours she cried, the bit of rock in her clenched arms fleeting comfort to a heart that was once more breaking.

Adrian was gone. She was too late.

―――――

ONE WEEK LATER...

"WATCH THAT TRUNK, will ye. Bunch o' lubbers, the lot of ye. Get on with it!"

The ruddy-faced captain stood on shore by the plank, smoking his pipe and hauling expletives at four lanky, green-at-the-gills youths.

Aided in small measure by the faltering daylight, Emmaline observed Captain Finlay MacGregor's stocky, weathered form as she approached and wished, despairingly, that he would be able to help her. He was her last and only hope, as she had already interviewed three other ship captains who insisted they'd never welcomed a man of Adrian's—or Adam's—description on board their vessels.

The targets of MacGregor's temper inched up the narrow gangway with aggravated faces, and awkwardly attempted to transport a series of bulky wooden trunks onto the ship's freshly scrubbed deck under their captain's watchful eye. Shellback that he was, a worldly sailor to the core who'd made his home belowdecks for more than a score and ten years, the captain should know well the pitfalls of leading a sloppy crew into oftentimes dangerous unknown waters and locales.

During the last decade he'd ruled his floating domain, a vessel he named *Trinity*, with an iron fist. It was said around these parts that two years under Captain MacGregor's command would season one in sufficient preparation to beat the toughest odds in a sporting match against Old Nick himself. It was also said that underneath his rough demeanor and language lay the heart of a man who would give his very life for those in his care.

Prior to these last few days, Emmaline hadn't had much experience in dealing with MacGregor's kind. The man in front of her possessed a huge forehead and bushy eyebrows. He peered at her with intelligent eyes that blazed amidst wrinkled, leather-like skin and a shock of cotton-white hair—or what was left of it on his balding pate.

"Captain, I was wondering if you could be so kind as to allow me a few moments of your time. I promise I shan't keep you long."

She'd dressed to fit in—a commoner—and disguised herself as best she could. It was unacceptable for a woman of stature to travel alone to a place like this, and she'd have drawn a crowd. She was already risking enough as it was.

MacGregor pinned her with a severe look. "Lass, ye must be right mad! This be no place for the likes of ye. If I were ye, I'd turn me heels and go back to me husband where I belong."

"Please, sir. I shan't take long."

Upon hearing the discrete stab of anxiety in her voice, MacGregor softened his demeanor.

"What'd ye want to know, lass?"

Emmaline gave the captain as detailed a description of Adrian as she could.

"Have you seen this man?" she asked, encouraged by the sudden glint of recognition in the captain's eye.

The captain told her of *The Scotsman*, a ship operated by a Scottish trading concern. It paid a short visit to the port of Leith about every six months, just long enough to unload cargo and take sail to new destinations. Sometimes, it would be gone within a day or two.

It appeared that a man of Adrian's height and countenance had taken a post under the command of a fellow named John Ballard. According to MacGregor's calculations, the vessel should be due back in a couple of weeks.

The captain's words instilled in Emmaline something she had not felt in a long time, especially since the day she located Madeleine's Scottish home—a feeling of accomplishment and optimism, one that enforced in her the audacity of believing in a real future with Adrian. Although hope had kept her sustained all these years, it never felt as strong as it did at this very moment.

A yawl negotiated the agitated waters in the distance, the half dozen toiling oarsmen in it surely thankful for the benevolence of a starry night. Three massive wooden spars that made the masts of the larger ship sailing torpidly not far behind glistened in the soft illumination provided by a gibbous moon. The surface of the water reflected the two bobbing forms as the waves danced around them in a glittering chiaroscuro frame. Emmaline marveled at the picture. The world looked suddenly beautiful.

An overwhelming elation gripped her. After thanking the captain, who once more admonished her for her carelessness in venturing out alone, she walked away, her mind whirling faster than a child's spinning top.

———

NINETEEN DAYS, four hours and thirty-six minutes later.

According to her Breguet-style silver pocket watch, that much time had passed since Emmaline's conversation with MacGregor. She'd taken his cue to give more regard to her personal safety, and elected to disguise herself carefully—so carefully that if one didn't look too closely, she came across as one of the typical lowbred, gangly, callow youths who swarmed into town fresh off the docked ships, ready to gambol in an evening of unabashed drinking and other earthly pursuits.

She snapped the glass case closed and pocketed the watch. Underneath her jacket, she also carried an ivory-handled poniard that had previously belonged in her father's varied collection of weaponry; one of those objects she would never bear to part with, it made her feel safe. Besides, she was knowledgeable in wielding the sharp, pointed blade to best advantage.

The prickly woolen jersey she wore made her skin itch abominably. Garbed in faded breeches that—she could only guess—had probably once been black as coal; worn, dusty boots; and a cheap but thick overcoat, which at least served its basic purpose to protect her from the hiemal climes, she made her way through streets and alleyways, and made sure along the way to take a thorough peek inside the taverns most frequented by scallywags and sailors. All the while, she took care to avoid attracting unnecessary attraction, and mingled with the townsfolk and seamen as best she could.

A place in particular, she hoped, would contain the one person she wanted to see. When she had asked about the crew of *The Scotsman* a few days earlier, she was told they liked to frequent *The Seven Tides*, one of the establishments located less than a block from the docks. The ship would be making a transitory stop, so the crew had to keep themselves as close to the port area as possible.

One more turn and she'd be there. She bowed her head and adjusted her wide-brimmed, shapeless hat to ascertain that her hair was securely tied underneath the fabric. It wouldn't do to blow her disguise.

Around midnight, the street traffic somewhat thinned as many men had settled into their chosen pleasures, or perhaps, sleep.

The door of the tavern was kept closed to stave off the biting cold. Emmaline lowered the hat's brim over her eyes, willed her roiling stomach to calm, and closed her fingers around the rough edges of the wood to inch the door open just a little. The panel creaked, but nobody inside noticed; they were too intent on whatever they were doing.

Her eyes scanned the inside with predatory precision. About thirty heads were scattered on miscellaneous tables, mostly sailors who indulged in a rare few hours of shiftlessness after imbibing pint after pint of cheap ale. A couple of ragged-faced swabs stammered out lewd ditties, each one determined to outwit the other in a contest of slurred notes. Others gambled away their measly fortunes, trying to keep their eyes on the cards and off the half exposed mounds of big-breasted women who draped themselves lasciviously over their laps.

A group of three men to the far end of the room were fully engaged in a trivial quibble, pettifogging about who'd deserved to win a fisticuffs challenge held earlier that day at the docks. Should it have been ol' Tom or Willy, the new boy? Did ol' Tom cheat, fearing that the younger, swifter opponent would too easily take his title?

An old sea dog plied his companions with a lengthy sea yarn, a braggart longing for the ears of others as he related his fanciful adventures. The flimsy veneer of his animated storytelling, however, could not disguise the weariness that soaked through his face and limbs, all beaten by the intemperate moods of the oceans he'd crossed in his lifetime.

Emmaline felt like she'd just stepped into one of her father's nautical novels.

One figure, however, caught her attention. Unlike the others, he sat alone at a table. His fingers trailed along the rim of his mug, his head bent forward in deep thought. Something about the way his golden hair fell over his brow, the way he sat with graceful stillness, the way he moved when he shifted restlessly in his chair, hit her like a ton of bricks. Goose pimples sprung all the way down her arm and a sharp tingling started at the back of her neck.

The man was Adrian. She was certain of it.

Emmaline let the door go and pressed her back against the wall by the entrance. It took a moment to quiet the frantic beating of her heart and tamp down tears of happiness. Now, the hardest part would be the waiting. She shook the nervous excitement away and braced herself. More than ever, she couldn't afford to make any mistakes.

A dark shape materialized about fifty feet away to her left. The man she had paid to trail her waited for her cue. The promise of more coin after the task was completed ensured that he would not renege on their bargain.

When Adrian exited the door, he would most probably start walking toward the ship. She would then signal to her man to follow and do whatever was necessary to restrain him.

Underhanded and dreadful, but it seemed the swiftest way to get him where she wanted and proceed with the blood ritual to reunite them. The most important part of her stratagem was that he still be alone when he walked out, or things would be considerably more complicated. She hadn't prepared for that possibility.

She retraced her steps and hid in the shadows of an arched doorway a few feet up.

Then she waited.

And waited.

At least an hour passed. The icy cold that rushed in from the north bit through the fabric of her clothing and leached to her skin. Her body turned stiff with lack of movement. Every breath she exhaled created billowing frost clouds. Exposure to the raw Scottish elements gave her a distinct appreciation for men's love of brandy. She'd gladly sell her soul to the devil just to feel that heat glide down her throat—liquid fire permeating her body, from the top of her frozen head to the chilled tips of her toes. She imagined the sensation vividly, hoping it would keep her body temperature at a tolerable level. Luckily, the thick gloves she donned kept her hands relatively warm.

This evening reminded her of another cold winter night—the night of the Annual Ball at Belvoir, the night she danced the waltz with Adrian and stole a passionate kiss behind the potted plant.

She cleared her head and forced her thoughts to the present.

How long was he going to sit there?

Most of the patrons had already stumbled out and dispersed. Inebriated, they tottered toward their sleeping quarters. The town was mostly quiet, with the odd noise or conversation traveling through the hollow alleys.

Despite the cold and discomfort, she recognized there was peace to be felt in standing there, listening to the subdued sounds of the dark hours. The occasional sign of human activity echoed through the streets, but other than that, it was mostly just her, the slumbering town, and the black sky waiting together in companionable silence.

The creak of the tavern door startled her. A man emerged.

She caught a glimpse of a proud, beautiful profile, and strands of sun-kissed hair that was longer than she remembered. His clothes were coarse, but the man was one and the same.

Adrian.

She hesitated, her excitement so powerful she found herself glued to the spot, at a loss on how to proceed. So engrossed was she that she only noticed the four ruffians, grotesque in size and form, when they'd already closed in on him with obvious criminal intent.

A sickening whiff of stale tobacco and unwashed bodies filled her nostrils, and put her senses on alert. They hadn't seen her in the shadows and swaggered to him, comfortable in the belief that no one would hear their shenanigans.

"Oy, there, feller, where ye be goin' so late, ey?"

"Want te grab a pint wit us, will ye?"

"Aye, he will. He wouldna say no to a right friendly chat."

"'Sna good te walk all alone at nicht, cin get you'n tribble."

All four together formed an impenetrable wall of muscle. Adrian shifted slowly, like a panther on the hunt, elegance in his movements. Emmaline watched the corded veins in his neck strain as his jaw muscles clenched. He was no meek opponent. His body was larger, more defined. He fisted his hands to betray the guardedness that simmered under his surface nonchalance.

"Evening, sirs. I regret to say that I must decline your invitation. I have other plans tonight."

That voice. Despite the hard edge, it filled her with wholesome delight.

"Oy, here's an English feller to boot. Ginna enjoy this one."

"Aye, brither. Those boots look right nice, dinna say."

The thugs drew their gully knives to demonstrate that they meant business, and shifted them in their beefy hands so the polished blades glimmered wickedly in the moonlight.

"Let's make this quick, gaffer. Got a pretty piece of laced muslin waitin' fer me so I din't have all night."

"I think you may want to think twice about this," Adrian warned as he unsheathed a wide knife with a sword handle, much like a short cutlass, or a handier, easy-to-carry version of one.

Emmaline recognized it as a deadly boucan knife suitable for hacking through skin, sinew, and bone. The sight of it made her wonder both how far he had traveled and what he'd been through. She once read in one of her father's books that in the not so distant past, those kinds of knives were quite common among sailors who cruised the Caribbean waters.

Tilting his chin at an obstinate angle, his eyelids half-closed, he measured his foe.

"I believe I just expressed my regrets, kind sirs," he reiterated when they moved not a hair out of his way. "What do you say you bid me good night and take your leave?"

The four men signaled each other.

"Dinna think so, lad. We have business ter take care of first," the ugliest one of the lot responded with peevish boldness.

"Can't say I didn't warn you. Which one first?"

Emmaline forced her eyes away from the unfolding scene to look to the left. Her man had vanished, probably too scared to meddle with the likes of these types.

Change of plans. Intervention would have to come first, regrets later.

She couldn't—wouldn't—let Adrian fight alone.

———

ADAM WIDENED his stance and prepared for a dirty brawl. It had been a while since his last skirmish, and God knew he needed to vent right now. There were moments when not even drinking a stream of liquor would assuage the hopelessness that consumed him.

This here was a perfectly good opportunity to take out his frustration. The knife play would give the whole affair the dangerous edge he needed.

Because he had absolutely nothing to lose.

As one of the giants approached, Adrian slashed the air with his blade, sliced through the man's shirt and nicked his bicep.

Good start.

The sight of blood set free his inner beast.

"Come on, dandies. You can fight like men, I hope," he taunted them.

He secretly wished this could be a real threat on his life. Perhaps on the other side, he could have found the answers he sought. But all he was able to do was fight for sport—and stay on the same ship a while longer. He had no desire to play dead and to have to think of a change of scene.

At the corner of his eye, he spotted some movement. Then, a body materialized before him, seeming to originate from the dim recess of a doorway. The figure moved with caution, a knife in his hands.

Adam groaned inwardly. Not another of these brutes!

From the mystery man's build, he looked like he could be young. Adam couldn't be sure as the stranger never spoke and a large, ridiculous hat hid his features.

To Adam's astonishment, the stranger walked past the thugs and turned around to stand at his side. Without a word, he lifted his knife —a rather fine, delicate-looking weapon for a common street boy.

Well, well...

"Let's see what you can do, young man," he whispered to his new companion-in-arms.

Adam caught the faintest of smiles curve the stranger's peculiarly feminine full lips, the only part of his face he could somewhat see, but when the four miscreants circled them, all speculation fled his mind. He hoped this boy knew what he was getting himself into.

In silent agreement, the two moved back to back, each aiming to ward off two attackers. Adam soon found that his ally had a way with the poniard that only years of practice could bring. When he managed to look, the boy had literally cut some holes into their opponents' strategy. One had blood liberally oozing from his leg, the other a long gash on his face, which would have him forever carrying a scar.

A soft grunt alerted him to trouble. One of the thugs had strong-armed his companion and gave him a rough push. Quick on his feet, Adam stalled the forward momentum and caught the stranger in his arms as the silly boy held on to his hat. The action brought their bodies flush together.

A vague memory stirred of him chasing a dark-haired, beautiful woman, like the one from his dreams. At one point, she tripped and he was there, right behind her...

The vision suddenly vanished, replaced by a feeling of ... *arousal?*
Damn.

The boy tarried in his arms and at such close range he could distinctly feel—yes, he had to be right—two sizeable swells of flesh, more commonly known as breasts. He questioned his deduction for a moment but that shape was unmistakable.

Adam's mind reeled. The boy ... no ... the person ... the lady kept her head down so he still couldn't make out the face but the body clinging to him was without doubt that of a woman.

His manhood was determined not to be ignored and his cheeks flushed hot with shame. Was he stark raving mad to entertain such ideas when lives hung on the line? This was definitely no time to be thinking what he was thinking.

But this boy was definitely *not* a boy! It was a woman—a formidable, knife-wielding, very interesting woman. The chit would have some explaining to do when this was over.

And when their discussion was done, perhaps she'd be amenable to a different sort of game. One that his now violently raging appetites wouldn't let him forget until he indulged them with an agreeable female—for, surprisingly, this was the best he'd felt in a long time. His body thrummed with excitement and energy. Having this chit near—it couldn't be the fight?—did this to him. The heavy heart, the constant weariness were gone, replaced by the bright spark of awareness and anticipation. She intrigued him; more than that, she aroused his senses in a way that was far from normal for him.

What was going on here?

Taking advantage of his distraction, one of the ruffians grabbed the girl from his grasp and threw her on the ground. Her head hit the side of the stone wall, and she was knocked senseless.

Adam rushed to her aid. His move proved a bad one when one of the adversaries drew up behind him and hit him on the head, so hard that he felt himself fall deep to the bottom of a burning cauldron.

He couldn't move but the roysters' victorious laughs drilled painfully into his ears. It was over. They were both dead meat ... especially his brave champion.

Vaguely, he heard screams. Inwardly thankful, he recognized some of the voices; he'd been sailing with them for a time now. He'd sigh with relief, if only he could.

Heavy footsteps ran in the opposite direction of the voices.

Must be the bastards making their escape.

The woman, is she well? Please attend to her...

He couldn't speak, although he did hear a choked sound, a groan, and realized it was his own.

I can't move.

"Bill, check this one here. Bull's ballocks! It's a lass! Why don't ye take her inside and ask Mary if she'd take care of 'er? She'll not refuse ye. Lizard and I'll get Alvar on board. Doc'll see ta him."

His mates were here to collect him. Time to leave the port.

He wondered about the girl lying unconscious beside him. Would he recognize her if he met her again?

He'd never seen her face. And most likely, he'd never meet her again.

On that thought, the void claimed him.

————

When Emmaline came to, she was being tended to by a kindly-faced, plump woman.

"My name is Mary," the woman said. "I'm the taverner's wife."

Try as she wanted, Emmaline couldn't get more than a croak out of her throat.

"Hush," Mary soothed, pressing a cold compress to Emma's forehead.

"Where ... he?" Emma managed to ask. "Need ... see ... him."

Mary's face fell, and she pressed a warm, fleshy hand to Emmaline's cheek. "He's gone, love. *The Scotsman* is back at sea, will not return for another three months."

Emmaline crossed her arms against her chest and shivered as a fast-freezing cold threw her heart into the clutches of despair. She sobbed against Mary's bosom, but somewhere into breaking down, she steeled her spine and straightened. Adrian would not slip from her hands a second time!

Because love was stronger than magic.

The best course of action seemed to be to wait, and Emma lodged at the inn, alongside Mary, waiting for *The Scotsman* to dock into the harbor once again.

But all was for naught ... because Adrian was not on board the ship when it returned. She learned that he had left the crew and nobody knew where he'd gone. It was as though he had left Earth to live on some parallel universe.

If she could've died, Emma believed she would have in that instant because she knew. She knew without a shadow of a doubt that Madeleine had been right.

She'd never see Adrian again.

———

TEN YEARS LATER, 1827.

EMMALINE SAT on the garden bench at her elegant country cottage in Somerset and observed her blooming rosebush. Her mind traveled to a decade past, to the last time she'd seen Adrian in Leith. It felt like several lifetimes ago. A cruel, uncaring Fate had reunited them for a fleeting moment, nothing more.

Her cousin had acquired that house in Somerset for her, after all, and she settled there after convincing the baron it would be for the best, that she wanted to move on. Only the implication that she might get Adrian out of her head brought him to acquiesce to her suggestion.

The most difficult task was to find information about the Valthreans, to learn more about herself. It was the natural thing to do at this juncture but she couldn't just waltz into a library and ask for it. Furthermore, despite the odds, she'd never given up on a reunion with Adrian.

No, she would never give up.

To her amazement, she had discovered over time that Valthreans were everywhere. All one had to do was sit in a crowded park or theatre and they were there, mingling with unsuspecting humans.

One day, she plucked up courage and left Somerset to attend a violin concerto at the Theatre Royal in Bristol ... without drinking her concealing potion.

A quick scan of the crowd gave her five possibilities. The right moment came when an elegant woman in a green and white striped satin gown glided past her on her way to the refreshments stand. Tendrils of energy floated around them. The woman stopped and turned to her.

Emmaline smiled at her knowingly.

"Forgive me for being too forward. I know we haven't been properly introduced, but I seek help," she said beseechingly.

The woman's narrowed blue gaze fell on her face. "How can I help you, dear?"

"If you allow me." Emmaline stepped a little closer to her and kept her voice low. "I'm looking for someone who is very important to me but it's very hard to achieve success without proper guidance. Is there anyone like ... like you and I, who can offer information? An office, maybe. You see, I have no one to ask."

"I understand perfectly," the lady said in acknowledged sympathy. She fished a card from her reticule and pressed it in Emmaline's palm.

"Take this. I hope you find what you're looking for. Enjoy your evening."

With a parting nod and kind smile, she left.

Emmaline held the card up with trembling hands. Her gaze traveled from the departing woman to the fancy print.

The Versus Club
Clement's Lane,
London

THE NEXT DAY, she packed her trunk and headed for London. The Versus Club was located in an unassuming building up a short, narrow road across from the Church of St. Clement. A respectable area, but not quite Fleet Street, and the church drew people away from the nondescript immediate surroundings. Clever place to maintain a degree of anonymity.

She pulled a rope to ring the bell and waited. A pointed nose appeared behind a small square window cut into the door. It looked unnaturally large between beady eyes, narrow lips, and a missing chin.

"How may I be of assistance?"

"I want to learn about me ... about the Valthreans, please."

Undisguised notes of urgency leaked from her voice. *Could she have explained herself better?*

The man's narrowed eyes assessed her thoroughly. She had gone on a limb and again forwent the potion, trusting that her scent would serve as her calling card.

It did. The door opened and the man preceded her up a flight of stairs to an enormous room stuffed from floor to ceiling, from one end to the other, with books, maps, pamphlets, and papers.

"The library is at your disposal, Miss. Here you will find information about all things Valthrean. If you have any questions, please do not hesitate to ask. We are open at all hours."

"Where do you suggest I start, kind sir?" she asked, not a little awed as she looked around her.

He went to a shelf behind her and found a small volume.

"This book will tell you about the Valthrean origins and give you useful information about the structure of the Council."

He placed the book in her extended palm.

"The Council?"

"Governments are not the prerogative of nations," he explained with a lopsided smile. "Valthreans need leadership, too."

Emma felt sheepish in admitting her ignorance of things that affected her on a personal level.

"It takes time to learn everything," the man said mercifully.

"Thank you." Emmaline smiled.

"May I introduce myself? My name is Edward Finley, librarian. I have been a Valthrean for ninety-seven years," he confided with a slight bow of the head.

"Lady Emmaline Deramore. It has been twenty years." Generally, they'd need a third person to introduce them in polite society, but nothing was normal about this situation. *Their* situation. At this point, she had no use for strict formalities when it came to this.

"Enchanted."

After showing her to a seating arrangement of two overstuffed leather armchairs with a square walnut end table between them, he bowed again and disappeared behind a desk.

Emmaline sank in one of the chairs, opened the book at a random page, and thought about Mr. Finley. That was decidedly the most peculiar introduction she'd ever had—and the most authentic.

Although she'd always be ready for Adrian and search for him until the end of time if need be, she was nothing if not a realist.

She'd lost him, but she still had a life to live—one without her beloved, but a life nonetheless.

Perhaps she had a home after all, and if she was willing to open her mind, an extended family.

Unless she let guilt and her obsession condemn her to a life of loneliness....

PART II

War

CHAPTER 9

"...signs of nobleness, like stars, shall shine
On all deservers..."
[Macbeth, Act I, Scene IV]

DECEMBER 3, 1944.
London, England.

"THE ORACLE HAS SPOKEN."

Massimiliano "Max" Damiani observed as Neil Waterstone eyed his only remaining family, Cam, who stood over the chalice, lost in another world as he gripped the table's edge on either side. A long, very long time ago, the brothers had been known as Nila and Candaka, borne from a long line of Kashmiri craftsmen and fishermen.

Two of the oldest Valthreans in existence who'd set up roots in Europe after fleeing their home over two millennia earlier, they'd known the very man for whom the Valthrean brotherhood was named. Together, after his tragic death, they established the rules and ethics that formed the core of their beliefs and the way of life for their then small community. Following the unjust persecution they suffered at the behest of the merciless King Aravala, and the way their lives were uprooted, they could be commended for fast adapting to a different existence—and that included eventually changing their names to more palatable ones for their hosting culture in the West.

After their parents opted to embrace their old age and die a natural death, they became each other's anchor. The rest of their family had lived in other villages and they never saw them or their country again.

Now, the Valthreans occupied all corners of the globe, raised in all walks of life like any society, but the central governing body remained in London, with additional headquarters in several cities over the world.

Neil had shared with him that he never wanted to see how his childhood home had changed, how the people there lived now. Max could tell, those long ago memories still haunted Neil—a feeling he related to. Perhaps it was one of the reasons why he respected and liked the man so much. The fact that the Cult had kept alive Aravala's culture of evil and greed brought home the fact that Neil was far from avenging all that he had lost.

A thirst for revenge—now *that* Max understood perfectly.

What Max didn't have, though, was someone like Cam, who, luckily, was a bit less philosophical about life than his brother, and good at keeping the balance. Only Cam could yank Neil out of the doldrums and force him to live. Max was pretty good at that on his own but there were times when the devil inside had the better of him. In the very bad moments, he needed a boost to help him summon the strength he lacked, but that was a need only his soul knew and no one else.

The Demon's Chalice—one of the sacred chalices from India currently in the hands of the Council—glowed beautifully with all the colors of the spectrum. The sight was more comforting than blinding as the different hues blended and separated with shifting hypnotic swirls and shapes.

The only Council member trusted sufficiently to witness such a magnificent spectacle, Max followed the elder Neil's gaze. While waiting for Cam to descend from his high and wind back through the magical veil into reality, Max lounged on a wing chair in his casual solid black utility suit, the acceptable attire for these austere years. His only claim to vanity was a genuine silk necktie in a burgundy design he'd had custom made in Como, Italy. Tonight, a Stand Down Party for the Home Guard would be held at the Royal Albert Hall and he had a pass. He didn't care for going, although he would. Nothing drove depression home more than hanging around the most blatant reminders that they were at war.

"Things are going to get uglier before they get better," Cam finally spoke.

Max curved his lips in a sardonic half-smile. "Don't they always?"

"Come have a seat," Neil urged, putting a hand on Cam's shoulder and steering him toward another chair to Max's left. "You need to replenish your energies now."

He sat him down. Cam once admitted he felt a bit dizzy after drawing his power from the chalice—a talent he'd acquired after some years of experimenting with it, in a manner following their founder's footsteps. Now that he had tapped into this ability, he was saddled with this secret and highly protected position within the organization. No strategy would be implemented by the Valthrean Council—or at least by Neil—without first consulting Cam.

Neil stood next to Cam, his arms crossed and brows knitted in thought. The pair was quite a sight. Both casually clad in slightly crumpled trousers and jumper, the brothers looked like they hadn't slept in days. Years of war were getting to them. They couldn't deny they were worried and overworked, thus neglecting themselves.

"You two boys each need two things and fast," Max said, looking from one to the other. "A willing woman, and more drink than you can handle. Why don't you come with me tonight?"

"Paperwork," they said in unison, Cam with a grin, after which

Neil added, "And decisions to make. We must prepare for the Council summit. Wartime brings added responsibilities and I think we've pussyfooted long enough."

Max knew what he meant. The Cult of the Snake had resorted to all sorts of dirty tactics to influence the outcome of this conflict. They colluded with the Nazis, facilitated corrupt police in the occupied countries, and caused the death of many good citizens to further their interests. Neil and Cam had done their best to put the brotherhood to good use for the allies, but careful organization and more hands-on influence was needed for this to end well. Too much was at stake for the future of the world, and they were all a part of the outcome.

"We've done pretty well so far. See how it turned out in Malta with our protection of the convoys, and then the battle at Al Alamein. Our support helped decimate almost a third of the Axis force there."

"The Germans should not have made it this far," Neil argued. "Yes, we're holding them at bay, but the cost is high." Neil linked his hands behind him and paced the room.

Max crossed a foot on his knee and rested a hand on his ankle. "We cannot prevent human deaths, Neil. We can only provide a few extra minds and bodies and some wise advice in the right ears. Case in point, Montgomery had a great victory in Egypt and he owes much of that to us."

"Yet, over thirteen thousand men were killed."

"Hitler and Mussolini lost over thirty thousand, damn near forty thousand."

Max would admit however that sometime into the future, aside from defensive tactics in aiding mortals, they needed to come up with a clear and decisive vision in handling the Cult problem once and for all in this changing world.

Neil unlinked his hands and plopped himself on the edge of the couch across from them. Leaning forward, he rested both elbows on his thighs and let his hands droop between his legs. Thick brows furrowed over a face that, although appealing, looked older than it was because of deep worry lines and a hard line of a mouth. Raising a hand, he pressed two fingers on the bridge of his nose and took a deep breath.

"It's not over yet. I can't get around all the military and civilian lives lost in Normandy and more of that as the troops move toward Germany. Our men are having a hard time although they're putting up a good fight. The Germans must be stopped soon."

"That's one thing I can't argue with."

"But first, we have another problem," Cam interjected.

Cam was generally more carefree and relaxed. Although just as burdened as his brother, especially with his role as Oracle within the brotherhood, his eyes always gleamed with optimism and mischief, adding to his already considerable charm. Right now, though, that lightness was replaced by a dark and troubled expression.

"A doctor friend of mine wrote to me a few months ago about a bizarre case at the V clinic. Apparently, it's been going on a while but he decided to run some special tests in the lab and what he saw was strange enough to inform me about it. He sent me another letter..."

Both men gave him a puzzled look.

"It's a woman. She's been going there a while as she gets sick pretty often, too often, in fact. The blood tests revealed three different types of blood, all incompatible. But the curious thing is that one of the blood types belongs to an immortal and it's ... *tainted*, for lack of a better word."

"Tainted?" Max asked. "Meaning, diseased?"

"No, there's a mixture of properties in that blood—and it's not any known sickness. The traces he found were of strange substances. Not sure what to call it except stuff that those who dabble in the Occult tend to use."

"You mean a witch?"

Cam nodded gravely. "Something like that, I suppose. It's the first time this has happened, as far as I know. The implications are several, and I don't like the look of it."

"You mean that witchcraft can kill us?"

"Or at the very least, weaken us, steal our power and our well-being. It's something the Cult could use against us, and that would spell disaster."

For once, Neil was speechless. Perhaps he was too tired and he'd officially given out. He leaned back on the couch, his eyes staring at the wall behind them. Max searched his brain for answers.

"But perhaps the question that screams loudest at me is—why now?" Cam added.

"I think someone should speak to this woman," Max suggested. "Neil?"

Neil started and nodded. "You should go, Max. If anyone can find out, it's you."

"Where is she and what's her name?"

"Emma Degrave. She owns a sweet shop in Bromyard." He paused. "But Doc said she hasn't been to the clinic since early in the year with strong influenza symptoms. He said she seemed to respond to treatment but still, he's a little concerned that he hasn't seen her since."

Small town in Herefordshire, in the West Midlands.

Way down the sloping corridors of his mind, the name rang a bell. *Emma.* A similar name, another region—Hertfordshire. Completely different place, a different time, but it was easy to get the two confused. Madeleine's face also materialized front and center to taunt him as it often did but again—why now? Wasn't Hertfordshire the area Madeleine had lived in once? He remembered that long ago case she was tangled in, of a man she'd kidnapped and spirited to Scotland....

What had been the aggrieved woman's name? *Emmaline ... Emmaline Deramore.* That was the one Madeleine had wanted to kill. He'd done his homework well before setting her up.

After Madeleine had eluded him, he'd needed to move on, leave the country for a while, find some peace.

But here he was now, thinking about it again. This woman's name was Emma, and some sort of hocus pocus was involved. Something about this business wasn't right, his gut felt it. If Madeleine had her dirty fingers in this pie, he wanted to know if she was alone or if the Cult was behind her.

"I promised someone I'd give a lecture at Cambridge in a couple of days. After that, I'm all yours."

————

A FEW MONTHS EARLIER, on April 9, 1944.
Bromyard, Herefordshire, England.

"HE'S SUCH A FINE MAN, EMMA!" Mary Jane Hargreaves barreled through the door at *Sweet Lullaby*, bringing in with her a cool rush of air. "I love him to bits. Look what he made for me!"

She squealed in delight as she handed Emma a handcrafted card with a drawn heart and teddy bear. Inside was a handwritten poem.

Emma closed the card without reading it. "It's too personal."

"No, no! You're my best friend in the whole wide world and I want you to read it. James wrote that himself, you know." On a throaty laugh, her face lit up like a thousand light bulbs at the village fair, she took off her coat and leaned on the counter, ogling the almond encrusted chocolate and brandy truffles with zealous longing.

"Here, have one before your eyes pop off."

Grinning, Emma handed Mary Jane a bite sized piece of heaven that the girl savored to the last bit.

"All right then. Mary Jane, I must say, you look wonderful today."

"Don't you like it?" She did a pirouette in her new green dress that fit her like a dream. "Mrs. Essame had it at half price. I couldn't believe it!"

"I wouldn't carry that off. I'm too tall to look graceful in anything."

"Are you joking? You're gorgeous with that skin and eyes! And the hair! Wish I had your figure and it's hell sometimes to find something that feels and looks as good as this. I'm short and a bit stubby."

"Oh, do shut up now. I bet your James would have something to say about that, too. So, what's the plan?" She winked.

Mary Jane handed her the empty pastry case and looked down at her shoes. She suddenly looked crestfallen.

Baffled, Emma came around the counter and placed a hand on her friend's shoulder. "What on earth just happened? Did I say something wrong?"

"Um, no, I just … I remembered what I came here to … s—say," she sputtered.

She lifted her gaze, her blue eyes big and round and deep like a puppy's, framed by a rosy face and wavy chestnut brown hair. She looked more eighteen than twenty-six.

"Emma, I just…" She bit her trembling lip. "I just can't let him leave without me. I'm a nurse, so I'm volunteering with the American field hospital. They leave for France in May and need all the help they can get. I already spoke to Dr. Coyne at the clinic. He said he'll … he'll keep my job for me if I wanted."

She sobbed on the last word and Emma hugged her tight.

"Mary Jane, working in an army hospital is not the same as here. You'll see unspeakable horrors and…"

"Emma, I made up my mind. Be happy for me. Be proud, please?" she said in a firm tone against her chest.

Emma's heart broke at the thought of losing a dear friend—something she hadn't had in so long—but how could she not support her? Emma had never seen Mary Jane this blissful since she met her eight years ago after setting up roots in Bromyard with her shop. They'd bonded in the best way girls ever could—over chocolate cake sandwiches and custard tarts. Emma's sought-after delicacies drove the town wild, including Mary Jane Hargreaves, and the rest, as they say, was history.

Emma knew that her kind and cheerful friend had never felt the fulfillment true love could bring, and now she finally had—all thanks to James Rockford, a twenty-three-year-old medical student from New Jersey who'd left his studies to join the Enlisted Reserves two years earlier. He'd been assigned as a surgical technician to the United States 42d Field Hospital that was on its way to Normandy to offer medical expertise and supplies. They'd travelled the Atlantic to Glasgow and from there, trucked to their little town in Herefordshire.

Since January, the Americans had made themselves comfortable as they prepared to face the real deal in France. They pitched ward tents and Nissen huts to live in, while getting acclimated to the British way of doing things.

Bromyard's fourteen pubs were happy for what they called the *Yanks'* custom, and bar jokes abounded about these fellows who'd taken them by storm and made the local girls swoon. Yet, many of these men were decent folk with families anxiously waiting for them back home. Even though they wouldn't be on the frontlines of the action, their lives and those of their patients would still be in danger once they crossed the Channel. Some looked so young, giving the impression that they shouldn't be away from their parents, let alone drink liquor or sink deep in the unfathomable horrors of a war.

Since they arrived, the twelfth century Parish Church in Bromyard burst at the seams with worshipers on Sundays—and that was where Mary Jane had met her beau nary a week into the men's stay.

She being three years his senior didn't deter their budding romance, and soon it bloomed into something much more serious. Something that took over Mary Jane's life and changed her—for the better, as all young love does. Emma had no doubt that James didn't just see her as a passing fancy; he really cared for her.

Emma was happy for her because Mary Jane—along with the Bromyard community—had given her a purpose. Thanks to this new home and people to care for, Emma had bought herself a few years of peace and contented living. She wouldn't leave idyllic Bromyard unless she absolutely had to, and one day she knew she would.

So no, she wouldn't stop this lovely young woman who'd shown her friendship and made her welcome—but did she have the gall to let her go alone in that minefield?

As Mary Jane cried quietly in her embrace, Emma came to a decision. She pulled her back gently.

"Darling, please stop crying and clean up that pretty face of yours. I'm about to close for lunch and there's something I must tell you. Shall we go to the Falcon for a pie and ale?"

They had more than an hour before Mary Jane had to meet James for a stroll and coffee. More than enough time for Emma to disclose her ideas. Sudden as they were, as time passed they seemed more and more like the right thing to do. She wouldn't have any regrets.

"I'm coming with you. End of story," Emma insisted upon Mary Jane's gasp. "Please pull your chin up from the floor. It's dragging behind your seat," she teased.

"Are you mad? What about the shop?"

Emma swallowed a mouthful of delicious, rich steak pie and mash. "I'll ask your mother and aunt to help while I'm away. And you know they'll both agree, since you're so adamant about this, that I should be there to make sure you're all right. They'll feel better knowing you're not alone. See? This will make your job of telling them your news easier than you think."

Mary Jane snapped her mouth shut. "You're evil," she said. "Did you think all this up on our way here?"

"Certainly." She winked and tipped the beer glass for a long swig.

"But ... the sweets..." she protested lamely.

"Lizzy can continue to make our staples in the back kitchen, and Sue comes in to clean up every day. Easy peasy. Now let's finish this food. I have a hankering for some ice-cream after this."

Mary Jane picked at her chicken salad. "I can't believe you can eat so much. Where do you put it?" she grumbled, but the look in her eyes was one of affection.

They ate in companionable silence until it was time to part ways. Emma walked back to her shop and prepared her selections for the tea crowd. Her freshly baked fruit tarts would surely go quickly today. She arranged those on the upper tray, with the cakes and sweet pies at the bottom.

Convincing Mary Jane hadn't been too difficult. Deep down, she'd be relieved that she wouldn't have to face it all alone. If only life were easier, but if wishes were horses, then beggars would ride. Life always made the rules; if nothing else, Emma had accepted that, and now her decision was called for.

Before leaving she'd hop to the V clinic to see about a stronger vitamin that would keep her through the harsh journey and the coming winter. She didn't know when she'd next be able to access

Valthrean healthcare if needed and that was daunting—but she couldn't let this pass. Mary Jane needed her.

She plucked the rose she'd attached to her belt and pressed it to her nose.

Better dry a few of these and take them with me, she thought as she caressed a velvety petal. There wouldn't be many of these beauties to easily find where she was going.

For by hook or by crook, she'd be seeing Mary Jane to Normandy in a few weeks.

———

AFTER WHAT SEEMED like an interminable wait in the bleak Welsh weather, where they waited to board for the Continent, they left for France in June. Emma had made sure that she and Mary Jane traveled on the same ship with James as each platoon made the journey on a different vessel. Still, there wasn't time or permission for dalliance as the business they were on couldn't be grimmer. Emma doubted many of the men knew exactly what they were getting into, but they could guess, and that was possibly worse. A somber mood permeated every nook and cranny of the ship.

Finally, their ship reached Utah Beachhead, as the Americans code-named it, in Normandy. They could tell they'd arrived by the sounds of blasts from mines and torpedoes that targeted one of the platoons. Through the incessant noise of guns and fire through the night, Emma found it hard to sleep.

Eventually, the blasts stopped. They disembarked and set up four hospital tents in a large field in Sainte-Marie-du-Mont. The worst wake up call came at seeing the open space carpeted in gruesome hues—wounded men in litters waiting for assistance, others standing up, staring aimlessly at the others. Mary Jane assisted in the Surgery Section with James and various medical teams. After quick training in the weeks prior to and after departure from Bromyard, Emma could make herself useful performing first aid and non-sterile tasks to assist the surgeon and nurses. Help was always needed, as much as the funds she'd generously donated for the running of the army hospital.

The introduction to Dr. Nigel Pearson, the one and only qualified surgeon, proved to be her first encounter with a Valthrean since she'd left home.

"How do you do, Miss Degrave?" He took her hands in a firm grip, which belied his mild voice.

Dr. Pearson's skills were milked beyond imagination as scores of injuries passed under his capable hands on the operating table. If he weren't of unusually strong constitution, he would have balked under the pressure.

After him she ran into some others—from those who ran the hospital to civilians to infantry men, they all did their part in easing the workload. Emma did not think of using her concealing potion at this time. What did it matter if she did?

Mary Jane impressed her with her unparalleled focus and guts. She was the consummate nurse with nerves of steel and a sturdy stomach. One time, Emma insisted upon joining her friend into surgery, despite Mary Jane's warning to stay away from the extreme. The sight of the surgeon sawing off a gangrenous leg had Emma rush outside and retch until she hadn't a spot of food or drink left in her. That had been the last time she walked through the blackout curtain in the surgery tent during an operation. She'd rather have been the girl at Graves Registration, recording the stats of the dead before they were buried—and that was the crummiest, most depressing job she could imagine.

Finally, they packed everything up and trucked farther into France, through piles of dirt, stone, and bricks that had once been villages.

Then, in August, under the comforting Paris sun, James proposed to Mary Jane to the cheerful sounds of the French Resistance guerillas —the maquisards in their Basque berets—who drove past the field hospital station off of Orleans Road in a noisy carcade after the liberation of their city. James had Emma and a couple of his buddies as witnesses. Mary Jane jumped into his arms and planted a solid kiss on his lips, her face streaked with happy tears.

"Yes!" she shouted many times over.

Happiness thrummed in their hearts that day—a welcome diversion.

The lovebirds vowed to marry as soon as the war ended, which they were optimistic would be soon. Then again, people in love tended to look at the world through rose colored glasses. Emma hoped they were right, and never uttered a word of discouragement.

To her, every day came to witness new nightmares—images of blood and pain would be impressed in her mind. The only way to cope was to become an automaton, to do her job and let the painful sights and grating sounds become a blur in her conscious state. That was another thing Mary Jane had taught her after citing it as the reason why she functioned so efficiently as a nurse.

Easier said than done.

Only at night did the monsters return to haunt her—thoughts of tortured screams and extreme anguish and obscene smells and destruction overwhelmed her to the point where she could hardly sleep sometimes. This happened more on days when they had to deal with some particularly difficult cases, or faced an undue number of deaths.

In mid-December, their party reached St. Vith in Belgium via Holland and set up the hospital in a once beautiful three-storey house in town, now badly damaged by shellfire. All around them, fir trees sloped down over the picturesque hills, bursting through the white snow, which in some parts was two feet deep. Nonetheless, in the daytime the weather was nice and the sky clear, while night brought with it a murderous chill.

Emma had finished her second breakfast in St. Vith when she decided to take advantage of the few hours of sunshine and walk down the cobblestoned streets. Her feet crunched on the fallen leaves that dressed the ground in pretty earth tones. It helped her de-stress. Mary Jane was still sleeping off the long day they'd had organizing things. She could afford it. The hospital's sole occupant recovered peacefully.

The birds chirped, the air blew crisp and pleasant. The town stood quiet—almost too quiet—as if the worst had left them for good. Ever the realist, Emma feared it wouldn't last.

Soon, she was proven right when the streets became muddy and mucky with hectic activity. Soldiers and civilians milled about, as if in a daze. Some ran about, speaking in terrorized tones of the advancing Germans.

Emma ran to the hospital and climbed the stairs to her room to wake up Mary Jane, but the bed was empty. She went downstairs to the cellar that had been converted into a mess room and bumped into her friend, making her spill half of her coffee.

"Goodness, Emma, what a fright! Did you just come in? I've been looking for James. Everyone's outside but he's not there. What's going on?"

"It's the American soldiers pooling in…"

"Let's go out and see. Maybe someone will tell us."

They exited the hospital and watched as more soldiers clambered down the hills into town. They looked much more terrified than their leaders. James was nowhere to be seen. From then on, everything went to hell in a handbasket.

Emma felt herself crash like a military glider on concrete at Mary Jane's stricken expression that rang all the wrong bells in her memory bank. Silently sending up a prayer, she steered her friend back from the press of the crowd.

"All right, where would he likely be at this time?" she asked. Level-headedness was the only thing that could keep them afloat in a rough sea.

"Uh, perhaps making the rounds, giving injections … but we only have one patient! God above…"

"Calm down, please. We can't accomplish anything by losing our heads."

"But—"

Just then a familiar face showed up in the hospital doorway. Emma heaved a sigh of relief.

"James!" Mary Jane screamed, and launched herself into his arms. Then she hit him hard on the chest. "We've been looking *everywhere* for you!"

"Well, clearly not everywhere," he teased, inviting another sock, this time on the arm.

"How could you?"

"Ouch!" he protested, rubbing on the offended arm. "I was just lookin' for Walt and Joey. They heard of some do at a cool dance hall in Bastogne and decided to join the party. I warned them not to defy orders..." He looked up the hill and frowned at the sight. The fog had thickened, making visibility difficult. "I don't like this. It's been going on for hours."

A truck rolled up to the hospital. An officer came out. "It's not safe to stay here," he said to them. "If you guys want to leave, you can join us, but we're not hanging around."

"Wait here," Emma said.

She rushed up to her room and grabbed her bag and Mary Jane's that were always kept packed just in case. After throwing in some basic necessities they'd used that morning, such as toothbrushes, their I.D., and soap, she flew down the steps to join the others.

"Here." She handed Mary Jane her bag and slung hers on her shoulder. "Let's go now."

James stopped them. He also had his duffel bag in hand. "You two go. I have to check on my buddies then—"

"Get on this caravan and decide later. You'd be putting yourself at risk if you head off on your own." James hesitated at Emma's words. "All right. I'm asking for selfish reasons. Please come with us or Mary Jane will drive me mad. And keep in mind if you came back unhurt, it wouldn't be for long."

Mary Jane nodded. "Wise words, indeed."

Grinning, he followed them, Dr. Pearson, and more staff onto the back of a 42d Field Hospital truck that soon blended with the other vehicles on the jam-packed road. They headed not onward toward Germany, but back from whence they'd come.

Emma looked out the back and tried not to stare at the handsome dark-haired man sitting in the jeep behind them and who wouldn't tear his eyes from her. She'd noticed him just before they left but didn't pay much mind. Now, she found him unnerving.

She turned her head and linked her hands tight on her lap.

Only once did she look back after leaving the hospital and all their equipment behind and realized the jeep had disappeared behind another truck.

———

They'd barely settled at a convent in Vielsalm for the night when James started talking about heading to Bastogne.

Mary Jane's breath hitched. "I have a bad feeling about this, love. Can't we just ask around? They could have been on one of the trucks."

"At the snail's pace we were going, I had the chance to check our trucks. No sign of the boys there."

He had jumped out and peered inside all their unit's vehicles when traffic was at a standstill.

"The Germans are all over. God knows where they're hiding," Mary Jane rasped, in a tone that showed her temper was stretched to the limit. Like everyone else here, she was tired, hungry, and cold. "You heard the nuns. Many Americans were found massacred close by."

Les Boches, the nuns disparagingly called the German soldiers. They were a very real threat at the moment.

James gathered her in his arms. "I don't want to leave you but ... I have to try."

Mary Jane pulled back. Her expression turned belligerent. Emma stifled a groan as she knew what was coming. According to that stubborn glint in her eyes, James was toast.

"Then I'm coming with you," she said. "And I won't hear any complaints."

Emma shook her head when James sent her a silent plea. Mary Jane looked from one to the other and waved them off. "Now, when are we leaving?"

James stuck his bottom lip out, reminding Emma of a pouting child. "Perhaps I'll just stay, then."

Mary Jane narrowed her eyes into slits and crossed her arms, shifting her body to favor her right leg. "James Harold Rockport, is my eye green? I'm not letting you out of my sight so you can slip away when I'm not looking."

He looked so tortured that Emma felt sorry for him and finally spoke out. "James, I'll come as well if that's okay. If you feel danger close by, I'll drag this girl back here, even if I have to carry her over my shoulder."

Mary Jane glared at her but she didn't flinch. She wanted the young man to know she meant what she said.

James sighed. "I sure as hell know this makes no sense and I probably need to be tarred and feathered to let you gals—"

Mary Jane silenced him with a hot, lingering kiss. She hooked her arm in his. "Fine then, we're all sorted. Let's get our things and be on our way, darling."

"We need to be here by morning," Emma warned. "Before everyone gets up. They told us we leave at daybreak."

They weren't authorized to take a jeep—or go anywhere for that matter—but James managed to finagle the keys to one. Emma resolved not to ask him how he'd accomplished that.

They bundled up, knowing that the night air would hit them hard. It would take a lot less time to travel the thirty something kilometers on an empty road, but it wasn't the shortest of drives.

Emma felt a strange excitement; she figured her adrenaline levels must be shooting through the roof. She hadn't felt this good in a long time, although it had been a while since she'd caught a bug. Even with all the diseases and agony she faced each day in this war, she'd held strong. Perhaps the vitamin Dr. Griffiths had prescribed at the V clinic was starting to work its magic.

About eight or so kilometers down the road, they got a flat tire.

Cursing, James turned left onto a country road and set out to change it as fast as possible. It wasn't the best of places to stop at night as Germans could very well be combing the area.

Unable to summon the patience to stay in the car, Emma let herself out and paced up and down. Headlights shone bright down the main road, from the same direction they'd come. With the dips and bends in the road, the lights disappeared and reappeared only when the car was almost upon them. James stopped tinkering with the tire and his body stiffened. Their lights were on and no one moved a muscle to switch them off. Emma wanted to kick herself for just standing there.

They were lucky. The driver kept going past them and soon became a speck in the distance—but not before Emma could catch a flash of golden hair and a square jaw that caused her senses to sing a loud tune. His was a filthy face, covered in dirt and dried blood—but even the little she saw seemed beautiful and ... *and what?*

Her emotions took a wild leap. She wondered where that soldier had been and who he was. He certainly was in a hurry.

She crossed her arms to still the trembling.

"Are you cold?" Mary Jane asked from behind her. She too had come out of the car.

"I'll be fine," Emma said in a clipped tone.

No, I won't.

What was that? Why did she feel this way?

Only one thing dominated her mind at that moment—she wished she could have seen his face more thoroughly.

Would his eyes be blue like a summer sky?

Would his right jaw be blemished from a reckless act of childhood?

Chances were, she was delusional.

Adrian wasn't here ... or was he? Her eyes were surely playing tricks on her. It was to be expected in these circumstances.

James' wrench clanged on the ground, making her start. Yet, that feeling remained, that part of her intuition that screamed for validation...

"*Siehe da, was haben wir denn hier?*"

The voice came from behind her and reached her ears by crawling with sharp talons up her spine, nape, hairline, and lobe.

They all turned around in its direction.

"Well, well, see what we have here," the man repeated in heavily accented English after checking out their uniforms with downturned lips.

More men stood behind him. Where had they come from? Trees flanked the road on both sides and Emma spotted a house not too far away. It looked like they had been waiting for an opportunity such as this.

From mere steps away, the imposing man looked straight at Emma with an expression of distaste. She knew why; his scent betrayed him.

She'd never met a Cult member this close before. He would be one of them. No upright Valthrean would sink so low as to side with these monsters.

James stood slowly, cursing loudly as the ragged group of Germans —seven soldiers and the immortal who appeared to be some field-grade officer as his coat had epaulettes—rounded the car with guns trained on them. The panzers' black shoulder straps and grey embroidered eagle with triangular backing stared them in the face, the sight of them feeling worse than a freezing shower in the snowed-in forest.

Emma took stock of the situation. All she had was her poniard, which wouldn't be much help against six machineguns, and she'd left it in the vehicle, anyway. Add to that, James was unarmed—and he'd barely ever held a gun, let alone knew how to use it. How could she tackle these men one by one without putting her friends in serious danger?

She wished Mary Jane had stayed in the car. Her eyes had grown round as saucers and she whimpered, rooted to the spot.

Panic attack.

Please, don't draw attention to yourself.

But the lead German had already honed in on her fear. He lowered his gun, walked brazenly up to Mary Jane, and trailed a gloved fingertip down her cheek.

"*Süßes Früchtchen.*" He threw a mocking look at Emma, as if letting her know he had something special in store for her next. "Pretty bitch."

Emma caught James in a steel grip before he flew at the man and marked his death sentence there and then. "Don't," she whispered to him.

The boss nodded at his men and like lightning, the army ants moved to restrain them. Emma had two burly ones grab her by the arms and waist. One shoved the barrel of the gun painfully into her ribs. The seventh soldier held his gun at the ready lest one of them should attempt to escape.

But what worried her most were the leader's cold words. "I want this one first." Then he spoke in German and the soldiers dragged Mary Jane to the ground. The man got on his knees and roughly hiked up her skirt. Mary Jane squirmed and moaned like a glued mouse, too terrified to form a coherent plea.

James screamed a litany of foul words and tried to break free. Sweat trickled down his flushed face as he struggled. One of the soldiers raised the gun, ready to clock him in the head but the field-officer rapped a harsh order in German.

"Let them watch," he sneered.

The German was on Mary Jane now. Unable to fully see with the man's hulking form above Mary Jane, Emma heard the sound of a belt being unbuckled and her eyes stung with moisture. She wanted to scream and kick and hurt these bastards, but she had more sense than that.

"Whore, you're going to like this. You're not my type, but it's been so long I could fuck a four-legged dog right now."

Then he said something else in German, perhaps translating his crude comment or adding something for the benefit of his constituents.

The soldiers' laughter rang cruelly into the night.

Uncaring that her tears fell freely, she turned her head away from the sickening sight, closed her eyes, and tried to think through the fog. Chaotic thoughts tumbled around her brain with deafening thuds that sounded as real as the bite of the wind on her face. The pressure on her waist and arms eased as she gripped at straws.

She braced herself when that unique scent of immortal presence overpowered her again. Someone grunted, then groaned. The air around her moved and something hit the metal of the jeep.

God above, had he done more than rape her? Had he finished so soon and come for her? Her heart sagged in a weighty mass as she told herself that she should have stopped them from this foolhardy escapade…

Not this road again—guilt was nothing but a sore loser. She started to resign herself to the fact that she couldn't have prevented this from happening. Taking a deep breath, she opened her eyes.

But the first thing she saw was two Germans lying in a heap on the ground on either side of her.

Mary Jane was still on the ground, worse for wear but seemingly unhurt as a man tussled with the German a few feet away. When he'd managed to pin him long enough to stab him, the bastard made horrible gagging, wheezing sounds before finally going quiet. The man stood and put something in his pocket before turning to her.

And she instantly recognized him. Dark, handsome, with a dangerous air about him.

The man from the jeep! The one she'd seen earlier, who seemed especially interested in her.

"You…"

He bowed. "Massimiliano Damiani, at your service, madam. And these are my colleagues."

He motioned behind her. A stunning woman impeccably dressed in a luxurious fur-lined coat and fashionable black shoes moved over one of the bodies, smoothing invisible creases from her clothing. The last thing she looked like was a person who'd just felled two big Germans in the blink of an eye. A pretty black beret fit becomingly over shoulder-length glossy black curls, intelligent brown eyes, and a face that artists would kill to paint.

She smiled at her with even white teeth and perfectly painted red lips.

"Enchanted," she drawled in a sexy lilt that was better suited to intimate conversations than a dubious introduction on the side of a dark road—after a quick scuffle. She had all the qualities of a femme fatale, like those in exciting Hollywood movies or glitzy magazines.

"The lady is Miss Viviane Cross, and the kind gentleman who dispatched the other three over there is Mr. Nathan Hart."

Hart leaned casually on the car next to James, his arms and legs crossed. Tall and solid as an oak tree, with brown hair cut close to his head, he had one of most ruggedly attractive faces she'd ever seen. Emma surmised he'd look much more likeable if he wiped out the "been there, done that" expression from his face.

Then, there was this other man—Massimiliano.

"You can call me Max," he said. "All my friends do."

"Are we friends?" she said with a raised eyebrow.

His lips curled upward. "Something tells me we will be."

"You're—" ...*like me,* she wanted to say, but wouldn't give herself away in front of Mary Jane and James.

Max seemed to understand. He simply nodded and said nothing, his eyes telling.

"You're lucky we happened to be here for you and that the clear moonlight allowed us to see you. No one with good intentions should be out on these roads at night, especially if they're unprepared."

Emma went to Mary Jane, who'd helped herself up. She took her in her arms and let her cry on her shoulders until James came to take over. Luckily, the German hadn't had time to finish his business and all she experienced was the shock of it all, more than physical pain.

The man—Max—addressed Viviane. "Do you think she can make it to the house over there?" He pointed to the small building a few feet down on the right side.

"We'll take it slow."

James and Viviane each took one of Mary Jane's arms and gently guided her away.

"It's vacant now," Max smiled wickedly as he looked at the ground littered with dead Germans. "There's a bathroom and clean water. And that one..." He pointed at the leader. "He's dead."

"How?" Emma asked in surprise.

"You should know we're not completely invincible."

Understanding hit Emma like a ton of bricks. *Cobra poison.* How had he done it? Knife? Syringe? She was intrigued.

"Ah, now I know what you mean by being prepared," she said, her pulse starting to wind down.

"We've been looking for you, Miss Degrave."

"How do you know me?" she asked in a guarded tone.

"I represent the Council. Dr. Griffiths brought you to our attention."

The Council? Her doctor?

"I thought there was such a thing as doctor-patient confidentiality." She flexed her fingers that felt stiff under the wool of the gloves and forced a shaky smile.

"Please don't blame him. Trust me, he wouldn't have told us were it not for the greater good of our organization."

"Told you what?" This conversation was really starting to annoy her.

"I hear you get sick a lot. You did some tests."

"Yes, but what does that have to do with anything? It's my business."

"I'm afraid it's more complicated than that, Miss Degrave."

"Cut the crap and call me Emma, please."

"That's an unusual way to drop the polite form." He laughed, his eyes dancing, and that irked her more.

She kicked the dirt around her. "Yes, well, what on God's earth do you mean?"

"Those tests yielded some interesting results. I need to discuss them with you, and I need you to return to England with me for more tests, if you may."

"You can wait if you wish. I'm staying here as long as Mary Jane wants."

His expression softened. "The Council needs you, Emma. There is a lot I need to tell you... Please, do it for yourself, at least. I know what happened to you. ... Perhaps we can help. Talk to us."

He sounded rather desperate and his words hit a nerve.

"I—I've been unsuccessful so far."

"Yes."

"I'm not sure how you could do anything for me."

That vision of blond hair and the familiar profile in the jeep a short while ago returned to her mind. Her jaw clenched painfully around a sob.

What if...? Could she still hope?

The diamond-studded question—Could she ever refuse help?

But first came responsibilities.

She looked up at Max. "I have a proposal. I stay here with my friends until the war ends, and when I get back to England, I'll do whatever you ask. I'll even come to meet you wherever you are. I swear."

"You're making my job very difficult, Emma."

He ran large hands through his hair. Some strands were too short to hook behind his ear but too long to stay put. A few fell over his face, suggesting something even less civilized beneath his already roguish veneer.

"Some say the war will soon be over although I'm not sure ... and I'm sorry but I can't leave them to fend for themselves. Look what happened today."

"Even though you were here, you couldn't have helped. You can't deny that. Cult members have been recruited in good numbers by the Nazis."

"Still, I'll make sure this doesn't happen again. I need to be the voice of reason."

"How—?"

She shook her head, standing her ground. "That's the most I can offer right now ... Max."

Her calling him by name put her in the category of "friend." They both knew that was as good as a shake of the hands. A vow she would keep—because she'd do everything for a friend.

"Fine," he said after a thoughtful pause. "So be it."

She was grateful when the others came to break the awkward

silence that ensued. After James finished changing the tire with Nathan's help and Mary Jane was safely inside the vehicle, their three saviors trailed them back to the convent like guardian angels at their backs.

Their plans to go to Bastogne had been abandoned. Later, Mary Jane slept somewhat peacefully with Emma sitting by her bed, watching over her like a hawk. She hoped the nightmares wouldn't riddle her too long. Judging from James' concerned glances and gestures of affection, she would come out of this smelling like the rose that she was.

The next day, they loaded the vehicles and continued on their way, toward Sedan in France. Keeping busy and helping to ease the suffering of others would also help Mary Jane get out of her personal misery. As a nurse, she was well-trained in doing just that.

At departure time, Emma gave a cursory glance at the inhabitants of the other vehicles. Max and his associates were nowhere to be seen this time, and somehow, she had an inkling that he would respect her terms. She was sure she wouldn't see the man again for a good while.

CHAPTER 10

"Come what come may,
Time and the hour runs through the roughest day."
[Macbeth, Act I, Scene III]

Tivoli, Italy, Spring 1946.

THE SIXTEENTH CENTURY Italian beauty was every bit as majestic as she'd heard, despite the wounds it still nursed from the recent war. Lush gardens, glorious sculptures, opulent fountains and whimsical water structures, exquisite masonry and breathtaking interior—all conspired to make the work of superior architectural and landscaping art that was Villa d'Este.

Even the bombings it took recently wouldn't mar the unique beauty of this behemoth in smooth stucco and lusciously carved marble, an exercise in exalted loveliness. One would not have to think hard to understand why Liszt chose this very location as a venue for one of his concerts late in his career.

Oblivious to the magic surrounding her, Emma roamed the grounds feeling like a cat in a cage. The war was over and James and Mary Jane had tied the knot. Amid much hugging and tearful good-byes, her friend had crossed the Atlantic to settle with James' family in New Jersey, where he would also finish the last few years of college. Once again, Emma was alone and facing more decisions. Bromyard wasn't quite as pretty without Mary Jane's bubbly presence, but everyone had their road to travel, and her friend had found hers.

Mary Jane's last letter came four months after her move. Emma could fairly feel the woman's mad excitement leap off the page as she read about her new pregnancy and how James was beside himself with pride and anticipation. She promised to send pictures soon after the baby was born.

Meanwhile, for Emma, the time of reckoning had come. She was in Italy to meet Max as she'd promised him way back in Belgium. When she requested a meeting at his headquarters, they told her he was stationed in Rome, so rather than expect a visit from him, she decided to leave her shop in capable hands and take a well-deserved trip. She was even considering selling it and moving on.

Max would tell her what the Council wanted and possibly, he'd help her with other things—such as Adrian.

Since she'd seen the soldier in the jeep—a dead ringer for Adrian—the tenuous peace she'd found in her new life had started to erode.

She walked in leisurely strides, while the vibrant scents of spring drifted on the invisible wings of the gentle afternoon breeze. Yet, inside her, it was the dead of winter. Unrelenting black clothed her body and just as black was her mood.

Was she insane to keep hoping after all this time? Was it so wrong to dream that one day she might just find him?

It could be.

Perhaps there had to come a point when life ought to be accepted the way it was.

Warm sunlight pierced through the branches of the tall redwood trees and danced with the shadows in her path as she took inventory of her life. As luck would have it, there were scarcely any visitors to the gardens today. Her thoughts lingered, entirely unimpeded, while she strolled through the deserted terraces.

There was still time until the meeting. Right now, she wanted to find a secluded spot where she could sit and wallow in her misfortunes, and yes, pity herself a little. To her right was a darkened path, away from the restoration crews, flanked by a string of fragrant cedars. Their scents mingled with far-reaching wafts of crisp cypress and pine. She wasn't sure where it led, but it looked just right for her purposes. It did not seem to be one of the most coveted spots in the gardens. More redwoods towered behind the cedars on both sides, giving the little area a rather sinister cast—all somewhat befitting her current disposition.

The shadows deepened as she progressed into the enclave and each step into the darkness seduced her into introspection, brought to the fore engrossing thoughts of Adrian.

He had to be somewhere on this planet. Doing something. Being somebody. But where was he now?

Beyond rationality, she was never able to fully let go of him. She had neither the will nor the desire to give her undivided love, her whole being, to another. Although there were times when temptation knocked on her door, she never opened it. A few moments of captured pleasure were enough to help her weather the bad days. Casual relationships, she could handle ... sometimes. But anything more, she would not permit herself to give or take.

It stumped her how her memories with Adrian were still so vivid —the musky smell of land, grass, trees, and horses on his clothes after a day of labor, the rolling pasture they explored in their youth, the softness of rose petals, the rich velvet of his voice, eyes as blue as the ocean, the golden light of the sun in his hair, the sound of pleasure. There was nothing in this world that did not bring her some recollection of better days with Adrian at her side.

How good it had felt to make love to him, to touch him and feel him. To inhale his essence, his skin! His skin ... she had loved every inch of it. The sweat that rolled off his back when he lay on top of her, possessed her, and the intensity of his caring for her. He was nature and emotion rolled into one inimitable being, *her* being.

Time had changed her; inevitable when constant change was all around her. Nothing drove this assertion home harder than the last war that had rocked the world.

On a physical level, she had vigor to equal any man's. Luckily, she was not the warring type and she avoided all type of conflict. Always cautious, she'd learned how to skirt the periphery of her world. But her memories were her survival, and the strength they granted her had proved both useful and welcome throughout the years.

In this sense, Madeleine had lost her battle against Emma. She'd meant to break her. Instead, she enabled her transformation into the quintessential survivor.

Letting go was not an option.

For this reason, she always tried to choose a name as similar to her given one as possible. Emmanuelle Dalton, Emma Dacres, Emmaline Dagnall. For her, each assumed life brought new roles and challenges and therefore, also a completely new identity. In the last decade and a half, she went by Emma Degrave. This was her special way of coping with the odds. Each new identity became a rekindling process not only on a personal level, in affirmation of her as a person reborn to a new life, but also one to embrace the changing world around her.

A slight breeze softly caressed her cheeks. It felt sensuous, much like a man's touch. Adrian's touch.

It had been too long since she'd enjoyed the feel of a man in her bed. After her meeting this afternoon, she would go to her Roman hotel room in Via di Porta Pinciana, change into something sophisticated and feminine, and walk two blocks to the dancing establishment she'd spotted last night. It would be teeming with single Italian men seeking a woman's attention.

Satisfied with her plans for the evening, she slowed her pace, perked her ears, and listened to the birds chirping, the leaves stirring, the ... moans?

The sounds she'd just heard were either human or feline. And she didn't think cats could emit such impassioned noises, so that left only one option.

She halted for a few seconds, training her hearing in the direction of the commotion. Again, a whimper, a sigh.

The sound came from behind the tree directly to her right. Careful not to alert anyone to her presence, she softly treaded toward the foliage. She peeked around the first tree and heard a groan. A distinctly male sound, this time.

The same voice then spoke in native Italian.

"Dio, Anna. Quanto mi sei mancata." God, Anna. How I have missed you.

A woman murmured something unintelligible.

A couple, having an intimate moment. Emma knew she should have minded her own business and left the two lovebirds alone, but her legs had a will of their own. Hearing was not enough, she told herself. She had to see.

She took a few light steps into the forested area, the solid tree trunks and thick leaves a perfect source of concealment. Cleverly hidden behind a cluster of bushy cedars and another spattering of sequoia trees was a small peaceful clearing, in the center of which lay a small marble fountain adorned with the statue of a nymph holding a water-spouting urn. Not unlike one of the nymphs that once decorated the conservatory at Belvoir. A couple of limestone benches completed an intensely idyllic setting, perfectly located for a mid-afternoon tryst.

The couple sat on one of the benches, and hung on to each other with passionate intensity. Emma could not see the man's face as his head was bent, buried in his woman's shoulder. His whipcord-lean figure clad in an elegant, tailored suit screamed youth and virility. His Borsalino hat sat behind him on the bench, leaving his curly black hair exposed for the woman's fingers to tangle in, massaging with loving strokes.

It was like looking into a modern rendering of a Renoir painting infused with sensuality, an image of innate exquisiteness.

The man's head lifted to bring his profile in her line of sight. His hand tenderly caressed his lover's cheek, and in so doing brushed away a trail of tears. Upon seeing the expression of pure devotion in his eyes, Emma's heart constricted. A painful, burning lump swelled in her throat and her mouth went dry. She knew she should go, but she couldn't get her eyes off them.

"*Non ti lascero' piu'. Te lo prometto, amore mio,*" he said, and locked his lips with hers in a searing kiss.

Emma bit her bottom lip. *I won't leave you again. I promise, my love.* Those were his words. Words that took her back to another life.

The woman finally broke the kiss, stood, and walked into the embrace of his thighs. She wrapped her arms around his shoulders and bent her forehead to his. She had long, unbound auburn hair that spilled over his head, and enveloped them in a private world.

The man kept her pinned to him. He skimmed his hands over her grey and red patterned dress, exploring her hips, her sides, her breasts, then back down and around her waist. He leaned forward and pressed his face to her belly as she stood, while she returned to toying with his hair. Her other hand caressed his face in loving strokes. Then she gasped when he turned his head and kissed her through the dress, below the stomach, right on her secret place. He lingered there and breathed in deeply, as if trying to capture her essence.

He dipped his hand down and up her dress—up to that place where his lips were still pressed—and she moaned in delight as he touched her in ways that made Emma squirm with a mixture of need, self-pity, and disappointment. But above all, desire. For the man got his lover to soar higher and higher until finally, her body slumped over him, its passion slaked.

Only an emotionally charged affair could produce such ecstasy. These two meant the world to each other, at least in this moment. There were things that a skillful lover could not achieve without investing their heart—and the eyes told everything. From her vantage point, Emma could tell fake if she saw it, and there was none of it here.

A gust of despair caught Emma by the throat. A pool of tears stung her eyes as she observed the sensual vignette, completely in thrall. She didn't want to cry. Not now, when he'd maneuvered the woman on his lap with her legs wrapped around him.

Emma knew when to cut her losses. She tore her gaze away from the pair to glance at the fountain with its intricately carved basin that supported the statue of a water nymph.

After a while she heard the man say, *"Ti amo. Sei mia per sempre."*

He loved her and she was his forever.

This place was the definition of splendor and tranquility. It reminded her of the feelings she'd get when she stood by the Ver early in her lifetime, and watched the undulating meadows and chalk hills that surrounded her long ago English home. That last day with Adrian she had experienced this harmony in the stillness of nature.

"Look at the water," he'd said. *"Look at the waves of hills, trees, and the vast lands in front of us. So delicate yet so raw, so real. So strong. They have been this way for centuries, and will be so for many more. They just are. This is how I feel about you, Emma. This is how I love you, in the purest and most natural of ways. You are meant to be mine. You are in my blood."*

Words she'd never forgotten, said in a deep baritone that had etched itself in her soul.

She could not bear the sight of such joy any longer; too painful and frightening like a fresh, deep wound. Feeling deflated, she turned around and made her way toward the meeting place. After all, the appointment she had was the only reason for her visit here.

And after being witness to such passion, such love, she changed her mind about her plans for that evening. The prospect of a night of meaningless sex was no anodyne to an injured heart. She made her way back through meandering routes and connecting terraces to the front of the villa, bypassed the Fountain of the Goblet, and followed previously obtained directions to the Grotto of Diana.

A descending path led her to the intended destination, a place so grand it made her hold her breath in wonderment. Minerva and Neptune told their stories in elaborate mosaic and stucco representations while the Muses observed the world with sparkling, bejeweled eyes. Together, they joyfully celebrated the happy marriage of mythology and art.

Transfixed by the depiction of Daphne's metamorphosis into a laurel tree to escape Apollo's lecherous plans, her thoughts flew into the scene. In her wild musings, Adrian called her name as she desperately vied with Fate to reach him. But each time she managed to get within touching distance, his body was suddenly engulfed in a crushing tree bark, and thick branches and leaves sprouted from his head. His handsome face radiated through the heart of the tree. She could see it, yet, never touch it.

Lost in the tunnels of her own mind, she started when a rich, lightly accented voice said, "A quite appropriate meeting place, don't you think?"

She turned around to behold its owner. He had come.

His large frame made the space feel like a rabbit box. Fleetingly, she had an insane urge to cut a wide berth between herself and the man, and in that moment she felt sorry for any woman who caught his sybaritic interest. There would be no chance of resistance as he cornered his prey and restrained her with invisible ties. His body and mind were a nation unto itself and with their power, she had no doubt in her mind, he would exercise sensual hegemony. He was one of those rare people who could make others melt in a puddle in his presence, just by *being*. The only person she could think of who matched that sort of charisma on all fronts was Adrian.

But right there, standing beside her, was Massimiliano Damiani. She'd learned a lot about him in her research at the Versus Club. Renowned bounty hunter, respected scholar, Occult expert, and self-proclaimed hedonist. Achingly handsome. He could find anyone, anywhere, it was claimed.... Those were the words that compelled her to finally seek him out. Perhaps his suggestion that he could help her had not been an empty one, after all.

On the personal front, he owned the reputation of having a heart immune to emotional capture, and earned the soubriquet of "epicure of pleasure" in certain circles.

Emma assessed the man next to her. She was not privy to his full heritage excepting his obvious Italian one, but she saw the possibility of his unique, swarthy looks being the product of Gypsy blood.

"You couldn't have made a better choice," he added.

"I'm not certain I understand what you mean."

"Diana is the goddess of the hunt. And you are on the hunt, are you not, Emma?"

"You know that already."

He smiled. Not a big grin but a barely-there smile. "Thank you for keeping your promise. If you help us, then we'll see about returning the favor."

His tone was matter-of-fact, but the message was clear. He was telling her in no uncertain terms that he called the shots in this exchange.

"I scratch your back, you scratch mine. But that is only fair when both sides get what they want," Emma countered fractiously. "My case is not an easy one. Why would you even want to help me?" she added after a pause.

He examined her through mesmerizing brown eyes. The odd look that crossed his face and the telltale pulse in his jaw betrayed genuine concern. "Perhaps I am tired of watching some suffer for the sins of others."

"I wouldn't have thought you bothered with emotional matters." The words slipped through her lips before she could reclaim them. She worried her lower lip with her teeth, irritated with herself for having been so discourteous. She needed to tread carefully, especially since this man's help was vital to her.

His lips curled upward at her impulsive comment. "That's what they say. And who am I to argue?" he parried.

The bent of irreverence had returned to his tone. Her muscles relaxed and she gave him an indulgent smile. They left the grotto and strolled leisurely, side by side.

"You have an old spirit, *Signorina*."

Emma nodded. "As you know."

"Indeed," he acknowledged. Then, unequivocally, he added, "I am no threat to you."

"I didn't expect you to be, not after what you did for me and my friends. I'll never forget that."

"True, but one cannot be too careful these days."

They stared at each other for a while and took measure. Emma decided she rather liked this man's unflappable frankness. "I have discovered that if someone or something needs to be found, you are the one I must hire."

"I suppose that is a statement, not a question."

"In the articles I read about you, the word is that you have unparalleled instincts, which is what makes you so successful at what you do. It also says you are the foremost expert in Ancient History and the Occult. So why..."

"Have I chosen bounty hunting as a profession?" he finished for her.

"Yes ... I don't mean to pry, I'm just curious."

"Loss is a hard thing to deal with. What I do gives people hope."

"I suppose there's a lot of sense in that. How long have you been in this line of work?"

His brows rose. "A very long time. But tell me first, what happened to you?"

Emma nodded. "I'm looking for my fiancé, Adrian," she confessed. "A long time ago, a woman, Lady Madeleine de Brandeville, kidnapped him before our wedding. She changed their names to Marie Colette Marchand and Adam Alvar, and married him herself. Later, both she and Adrian disappeared. She stole him from me, and I've been looking for him."

She stopped at a terrace and leaned over a stone balustrade. "Before she left, Madeleine turned me, and she put some spell on me. She said that it would only break if one of us died, and I could never see Adrian again. Getting sick ... it didn't start right away, but over time, it got worse. The last vitamin I took helped a little."

She could not help but notice that he'd stiffened as she related her story.

The planes of his face had gone hard. He hooked his hands behind his back and took a deep breath. "I will help, and not only because I come with the blessing of the Council."

"Not only?"

He let the silence stretch between them. "I have no choice but to explain a few things to you. In confidence, of course."

"You have my word," she said.

He gave a curt nod. "I knew the woman you speak of, Madeleine."

Emma's jaw dropped to the ground. This was *not* what she expected to hear. Nor did she expect to learn that there was a connection between this man and Madeleine and possibly, Adrian. Her heart skipped a beat at the staggering statement but she was determined not to distract him. She needed more answers.

"Why?" She felt a trifle dumb in asking that question, yet, she had to.

"You want the whole story or an abbreviated version?"

"Max, I want as much information as you can give. My life is full of blanks. Perhaps you can fill some out."

He bent his head as he gathered his thoughts, so long locks of his glossy hair fell forward like a raven's wing, partially hiding his face from view.

"My entire family died during *la Terreur* at Madeleine's instigation."

The Reign of Terror? She veiled her surprise and bade him to continue.

"I'm only half Italian. The other half is French. My mother was very beautiful and she and my father were deeply in love. His name was Federico; he was the eldest son of the Marchese di Carcaterra. My mother, Maribelle Christine, was the youngest daughter of the Vicomte de Montignac. They met at a ball in Paris during my father's jaunt through the Continent. He once told me that the second he laid eyes on her, he vowed never to leave her side.

"They married and had two children—myself and my baby sister, Elise. My father was exceedingly concerned with the political unrest in France, and several times, he begged my mother to leave. He wanted us to go to his father's seat in Italy and settle there. But she refused to leave the city she loved so much. My father stayed with her and did his utmost to protect us all."

He looked at Emmaline and she nodded in encouragement, wanting him to continue.

"Unfortunately, my father was a very handsome man and he caught Madeleine's eye. Numerous overt attempts at seduction, however, would not bring him to heel and drop him at her feet. She didn't know that he would never entertain the slightest wish to betray my mother and that hers was a lost battle from the outset. Her jealousy exceeded all sense of proportion."

As she felt toward me, Emma mused.

"In the meantime, the Queen's head rolled and Robespierre administered the Reign of Terror with an iron fist. Madeleine joined the cause, so to speak, motivated more by self-interest than patriotism, of course."

Emmaline's brows furrowed. "But I thought Madeleine was an aristocrat. How was that possible?" she remarked.

"Aristocrats were not the only ones to lose their heads under Lady la Guillotine. There were so many others, members of the lower or middle classes and even clergy, who were labeled a threat to the new revolutionary government. But to answer your question..." His lips curled up at the corners as he injected irony in his voice. "Madeleine was whatever she wanted to be. In truth, she was no aristocrat but an accomplished liar and opportunist. She didn't even go by de Brandeville back then. She changed identity when she got to England."

"What was her name, then?"

"Madeleine Sophie de Rais."

Emma gasped at the mention of that infamous surname that once belonged to one of the most cold-blooded serial killers in history.

Max nodded. "Quite. The youngest daughter of an inconsequential noble family with more madness than wealth to speak of in its lineage. Supposedly, they disowned her at a young age."

What had hardened Madeleine so much that she'd act this viciously? What had happened to her?

"Can't say I'm surprised at her lies, but then I have seen her darker side," she quietly responded.

"As have I. Everything happened so fast after she got chummy with Robespierre's thugs."

He closed his eyes briefly, shutting out the world as he relived his private ordeal. He looked at her—no, *through* her—with a degree of torment she'd never seen before in a person's eyes. His silent message coded him as utterly ... *damaged*. Her throat burned in reaction; her eyes threatened to spill.

My God, Max, what happened to you?

Then he focused back on her, a little startled, as though he was seeing her for the first time.

"One day, I may tell you the whole story. I—I just can't right now." His Adam's apple bobbed like a buoy in disturbed waters.

"Max, I'm so sorry."

His gaze shuttered. "Don't be. I've come to terms with my past."

"Have you? You seem so intent on living carelessly. I've made it a point to learn about you and your wild exploits before this meeting."

His eyes narrowed. "Perhaps I know how love and devotion can destroy a person. I would not freely succumb to such a fate."

"I think that when it happens, you'll have no choice but to submit to it," she countered with a sad smile.

"Not if I can help it," he smiled back, demonstrating all his God-given charm.

"Can you tell me more about Madeleine?"

"I'd seen her ... do some things." A pause. "So I took my chance. I made straight for Madeleine's house and confronted her, told her I saw what she had done and that she owed me a debt. If she refused, I would tattle to the revolutionaries that she'd been seen consorting with the Duc d'Orléans prior to his arrest and execution."

"Philippe Égalité."

He nodded. "Correct. I was fully cognizant of the fact that his obscene wealth had caught her interest while my father's person aroused her passions. But neither of the two fell in her web."

"Why was she worried about execution? Is a Valthrean not immune to physical harm?"

"True, but she wouldn't want the world to know her secret, would she?"

"That makes sense..."

"I went to England with her. It took no great effort to charm a sexual creature like Madeleine."

He fisted a hand and drummed it absently on the balustrade. "My thirst for revenge took over my life. I made sure Madeleine took me as her lover. I learned all the tricks I could to keep her interest."

Again, the raw anguish in his eyes. Time is supposed to repair the heart, but it's not always that simple.

Disgust laced his voice. "I insisted on separate lodgings for the sake of appearances, but for years, I watched her interest in the Occult grow. It became more of an obsession to her and one day, she told me about the ancient Valthrean object she'd acquired through a past acquaintance of hers in France. She said she had a surprise in store for me, one that would make up for all the *inconvenience* she'd caused me," he said with mounting scorn. "She'd taken everything I had, everything I treasured, and that's precisely the word she used."

He crossed his arms and observed the gardens below before turning to her, an unholy light gleaming in his eyes.

"When I gained all I had to gain, I left Madeleine's protection. For years, I focused on building my fortune at the gambling tables, but I never lost sight of her. I believe she quickly realized the mistake she made by sharing her secrets."

Still perplexed, Emma asked the one question that stood out in her mind. "Why did you wait so long to take your revenge? Why befriend her?"

"I bided my time because I wanted no mistakes, and I wanted to take what I could from her. Does that make me just as bad?"

Emma rubbed her arms that suddenly felt cold and shook her head.

"Then one day I acquired this from an African trader; it was just what I needed."

He slid his hand in his jacket's inner pockets and retrieved a black velvet pouch. After he made sure nobody was watching, he surreptitiously unveiled its contents. The object was like nothing she had ever seen. It had a snake-like shape, about ten inches long. When he pushed the button at its base, the mechanism prompted a tiny hole to open at the center of its hood. Another push, and a two-inch needle shot out.

"It is beautiful. Is it a vaccination device?" She reached out to touch it and he checked her.

"Careful, it's called *The Bite of the Cobra* and can be dangerous if not handled properly. It contains a vial inside. Snake poison. I now use it for self-protection."

Swiftly, he folded it back in its case and returned it to his pocket. "It appears that its provenance is Indian. There's a rumor that the Snake King designed it so his mercenaries could destroy the Valthreans but of course, there's no evidence to that effect."

"But I thought inoculation was a British discovery."

"The English like to think they've invented everything. Such delusion has caused an awful lot of trouble," he reparteed.

Emmaline grinned. "But aren't you a little afraid to carry it around in your pocket?"

He smiled. "I probably would be if I didn't know how to use it."

"What happened next, then, with Madeleine?"

"When the time was right, I tracked her to Scotland. The rest, you already know, except one thing. She wanted to hire me to kill someone." A shadow crossed his face and his eyes darkened.

"Who?"

"She never did tell me but I found out anyway." His eyes pierced through her. "You know my answer." He pronounced each word slowly, attentively.

Emma bit her lip on a gasp. She shouldn't be surprised, after all, should she? But why would the woman want to kill her after so many years? Adrian was with her, away from his old life. She'd taken him and kept him. How was Emma a threat?

"She wanted to kill me," she whispered.

Max showed no surprise at her comment.

"I always wondered why she was so keen on having my fiancé. She sacrificed her life in England to take him from me and I find it near impossible to believe she did it for love. Could she have had an ulterior motive? Maybe something to do with the Cult of the Snake. ... And then, why kill me?" She echoed her thoughts, as she scratched a spot on her temple.

"All conjecture," he said. "As for killing you—clearly, you were a nuisance."

"You mean to say there's some connection between me and Adrian ... something I never thought of. I—" She stopped suddenly, a crazy thought materializing in her mind. "What if my health was somehow connected to this? I have no idea how, and it's insane to..." She waved her hand about. "Ah, I have officially run out of opinions...."

"You're making sense."

Excitement seized her heart. "Here's another thought—if she wanted to kill me, her magic must be flawed." She looked up at Max, who stared at her with his arms crossed across his chest.

"So go back. Tell me about Madeleine's visit," he asked.

She related in detail Madeleine's hand in Adrian's disappearance. "Can you help me find him?"

"There is no Valthrean in the civilized world who I do not know about. If he's here, I will find him," he said, echoing what she'd read about him. "If he's hiding somewhere, we'll just have to wait until he resurfaces. A man cannot elude detection forever."

"How could you possibly know every Valthrean?"

"Look how we found you. It is my business to know such things."

Some sort of rebuff would have sounded weak. He had given her the truth—she had no gripe with that.

"As I already stated, I have resources. I won't say more. The only thing you need to know is that I will help you," he added flatly.

That cryptic remark held the door open to a thousand suppositions. His mention of *resources* also put her in mind of the words uttered by the witch she'd visited in Redbourn at the start of her quest.

So perhaps also like the witch, he had a great many secrets, along with all the regrets, self-hate, guilt, pain, and recriminations. She understood all of that.

"One question," she said. "Why did you confide in me your acquaintance with Madeleine? You could have easily avoided mentioning it."

He sighed. "Call it intuition, if you may. Our connection to Madeleine and the dark shadow she flung on both of us is a tragedy that we share. We both live with it, day by day. You, perhaps more than anyone, deserve to know about it."

With this statement, Max offered her a glimpse of his true self. The man had so many layers to him it would take an extraordinary woman to peel them one by one and find the gem beneath. Yet, with her, he was as frank as can be, and she didn't even have to try very hard. He had done his homework and decided to trust her, sight unseen. It was more than she could ever hope for.

Emma accepted his explanation and offer of assistance, infinitely grateful. A spate of unadulterated relief ransacked her senses.

"I must tell you that it's our business to keep track of all Valthreans to make sure that loyalties are not ... how shall I say this ... *misguided,*" he continued.

"*Our* business?"

"The Cult of the Snake is growing in numbers. The war has been a crucial time for us, and it remains necessary to keep an eye out for things and maintain the balance. I'm sure we could find good use for someone such as yourself..." He let his voice trail away, dragging the suggestion between them.

"I sought out the *Versus Club* because I wanted to know about myself, even though trying to find Adrian has caused me to live free of commitments and concerns. I made some acquaintances but haven't formed any real bonds."

His answering look was one of tacit understanding. "Before you go," he said somberly. "I must warn you. Watch your back. Danger is always brewing in our world."

"Someone gave me that same advice a long time ago but nothing ever happened."

"You have been fortunate."

Or because I've been taking precautions, except for today, she thought.

"Some of us have an agenda of their own, they're renegades. The Council is regrouping, preparing for the inevitable."

"I got it covered, I promise."

"I hope you are. Be careful who you trust."

"I trust you and you're going to help me. I appreciate that."

"Please don't thank me just yet. There's a lot of ground to cover, and you owe me a trip to London to meet with the Council and submit to further testing."

"Max, I have waited this long. I'll manage, whatever it takes."

"My offer doesn't have an expiration date."

"I've been thinking lately that I'd like to get more involved."

He perked up his ears, interested. "How?"

"Let's set up that meeting. Aside from the agreed agenda, I believe I have something else that the Council would be very interested in."

CHAPTER 11

"I have lived long enough: my way of life
Is fall'n into the sere, the yellow leaf;
And that which should accompany old age,
As honor, love, obedience, troops of friends,
I must not look to have; but in their stead
Curses, not loud but deep, mouth-honor, breath,
Which the poor heart would fain deny, and dare not."
[Macbeth, Act V, Scene III]

PRESENT DAY.
Deep in the Kashmir...

UNDER THE SPINNING tires of Adam's jeep, the earth rumbled and the ground shook in discontent. The air hung heavy with the shifting dust of centuries and the biting cold had turned vicious enough to swathe the fires of Hell in a frosty haze. Another hard winter waited eagerly at the door. This particular day, God had painted a lackluster sky and overpopulated it with moisture-filled gray clouds.

The rain would come any minute, and when it did, would pound the earth mercilessly to remind man of just how powerless he was in Nature's hands. After staying in India, a country ripe with consummate hagglers and hustlers, Adam wished he had the power to negotiate the state of the weather. The earth was angry today. He needed to finish his business here and rush back to his hotel room, but he seriously doubted he'd make it.

As he sat behind the wheel of the rusty four-wheeler, he cursed under his breath and wondered if the engine would survive at least another few hours before it exhaled its last breath. The ground shook again. What the hell was he thinking? And more importantly, what the fuck was going on?

As a multitude of thoughts and invectives careened through his head, the tops of thatched roofed homes, farms, and ramshackle buildings came into view. He was finally at his destination. Anywhere in Europe he'd have made a similar trip in just over sixty minutes, but bad roads and a wheezing motor prolonged his journey northwest by over two hours. Luckily, he had the foresight to leave his hotel room in Srinagar very early, way before dawn.

The mountain village of Jabala was located in the heart of Indian Kashmir and this was where he'd agreed to meet his contact. Why he didn't agree that Abid meet him in the relative comfort of the hotel café as the man had originally suggested, he did not know. In his almost immutable state of fitfulness, he thought that anything would be better than to spend time in his tiny room, caged within four oppressive walls.

He put his foot on the accelerator, and milked the jeep for all it had. *Faster, dammit!*

Had he any sense, he would be soaking up the sun on some tropical island far from here, but he was never one to resist a worthy venture.

And, this trip promised an interesting outcome. He had been introduced to Dr. Abid Kothedar, historian, when he arrived in the Kashmir to trace the steps of the great Greek philosopher Appollonius of Tyana, a man who lived around the same time as Jesus Christ and was born in the area where the city today stands on Turkish soil. He was always on the lookout for interesting artifacts. And what better places to find them than in the remotest corners of the world, places as yet untainted by the sophisticated complexities of so-called "advanced civilization?"

Although his study interests were broad, he preferred collecting early to mid-nineteenth century objects, particularly of British origin. In a way, a perverse attempt to hold on to his roots, or perhaps it reflected a hope that he would one day wake up to the clear remembrance of his past—something more than dissociated snippets and random imaginings.

He had learned enough about himself to know what he was, what he had become. Eschewing both Valthrean and human company, he preferred solitude—with perhaps the comfort of his dusty relics as company. Meanwhile, his life consisted of erratic attempts at giving credence to his own identity. By fostering an interest in the arcane, he felt that in some fantastical way he could succeed in piecing together his broken soul.

Anyone could dream.

The village wasn't large, but suddenly he felt impatient to get this business over and done with, and get the hell out. He tried to focus on the object of his visit, and ignored his screaming gut.

What he'd learned in his preliminary research into this new endeavor was that, ever the willing scholar and constant traveler, Appollonius—along with his friend and fellow scholar, Damis—embarked on a thirteen-year-long journey eastward, all the way to India, in search of philosophical knowledge. It is recorded that the two men spent four months in this area, learning from the so called Sages of Kashmir. Despite his affluent background, Appollonius was aware that the world was a bigger place and he was determined to see it with wisdom as his guide. In his search for the spiritual, he held the instruction passed on to him by the Sages in high regard.

The philosopher spent much time worshipping at the Temple of the Sun, which, in his time, had been a rare example of magnificence. The structure had been built on an elevated plateau with the Himalayas as a backdrop, a few miles outside the summer capital of Srinagar in the Valley of Kashmir. Srinagar itself was said to be home to *Sri-Naga*, the mythical seven-headed Serpent King, venerated by early Naga settlers as the god of the underwater. Legend has it that among other things, these Nagas, or Sages, also instructed Appollonius in the arts of magic, and thus, rounded up his education in the esoteric.

During one inquiry into this slice of history at a museum in Srinagar, one of the clerks referred him to Abid, who was considered an authority on the history of the region. He contacted him by phone, and Abid enthusiastically told him about an ancient book of magic he'd found on one of his casual expeditions. Abid suspected it had been written by the Sages some three centuries before the birth of Christ, around the time when Srinagar itself was erected by King Asoka, the regnant who took over the Naga king Aravala's kingdom.

Asoka was responsible for proselytizing Buddhism to the Snake Cult. According to legend, many followers of the Serpent King, realizing the power of the Buddhist belief, eventually converted. Adam's new friend Abid expressed his hope that the tome was not the only one in existence.

Drawn to this story and feeling great respect for Abid, a brilliant but unpretentious man, he immediately arranged to meet with him in person to examine the treasure first hand. If it was what Abid claimed it was, he intended to place a bid on it before the man presented it to the local museums.

When he reached a small wood and stone house with white windows and doors at the edge of the village, Adam parked and got out of the vehicle.

Suddenly, the ground moved again, but this time it gave no warning. A ways up the road to his right, large chunks of rock dislodged from the side of the mountain and, with a horrific thrum, rolled down toward the village, dragging with them an astonishing amount of rubble.

"Damn."

This place had boarded a speed train to hell.

People stopped in their tracks and looked at the scene that unfolded before them like a 3D movie screening. They just stood there as if detached from their bodies. As if they were not actually there, watching huge boulders literally hurtle toward them and their humble abodes from the promontory above.

Then the panic started.

A small-boned, scrawny man with a thick black moustache and traditional dress opened the door of the white-windowed house and ran toward him. It had to be Abid because he was holding a large book in his hand. Adam didn't miss the terror glazed on his face.

No time was wasted on introductions. Abid had recognized him immediately. After all, he didn't have much opportunity to meet many foreigners in this part of the world.

"We must get out of here. Quickly," he said in a thick but melodious accent.

He carried nothing with him except the book. He'd rushed out of the house with only the clothes on his back.

"Please, let's go!" he shouted when Adam hesitated. His penetrating voice dripped with alarm. "All my belongings are in that house but life is more precious. It will happen any second now."

They jumped into the jeep. Thankfully, the engine started without preamble and a u-turn later they were back on the road.

"What will happen any s—"

Before Adam could finish the question, he instinctively slammed his foot on the brakes. About fifty feet away, the land moved and the mountain started to slide.

Shit.

They heard a bloodcurdling scream coming from somewhere behind them, and a woman shouted in the native Urdu, *"Zalzala! Zalzala!"*

"What are they saying?" he asked the petrified man sitting next to him in the passenger seat.

"It's an earthquake. She just said it's an earthquake."

They watched the landslide bury the road and block their only route of escape. There was no way out.

"Holy shit. Get out of the car. Now!" he shouted at Abid over the fracas.

Under any other circumstances, he would have wanted them to stay in the car for better safety. But the road was narrow and he was afraid the falling rocks would nudge the car off the precipice—something he certainly didn't want to happen.

They ran back toward the village where the people drowned in a state of chaos. He tried to collect his wits and search for some cover.

"We must find an open space, away from the buildings."

They sprinted away from the madness, but time was not their friend. Within minutes, most homes within viewing range were razed to the ground, their roofs precariously perched atop a pile of rubble. He heard the sobs of the injured and of those who lost everything they owned in the blink of an eye.

Just then, he became aware of the muffled wail of a small child. A man shouted desperately, "*Madad karnaa! Madad!*"

He and Abid looked in the direction of the voices toward a house that was no more. The walls had collapsed like a deck of cards. Abid spoke above the loud clutter of voices and falling rock. "That man said his wife and baby boy are in there. He needs help."

From the look of him, the man was a farmer. With desperate, bare hands, he dug into the rubble. Overtaken by a frenzied need to help, Adam ran to the man making sure to avoid the shower of debris.

Abid followed, still clutching the book in his shaking hands, and stood a few steps away, his face devoid of color. Others joined them to assist in the efforts to unearth the man's family.

Together, they dug their bare hands deep into the dirt and wreckage and shoved it aside. But the tremors persisted and more rocks slid down the side of the mountain. From the corner of his eye, Adam caught a particularly large one that began to roll in a straight trajectory toward them.

"Abid, move away!" he cried to the clueless man but someone clutched Adam's arm and held him back before he started toward him.

It was too late. The boulder plummeted at a murderous speed. At last, Abid looked up and watched the rock come at his head. The split-second action signaled the final seconds of his life.

"No!"

Adam rushed to him and pressed his hand to Abid's pulse. Abid lay bloodied, barely breathing. Tears stung his eyes. Numb and unashamed, he let them fall to the ground.

Adam wouldn't dare move him for fear of causing more pain. Blood and dust dried on his lips and face, and he struggled to catch air in his lungs

"Take ... the book ... it's yours ... take c-care of it..."

With those words, Abid's reserve of strength was depleted. In the next heartbeat, he was gone.

For a while, Adam lay motionless in the midst of disorder. He waited for the numbness and desperation to be replaced by the more tolerable emotion of anger.

Why take him? Why not me? Haven't I lived enough?

But you cannot die, a little voice replied in his head.

If he didn't do something now, he'd sink into himself, deeper and deeper, until there was nothing left.

His hands trembled. He shivered all over, but not from the cold. Sometimes, it was near impossible not to fall apart, to hold himself together.

He curled his fingers around the book and forced himself to set it aside and return to the task he had charged himself to do—to help the farmer get his family back. He had no time to wallow in anguish.

The tremors subsided and for the first time he looked around to see—really see—the devastation around him. The village was practically leveled. It did not take a rocket scientist to conclude that a long time would pass before these people would be able to rebuild their homes and overcome personal losses, if ever. For most of them, life would never be the same.

He thought of the privileged existence some like him lived, and how problems could be weathered with money and the right kind of insurance. Others were not so lucky. After losing everything, all they were able to do was wait for fate to turn and smile on them once again. Life was that simple and that hard in this neck of the woods.

For the longest time, he'd stayed away from England and spent his days traveling and seeing the world for what it was—a great, big mass of problems. Still, it was home. To him, it represented a constant search for understanding, for grasping the unfathomable mystery that was his life.

Sometimes, he would declare a truce and buy himself moments of oblivion, such as two weeks ago in India when he spent the night with a cheerful Swedish tourist he bumped into while he browsed the market wares. Eleonor showed him a few hours of pleasure but when he reached within himself, he only found desperation, for all he was doing was to try to catch a glimpse of something familiar in the arms of a woman. That didn't happen. It never did.

Physical release was simply a way to stop him from going completely insane. A few moments meant to keep him grounded in the present. Most of all, it helped him forget about the darkness that was his past.

The past. It was a black hole that suctioned him into a purposeless existence. In this moment as in any other, he asked himself that eternal question—*Who am I?*

These days, he rarely experienced strong waking visions, stirrings of memory, as he had many moons ago when he and the female stranger fought four thugs for survival. He only had the visions on rare nights, in the moments between weary wakefulness and restless sleep. She came to him mostly on the really bad days to revive that iconic verse of Byron's through the vision in his mind—because she was indeed an ethereal apparition that walked in beauty like the night and the stars illuminating it.

It had been a curious encounter, the one in Leith. It awakened in him something that connected him with the man he may have once been. He thought about that sister-in-arms on occasion and tried to create her face from imagination. Was she pretty? What color were her eyes? Did she possess thick hair, or was it straight and silky?

He'd built an imaginary life for her, too. He wondered what her passions were. If she had a good life.

But he had to get his mind off that road. For now the woman was long dead and he was still here, clutching at life.

Perhaps it was time to return to his roots, to once more set foot on English soil. For too long, he'd run away from it. As soon as he got himself out of this calamitous mess and saw the man's wife and child to safety, he would go to the city, pack his bags, and leave India.

At that precise moment, a persistent drone and alarmed voices stopped him thinking. It was all he could do before a vicious tightness formed in his chest.

Not again?

In the seconds before blackness enveloped him, another familiar vision of flowing dark hair and graceful feminine curves entered his mind. And now, as always when she appeared to him, he was at peace.

Who are you, my dark temptress?

She rarely spoke to him, but her soulful brown eyes communicated her torment. He was certain she needed him as much as he needed her.

My comfort. My only respite.

He wanted to talk to her, to ask her what she would think about his return to England. On some visceral level, he was sure it was what she wanted from him as well. So return he would.

What would he be this time?

He rather fancied the idea of a place to display his collection of bizarre objects. It was an idea he'd mulled over a few times and never acted on. The work would suit him—odd things for an odd man like himself. He wanted to chuckle but his body didn't allow him to.

Pain sank its claws into him—a second wave that knocked him over like a bowling pin hit a strike. He let go then, just like that time in the very distant past after he was waylaid by four nefarious felons, and fought them with the assistance of a fearless stranger.

———

THAT SAME MOMENT.

Marina di Ragusa, Sicily.

EMMA STOPPED AT AN ICE-CREAM STAND, a *granitaro*, set up on the promenade alongside the beach and bought herself an almond granita, her favorite Sicilian treat. A lukewarm wind whipped at her face as she walked to a wooden bench that faced the expanse of sand and sat to observe the random spattering of tourists who lounged on colorful beach towels, fully clothed.

A couple of fearless jocks took a dip in the sea and braved the freezing water. They were hardcore, professional swimmers who sought this thrill year round.

She took a spoonful of ice and let the burst of flavor melt on her tongue. As she chewed on the small bits of almond, she noticed the empty tables and chairs outside the restaurants, and the few stores lined at the basement level of the building to her right were begging for customers.

Emmaline enjoyed watching the steady motion of low waves that rolled idly inward. Nothing beat the privacy of visiting a summer resort in the off season. By late spring, the beach bums would start to swarm in, and the quasi-deserted fall and winter paradise of Marina di Ragusa would be invaded by the screams of children, the shrill chidings of their mothers, youths in search of adventure, and the deafening beats of the latest dance music. By August, mostly *Ferragosto* time when the bulk of Italians took their vacation, the chaos would be in full swing.

The salesgirl from the one and only shoe store on this strip walked up the few steps to the square and leaned back into the railing. She nodded to her before she opened her pack of smokes and lit one up. The first inhale was a deep one that came with a heartfelt sigh of relief. A die-hard smoker who could only take the occasional break to indulge.

Emma admitted this little seaside town was charming, but she'd never set foot here in the summer. Since her arrival the previous day for a short weekend break, the sun and crisp breeze worked together to create the perfect temperature. Not too hot, not too cold, a perfect usher to the spring, and a stark contrast to the icebox that was downtown Birmingham right now, the British city she'd just visited on business.

She'd made it half way into her cup of Italian ice when the pain started. First, there was the throbbing in her head. It started out faint, like a dozen ants pounding little hammers in different parts of her brain. Then the aching merged into a bigger, contained mass that brought little black dancing spots in front of her eyes.

She shuddered and clamped her lips to suppress a wail. The cup slipped from her hand when the muscles in her arms contracted hideously. Creamy white syrup spilled on the gray concrete. The cramp spread to her shoulders and neck, where violent spasms rocked her upper body until they knocked her from the bench onto the hard ground.

Words failed to come out of her mouth, and she couldn't move her arms to lift herself back up. To breathe was difficult. Her hands were bunched mid-way into fists as the muscles in her fingers refused to relax.

The young lady from the store discarded her cigarette and ran to her.

"*Cosa le succede, signorina?*" she asked.

If Emma could talk, she'd respond she had no clue what the hell was happening to her.

"*Adesso chiamo aiuto. Aspetti qui,*" she said and ran inside a restaurant to get one of the waiters to help.

Emma would have laughed out loud at the girl's instructions to stay put. If she could.

Who's going anywhere?

A pimple-faced waiter sat her up, grabbed her from the back, around her torso, and gently lifted her on her feet. Then, he and the girl placed their shoulders under her arms and kept her moving.

"*Scendiamo di qua. C'e' una poltrona comoda dentro il negozio dove la possiamo far sdraiare.*"

It was a suggestion to take her inside the shoe store and place her on a comfortable chair.

They hauled her down the steps and into the shop. Emma noted they passed by the cutest red suede t-strap wedge shoes she'd ever seen before they deposited her carefully on an overstuffed armchair at the back of the store.

Don't panic. Look at the pretty shoes, and it will pass. It's only a cramp.

The good thing was that the spasms had distracted her from the dull, persistent ache in her head.

"Meglio chiamare un dottore."

No, no doctor! It will pass.

The girl picked up her cell from the counter and looked through her contact list. *"Non credo di avere il suo numero di cellulare."*

Good, she didn't have the doctor's number. Please, let it pass. I want out of here.

"Mario, sai se il Dottor Scacchi e' in clinica oggi?"

"Credo di si perche' non abbiamo classe con lui di giovedi'."

Emma groaned inwardly. Perfect. This Mario, the waiter, was also a medical student who didn't have class with the good doctor on Thursdays because the man was on clinic duty. She hoped the kid wouldn't offer to examine her himself. He looked young enough to be a freshman.

While the two locals scrambled to find a number, the muscles in Emma's hands started to relax and she could now move her fingers. Slowly, the feeling returned in her arms, too. The vise around her lungs had fallen away.

"No, stop!" she shouted, louder than she intended. Her voice was back! "Please, thank you for your concern, but I'm feeling better. I get cramps sometimes," she lied. "It's nothing serious."

Another sharp stab of pain arrowed through her head and this time she cried out. She raised her hands to her temple and held them there until the pangs subsided.

Her two good Samaritans stared at her, looking unconvinced. Perhaps she needed to explain in a way they could understand better.

"Sono riconoscente per l'aiuto, ma mi sento già meglio," she explained,

while she gingerly moved her arms to demonstrate that she was mobile now. She wanted to express how grateful she was for their help, but she was already feeling better.

When her body started to return to normal, she slowly stood and thanked them again, bought the red wedge shoes without trying them on, and left the store.

What had just happened?

Her body had been assaulted like a freak tornado barraging through a town and then, left everything intact.

She was healthy, just had her required twice-yearly physical at the V-Med Clinic inside the Birmingham HQ. Valthreans couldn't die and their bodies were strong enough to heal themselves in most cases, but in some instances, there could be a kind of deformity, immunodeficiency, or ailments that caused prolonged distress if left untreated. This could be avoided with regular check-ups and specialized prevention treatments where necessary.

In her case, this was especially important. After Max had taken her for additional tests, nothing more was found apart from what was already known. The blood they'd drawn before her move to France with the field hospital was studied over and over, its properties discerned. Traces of specific herbs and substances were found, such as the chickweed that affected her memory. However, it would be impossible to determine the amounts, or whether there was more that wasn't showing. Furthermore, no one could yet understand how the potion had worked except that the magic of the chalice had made it possible.

What mattered most though was the implied meaning that witches' spells worked on the Valthreans—and not in a good way.

They'd decided to keep an eye on her, especially Dr. Griffiths, but apart from frequent bugs and viruses that affected her more in winter, nothing else seemed to be wrong. The latest results had come out fine —all negative.

So, what happened moments ago made no sense.

As she walked through the Lungomare Andrea Doria to her hotel, Emma felt no discomfort or pain, not even the slightest remnant of what had just occurred inside her. Baffled, she entered the lobby and retrieved the keys to her room from the front desk. The welcoming mossy green on the walls of the Hotel Terra del Sole, complemented by modern minimalist furnishings in warm earth tones carried from the common areas to the individual rooms, soothed her jangled nerves.

She went straight to her room and threw her jacket, purse, and shopping bag on the armchair by the leather-upholstered bed. Her laptop was open as she'd left it, on the wenge veneer of the desk top built into the wall. She input her username and password and opened her mailbox. Nothing new.

After calling room service and asking them to deliver a grilled fish platter and vegetables to her room in an hour, she took a quick shower and propped herself on the bed. There was no way she was going out to a restaurant tonight, even though she itched to break in her new shoes.

She reached over her nightstand and absently grabbed a bag of mixed nuts she'd snagged from the mini-bar. A knock on the door signaled that dinner had arrived.

She switched on the flat screen while she ate. Perhaps she'd catch a classic movie somewhere, even if it was dubbed in Italian. She was happy to see that a number of American and British channels were offered via satellite. A hop to the pay-per-view channel told her that *Dangerous Beauty* and *Mr. Smith goes to Washington* were on offer. Perfect.

When she finished her movie marathon, it was late but she wasn't tired yet. She grabbed the TV remote and did a bit of channel hopping. The news was just starting on CNN.

First item of the day, a 7.6 magnitude earthquake in the Kashmir region that practically razed the Indian-controlled village of Jabala to the ground. Live airtime was granted to the on-site journalist who gave his first-hand report of events from Srinagar, and who recounted the extent of the devastation.

A picture replaced the journalist on the screen. A CNN exclusive. It was a close up of a young man laid out on a stretcher, being carried off an ambulance into a hospital. His head fell sideways, left side down, toward the camera. The reporter said that the wounded man was a British national who happened to be in the area where the earthquake had done its worst.

Emma sat up straight and narrowed her gaze on the screen.

The shape of his face.

His square jaw. *The thin scar above that right jaw.*

Her heart skipped a beat. "Bloody hell."

The still was replaced by the reporter who said that the man, whose name was Adam Derringstone, was lucky to have been found straight away. American military helicopters landed on the scene within a couple of hours of the incident. In similar circumstances, help normally took days to arrive, but the authorities were prepared after a similar disaster had occurred a few years before.

Emma shot up from the bed and rushed to her computer. Fat fingers got the password wrong and she spat a foul curse. Second time a charm, she logged on to wi-fi and typed in the CNN website address.

The story was up already. She clicked on the headline first and then, pictures. The man in the stretcher was the first one in the series.

She clicked on it and maximized it. Her eyes were glued to that scar. That face.

"Oh my God."

The earthquake happened around the time she was on the promenade this afternoon.

A coincidence?

Adam Derringstone.

She got up and started to pace. A couple of steps, and her knees jammed into the side of the bed.

"Ow!"

She rubbed the offended spot, then put a thumb in her mouth and nibbled hard.

"Ah, what shall I do?" she asked frantically as she ran a hand through her hair.

Calm down. Panicking won't get you anywhere, Emma.

She returned to the computer and pulled up Google. Her fingers stilled on the keyboard before she typed in the search box.

The results yielded a number. She grabbed the phone and dialed. An efficient voice answered in native tongue, most likely Koshur.

Emma spoke to the woman at the Shri Maharaja Hari Singh general hospital in English, and asked to speak to Adam Derringstone.

The woman informed her that most patients were resting at this time. "I can pass the call if you wish."

Emma bit down on her lip. "No, that's fine then. I'll try tomorrow. But—can you tell me how he's doing? What happened to him?"

"I am sorry, madam," the woman replied in a calm, accented voice. "I am not at liberty to divulge that information over the phone. The doctor or nurse will speak in person to family members."

But I am family, Emma wanted to argue, but didn't. It would have been useless.

She thanked the woman and ended the call.

It would be a long night until she was able to call again. And when she did and got through, what on earth was she going to tell him?

PART III

Reckoning

CHAPTER 12

"I had most need of blessing, and "Amen"
Stuck in my throat."
[Macbeth, Act II, Scene II]

MONT SAINT-MICHEL ABBEY.
Normandy, France.

THE HEATER NEEDED to be replaced. Again.

Madeleine rubbed her arms vigorously as the dampness in the air seeped into her skin, and she put on the thick cardigan she'd draped on the back of her chair. She missed the good old days when a simple roaring fire in the grate would ward off the winter chill. These new machines and gadgets they kept bringing to her did not make life easier, except perhaps a few things—such as the television that kept her amused in the long hours spent confined to her quarters and private yard, which were separate from the cloisters where the monks resided.

She looked up from her desk in her living area, out of the diamond-paned window that offered views onto the vast sea and nothing else for as far as the eye could see. A view that became increasingly dull as the days and years passed. How many times could she observe the bright sun in the sky, the gray clouds, the occasional boat, or the changing colors of the sea?

How many times would she sit on her bed, her beautiful engraved locket in her palm, and childishly dream of an imaginary life with the man she desired?

Golden hair and blue eyes—and a daughter with bouncy locks and a bow-shaped mouth that looked just like him. She could have lived such an ordinary existence, without the decadence, she'd convinced herself. He'd have saved her from those dark cravings....

For endless years, she'd floated in a fog, her wants and needs tucked away in a dungeon of their own.

"You'd love this dress, Adam, darling," she said to the face sketched on the sheet of paper she'd propped up before her. She smoothed a hand down her figure-hugging, turtle-necked black dress with long stretchy sleeves. "It would have caused a quite stir in our time. Scandalous." She chuckled.

Everything she asked for was provided to her—except any demand to leave the oppressive medieval abbey that was her prison.

She looked down at her notepad where every spell she'd ever created was written neatly and in order. She'd penned a few new ones, but without the chalice, or a real collection of herbs and spices, she could only work off of her head.

What an idiot she'd been to escape without it. How could she have known St. Giles' intentions when she had requested an urgent meeting after her encounter with Max? She'd managed to elude castigation for months but after they found out about the chalice, St. Giles' masters were very displeased. By the time they sent someone to retrieve it, both it and Adam were gone. As punishment for causing so much trouble, he'd sentenced her to a life locked away from the world. She was lucky they hadn't sentenced her to death, St. Giles tritely stated.

For who knew where the chalice was now? Certainly not in Cult hands ... not since Claude's brother had foolishly put it in his safe-keeping a long time ago. The man had probably been severely dealt with, so she considered her banishment here a lucky escape from a worse possible fate.

He'd brought her here tied and blindfolded like a common criminal, after putting her on a boat and whispering in her ear of the dangerous quicksand that surrounded the property at low tide should she think to escape. She was sure he'd lied and exaggerated just to scare her. Who did he think he was? Her new lady's maid spoke French and soon confessed where he'd brought her—up high in a medieval building surrounded by water. In a godly place inhabited by monks who weren't allowed to get close to her or speak to her.

Completely cut off. Alone.

"I have a special arrangement with the abbot. You will be pleasantly surprised with the accommodation," he'd said, very satisfied with himself.

The bastard.

He'd provided her with a fresh wardrobe and all the basic comforts. Since that time, he'd never visited her. How she hated him.

Fine. She resigned to staying here as long as they wanted. Better alone than die—and kill her they would if she defied them. More time to work on variations for these spells...

The door knocked and someone came in. Madeleine picked the pen and added lodestones to a particular recipe.

"You're too early. Leave it on that table," she motioned absently with her free hand, "by the door."

"Is this how you greet an old friend?" said a deep voice behind her.

Madeleine froze. The pen slipped from her hand when her mind stopped functioning. To move at all at first was difficult, as though her motor skills had regressed to an infant's. Cold sweat formed at her brow and along her spine. How the man managed to make her shake like a leaf with just the timbre of his voice, she never could understand.

She just learned he still had that power.

"St. Giles," she said.

Slipping the pencil drawing of Adrian beneath the pad in a last second bid for privacy, she slowly turned around to face him. He hadn't changed much, except of course that his clothes had moved with the times. In a perfectly fitting black suit and navy blue and white tie, he was the epitome of modern elegance and deceptive charm. Much like a mature male model in one of those exclusive fashion magazines, oozing confidence and sex appeal. She always thought that whoever took those pictures knew what made women's instincts scream in delight.

He gave her a toothy smile—something she rarely remembered him doing, if ever. To her, he'd always seemed so forbidding and serious.

"St. Giles," she repeated, licking lips that had gone drier than the noon desert.

"What a pleasure to see you, Madeleine," he said, still smiling. "I've been thinking it was high time I did."

————

REMBRANDT 96, *a boutique hotel in the Canal Loop area, Amsterdam, Holland.*

Room 12.

EMMA'S LAPTOP screen flashed on with a beep. The machine sat on a small maple desk in a shadowed corner of the standard issue but comfortable hotel room.

Outside, a row of streetlights dispensed decent enough illumination for a night without stars. From the middle floor of her room, she did not have a view of the rooftops of Amsterdam, but the smooth-surfaced canal that divided the street below her into two wide sidewalks linked by the occasional bridge provided the picturesque view that one would expect from a visit to this city. The characteristic trees were sparse here; they flanked the canal only at odd intervals.

People strolled by, mostly tourists hastening to create an illicit memory of the large display windows in the nearby Red Light District. Nobody came to Amsterdam without stealing a taste of its forbidden fruit. For many, the promise of legalized sex, drugs, and escape from a responsible routine was hard to resist.

In addition, the Red Light District's proximity to the University of Amsterdam made these erotic tableaus an ideal site of employment for female students looking to make more money than they ever would with a low-paying waitressing or shop attendant job.

The tourists would have occasion to gape at young, statuesque, rose-cheeked girls of barely legal age, who worked alongside seasoned prostitutes and active members of the *De Rode Draad,* the official prostitutes' trade union.

The older ones who'd been round the block a dozen times would be hanging around the Prostitute Information Center in the lewdest of outfits that barely covered too large or too skinny aged bodies. This was how one would try to outdo the other, in between idle time spent chain-smoking and talking about the good times—when they had all of the men's attention.

But the young girls, the ones most men wanted, didn't have time for idle chat. They'd keep to themselves. Smart, beautiful, and raised in open-minded tolerance by their permissive Dutch families, they'd stun the crowds in lacy or sports lingerie that clung perfectly to their toned curves. It is not unheard of for them to balance some enormous textbook on fractal mathematics or particle physics on their laps to prepare for the next big test while they waited for the next eager client to ring their door bell for a private session of earthly pleasures.

Emma had strolled through the area a few days earlier and felt sorry for those women who were over the hill, and clearly struggling to hold on to their youth, to continue to make a living the only way they knew how.

All of this was a world apart from her quiet room over the canal.

In many busier streets of the city center, the Dutch capital reveled on, uncaring of the turmoil a lone woman in a hotel room was going through. Of the upside-down thoughts and conjectures that whirled and whirled in Emma's mind, forming the face of a man as old as her memory, as her heart.

Echoing that private squall of feelings that brewed inside her like a barrel of Adrian's long-ago favored Hertfordshire hops, the charcoal-gray clouds hid the moon and all its shiny cohorts from view, preparing for a good rain. Even the brightest of them all, Sirius, was nowhere to be seen through the thick curtain that cloaked the unwelcoming sky.

Emma looked outside the window from her seat at the small corner desk and sighed. They'd said on the news that tomorrow would be another dreary day. It would probably rain.

She walked to the bed and dropped a folded sweater in her half-full suitcase. Tomorrow, she was checking out to take the train to Maastricht, where she would be attending an important event at the Maastricht Exhibition and Congress Center. Luckily, the hotel she'd booked there, although not one of the most exclusive offerings nestled in the midtown area of the south-eastern Dutch city, was clean and conveniently located within a short walking distance from the venue. It provided all the amenities she needed, including a fitness center she could visit every evening at the end of a long day.

The fine arts and antiques fair in Maastricht was probably the biggest and most popular event of its kind in the world, and she was glad she'd made the decision to attend. *The Purveyor,* an elite publication on worldwide antiquities and treasures, had picked her from a pool of writer candidates to report on the convention this year. If they liked her work, she was confident it would lead to a more permanent professional arrangement.

Her plan was to attend the lectures, make connections, and get to bed early. She was not interested in painting the town red—she'd seen Maastricht before, therefore, sightseeing wasn't a priority.

Amsterdam, however, was different. She wanted to relax, to distract herself before her departure. Yesterday, she'd taken a leisurely stroll by the canals around lunch time. Later in the day, she'd opted for an early supper, then, spent an hour at the gym next to the hotel and followed it with a long soak in the bathtub.

With the exception of tonight, she'd skipped the myriad options for entertainment all around her but this evening, she'd decided to go to a Bach dinner concert. It was a much needed break from her constant thoughts of Adrian. Because since she saw his face in the news, she couldn't think of anything else.

Adam Derringstone.

A strange name she had no connection to.

The concert kept her interest but later, as she walked through the streets, the thoughts returned in full force. She gave up on fighting them, and instead slowed her pace and welcomed them.

She took it easy getting back to the hotel. By the time she bathed and finished drying her hair, it was running on midnight. Snuggled up in a fleece jogging suit, she prepared to finish packing and wrap things up for the day. After checking her messages, she'd dive into bed.

A computer prompt popped up with another loud beep. Emma sat back at the desk, typed her username and password, and waited for the customized red rose petal desktop screen to load. It only took a few seconds.

A yellow envelope appeared at the bottom right corner of the screen. Palming the mouse, she moved the cursor and clicked on it. It seemed to take forever for her mailbox to open.

"Damn slow connection," she grumbled.

Finally, the hourglass cursor returned to its arrow shape and the page appeared.

One unread message stood out in bold text. It was from a familiar sender and said "*Updates...*" on the subject line.

"Let's see what you've come up with, Max," she whispered to herself.

She clicked on the title and read.

WAITING *on word from some of my connections. I received the usual replies from India earlier today. Unfortunately, I have nothing to report so far. But we'll find him, I promise. Don't give up.*

. . .

HEY, *how's business in Holland? Has the convention started already? I'm in Ibiza with a lady friend for the week. Will be in touch. Stay safe.*
    Max

DON'T GIVE UP.

Easier said than done. A time or two, she thought they'd had some good leads, yet on each occasion they fizzled to nothing.

She'd seen Adrian's picture on television, knew where he was, but obstacles were still there, undeterred, to keep them apart. When she'd called the Srinagar hospital the day after seeing him on television, he'd been moved elsewhere—that was all they told her. Another ward? Another hospital? Where? She had no idea. The frustration tore at her.

Were it not for Max's calm intervention, she would have gone on the next flight to India but he promised he'd get to the bottom of things....

It could be another near miss, like the one in Scotland. If she failed this time, would she have the will to keep on searching?

She studied a spot on the wall and mulled over Max's message. So another day had passed without news. She was used to such days. Grasping the edges of the monitor with the flats of her fingers, she pushed it down and the computer shut off automatically.

Time to go to bed and get some sleep. The first day of the fair, Ranieri, a preeminent expert on the Italian Renaissance period, was supposed to give a two-hour lecture on Knight Hospitaller writing and art in the auditorium. His talk would be followed by an exposition of manuscripts of interest which she was keen on having the opportunity to peruse. Events such as this presented numerous rewards in the form of both useful contacts and insight.

And most of all, they kept her mind occupied.

After a stop at the bathroom to brush her teeth, she slid between the crisp white cotton sheets and pulled the thick eiderdown up to her shoulders. It was comfortable and warm, and instead of counting sheep, she let her mind drift to the whirlwind events of the past few weeks.

After meeting Max at Villa d'Este—and after she'd fulfilled her end of the bargain with the Council—she'd formed an easy friendship with the man. She admitted it felt good to have somebody to talk to. It was all the better because that somebody understood who and what she was.

In those post-war years, she also had the opportunity to get to know two mid-level Councilmen, Nick Lucas and James Flannery, who both had military backgrounds and worked in the field of Valthrean Defense and Emergency Preparedness. They gave her further insight into Valthrean politics.

To her disappointment, the highest-ranked leaders of the Council would remain concealed behind a thick curtain of bureaucracy, from where they'd pull the strings and give out directives in total secrecy—that was Council policy. Max told her only a privileged few were granted clearance to meet them.

"What are they like?" she'd asked Max.

"I'm not at liberty to discuss such things," he replied evasively.

Emma thought of the images she'd seen in the mirror, so long ago, at the witch's cottage in Redbourn. Images that had played like a modern cinematic movie before her eyes.

She wondered if Nila, Candaka, and the other Nagas had made their escape, and if they survived, would they be on the Council today?

Perhaps she didn't have clearance to meet with the top Council members, but the recipe handed from the witch in Redbourn blew their minds away, although she was a little surprised that in all this time, the Valthreans had not managed to acquire such an asset. Or even that they never heard about it, or considered the usefulness of having such an effective weapon of defense.

General Flannery declared that in his lifetime of two hundred and fifty something years, he'd never come across anything like it in the Valthrean patent list. Before her case, they'd never even considered the usefulness or otherwise of witchery in their affairs.

"A herbal potion to kill the pheromones we give off, a sort of cloak to suppress our distinctive scent?" he roared in a Texan accent. "By golly, to a common mortal it may not be much to write home about, but to a Valthrean. ... Holy guacamole, it's pure genius!"

"The ultimate defense shield," the younger, handsomer, and more formal Lieutenant Lucas agreed. He was clearly a man of few words, a necessary balance to his gregarious companion.

"I can make this for you in whatever amounts you desire, and I'll offer it at a good price," she proposed. "The actual recipe stays with me."

Lucas and Flannery looked at each other. A silent message passed between them.

"You can discuss this and get back to me later if you like."

Flannery turned back to her with an ear-splitting smile. "You have a deal, lady. I'll have my assistant contact you for another meeting," he guffawed, an action that made his bushy moustache vibrate.

It took some years before the logistics of production were figured out. Only a few from the inner circle were allowed to test it at first while Max was charged with coordinating a small, elite Valthrean Secret Service to support the various military and investigative teams. It was a staggering task that involved endless considerations and strategic planning, but Emma knew that Max loved to keep busy. She also appreciated that she could do something for her people while opening doors for her future. She'd finally become a part of something bigger than herself.

Eventually, Max started to badger her about taking on more responsibility by contesting the elections as Junior Councilwoman. "You'd be good at it."

"How do you know? You haven't known me long."

"I know how tenacious you can be. You'd be unstoppable."

"Just because I'm trying to reclaim my life with Adrian doesn't mean I can be that way in everything I do."

"You don't give yourself enough credit," he argued.

"I'm not in the mood, and that's the end of it," she responded firmly.

After that day, he never mentioned it again.

Meanwhile, she spent a few months brushing up her knowledge of

Italian and developed an addiction to a morning dose of cappuccino and chocolate cream pastries liberally dusted with confectioner's sugar. They were almost as good as lemon scones and jam.

Hell, they *were* as good as scones and jam. Although she'd never admit it to Max, who thought the sun rose and set on Italian cuisine, a glass of strong Barolo, and amusing company. The Italians possessed an atypical, in-your-face sense of humor that was alien to her, while Max was right at home with it.

"It's all about conviviality and adaptation," he'd explain. "A car moves when all the wheels turn together. The smoother they turn, the better the ride."

Perhaps he was right. She was too focused, too serious for her own good, and she needed to widen her perspective. Max could afford such a statement; he was as free as a bird.

Max was not the average sort of bounty hunter. He traveled in exclusive circles and could afford to pick and choose his assignments at his own convenience. His selectivity made him a very desirable catch for prospective employers.

Yet, he had the constancy of an invaluable friend. He instantly championed her quest for Adrian with no-nonsense diligence, and he supervised her treatment like a mother hen when she'd consented to subject to it. She had much to be grateful to him for. He gave her hope, as well as a place to belong. One day, when she'd have to start afresh elsewhere, with another identity and life, her newfound friends in the Valthrean world would remain in the picture. They were one big thing in her life she wouldn't have to give up.

At some point, her mind shut down in sleep.

It didn't seem long afterward when the ringing in Emma's ears became louder and more persistent. It yanked her into a reluctant state of being which teetered between wakefulness and sleep. The trilling peal was as maddening as an importunate fly buzzing about her face and refusing to let her be.

The ringing stopped. Then started again.

She knew somewhere at the back of her mind that it was the phone asking her to pick up, but she wished it could be a dream and nothing more. If she had the energy, she'd fling the blasted thing against the wall and see it break into a hundred pieces.

Finally, she opened her eyes and looked at the alarm clock.5:44. Who the hell would be calling this early in the morning? Her hand snuck out of its quilted cocoon and reached out for the hotel phone. She lifted it off the base and set it to her ear.

"Yes? Emma speaking," she tried to say but her voice broke midway into the second word. She licked her lips and cleared her throat.

"Emma, what took you so long? Listen to me carefully. Pack your bags and get yourself on a plane back to Rome."

"Max? I thought you were in Spain. Do you know what time it is?"

"'Course I know, it's early morning, and it's time to get up. I'm on the way home now and you need to get back over here."

"Max, it's not even six o'clock! Stop being bossy. I have a train to catch in three hours and I need to get some more shuteye before breakfast. Can't it wait a couple of days? What's so important anyway?"

"Emma, I think we have him."

"Him?" Emma sifted through the cotton wool in her mind but her thoughts registered a blank page.

Slowly, very slowly, a bold handwriting became clear in her fogged mind, like graffiti designs on the wall. Suggestive, meaningful designs so daring and bright, they kicked the remnants of sleep out of her system.

Max's words hit her like a bold Marquee lit with a thousand light bulbs and pushed up close to her face.

"Yes, *him*," Max echoed.

———

IN ROME, Italy...

. . .

EMMA WAVED Max in her tiny apartment and saw him into the kitchenette where he grabbed a bottle of water from the refrigerator, twisted the top off, and swigged a quarter of it in one gulp.

"Just the thing."

He continued to sip as he trailed Emma to the bedroom where she busied herself unpacking her luggage. She was too nervous to sit still and do nothing.

Less than an hour earlier, she'd walked off of an abnormally hot late summer afternoon that raged over the nearby *Piazza di Spagna* with her luggage. In the square, the lackadaisical tourists flurried louder than spirited cicadas in the heart of summer, swarming to the wide Spanish steps and the *Fontana della Barcaccia* at their base as if it were their only source of light.

From the corner of her eye, she watched him stop at the entrance to the room and lean casually against the door frame, one hand in his jeans pocket and the other dangling the bottle at the neck. She went back and forth in jerky movements, while she tried to dislodge a lump the size of Australia from her throat. Mercifully, he said nothing.

Hands trembling, she looked up at him as she pried open a chest of drawers and slid a folded sweater inside.

"Tell me," she asked curtly.

"Good afternoon to you, too," he remarked with a raised eyebrow and mouth bowed in humor.

"Don't tease. Not now."

Regarding her intently, Max nodded and sobered up, duly chastened. He knew when it wasn't a good idea to push the envelope. He'd probably never seen her so agitated except that time in Belgium.

"Let's see," he started. "It seems that our mark has acquired a building in London not far from Trafalgar Square. The notice hanging outside states that it is being converted into some sort of museum. I'm not clear on the details yet."

"Has Jack given you any updates since we spoke last?"

Max shook his head. "He's due to call me sometime this week. I left him a message asking him to send over some pictures ASAP. The name Adrian's using, as you know, is Adam Derringstone, and he fits the description. Gil, Jack's sometimes work partner and a Valthrean, confirmed he's one of us. Jack told me the man doesn't go out often so getting a good visual to compare with the shot from the news broadcast is a bit of a challenge."

"Adam," she whispered the name Madeleine had given Adrian. Then, her brow furrowed in concern. "You said he's good ... this Jack? Can he be trusted with this?"

"You worry too much, Emma. Jack Steele's job is to find out stuff, and he's one of the best in the business. What's great is that he doesn't ask questions, and he's shown his loyalty time and again. He's a professional, does what he needs to do, and won't raise suspicion."

"How can you be so sure?"

Max grinned at her. "Emma, the ever cautious one."

"Well?" she insisted, ignoring his barb.

"I've worked with him for about five years and he's reliable. Plus, although he knows about us, he's not one of us. ... He's what we'd call an ally of the Council. We use people like Jack when we don't want to attract the wrong kind of attention. He's sworn to secrecy, a privilege only granted to a few."

Emma contemplated Max's words. "I just don't want anything to go wrong. It's different this time. It's *real*."

She rubbed her arms and stifled a shiver. Her body was on edge, a nervous wreck since she left Holland in haste last night. She grabbed a pair of black mohair gloves and pulled at the soft flyaway threads.

"I packed these for nothing. It wasn't that cold in Holland," she muttered. She wanted to bury her face in the soft wool and let it absorb her tears. It would be so easy to break down and cry, to let herself go numb and weak.

Max walked toward her and stilled her fidgeting with his warm palm. Then, he caught her chin between thumb and forefinger and pierced her with a serious gaze. Even while desperately trying to hold her tears back, she thought he looked very handsome when he wore a staid expression.

"Emma, I wouldn't dare take this lightly. I know how important it is for you and I hope you understand that."

This was probably the most openly compassionate she'd ever seen him. He must be truly worried about her. If he acted more this way, women wouldn't stand a chance—although she wasn't sure he needed more adulating females to fall at his feet. He had probably broken more hearts than she had lived years.

Emma's eyes stung. She swallowed with difficulty and nodded. "Thank you for being a good friend."

"Don't be fooled," he replied as he let go of her. "I'll have to cash in some day." His lips stretched in a wide smile, to throw into relief the fanned lines at the corners of his eyes.

"You rascal," she countered with a chuckle as she shook her head.

Just like that, he was back to his trademark flippant self.

Max put on an innocent expression and leaned back. "What?"

Of course, his cavalier attitude didn't deceive *her*. "You keep going on with that act. One day you'll get your just desserts, I can promise you that, and I'll be sitting on the sidelines watching you. Laughing my arse off."

At the look of mock horror he gave her, she patted his cheek and started out of the room, snickering.

"Going to fix some food now for an early dinner. Want pasta?"

"I'm starving so I accept the offer, even though you laugh at my expense."

"Believe me, Max, when you're caught hook, line, and sinker in love's net, that's when I'll *really* be amused. I can't wait," She waved a finger in the air to make her point.

"Such a dire fate is not in my plans, I'm afraid. I hope you're not planning to wait for that because I'd hate to disappoint you," he said dryly.

"But Max, of anyone in the world, you *must* know I'm used to waiting."

She looked over her shoulder and shot a sly glance at him before she disappeared into the kitchen. After all the hurt he'd experienced, she understood his hesitation to give anyone the keys to his heart. But she'd busted through those locked doors inside him, saw him for what he was, and she had learned to love him like the brother she never had.

247

He loved hard and fast. Just like he had let her into his life, amazingly, within the span of weeks, and he could do the same with someone else, one day. Someone who loved him as much as a woman could love a man. She was glad she'd secured this little place in Rome to be close to her friend. It was one of the best decisions she'd ever made after what happened in Sicily.

She put a pot of water on the stove and stuffed a bunch of fresh basil, mint, garlic, and some toasted slivered almonds in the food processor, the first ingredients for her favorite homemade pesto, modified from the original recipe. When she seasoned it and added parmesan cheese and olive oil and switched on the machine, the room burst with the mouthwatering bouquet of fresh herbs.

He inhaled the air, pure delight on his face. "Italy's good for you. I need to visit more often."

"I'd learned to cook long before I came to Italy. It relaxes me."

"Lucky for me." He grinned.

They ate and moved to the L-shaped couch to take their coffees. Max crossed a leg over his knee and sat back. Emma sat counter-corner from him and placed their espresso cups on black leather coasters on the glass coffee table.

"I haven't eaten so much in a long time," he sighed, rubbing his belly.

"Seeing that I boiled a whole packet of pasta, of which I had a starter portion, I hope you're right. There isn't a single strand of fettuccine left in the pot." She looked him over. "Where do you store all that food?"

He frowned back at her. "I had to push you to eat a few forkfuls."

"Shut up and drink your espresso." *Cut me some slack, Max. I need a distraction.*

"I received a message from Neil last week. He shared an interesting theory."

"What is that?" she asked, relieved for the change of direction.

"He thinks there's a mole in the organization. I think that the last operation to foil a small arms transfer in Angola at its source in Southampton failed miserably because the Cult had inside information. There have been other instances, too, like Gil's run-in with one of their thugs during a sting in Prague. One of our six agents was destroyed by mortals because it was clear they were prepared for us."

"You think that someone tipped them?" she asked. "Hang on now—you said killed by mortals?"

He nodded. "The Cult of the Snake is using more mortals for their dirty work these days so they can stay where they like to be, in the dark where no one can see them. We need to make a list of who can be trusted and who cannot. We have to constantly screen for spies," Max said, clearly worried.

Emma propped her feet up on an ottoman, and sipped on her espresso, wishing she'd made a cappuccino for her, even though it wasn't the custom after a meal in Italy.

"I've been telling the Elders we need to mobilize, and fast. We need an internal affairs division aligned with the secret service, to utilize our intel and investigation resources their full extent."

"Weren't they going to offer you that responsibility?"

"It's too big a job for one person." He gave her a pointed look. "Or two. I have reliable people working with me but we need more manpower. The Cult is using magic to keep us away from their doings. I don't like where this is going."

"I know that all the original Valthreans ever wanted was to live a peaceful existence and blend in with the humans, but I cannot understand why the Council hasn't organized itself more heavily before now. They were aware of the threat, weren't they?"

"The threat was there but it wasn't, if you know what I mean."

"But wouldn't the Cult of the Snake have acted by now? Why wait two thousand years to get even?"

"Someone's been biding their time. Perhaps there was nothing worth fighting for before now."

"That sounds far-fetched. History has presented numerous opportunities for individuals and groups to profit."

"Yet, only in the last few centuries have the Valthreans decided to contribute more heavily in the human world and help them with their decisions by strategically infiltrating key positions at all levels. Think, for instance, what the world would look like if Hitler had won the war or if Napoleon had reigned long enough to invade America."

Emma pondered that for a moment. "And today there are also corporate interests to contend with, as well as advanced technology, so we're dealing with a much larger playing field."

"Precisely."

"So the enemy has the same goal, but with different intentions," she said thoughtfully. "Some have always been followers of the Snake King but others are rogue Valthreans. They would be privy to our business. Rather than kowtow to the Council's rules and unite with the rest of us, they have their own agenda."

"On that note, Emma, more odd things have been happening lately, seemingly unrelated. I'm not so convinced it's not the workings of some larger scheme. In the last ten years, we've had twenty-six unresolved Valthrean deaths. After investigating the files, I found that all the victims were handling delicate business at the time. So knock me senseless, but I see a pattern here, and it's not pretty."

Emma's brows furrowed. "Let's rewind. What if..." She put her feet down and leaned forward, rested her forearms on her thighs and cradled the cooling mug in both hands. "What if Madeleine's hidden goal with Adrian was something along the same lines?"

"What do you mean?"

"Adrian was becoming an authority in the field of agricultural reform. He had many friends in high places all the way up to the Prince Regent, and he had his seat in Parliament, of course. Then especially, he had close ties to the British Foreign Secretary and although he wasn't that involved in state matters any more, the link was there."

"Are you saying that she was using Adrian to get entrée in those circles?"

Emma shrugged. "We'll never be sure of that, I suppose. But Adrian was also extremely rich, even by today's standards. He owned several properties, and his estate had become very profitable. Still, to me it makes no sense ... why him? A viscount. I'd expect her to angle for a duke, at least."

"Madeleine does what Madeleine wants. She's unpredictable. Still, seems to me he was a good catch, still," he said, as he stood up and negotiated the end table to go to the kitchen area.

"Yes, a great catch," she murmured. She suddenly found it hard to swallow.

She bent her head and contemplated her shoes. *Must* not *cry,* she firmly scolded herself.

From the side of the couch, Max reached out and put his hand on her shoulder. "It will work out, I promise," he said gently.

Right. From her experience so far, Max's words didn't even begin to hold water. She turned her head to look up at him. "Like it did for you?"

A shadow crossed his face. "It's not the same."

Emma covered his hand with hers. "You're right, it's not the same. I shouldn't have said that."

Maxed squeezed her shoulder and walked to his fancy coffee machine like the ones found in bars to make himself another espresso. "Forget about it. You don't have to walk on eggshells with me."

Emma smiled into her coffee cup. *Thank God for Max.*

After that evening, a week passed in torturously slow motion until one afternoon, after lunching on a take-out *tramezzino* sandwich, Emma found herself staring at the title of an e-mail on her computer screen.

Pictures.

Her right forefinger hovered on the mouse button and she pressed her thumb down on the mouse pad to control the shakiness in her hand. She clenched her eyes shut for a brief moment—like a terrified child bracing for the dreaded prick of a flu shot—and depressed the left mouse button. Then, she downloaded the first of three attachments without sparing the message text a glance.

The digital picture showed the back of a tall man with darkish blond hair, a bit on the long side, walking in a busy street. He wore medium-rinse jeans and a well-cut tan suede jacket.

Immediately, the hair on her neck rose to attention and a tingle shimmied down her spine. She couldn't see his face but something about him, about his form and stance...

She opened the other two files in succession. The first was another back shot which she guessed was taken a few seconds before or after the one she'd just seen. That tiny flare of recognition lingered as she glossed over the image. The third and last picture, however, was the one that stopped her in her tracks. This time the man's face was partially turned toward the camera.

He'd hooked his hair behind his ear but a few rebel strands fell down over his face. Still, she could see the sharp angle of his jaw, his nose and an eye. The camera had caught him looking left. He seemed to be checking for oncoming traffic before crossing the street without the aid of a pedestrian crossing. It wasn't a close up of Adrian but now she was certain.

It *was* him.

She wasn't sure how long she sat there, drinking in the play of light and shadows over his face, feeling detached from herself, and desperately wishing she could jump inside that picture. Time had stopped—much like one of those moments when a person falls into a hypnotized state while driving, without realizing it, and doesn't know how they arrived at their destination. When she came to, she minimized the image and read the message.

JACK TOLD me that once you give the go ahead he'll put together a package with some interesting information and send it over to you.

YOU HAVE THE PICTURES NOW. *Talk to me.*
  Max

EMMA HIT the reply button and typed three words: *Send the package.*

She didn't want to call Max right now. She wasn't capable of talking to anyone.

She pulled up the last image again and made it bigger. It hurt to look at it. It also hurt *not* to. Minutes ... hours ticked by, with her eyes glued to the screen.

When she sat up, the late March dusk had already crept through the windows, and cast a dim net over the room. The encroaching darkness didn't help her any to get out of her daze.

Finally, she tore herself away from the table, plodded to the kitchen and switched on the coffee maker. She needed something strong to gather her sprawled wits, as well as some nourishment. Grabbing an apple from a bowl, she bit distractedly into it. Her mind reeled.

What if she'd had a crystal ball back when she first lost Adrian—would it have told her about this moment? Would she have gone mad at the realization of how long it would take her, what she'd go through, to find him?

Without Max's help, perhaps, she wouldn't have been able to, or it may have taken her much longer.

And it wasn't over yet.

She wanted to jump on a plane to London and claim Adrian on the spot but that would destroy all her chances of getting him back the way they once were. Her most difficult challenge was yet to come because both she and Adrian were different people now, their personalities kneaded and molded by time.

Adrian was Adam—a completely different name for a completely different man.

They had each collected a well of experience in separate worlds. If a new bond was to form between them, they had to get to know each other all over again. She would have to gauge the situation, feel the energy in the climate between them.

Seeing his pictures brought this home to her with the momentum of a thunderbolt.

Would the man he was now be attracted to her? Or a more intimidating notion— Would he be the man she wanted by her side from here on out?

She had to dig up the courage to see this patiently to the end. Only then could they start building a new life of shared hopes and expectations.

She'd take a week and plan her approach. Max told her he'd loan her his London townhouse for as long as she needed it. It was a small, elegant place situated minutes from the Marble Arch tube station, where, he confessed to her, he planned to settle into in the near future. With things as they were in the Valthrean world, there were times he needed to be on call twenty-four-seven, and that meant living close to the Council headquarters in London.

In the meantime, she would come to terms with the fact that the process would take time. She couldn't blow her chances by doing something that would risk her losing Adrian another time.

It would be torture to be in the same room with him and not be able to tell him who she was. Searching for him, waiting all this time to find him, was one thing. But being so close to him and be compelled to act a part, without the ability of telling him outright what he meant to her until she had his trust and his heart—that would kill her.

But she was going to have to form a relationship with him based on a lie, and then she'd have to bide her time. Things between them had to progress naturally.

She told herself she'd waited this long, she'd wait a little more. If destiny would allow him to love her, to make him hers again, then she'd know it was all meant to be.

Max called her mad to make things so complicated. His idea was that she corner Adrian, perform the ritual, get his memory back, and be done with it.

True, that would be decidedly easier, but would it be fair to her, Adrian, or their relationship? A salvaged memory did not guarantee that anything would be the same between them.

She was adamant that this was the way it had to be. Kindling a new flame was the right way, the only chance she had to build a lasting bond.

While she prepared to go to London, she insisted that Max tell

Jack to keep an eye out for Adrian until her arrival. And when the time was finally right, she'd make her move.

Her mind made up, she put the apple down and poured her coffee, adding milk and three heaped teaspoonfuls of sugar as she'd take it back in England. She liked her coffee sweeter than her tea.

She opened the freezer and took out a portion of store-bought *lasagne alla Bolognese*. A skimpy salad wouldn't do today. She needed comfort food. A load of carbs, followed by a respectable mound of hazelnut and chocolate gelato.

After removing the pasta portion from the aluminum tray it came in from the *tavola calda* she'd brought it from, she plated it and put it in the microwave. She adjusted the settings to three minutes and waited for the rich smell of beef sauce, cheese, and béchamel to fill the room.

It gave her enough time to send a long, silent prayer to the night. A prayer she chanted over and over, as if she was trying to convince herself, more than a supreme being, of its necessity.

May God grant her the strength to be patient.

May her quest be finally over.

And may it be all right in the end, for this time she'd wrestle Fate barehanded to keep Adrian by her side.

CHAPTER 13

"What are these
So ... wild in their attire,
That look not like the inhabitants o' the earth,
And yet are on 't?"
[Macbeth, Act I, Scene III]

Back in Rome...

An elderly voice greeted her at the other end of the line.

"May I speak to Mr. Derringstone, please?"

"Certainly, madam. Your name?"

"Emma Deramore," she said, citing her name of the last twenty-eight years. The one she was most comfortable living with.

"Please hold on, Miss Deramore."

Emma tapped four fingers on her thigh in a rapid rhythm, the beat in sync with the erratic thumping of her heart. Spread on the table was a variety of newspaper and magazine clippings—the entire contents of the package Jack had sent her. For a whole week, she'd read them and reread them in the attempt to capture something of what Adrian had become, how he'd changed.

The Derringstone Museum of Oddities to quench London thirst for the bizarre; New museum to open doors behind Trafalgar Square; Derringstone: The Odd Newcomer.

Most articles talked about the museum itself and only skimmed over mention of the elusive owner. Adrian was merely described as a "reserved, private individual" and his apparent interest in world culture and history was given sporadic notice. Other than that, there were no more personal details except a couple of pictures of the building itself.

Emma saw it as meaningful that he had chosen a profession some-what linked to her current one. Although the perspective was differ-ent, still, it was a career that kept them both connected to the past through the objects they came in close contact with—she, as a writer and he, as a businessman and collector. She didn't regret closing down her sweet shop to change direction. The move had come at the right time for her.

She heard a shuffling noise at the other end of the line, followed by, "Hello, Adam speaking."

The rich baritone knocked her senses like the head-on collision of two high-speed trains.

The voice I've been longing to hear.

"I ... er, good morning, Mr. Derringstone. I was wondering if you had time to discuss a matter of business," she replied with bated breath.

"What can I do for you, Miss Deramore?" he said in a professional tone.

A twinge of discomfort shot through her neck and arm, and she clutched the phone like a lifeline. From there, all the tension in her body seemed to flow down and conglomerate in one little spot at the tip of her spine. She sat ramrod straight on an armchair, perched on the edge of the seat, legs and ankles flush together. In the pregnant moments of silence that followed, while he awaited her response, she ground her heel nervously on the rug and worried her bottom lip until she could taste blood.

Get a grip.

"First of all, I wanted to ask you if you would be willing to grant me a personal interview for publication in *The Purveyor*. My editor has already given his approval," she lied.

"I never give personal interviews. It is my policy," he said with finality.

Blast it. "I'll give you time to think about it, of course. Uh, perhaps you are also considering the acquisition of more objects to add to your museum collection," she improvised, scrambling for an in. "I have great connections with dealers in fine art and antiques."

"I am always on the lookout for interesting pieces, Miss Deramore."

"Call me Emma, please," she cut in, all too late realizing how testy she must have sounded. But how could she explain that she couldn't bear his impersonal address and that if she heard him call her by her surname again she might scream?

A slight pause. "Of course, Emma. And, you can call me Adam. I presume you have something in mind that you wish to tell me about?"

"Uh, I do have some clients who may be interested in selling," she said, wishing she had thought of rehearsing different scenarios. Then she remembered something she read in the papers about his interest in East Indian history and mythology. "But before I run anything by you, I was wondering if I could impose on you to provide me with some insight on East Indian history of the first century and earlier. I am not yet well-versed on that particular period and I want to make sure that what my clients may wish to donate or put on the market is worth your time..."

She let her voice fade, fervently hoping she'd sounded convincing enough.

"A friend of mine also has a particular object that she would like to learn more about and asked me to look into it before she decides to sell it," she added, pulling out all the stops. If this did not make him consent to meet her, she didn't know what would.

"I am honored that you contacted me, but I'm curious."

His tone took on a slower nuance and poured through her like thick hot chocolate.

"How did you hear about me? I notice that you're not calling from England, yet, as far as I know, the museum has not been mentioned in any foreign publications."

"You're right," she hedged. "I'm in Italy at present, but I plan to move back to London shortly. A friend of mine returned from a business trip and brought me some information about you and your establishment. He thought I might be interested in writing about you and he was right."

"I have no problem with you writing a piece about the museum. It's strictly personal interviews that I have an objection to."

She gulped. "I understand. There is also something else I must divulge."

A perceptible pause then, "Yes?"

"My friend who mentioned you to me is a Valthrean. He is a Council member."

His response was quick. "I have no dealings with the Council. I like working alone," he stated.

Don't I know it.

"What I can't understand is, how would you know about them? The Valthreans are the most secretive, clannish lot I've ever seen."

"I'm a Valthrean, too, and I assist the Council from time to time." At least in this she could be truthful.

She heard him breathe on the other end—the only indication he hadn't hung up.

"I hope this is not a deal breaker because I still need your help."

"Why me? I doubt they lack antiquities experts on the Council."

"Your focus on a specific part of world history makes your expertise unique. Then, as I told you, I have an article to write. The editor expects me to deliver by next month."

Another stretch of discomfiting silence. *Please, say yes.*

"If there is one thing I find deplorable, it is lack of honesty in a person. I appreciate you for coming clean right away."

Emma almost dropped the phone in relief.

"Can you give me a few details about the object in question? I may be able to help your friend better if I have an idea of what we're dealing with," he asked.

Off the cuff, she gave a brief description of an ancient Indian stone figurine she'd once heard Max talk about. She kept the details vague, aware that she was treading unfamiliar territory.

"That is odd. Something that old is hard to come by in a private collection; then again, in the rare case it is, the owner would not be at all casual about parting with it. I doubt many could even afford to acquire such a piece."

"As I said, Adr ... Adam, I am not a connoisseur. When I get to London, I'd like to set up an appointment with you. Maybe I can offer lunch in exchange for your time."

Right then, she could visualize a smile splitting his face.

"I'm sure I'll take you up on your offer. When do you plan to arrive?"

"Next week. I'll call you as soon as I get settled. "

"Certainly. I hope you have a comfortable trip."

"Thank you." She ran a shaky hand through her hair. Cool moisture tickled her skin. "All right, then."

"Your voice ... this may sound strange but, have we met before?" he asked unexpectedly as she placed her clammy palm on her lap.

"I'm certain we haven't. Why do you ask?"

She crossed her index and middle fingers, and hoped she wouldn't be suddenly struck by lightning.

"Nothing, just an impression is all."

"I have learned at my own expense that gut feelings are important. Perhaps you should heed yours," the little devil on her left shoulder urged her to say.

"Are you saying that we know each other?"

Her heart picked up a hammering rhythm. "I didn't say that."

"What was it you were saying then?" he replied, a hint of humor in his voice.

He seemed to be greatly enjoying their exchange, which emboldened her to go on. "I was saying that sometimes things are precisely what they seem."

"You must be an interesting piece of art yourself, Emma."

His husky laugh was molten lava on her nerve endings.

"Don't say that. For all you know, I may be dull and boring."

"I somehow doubt that very much."

Coming from his mouth, these words felt like an intimate caress, as if he had just reached through the receiver to brush her heated skin with a slow, knowing touch.

The tightness in her chest intensified and her brain went into overdrive. She had to end this conversation before she said something stupid. "You are too kind, Adam. I'll call you next week."

"That'll work, Emma. I look forward to it."

So do I. You have no clue how much.

She floated through their goodbyes. Not even the *click* that signaled the end of the call woke her from the dream world she had sunk in.

"Adrian," she said softly.

But nobody could hear her, only the late morning breeze breaking through the cracked window and the voice in her head that told her that what had just happened was not a dream at all.

———

Somewhere in London...

"Say again?"

Bree Wynter examined her eggplant-painted nails with assiduous interest, loath to look up and acknowledge the formidable man who crowded her space. A desk stacked high with files, stationery, assorted junk, and a twenty-one inch computer monitor wasn't enough terrain to separate her from St. Giles. It would take a canyon and a half between them to pacify her somewhat.

St. Giles' eyes bored into her and she squirmed a little, to her eternal shame.

"You should sit down," she said, waving at the chair next to him.

He ignored her.

"I said, the leaders demand you make yourself useful. Against my advice, of course."

Creep. "Yes, well, and how do you suggest I do that? Since Mom and Dad got out of the picture, I've been wondering how many ways they've blown my chances of advancement. And don't get me started about my sister—"

"Not everything they did was wrong. They raised you and supported you when you first joined us and swore allegiance to us."

"Not without a lot of noise and objections. Just thinking about it gives me a migraine." She winced.

"So far, you've kept your promise."

"You're saying I'm part of the team? Oh joy! All I do is sit around here and wait for you chaps to decide if I can do better than push papers and refill coffee mugs at board meetings."

"Everyone in our select group must earn their loyalty, and such things take a lot of time."

She tsked and crossed her arms. "By time, you mean the average lifetime of four to five humans, give or take? I could easily debate the fairness of that. I didn't see you give time to Stella van Kamp, the society girl who loves to parade her fake breasts at fashionable parties. Or Martin Maclaine who up and offered those twenty million to the foundation..."

"I see that the virtue of patience has eluded you."

She pulled an empty Styrofoam cup and crushed it—the next best thing to attempted strangulation of a top Cult official. A drop of cold, stale coffee fell on the wood by her keyboard. She fixed it with a frown.

"I think rather I was born in the wrong family."

"You can believe what you like, but if you want things to change, you should check your emotions and start thinking with your brain," he said without mincing words.

"To wait as I've waited, working for peanuts, you either have to be bat-shit crazy or totally masochistic. I think patience would high-five me for my stick-to-itiveness."

When she turned eighteen, she had one wish—to become one of the Cult's own. It took them nine miserable, long years for them to accede to that request. Even her father had stabbed her in the face, claiming she hadn't done anything to deserve it. She'd argued that what the Cult wanted was blind allegiance, and that, she would give willingly. Fuck, hadn't she *proved* herself enough? He had enough clout to facilitate her initiation. Thankfully, he at last relented and had her sorted before he blew his chances at gaining one of the Cult's most prized positions—Senior Advisor to the Grand Master and Chief of Central Intelligence.

If she'd thought her advancement would come quickly and satisfyingly, she'd been wrong on all counts.

St. Giles rounded her desk and sat at the edge, on her side. He leaned down, bringing his eyes close to hers like a criminal hypnotist intent on making her do unspeakable things.

"If you let me speak, I can tell you there's a way to remedy all that," he said, his breath warm on her cheek.

She swallowed hard and forced herself not to cower or cringe. "Okay."

"Remember that luxury apartment you liked in Knightsbridge?"

Did he mean the flat for sale she'd gone to see with an interested friend who she knew for a fact couldn't afford to pay a quarter of the asking price? A dream place fit for a celebrity, many steps up from Bree's nice but tiny one bedroom in Camden.

He moved perceptibly closer, and this time it was impossible not to back up just a little.

"That one," he confirmed, picking up on the play of thoughts on her face.

"How do you know? I haven't told anyone ex—"

"It's my job to know, my dear. Surely you know that by now?"

He lifted a finger to her cheek and trailed it down so slowly to her chin, as if examining every pore on her skin.

"You should thank your mother for the kind of beauty that can drive a man wild. Even one as old as me."

His lips curved upward and his astute gaze let her know he was as far from going wild as a Tibetan monk. He was fully in control of the situation, and this was an act to suck her into doing something he wanted her to do. Then again, he knew she had no choice.

He licked his lips then pulled back, breaking the spell and leaving her slightly dizzy.

"My mother? You know I don't look like her. I'm not blood."

"I meant precisely what I said. Your *mother*." He let his words sink in, then added, "The one who gave birth to you."

"But you—everyone said she was dead."

"No. I merely said she was gone."

What was she supposed to say to *that*?

"About that flat in Knightsbridge," he said after a pause. To her relief, he got up and paced to the bookshelf. He pulled out a book and leafed through it. "It's yours if you help us, all expenses paid. This can be a first of many perks, should you wish." He put the book back and flicked imaginary dust from his lapel. "You can thank me later for putting in a good word for you."

Bree suppressed a shiver at the implication of his words and tried to think logically. He didn't want her; he just wanted to use her, but who cared as long as she moved up from the stalemate position in the organization?

Were she an average girl, part of her mind would be screaming to run, but average wasn't one of her favorite words. Common sense urged her to take the offer. Indecision wouldn't give her a nice bank account. Caution wouldn't land the high life in her hands. A girl like her couldn't afford to be skittish in a situation like this, which could be the break she'd been waiting for. She doubted there'd be another chance if she refused this time.

"What do you want?" The tone came out harsher than she intended, but there were times when the fear of St. Giles and his influence didn't matter. When she couldn't give a damn what St. Giles thought of her—and this was one of those times. What he'd just disclosed to her was too big, too crushing, for her to care. But most importantly, the scent of money and power did the trick.

"You remember those classified files we discussed during the last meeting? They were pretty detailed." His terrible eyes settled on her again, ruthless and direct. "You're one of the few who know what's in them. Do you still want to think we don't value you?"

He was messing with her mind and he knew it. Again, she didn't care.

Get on with it now.

"Still, there is part of that file you haven't seen..."

"Why?"

"We need your mother to help us with some things to give us an edge over the enemy, and we just realized there's a connection between her and the person who created this little problem for us. As I don't wish for this information to get outside our inner circle just yet, she's our best asset right now. She has experience with, shall we say, certain types of magic."

"How do I factor in this equation?"

"You have a sharp mind and an interest in the dark arts. I want you to follow her closely, to let her teach you everything she knows." He linked his hands behind his back and approached the desk. "We don't want to keep our eggs in one basket. Who better than you to gain her confidence?"

"Does she know—?"

"She thinks you're dead, and she has no knowledge of her link to this case. It is best that she keep thinking that way. For now." His lips set in a grim line. "So, what's your answer?"

"All expenses paid" ricocheted in her head with an earsplitting clang. Over and over until it sunk in. She almost couldn't bear the excitement.

"As I said, the more you do, the more you earn," he added.

"You know my answer."

"Yes or no. I have a fondness for clarity."

"I'll do it," she retorted.

"Fine." He nodded. "Enjoy your day."

So this was it? Yeah, she wanted him to leave, but for him to dismiss her like one would an inconsequential bug—it was too much. He walked briskly to the door, not even allowing her to wrap her head around things. The wonderful things she was about to get for herself.

"Moron," she muttered.

"What?" he asked, without looking back.

He turned the knob and opened the door.

"Nothing."

Bree's mind worked overtime, already planning a new life at a new place. She hoped there wouldn't be any nasty surprises to put a wrench in her plans. If she kept her brains screwed on tight, she'd impress the lot of them, including the cynical St. Giles.

St. Giles opened the door wide but he stopped short of taking another step for there, on the threshold, stood a stunning, elegant woman with the most magnificent mane of red hair. Not a rich mahogany with natural red highlights like hers, but a bright shade that framed a perfect face.

But what gave Bree pause were the woman's eyes—green and big and almond-shaped, exactly like her own. She had no doubt then that this was her mother.

She instinctively clutched her stomach and winced, glad she was still sitting. For the first time, she wasn't so sure of anything anymore.

"Am I too early?" the woman said with a sophisticated inflection. "I couldn't stand to wait in the reception area so I decided to come up."

Bree let out a shaky breath, wondering at the same time how long she'd been holding it. The enthusiasm for St. Giles' proposal was short-lived—because now, the impact of what she'd just gotten into hit her hard.

She had to spy on her mother.

Her heart skipped to her throat and lodged there in a big, nauseous lump. A wave of panic propelled through her like a log sailing through an angry river, and hitting sharp rocks along the way.

Those eyes that looked so familiar met hers with undisguised curiosity. Was that shock she saw flash across them? If it had been, the woman didn't waste time composing herself.

"I hope this is not an inconvenience?"

St. Giles moved to the side and motioned to her to come in, his calculating expression however glued on Bree.

The part of her mind that had urged her to run from this deal mocked her now.

Is Knightsbridge worth all this, you think?

Somebody help her; how the hell was she going to get through this?

But get through it she would. If not, she wouldn't be Bree Wynter —the coldest bitch in London.

———

MADELEINE'S OLD RESIDENCE, *Hertfordshire.*

THEY'D KEPT it in good shape with upgrades over time, yet it remained at its core a stately house straight out of a Gothic novel. It wasn't overly large, but imposing enough. Madeleine felt grateful that it had been properly aired and cleaned, so she could sleep in her bed tonight. Even though 'her bed' was just a term. They hadn't paid maintenance and installed modern comforts for *her*, of course. The house had always been Cult property. She didn't own one chair, one set of sheets, or one kitchen pot in this house. All she'd ever had was the right to use it for as long as it pleased them.

St. Giles had promised things would change. She'd have her own bank account, and eventually, her own property, although it would probably not be this house but something smaller and unassuming, perhaps in the same area. She wouldn't put her hopes up.

The most exciting aspect of the deal, however, was that she'd have a new chalice to work with. She'd expressly requested it, meeting St. Giles' resistance head on. If the Cult wanted her to employ the full extent of her skills, this requirement topped her list.

He'd never told her how many of the seven chalices of legend the Cult possessed today—that sort of detail was top secret. However, he did consent as long as the chalice came and went with Bree Wynter every day. Once trust was lost, it wasn't easy to earn it back.

Madeleine disliked a condition that took power from her, but if there was one thing she learned from her extended stay at the abbey, it was to be patient. Her old plans had not been discarded, only filed in the back of her mind, like cold cases gathering dust before new clues and new opportunities came along. Being back out in the world was her cue that endurance eventually pays.

The next morning, the girl came early. Madeleine opened the door herself as St. Giles didn't want any employees running around when she was working. A couple of maids and a cook would come on Saturdays, the one day when Bree wasn't scheduled to visit. The place would be thoroughly cleaned and meals prepared in advance and put in the freezer in portions for the week.

Bree greeted her with a smile and wheeled a medium-sized piece of hard luggage inside. "Where shall I put this?" she asked, sounding neither bored nor enthusiastic.

She didn't have to say what it was.

She took the suitcase handle from the younger woman's hands and started upstairs. "Follow me."

"Sure."

Madeleine chanced a surreptitious glance at the college-girl-look of jeans, heeled boots, and stretchy bubblegum pink sweater. Bree came across superficially as the pretty princess type, a bit spoiled and doll-like, but Madeleine wasn't fooled. Astuteness lurked behind that made-up, almost vacuous exterior.

She found that charming, although she still hadn't decided whether she should be pleased or annoyed with this collaboration. Time would tell.

Bree climbed the steps behind her. From the large mirror ahead, Madeleine caught the young girl's roving eye. Calculating, assessing, weighing. The world was full of useless young girls who had no understanding or respect for something that was bigger than them, but for some zany reason she couldn't explain, Madeleine hazarded a guess that Bree wasn't one of them.

They entered her parlor, her most favorite room in the world that she'd missed more than anything in all the years away.

"I was about to have coffee. Sit down and let's have a chat while I pour us some. Sugar and cream?"

"Black, one sugar."

"Bree." Madeleine smiled indulgently as she handed her a steaming mug and sat down in front of the girl. "I suggest we start on the right foot, first and foremost. So may I ask, what did St. Giles promise you in return for keeping an eye on me?"

Bree's eyes went big and round in her oval mannequin face. "Keeping an eye on you? I'm just here to help and learn."

Madeleine crossed her legs and took a long sip of instant brew. Disgusted, she put it down on the side table and bit into a shortcrust biscuit to chase away the taste of dishwater from her mouth. "This is foul tasting. I need to see about getting some real coffee into this house."

"I can take you to the grocery store. You'll also need a coffee machine…"

"I wasn't aware that your duties include chauffeuring me around."

"They're not. I just—"

"You just want to let them walk all over you."

That last statement clearly annoyed the little spitfire. Despite the fixed smile on her lips, she was sucking on the inside of her cheeks. Madeleine wondered what words she was biting back. The girl was good at play-acting, but not good enough.

Bree Wynter—what a name for one whose eyes flashed with emerald fire. Although fragments of ice swam in their depths, too. Ice that floated and swayed according to fluctuating moods and thoughts. The girl reminded her so much of a younger her, it unnerved her a little.

Madeleine realized that Bree had not yet fully learned how to tuck her heart beneath her sleeve, how to completely hide the play of emotions from her expression. Perhaps she'd lived an entitled life that hadn't forced these lessons on her at an early age. Or possibly, Madeleine's keen eye hadn't lost its touch.

The thought neutralized her a little, adding salt to a still raw wound. How much time she had lost! Where would she be today if things had turned out differently?

"How do you know St. Giles?" she asked, laughing inwardly as she caught Bree off guard again.

"Through my father. He's pretty much in everyone's business. It's his job, isn't it?"

"You still haven't told me what he promised you." *I'm not going to make it easy for you, girl.*

Bree frowned, then looked resigned. "A flat, and a promotion if things turn out well."

That card was on the table, now for the rest. Some things had to be ironed out before they started this cooperation. Madeleine couldn't afford to keep looking over her shoulder, to have her motives questioned for everything that she did. Still, it would be a gamble, but she'd slim the odds and buy as much dependability from this girl as she could.

"Why should things go wrong?"

"It's just hypothetical."

Madeleine's lips curled in a sardonic smile. "Right. I wonder how long you have been working at headquarters?"

"What does that have to do with anything?"

Madeleine shrugged and swung her crossed leg back and forth. "It's only a question. I think that if we're going to work together for so long, we should try to be friends," she said frankly. "We're both on the same side, aren't we?"

"I suppose we are," Bree muttered as she nibbled on a square of fruit and nut chocolate.

Okay then, I'll cut you some slack. "For me, let's just say it's been more than a couple of big ones."

"Big ones?"

"Centuries, darling. Centuries," Madeleine said on a sigh, patting her hair. "It takes serious work to keep it all together. I don't wake up looking this perfect, you know."

Bree grinned at last, seeming to loosen up. "All right then. I've had my job since the crowning."

"Queen Elizabeth?"

"Victoria."

Madeleine gasped in shock and narrowed her gaze. "They've kept you working in an office that long?"

"I think it takes time to become good at something." Bree blushed under her scrutiny.

"Time, yes, but this is exploitation. Mortals advance ten times more than you have in one lifetime."

Bree looked really flustered then, at a loss for words. Her mouth formed an "o" as though she was about to say something, but then thought better of it.

"I see now, dear girl, you are in complete agreement with me."

"I am grateful to St. Giles and my superiors," she snapped.

"Rubbish. You feel they don't appreciate you enough. You feel that what you're doing is beneath you. Fool yourself if you want to, but don't ever try to fool me."

Bree shot up from her seat like a propelled rocket. "We're wasting time here. When are we starting?"

Madeleine pinned her with an icy stare. "Sit down."

Putting on a truculent expression, the emerald-eyed hellcat crossed her arms and stood her ground.

"Fine," Madeleine said—in that soft tone that those who knew her well recognized as a threat. But this slip of a girl didn't know her nose from her backside. "I'll ask St. Giles to send me somebody else, then. Somebody a little friendlier."

"Then I'll tell him you're a liar, and that you're not cooperating!"

Madeleine could fairly imagine her stomping her foot and huffing in outrage.

"I'd like to point out that I've probably known St. Giles longer than you, darling, and what I know about him are things not even his own mother would know, if he has one."

Bree held on, taking stock. She looked like a brave deer facing a pack of coyotes as she weighed two sets of logic in her mind. What would she do—uphold her loyalty to the bastard St. Giles, or take a chance and play both sides? Madeleine pegged her, because this was precisely what *she* would do in this situation. To regroup and reposition herself for maximum benefit.

Let's drive the nail in the coffin, then. "Sit down, please," she asked in a gentler tone.

Bree complied, albeit not without a grimace.

Madeleine leaned forward and placed a hand briefly on Bree's knee. "Listen please, my dear. I have a feeling there is no love lost between you and St. Giles. The man simply suits your purpose for now. Why not let him believe what you want him to believe?"

"St. Giles gave me this position. I owe him a lot."

"You owe him nothing for holding you back. The same way I owe him nothing for taking away my life! He's a wolf who will eat you alive and spit your bones if he so wishes. A man like that, you must always watch."

Bree slumped forward and hung her head on her hands. "Sheesh, it's day one and I'm already fucking up. Give me a break, please."

"Watch your language, girl," Madeleine said sternly. "Didn't your mother teach you how to behave? I even taught myself all the proprieties."

Bree sat up straight at the tongue-lashing, her face creased. Emotions, like wild bats in a cave, flitted across it.

"*Proprieties?* Who even uses that word anymore?"

"I think you've forgotten where you came from. You think that by living in this modern world and embracing all the change, you have all the answers. But I'll tell you one thing, young lady." Madeleine waved a finger at her, her tone unsympathetic. "With people like St. Giles, you must handle them on their own turf. These men have lived a long time, and you won't win an edge by being cute like ... like those silly actresses on the television."

Bree stared at her in astonishment. "I don't believe you. Haven't you been living as a hermit somewhere?"

Madeleine tsked. "Even as a *hermit*, I've watched shows like *Gossip Girl* and *Glee*. Rather good, actually, but that's all fiction, like the sensational novels of my time."

"That was my time, too, but I moved on. I'm adaptable."

"There's adaptable, and there's stupid. I've watched the news and society gossip, and I know how the world has changed. But the number one thing is that you never forget your roots, not in our case. Once you do, you fail to play their game and then you lose."

White-hot rage formed a sizzling ball in her gut, an instrument of torture that twisted and burned and ate at the fringes of her sanity. Madeleine was familiar with this raw anger that came suddenly and consumed her so viciously. Resentment and a thirst for revenge were at its smoldering center, screaming bloody murder, and she usually calmed those chilling voices by doing repetitive things, such as drafting her spells or creating new drawings of Adrian.

You never forget. You never let go.

You simply deal with it.

"Madeleine?"

Bree's voice cut through the net of madness she'd caught herself in. Madeleine's eyes met the girl's worried ones and an alien tightness took hold in her chest. It had been a long time since someone had cared enough to look at her like that.

"Listen," Madeleine croaked, still a little shaken. "Somehow, we must work together, whether we like it or not. Don't you agree?"

Bree nodded, lips pressed in a thin line.

"I have a proposal for you. You tell me what it is St. Giles wants, and I'll teach you how to get anything you want. *Anything.*"

"You say I can't trust St. Giles, but how can I trust you?"

"Can't you see we're in the same boat? If I fail, you fail. Your fate is linked with mine now."

Bree leaned back, her eyes gleaming with cunning. She wasn't a fool; she was a gambler. Madeleine felt something like pride sneak upon her quite unexpectedly.

"It has to do with a file," Bree said. "They've kept some things secret, but not from me."

"St. Giles told me I'm supposed to come up with a new recipe, some sort of concealing potion for us. I'd never heard such a thing existed."

"It does, and the enemy is using it on us."

"So they have magic, too? Witches?"

"We're not sure, but we found out someone's heading that operation and their intelligence is using the potion as needed. You're backup, meaning your job is to find out what's in it as we haven't managed to get our hands on a sample yet."

"Why me? There are witches aplenty in this world."

"Not in the Cult, and St. Giles swears you're the best. Your skills, he claims, impress him."

"I see," Madeleine said, unconvinced. "I think there's something you not telling me. I also can't believe that Valthrean security is so good that nothing will crack it."

"It's almost impossible to get through that many levels of clearance."

"Yet, you have a mole."

Bree said nothing, but the answer was obvious. And the mole, unfortunately, wasn't high up enough.

"Who's the man responsible for all this?"

"Woman," Bree corrected. "We're not exactly sure of her role and how she got there, but we're working on that. Her name is Emma Deramore."

———

THE TIME HAD COME.

For two hundred years, Emma had missed him with every fiber of her being. Each and every year, decade, and century, life trailed behind her, and people, visions, and experiences came and went as surely as any river ultimately empties into the ocean. Meanwhile, without fail, she'd waited for this moment to come.

Since that fateful day when Madeleine's curse changed their worldly lives, all hopes for the future had withered, but she'd never truly believed him dead. An eternity of ordeals ensued from that encounter with Fate, but things would finally change now.

The last week of waiting had been more painful than a slow walk over blistering coals. Knowing that Adrian was alive and well, living his life a few hundred miles away, and not be able to see and touch him was the most excruciating sacrifice of all.

She looked down at the palm of her right hand and thought of the things the witch in Kent had bade her to do when she first set out to find Adrian. She'd kept those words close to her heart along with her memories. Soon, she hoped she'd have the chance to use that knowledge.

Since her initial meeting with Max, she had not allowed herself to believe this stroke of luck until she'd seen first the news, then the pictures; and even after all that, it felt like a surreal dream until she spoke to Adrian on the phone.

Yet, something that nagged her mind was that if Adrian could be found, what had happened to Madeleine's barrier? Madeleine had made it clear that with her magic she had created a permanent rift between Emma and Adrian to ensure they'd never, ever get close.

Only death could destroy it.

Of course, the news had reported that the British traveler had fallen into a short coma after being hit by a rock during the earthquake in India. When he was transported to another facility or ward, he must have still been in that state, and the reason why the nurse hadn't given her information was that he wasn't in a position to give consent.

That must have been the catalyst. The only explanation Emma could think of was that the spell had eroded over time, starting in Leith. Something must have happened before then to allow them to get to this point. Now, after so long, there was the coma—a macabre imitation of a state of death—and the barrier must have completely fractured.

If everything went according to plan, and she managed to see him, face to face, to touch him, talk to him, she'd have her confirmation.

Now, it would all be over soon, and she was ready. Wasn't she ready!

She stopped by the elevated statue of Anteros in Piccadilly Circus and asked directions from a middle-aged man in a powder-blue and cream Argyll pullover and dark blue blazer. "I'm looking for the Derringstone Museum of Oddities. I was told it is located somewhere around here."

"Certainly, Miss. You're almost there. It's right around the corner on the narrow street past that sandwich shop to the right," said the helpful stranger. His precise, old world manner appeared somehow displaced in their twenty-first century surroundings. Everything about him screamed old-fashioned, stiff-necked Brit to the bone, and she could have easily pinned him as a Valthrean if she didn't know better.

"Thank you, sir."

"My pleasure." An ethereal stream of frost exited his mouth as he spoke.

Emma felt his gaze burn into her back as she hastily turned away. In anticipation of meeting Adrian, she had not taken the usual concoction today. After her admission to Adrian, it would be best to venture out without its protection, but she didn't want to test providence any more than necessary.

A hard winter was settling early upon the city. Although still November, the merry notes of *Deck the Halls* reverberated around her, the anticipatory holiday atmosphere an antithetical foil to the threatening clouds and ominous gray skies. The cheery street decorations dwindled precariously between the buildings, and the dangling lights and random bells performed their own symphony as they daintily tinkled in tune with the occasional gust of wind.

She passed by a shop window outfitted with a long mirror and caught her reflection. It made her wonder what the man she'd just asked directions from had made of her bizarre top-to-bottom black attire. He hadn't been able to hide his discreet perusal of her three-inch boot heels and full-length leather overcoat layered over snug, boot-cut denims and a fitted whaleboned jacket styled in the manner of a Victorian corset. The coat's lapel was adorned with a single fresh red rose—right above her left breast, upon her beating heart.

She'd left her ruler-straight, waist-length ebony hair unbound, but had covered her head with a French beret. As she arrived at a crossroads, the wind cut through the early morning mist to lift the locks in soft, sinewy waves in front of her face. Her pace was assured, aggressive even, her mind intent on her mission. The streets were slippery this time of year, yet she did not falter.

Each hurried step as Emmaline's legs swallowed the distance toward the museum brought her ever closer to him.

To Adrian. To her man.

She turned the corner and a few feet away, a heavy door, painted the color of red brick, met her vision. Her pulse pounded as she approached it and lifted the heavy mermaid-shaped knocker.

Two determined knocks.

The door opened after an interminable wait. Behind it appeared a gray-faced old man with arthritic hands whose eyes were sharp but deeply set, a little too close together. He looked about as old as Methuselah.

"Good morning, Madam. Regrettably, the museum is closed this week for renovations in the new wing. How may I help you?"

"I am here because I have an appointment with Mr. Derringstone. I believe he is expecting me."

"Quite right, yes, my apologies. Please do come in. I will let Mr. Derringstone know you have arrived, Miss...?"

"Deramore, Emma Deramore."

"Right. Miss Deramore, please go ahead and take a seat in the salon right beyond this hall. It's the first door to the right. Would you like me to take your coat?"

"No, thank you."

He bowed curtly and turned away. Emma noted he was surprisingly nimble for his advanced age. He also sounded like the same person who answered the phone the times she called. She didn't note any other activity, human or otherwise, when she entered the building. Perhaps Adrian had given the workers a break.

She walked down the corridor to the salon indicated by Methuselah. The door was ajar and the room was inviting and warm, albeit a little dark. A fresh fire burned in the grate and sparse but tasteful

Christmas decorations graced the heavy mantle. They brought a drop of cheer inside the otherwise gloomy room.

The fireplace itself was quite a sight, carved entirely from an enormous slab of ebony marble. All decorative items had been carefully placed for maximum effect. She looked at the furniture and draperies. The owner had good taste, and he also seemed to have a predilection for rich velvet and damask furnishings.

Her eyes and mind continued to wander until a deep voice stroked her heart and put its beating into overdrive.

"Emma?"

Her back was to the door when she heard him speak her name. She allowed herself to close her eyes to secretly delight in the familiar intonation. Slowly, silently praying for composure, she rotated her body to face the person who had just walked into the room.

Her reaction could not have been stopped by an army of avenging angels. "My God, Adr—" Biting down hard on her lip, she managed to hold his name from escaping on a traitorous huff of breath.

How could she have convinced herself that she could be prepared for this moment? His overpowering Valthrean scent eddied around her, holding her captive. With both their auras enclosed within the small room, its four walls morphed into an airtight vitamin capsule teeming with live, explosive energy.

She should have been able to run to him and claim him, to kiss and embrace him and express her love openly.

And if life were fair, his face wouldn't register a blank right now.

She ruthlessly calmed herself down. The witch had been right. He wouldn't recognize her when he saw her.

"I'm Adam," he said.

She nodded, afraid to speak while pain stabbed her chest repeatedly, in the spot where her heart was soaring and breaking at the same time. After so many trials she'd trudged through, this could possibly be her biggest one yet. It hurt a hundred times more than she anticipated.

She put a check on herself. Her plan *couldn't* fail! It was imperative she not make any mistakes, that she be rational.

"I see you are very punctual. It's good to finally meet you." He walked over to shake her hand.

"My pleasure also, Adam."

She took his hand with barely contained enthusiasm and not a little trepidation. His handshake was firm, the caps of his fingers lightly resting at her wrist. Electricity shot through her at lightning speed and her traitorous pulse beat faster than the wings of a Club-winged Manakin. He must have felt it too because his pupils grew large and he hastily drew his hand back, as if singed from the brief touch.

She could see that his eyes betrayed some curiosity and yes, that quickly, she even sensed his instant attraction to her.

To a woman he deemed a stranger.

Rattled, she removed her beret and ran a hand through her hair.

Get a hold on yourself. How can a woman be jealous of herself?

"I'm looking forward to visiting the museum," she croaked.

"I hope it will live up to your expectations."

"I have no doubts, Adam."

Emma observed him as discreetly as she could while they conversed. He had changed. He looked older. There was no softness in his face, no boyishness left loitering in the sidelines. He was all man—dark, decadent, sexy. The angular shape of his jaw and chin, and the dangerous-looking scar she used to love to trace with her lips, gave him a forbidding air that she longed to unsettle with her touch. His hair was a more intense gold than she remembered and the faint lines fanning from the corners of his eyes gave him a weathered look that contrasted with the smooth-faced, sunny Adrian she knew.

Nonetheless, time had treated him well and added to his charms. He was a large man with a form fit for a god. Not the Norse god she remembered—her kind, sensible Balder—but a darker, more brooding version. Like Thor, the virile god of thunder.

He had it all, the charisma and frame of a physical man—wide shoulders, big arms, narrow hips, and thick, muscled thighs that civilized clothing barely concealed. The sophistication in his demeanor was still there, but with a rough-around-the-edges quality to it. In truth, he'd become handsomer, if that were possible. And he was well dressed in a quality chocolate-colored turtleneck, impeccably tailored black trousers, and polished black Italian leather shoes.

She stifled a sigh. *You're still to die for, my love.*

"Are you sure you have time to show me around? I know we had an appointment but with all the refurbishments going on in the museum, I do not want to inconvenience you."

Please, let me stay.

"Never mind that. I am happy to show you my domain. Shall we?"

Emma followed him out of the room while the air between them popped and sizzled. His aura glowed with colorful luminosity—if she were psychic, she may have seen red for a passionate nature, green for groundedness and love of the outdoors, a light blue to show his search for a serene life. In this moment, she fancied the red overpowering all other hues until they were barely visible.

Thank goodness, he wasn't immune to her. She needed to buy some time and allow them to get reacquainted. It had to work, she had no choice, yet the act of summoning the required patience was difficult to accomplish.

Then he smiled, and his face translated to the faithful image she held fixed in her mind. *That* smile with the dimple on the side. The one that always used to turn her insides to utter mush. And there was no doubt about it—it still did.

"I thought you would probably prefer to peruse our facility first before we sit and talk, so I took the liberty of asking my staff to have the rooms prepared earlier than usual this morning," he said.

He gave her a peculiar look. Her sixth sense picked up a trace of vulnerability, but it was gone before she pinned it.

"Thank you."

She looked away before emotion threatened to overwhelm her.

I want to spend every day with you. Eternity with you.

No matter who you are and what you've become...

Briefly, her eyelids fluttered shut to quash her inner turmoil. She took a deep breath and set herself to rights once again.

"Let's go, then." He extended his hand politely toward the doorway. "After you, Emma."

As she walked by him, his hand rested fleetingly on the small of her back and a wave of memories slammed her, along with the energy from his touch. The last time he had touched her like this...

"Are you sure we haven't met before?" His unexpected question startled her.

"If we'd met in the past, would you forget me?" she responded, inwardly shaking.

Her bold response seemed to startle *him.*

A faint smile touched his sensual lips. "I should think not."

She walked past him, close enough so he would catch a whiff of her rose perfume. She heard him inhale sharply. His instinctual reaction to her shameless flirtation drew an inner smile.

Another pang of jealousy nagged at her when it dawned on her that whatever attraction there was, it was merely physical. But she swiftly subdued the treacherous thoughts. She did not expect him to have lived the life of a monk for two hundred years. He would have taken lovers, but although it made sense, the thought did not make her feel any better.

"So, what's first?" she asked, forcing herself to brighten up.

"Let's take a look inside the Medical Room."

They entered a large space with an eerie feel to it. The dark, wood-paneled walls and subdued lighting spelled gothic mystery. "In here you'll find all sorts of unusual artifacts relating to the medical world."

She perused the array of deformed bodies, fetuses, and strange medical equipment, and wondered how Adrian had gotten his hands on these items. It must have taken years of hard work and generous benefactors. This begged the question—if he had lived a solitary life until now, how did he make it work?

The gruesome collection instilled sadness, rather than curiosity. The fate these people must have endured was not to be discounted; she'd seen too much grief throughout her lifetime to deny this simple truth. People suffering, unable to cope with the blows life dealt them. A feeling of melancholy took residence somewhere deep in her belly.

"I think I've seen enough," she said, averting her eyes.

She regretted those words as soon as she said them because her plan was to bide her time and stay in his company for as long as possible. How could she ever find a way to get to know him if she didn't? The more they were together, the better.

"I'm sorry, I shouldn't have said that," she corrected herself. "It's not fair after the kindness you're showing me."

"I understand. The display would have a disconcerting effect on many visitors. But to those like us, it can seem unbearable," he said with shuttered eyes.

Curiosity nibbled at her. "What about yourself? Does all of this disturb you in any way?"

He considered her question. "I try not to think about it too much." He paused, and linked his hands behind his back. "But I don't believe it's a bad thing to remember reality sometimes, to feel the pain around us and empathize. If one is more aware, then it's easier to make a change. We have too much time at our disposal. It is best to use it wisely."

There was no mockery in his tone. His practical wisdom was one of the things she always loved about him—the ability to dissemble any situation and bring it down to the bare bones, to its simplified state. He always believed that by understanding things better, it was easier to deal with them. This was one of the traits that apparently remained a part of him.

"Good point," she said, as she craned her neck to look up at him.

Had he grown taller?

Their eyes locked and time stood still. The pull was there, undeniable.

Love, I've missed you so! It's me, your Emma. Can't you see?

He was the first to break the spell. "The Crime and History Rooms may be of interest to you. We have some fascinating items in those sections."

His eyes twinkled with appreciation, a gaze that uplifted her. Welcome warmth trickled through her body in titillating waves. "Lead the way."

The History Room was about the same size as the Medical Room, only longer and narrower.

They stopped to look at the remains of what—or who—was called the "Soap Woman." What was left of her face emitted a disquieting message that she had to have suffered terribly in her death.

"The Plague," he confirmed.

"Was she mummified?"

"The soil where her body was buried contained a certain chemical compound that eventually turned her entire body to soap."

"Soap!"

"There is a similar display in Philadelphia, I believe, at the Mütter Museum, of a woman who died of yellow fever. She's baffled scientists for a long time."

"I wonder why this exhibit was not placed in the Medical Room?"

"Because we regard the Plague as an important landmark in British history," he clarified.

They walked on while he explained the rest of the exhibits to her. His knowledge was vast and impressive, but he was never condescending, and entertained all her questions, no matter how basic.

"Now there's something I really want to show you. Your editors will love this. It's in the Crime Room."

Guilt stabbed at her for deceiving him with a phony promise but she had no other choice. Their destination was only a couple of doors away.

"That exhibit over there..." He walked to a glass case fitted on a prominent stand in the center of the room. She followed his lead. "Take a look at this."

The object on display looked like a very old journal, and from the look of the paper and the style, it would be about a couple centuries old. Given her chosen line of work, she had a good eye for assessing the age of things.

He gestured at the yellowed pages. "This was for many years purported to be Napoleon's diary," he said, "but the experts have reason to believe it's a forgery. A very good one, but a forgery."

"How could they be sure? The period looks right."

He gave her an approving nod. "Your assessment is correct. But if you look over here," he indicated a sheet of paper on display to the right, "you'll see a scanned copy of Napoleon's letter of surrender to Wellington, which he sent after his defeat at the battle of Waterloo. Look at the slant of the words and the way he scripts his '*ds*'. They don't match with the writing on the journal."

"So it wasn't written by Napoleon. But why is this forgery so special or odd in any way?"

"Well, although it is a fake, it was written around Napoleon's time, as you have already guessed. Besides, the information contained in this document is of a very confidential and intimate nature. It discloses certain details about the Emperor that we do know to be true today but in his time were not widely known. I believe that this diary was written by someone who was very close to him, even intimate with him, not necessarily as a lover but as a confidant."

"Incredible. How long have you had this item?"

"Not as long as you think. An acquaintance of a business associate was kind enough to donate it to the museum."

"Big stroke of luck, then."

"I would say so." He smiled. "I expect this to be one of the most popular exhibits. I hope that the Naga book of Magic will do just as well as soon as I place it on exhibit."

"Is this your latest acquisition? I'd like to see it."

"Tomorrow, if you're free to meet again."

Yes! She tamped down a scream of joy. "I think I can make time."

He let her roam around the room for a while. When she made the full round of the displays, she returned to his side.

"Tell me about yourself," he asked. "You have recently moved to London from Rome. A bit of a wanderer, I presume."

So he'd skirted her questions and wanted to know more about her. It was just as well because she had no way of digging deeper into *his* life without arousing suspicion.

Unfortunately for the moment, outright sincerity was not an option for her.

"I've been around. A little here, a little there," she said with overly theatrical flair. "I don't want to bore you with details. And a wanderer likes a bit of mystery," she supplied with prim humor.

His eyes crinkled at the corners. "I see you have the gift of wit, as well as many secrets."

"So it seems."

He bent to speak low into her ears, his breath warm and arousing.

"I must find a way to pry them from you then," he responded, then straightened and looked at her as if to say he meant to follow up on that statement.

As they returned to the room where he'd first greeted her, the atmosphere between them was one of tightly coiled tension.

She kept nervousness at bay through conversation. They talked about his decision to purchase this building and turn it into a museum the previous year, and she shared some sporadic details of her work. They talked about everything and nothing, and she was careful not to disclose too much. Still, it felt so good to be with him.

There were moments, when his sense of humor and teasing nature emerged, that gave her glimpses of the Adrian she carried in her heart. Despite everything, the man she loved was still there. He'd just forgotten about *her*, but she'd help him remember...

She pondered the irony of it all while demolishing the delicious home-made lemon poppy seed scones that Hawkins—Methuselah had a name—fetched for them. Happily, she considered they could have made the perfect picture of domesticity as they sat and ate their treats in the silence broken only by not so discreet looks and smiles.

When they finished tea, they lingered, making small talk. It seemed neither wanted their exchange to end. Finally, he got up and offered her his hand.

"Let me escort you to the door. I'm sure you're tired after a long afternoon. We shall meet tomorrow at the same time."

Her hand glided into his and submitted to his steady grip, primed for the chords of awareness and yearning that strummed through her on contact.

"Sorry to harp on this but I keep having this strange feeling that I've met you somewhere."

She lowered her head and pretended to look for something on the tips of her boots. "Perhaps you have."

"But what matters is that you're here now," he said with a smile that dropped a rabble of butterflies straight into her belly and lower still.

Looking back up at him was a mistake because it caused her to start to crumble. She opened and closed her mouth, unable to summon anything to say.

He took pity on her and lifted her hand, turned it palm upwards and kissed it, all while holding her gaze. When she was completely suckered in, her body screaming to throw itself into his arms, he let it go slowly to open the front door.

Gentlemen didn't kiss a woman's hand like this in the twenty-first century. Such an intimate gesture would at best raise eyebrows or even draw ridiculing laughs. Good thing she didn't mind, she thought dreamily.

He cocked his head, gave her an assessing look, and made her feel like a puzzle he could not solve. "Until tomorrow afternoon."

"Yes."

She held his gaze, sketched his dear face on the canvas of her mind, reluctant to let him go for even an instant. It was impossible to resist reaching out to him that way, at least for a moment, to send him a wordless message by allowing undisguised happiness to shine forth through her eyes.

CHAPTER 14

"If you can look into the seeds of time,
And say which grain will grow, and which will not,
Speak."
[Macbeth, Act I, Scene III]

THE NEXT DAY, ADAM SAT BEHIND HIS DESK IN A FUTILE ATTEMPT TO focus on work. He stared at an invoice from the contractor company that was handling his renovations. In the half hour since he'd had it in front of him, the numbers made no sense and the typed list of supplies could have been written in Mandarin. At last, he gave up and set the paper aside while he took a peek at his watch—the latter an act he found himself doing every two minutes.

Last night, he'd spent way too much time thinking about a certain woman with almond-shaped brown eyes and silky ebony hair. A woman whose guileless smile and lithe grace held sufficient vivacity to heat an igloo in the Antarctic.

One encounter with Emma and she had already slunk under his skin.

Her beauty was undeniable, but many women were beautiful in specific ways. What haunted him most was her gaze, the way she sometimes looked at him with expressive intensity and an inkling of sadness. There were signs of longing in those stolen looks, as though he unwittingly held the only key to some secret drawer locked away in her soul.

It was not like him to fall head over heels under a woman's spell. Marie had taught him that lesson the hard way. In addition, there was the fact that it was uncanny to be so attracted to a woman he'd just met in person. Their phone interactions had been entirely businesslike, yet, even across the distance, there were unfathomable instances when the attraction between them was as palpable as the slick leather of his office chair.

What was this woman doing to him? *Why* was she so special? True, she was a Valthrean, but it wasn't all. This puzzling notion kept nudging at him from the depths of his subconscious. She created a yearning within him that was alien and far from comfortable. It tugged at his senses so powerfully that his perfectly built house of cards was threatening to fold around him. However, he knew from bitter experience that nothing good would come from trusting someone completely.

Still, it was even worse if a man wasn't brave enough to be true to himself.

After Marie, he'd preferred superficial relationships that didn't require him to compromise his way of life. Things were much easier and cleaner that way. No messy breakups, no second guessing, no unwarranted risk.

But Emma was different. He felt in his bones that he'd be making a big mistake if he let her exit his life before taking the opportunity to find out about her. When he saw her today, he wanted more than an impersonal discussion about work.

He wanted to get to know her.

Adam didn't know what to call this emotion that made him weak inside. He only knew that he couldn't remember ever feeling this way. But then, his younger years were still a mystery to him.

Perhaps before the darkness, something, someone, had existed in his life.

Someone like the woman in his dreams.

The ring of the brand new front door buzzer that had been installed that morning prevented him from drilling further into this line of thought.

His gut told him it was her. She was early.

Both eager and hesitant, Adam took his time to go and meet her. Hawkins would have showed her to the parlor and offered her refreshments, so it would not be impolite to leave her a few moments alone. Meanwhile, he tried to decide what to make of the situation.

Should he let things be or should he ask her out? The former would bring regrets, the latter a multitude of complications.

In the end, he decided he'd be all right as long as he kept the reins of their interaction firmly in his hands. He could not afford to lose control, and he was not going to.

The lunacy of his resolution dawned on him the moment he entered the sitting room and set eyes on her. She was pacing back and forth across the room. When he entered, she started so violently Adam thought she'd eject into the ceiling. She nervously rubbed her palms against her sides and released a breath.

That face. Adam felt his lungs squeeze as his own breath was knocked right out of them.

"Adam, it's you. I apologize for being early." She spoke in a siren's lilt. Clasping her hands together, she took a couple of steps in his direction.

Pleasure arced through him when he heard his name come out of her lips. Her passionate, personal tone caused his stomach to make a wild somersault.

"No need to apologize."

Today, she wasn't wearing a hat. Instead, she'd gathered her hair in a thick ponytail and draped the long locks over her left shoulder where they fell, insouciant, to her breast. A belted, waxed-cotton jacket stopped above interminable legs faultlessly snuggled in indigo-wash jeans.

She wore no jewelry, only a fresh-snipped rose pinned next to the funnel collar of her jacket. Yesterday, she'd also worn a rose on her coat—an interesting preference that fired up his curiosity.

"I can wait if you are busy," she offered with an apologetic expression.

"Certainly not. I'm glad you're here, and my work can wait. Have a seat, Emma." He motioned to the chairs.

Her mouth curved slightly upward. When she settled into an angled tub armchair, the exotic contour of her high cheekbones and the gentle curve of her jaw line came into relief. Distracted by an overwhelming physical urge to crush her to him and kiss her senseless, he stuffed his hands into his pockets and reined himself in.

"Has Hawkins offered you something to drink?" he asked, rallying a level tone.

"Yes, thank you."

Her full, bow-shaped lips moved sensuously around those three simple words, her diction unhurried and refined.

"Good. The book is in my study. I'll go get it, if you excuse me," he said, as he started to feel that his resolve to keep the upper hand was doomed to go to hell in a handcart. Fast.

He retraced his steps to the door and caved in to the temptation to turn back around and stare at her. It caused his body to react in wholehearted excitement. In a flash of instant awareness, cerulean fixed on brown.

Such striking, soulful eyes.

He'd seen a pair like them before. He even conjured dreams of them.

That's why he couldn't get her out of his mind.

Shaken by her resemblance to his nighttime Venus, he opened the door and rushed out as though the hounds of Hades were after him. What an outlandish notion to even imagine it could be the same woman. Merely a coincidence, nothing more. If it weren't for his interest in Emma, he'd never give the idea a second thought.

He needed to clear his head.

Adam deliberately bounded to his study and passed his cluttered desk to reach the wall behind it. Gripping the gilded corner of the hanging frame to an oversized watercolor landscape in the style of Turner, he pulled it toward him. It opened with a click to reveal the lock to a temperature-controlled, steel safe.

His fingers flew over the electronic keypad to plug the combination. With efficient speed, he retrieved a large wooden box and put the painting back against the wall. He returned to the parlor, cradling the box under in his arms.

He placed it flat on the coffee table and sat down on the sofa in front of it. "Perhaps you wish to join me here so you can see better."

When he opened the box and lifted the heavy book, he made sure to hold it from both ends. Carefully, he lowered the fragile manuscript on the table.

Emma got up and joined him on the sofa. She leaned forward to get a closer view of the Book of Magic of the Nagas. The tome was wrapped protectively in cloth. He unfolded the protective material, trying not to think too much of how receptive his body was to her closeness. She smelled of roses and woman and another, lulling scent.

Lavender.

He shifted uncomfortably in his seat, his trousers suddenly tight.

"I'm not going to open it until the expert sees it but even the cover is a work of art, I think. You're the first to actually see it since I've had it."

As soon as he uttered the statement, he realized its truth. She was the first he'd deigned to share this discovery with. The thought disconcerted him a bit.

"It's beautiful," she agreed.

He told her about his research into Appollonius of Tyana and the philosopher's adventures that took him to East India, including his encounter with the Naga sages in the Kashmir who spearheaded his learning in the spiritual and esoteric arts. He explained how these were a people with long-standing customs and traditions and how they had perfected the art and science of magic to a fault.

He also went in a little detail about their history, relating the story of the Snake King and his adversary, Emperor Asoka, the importance of the Temple of the Sun, and the myths surrounding the birth of the city of Srinagar. Finally, he told her how the Naga King Aravala was ultimately defeated by Asoka, who brought Buddhism to the Kashmir region.

Emma tensed beside him. "Aravala, you say? What do you know about him?"

"According to Eastern mythology, he was a ruthless king with immortal powers. I have not had much opportunity to focus my studies on him but it's an interesting legend, nonetheless."

She slid her hands between her knees and kept her eyes fixed on the book, but her mind seemed elsewhere. Her brows knit together in a frown. Lines of furious deliberation appeared on her brow while she chewed on the inside of her cheek.

"Are you all right? I hope I'm not boring you out of your mind with my rambling."

"Emma?" He nudged her when she didn't respond. "Are you there?"

"Sure," she uttered in a small voice, deliciously biting her bottom lip. "I was just thinking of something."

"A man always loves to hear a woman admit to thinking of other things while he's speaking to her," he teased.

She grunted. "I meant I was thinking of what you just said. Are you aware that the story of King Aravala is strongly connected to the Valthrean roots?"

"No, I'm not."

"Aren't you curious to learn about our origins?"

She shouldn't have said that.

"No," he retorted, hostility getting the better of him. "I didn't sign up for this. All I'm interested in is minding my own business."

The blood drained from Emma's face. "But don't you see? It's our duty to learn so we can protect ourselves."

"I can take care of myself and I don't need a bunch of secret society militants to tell me what to do or how to live my life."

Get a hold on yourself, man. Change direction.

He muttered a curse. "I don't mean to be hard on you."

"As you said, it's none of my concern. Please tell me more about the book," Emma atoned, waving a white flag. Strokes of embarrassment and desperation brushed her face.

"All right," he said, combing back his ruffled feathers and accepting her peace offering. "Your wish is my command."

She edged closer to him, part of her thigh flush against his. ... Shaken by the sense of intimacy, he labored doubly hard to school himself into maintaining a modicum of detachment.

"The script on the cover is in Vedic Sanskrit. This was the old tongue before the introduction of Classical Sanskrit and even the influence of Pali, the Buddhist language which was prevalent at the time in the region where this was found," he said, as his hand hovered deferentially above the symbols.

He wanted that hand to be on her bare skin. It would be soft as downy swan feathers...

"Are you saying that the people Appollonius came into contact with spoke a different language than that written in this book?" she asked, seeming engrossed by his explanation. Her face was more relaxed now.

"I'm saying that they likely spoke a more advanced form, if you wish, an evolution of the language," he corrected. "Vedic Sanskrit is a precursor to the classical version. However, this would also prove that whoever wrote this book preferred to adhere to ancient traditions, especially in regard to their use of written language."

"Have you had the text translated yet?"

"I engaged an expert in linguistics to assist me. Dr. Koul holds a professorship at the University of Mumbai but is currently on sabbatical. I'm flying him over next month and he'll be working from my office. It was fortunate for me that he accepted this engagement."

"How did you get him interested in the project?" An errant lock of hair broke loose from her ponytail and fell over her face. She pushed it quickly back behind her ear before he satisfied the impulse to do the same thing.

"He was a close associate of Dr. Abid Kothedar, who passed away after putting this priceless book in my hands. Abid respected him, and that's good enough for me."

Her hand was on her lap, mere inches from his. It would be so easy to lay his fingers on hers and caress them gently, to delight in the softness of her skin and mark out the structure of the delicate bones.

"You met Dr. Kothedar in India, I presume?"

"Yes, I met him during my travels," he said vaguely.

"He must have trusted you very much if he willed the Book of Magic to you."

"He didn't will it to me," he confessed. "I just happened to be with him when he lost his life." Although he hadn't known the man well, the memory of Abid and his tragic fate still tore him up inside. Such a brilliant mind didn't deserve to die that way. Adam had never discussed his experience with anyone, until now, with Emma.

Another first.

"Good grief. What happened?" Her tone held genuine concern.

"I had just arrived at his home in Jabala when a massive earthquake practically leveled the town. There were so many dead and wounded people that I lost count of the bodies lying all over the place. While Abid and I tried to make an exit, the road caved in, and huge rocks started to tumble down the mountain and created a barrier."

"You had no way out."

"We went back to find a safe place in the village, an impossible feat. Some people needed help. We were about to lend a hand when a large piece of rock hit Abid with extreme force. He never stood a chance."

"Oh, Adam, that's terrible," she said. Her eyes were bright with compassion and an offer of comfort.

It was getting harder to keep his distance from her but her sympathy rankled him. He'd never needed anyone to console him, to get him through the deep-rooted pain that lived in a corner of his soul. Being responsible for himself was a cheap and easy habit.

"Before he died, he said he wanted me to have the book," he said gruffly. "This was his baby, his discovery. It's the genuine article. Giving it the place of honor in this old place is the least I can do for him."

"What happened to you then?" she persevered.

"It's a bit of a blur. Like Abid, I got smacked in the head and ended up in hospital." He looked away from the hurt printed on her face. "I fell in a short coma."

"How is that possible, as a Valthrean—?"

"Perhaps something inside me refused to wake up. Perhaps I was tired and wanted to remain that way. I couldn't say. I hung around for a while after recovery, thinking things over." Too much information, but he couldn't hold back the pain that laced every word.

"Was that when you decided to come to England?"

He nodded.

"Enough talk of the past now," he said, buckling down.

It was clear that she wanted to know more about him, but with his last statement, he'd closed up her inroads. How could he explain to her that he couldn't remember part of his life, that he couldn't even remember how old he was unless he went by what Marie had told him?

"So you opened this museum," she said.

"Well, I had been toying with the idea of doing something like this for a while, and when the right opportunity came along, I took it."

"You have quite a story. What other places did you visit before India?" she probed, trying to get back on the saddle. She was certainly a persistent little vixen. How effortless it would be to let those big round eyes drag him down from grace and have him play to their tune.

Effortless, but fatal.

"It's your turn to tell me something about yourself," he said, turning the tables.

"Nothing I could tell you would possibly trump what you just told me." Guardedness swept over her face for the briefest of moments, quickly upturned by inscrutability.

So the lady was no stranger to mystery, either. What was she hiding?

"That's up to me to decide," he ruthlessly insisted.

"What do you want to know?"

"How long have you lived in Rome?"

"A few years."

"What made you decide to stay there?"

She took a little too long to respond, which gave him pause. "It's a city full of history and culture. I love it."

Adam pondered that response. She managed to say a lot of nothing in two sentences.

"There's lots of history in England, too," he countered.

"It's for the same reason you traveled, to see somewhere new."

"Where are you from, then?"

"Does it matter? So much time passed I barely remember any more," she evaded.

How could she say that? "It always matters where one is from," he argued with conviction.

"Perhaps, but now I'm alone and not answerable to anybody, so I don't know what the big fuss is about."

Was that edginess in her tone? He must have hit a nerve.

"I understand."

Remorse leaped into her face. He felt like a boor for purposely upsetting her.

"Please forgive me." She placed a hand on his arm. "I didn't mean to be rude. It's just that I am not used to talking about myself much, but that's no excuse."

"It's all forgotten."

The heat from her hand soaked through his sweater and penetrated his skin. He looked at her slender fingers curled over his forearm and then into her eyes. Again, he was sucked into their meandering depths. How long would it take him to pry all the hidden secrets from them, from *her*?

A slow, uncertain smile started to form on her face. When he gave her hand a reassuring squeeze, she broadened her smile. It transformed her face, blinded him.

Before he could arrest himself from blurting out banalities, he confessed, "You have a brilliant smile, the most beautiful I've ever seen. It becomes you."

If he'd betted with Fate he'd resist the urge to say those words, he'd have lost miserably.

Her tongue darted out absently to lick her lips. The guileless act caused him to stifle a groan. He had forgotten what it felt to be so attuned with the physical and emotional vibes of another person. His mouth went dry and he was painfully aware of his Adam's apple bobbing up and down.

Of their own volition, his next words rolled off his tongue. "What are you doing this evening?"

His hand never left hers.

She tightened her hold on his arm. "What?" she whispered.

Her knuckles brushed under his fingers. His thumb doodled lazy circles on the back of her hand.

"I asked what you're doing this evening."

"I have no plans."

"Care to have dinner with me? I've been working way too hard and need some cheering up. Believe it or not, I must also eat once in a while for fear of extinguishing myself."

He looked down at their hands. This *thing* he was feeling begged further exploration and he wasn't one to fear challenges. "So, what do you say? Join me later?"

He hoped he wouldn't scare her off because she looked suddenly fragile when she followed his eyes to his big hand covering hers. Then she recaptured his gaze.

"I'd say let's do it."

"Do you like Indian food? I know this little place near Soho where they make the most amazing Tandoori."

"Love that."

"I can pick you up for dinner at eight. If you're up to it, we'll follow with drinks at a quiet jazz club that's right next door to the restaurant."

"I'd like that, too."

Acting subdued, she gave him her townhouse address and got up, a little unsteady on her feet. "I'll let you get back to work, Adam. Thank you for showing me your treasure."

"My pleasure," he said as he stood. He shook her hand, held it a bit longer than necessary, and kissed her on the cheek, confirming that she was indeed smooth as silk. As he reluctantly put polite distance back between them, he wondered what the rest of her skin would feel like under her clothes. She seemed to have retreated into herself, shut off in a private world he wasn't allowed in.

"I'll see you tonight, then." Her hand left his, which filled him with disappointment and an ungodly urge to recover that physical link between them.

"Tonight," he said, letting her go instead.

———

MADELEINE MANAGED to open her front door holding five large shopping bags in each hand.

"I've never seen a trail of shops that long in my life!" she exclaimed as she set the bags on a bench in the hallway. "I'm glad I wore comfortable shoes so we could walk all the way to Harrods from Oxford Street. That must be my favorite."

"And when it gets really cold, we can go to Westfield. All you want under one roof, including lunch." Bree had followed her in, her arms also loaded, and stopped at Madeleine's blank stare. "You've never been to a mall, have you?"

Bree shook her head on a pained sigh. "So sad. I see there's a lot of catch up you need to do."

"Well, I know what a mall is. I've seen it on TV."

"It's not the same!" Bree countered as she walked toward the kitchen. "I'll go prepare the plates for the lamb curry."

Madeleine sorted herself in front of the hallway mirror, pleased to see her face flushed with a healthy glow. She'd forgotten the reviving smell and taste of charged city air, and the feeling of walking among many people.

What a welcome distraction from her obsessive thoughts of the last few days. Ever since Bree had mentioned that name, Emma Deramore, her hunger for revenge had grown until she changed to a ravenous beast on the prowl. A beast that hadn't eaten a crumb in over two hundred years.

She knew it was *her.*

She knew it deep down, like bottom feeder fish recognize the floor of the ocean and its hidden treasures and traps. With all the force of her base instincts, she refused to consider it a coincidence.

Bree had promised to keep her informed of any updates to the Deramore file and so far, she had kept her word. Said woman was in England, and she'd met a certain Adam Derringstone at some museum in central London.

Emma and Adam.

Could it be?

No, surely not. Her spell was foolproof. Under no circumstances could they be reunited. Unless...

Unless her magic had flaws. Unless something had happened to circumvent it.

Soon after, Bree gave her the concrete proof she needed. A trip to Emma's lodgings and the chance to see her nemesis for herself. Emma had done so well, she'd snagged some elegant accommodation in Mayfair. What a shock to her system! The sight of shiny black hair and a tall hourglass figure, and Emma's doe-like features taunted Madeleine still—awakened her demons. Not much had changed about the chit, except her dress and a certain maturity stamped on her face and the way she moved. The hardest thing for Madeleine was keeping a distance, but to be foolhardy was self-defeating.

For days, she deliberated this unpredicted situation from all angles and came up none the wiser. Thinking was going to get her nowhere except paralyze her to the point where action would be impossible. What she needed was to come up with a new, stronger spell, and in the meantime, a solution for damage control.

Madeleine was certain of one thing. In the end, she'd win both Adrian and the favor of the Cult. She walked to the kitchen where the spicy stew was served with a side of naan bread.

Bree grinned at Madeleine's nod of approval. "Microwave works wonders. A couple of minutes and *poof!,* you have a nice, warm meal."

"I love a world where you can buy anything ready to eat. Back in old days, we had only the pie shops or you had to go at an inn or pub.

But to take a cooked meal like this home, that was unheard of. Of course, we had cooks…"

"Who needs a cook in the house when you can easily get takeout? Plus it's less messy and impresses a man if you tell him you made it yourself." Bree winked at Madeleine, drawing a throaty laugh from her, then her eyes went big as saucers. "Oh, and there's delivery! Tomorrow, we'll order pizza."

"Order?"

"Kind of like when you were at the abbey. You told me people just got you what you wanted to eat, but on certain times. Delivery is way better. You order whenever you want, and food comes to your door still warm."

"I see."

"As I said, Madeleine, lots to catch up on. *Lots*." Bree stressed the last word with a sneaky look. If she had glasses, she'd be looking at her above them.

An hour passed in pleasant conversation before they went back to Madeleine's parlor. Bree said she'd never seen the chalice at work, utterly fascinated after Madeleine gave her a demonstration with a potion that would change the color of her eyes from green to blue for twenty-four hours, with just a saliva sample and the tip of a fingernail. It worked almost instantly.

"You said just a day and then they'll change back?"

"Yes."

"What if I want to snag a guy? How do I do that?"

"You have to bring me something that belongs to him. Something personal, and ideally, a few strands of hair or an item of clothing."

"Now how do I get that? If I got that close, I wouldn't need help."

"I thought you were resourceful," Madeleine teased as Bree leaned against the solid table and crossed her legs.

"Sounds like a load of crap to me."

Madeleine rolled her eyes. "Why, is there someone you want?"

"No, I was just being hypothetical."

"I noticed you like to say many hypothetical things, but I prefer concrete things. How about finding an attractive man?"

"Men have overblown egos, so one has to be selective," Bree theorized, tapping her fingers on the table. "Once I'm in Knightsbridge, I'll move in better circles…"

"Ah, the girl is ambitious. Good trait."

Madeleine washed her hands in a bowl of water with squeezed lemon, then dried them with a clean hand towel. She picked up her locket and started to put it back around her neck.

Bree moved toward her and motioned to the piece of jewelry. "You always have that on. Is it special?"

The young woman's eyes glowed with interest, but Madeleine held on to her golden treasure in a gesture of protection. She wrapped her fingers around it, almost as tight as the vise closing around her heart.

"It's only something I've had for a long time. I wear it because it's a habit."

"Can I see it?"

Why?—the question was on the tip of Madeleine's tongue. *Why must you glimpse my secret, my shame?*

Unbidden, tears formed at her eyes—seeped through like liquid through a hairline crack at the bottom of a bottle. With trembling hands, she relinquished the locket to Bree and turned away, angry with herself, angry with the world.

Simply, angry and desperate.

"This is lovely, such craftsmanship. Can I open it?"

No!

"Go ahead," Madeleine spoke through gritted teeth, although it was the last thing she wanted to say.

The seconds that ticked from then seemed interminable. She brushed away the tears, the pain, and worked at replacing them with ice. She was good at this—at turning a hot emotion into something that could serve her better.

"Is this hair in this pouch? It's very fine, like baby hair."

She turned toward Bree, somewhat composed, and saw her touch the locket's contents delicately with a perfectly manicured fingertip. More than ice, hoar frost had formed in a spider web around Madeleine's heart. Through the gaps of the crystallite strings, though, an opposite warmth radiated toward the beloved object that Bree now held in her hand. Ever since Madeleine had had it, no one else had touched it. No one had known of it.

It had been hers, and hers alone. A solitary secret to hold close, to safeguard from the very dark world she'd chosen.

"Yes," she let out, and suppressed the urge to snatch her possession back.

Madeleine expected to see the same interest on Bree's face she'd seen before. She'd braced for that impersonal expression—the look of someone who wants information that, really and truly, means nothing to them except to satisfy a sense of flavorless curiosity.

But to her surprise, her companion's expression was far from detached. Bree swallowed hard, as though something had stuck in her throat, and she looked about to cry.

"What is it?" Madeleine asked softly, feeling the air crackle between them with a violent energy that, if visible, would rival that which the chalice could produce.

Please, Bree. Don't ... don't do this. Close that locket. Put this behind you.

Some invisible force pulled with a cruel insistence at Madeleine's heartstrings. Yet, she couldn't acknowledge the fact, for if she did, she'd have to think thoughts she didn't want to think. She'd have to wonder what this strange connection she felt to Bree right at this moment meant...

She stared at the girl's beautiful blue eyes. Those eyes were really green, like hers.

Who are you, Bree?

Silly question. She knew who Bree was; she just didn't want to have this conversation.

"I don't know much about your family. Who does this belong to?"

"I..." *You just had to go and ask, did you, Bree?* "That was my daughter's."

There, she'd let it out. The memories ricocheted from space and time, back into her head—the daughter she'd birthed and never seen; the kind midwife who'd brought her a lock of her baby's hair after they informed her she hadn't survived the birth.

That soft, fine hair she'd never, ever parted with. Her strength, her solace. Her deepest regret.

Never again had she ever felt love like she'd felt that day, for a person she had never seen or held in her arms. Never again had she wanted for her life to change so she could care for a tiny being that came from her flesh, from her blood. And never again had she ever felt such surprise at her heart's capacity to feel a pure emotion as that love for her child—because it had been the one and only time.

Never again.

All she had left of that being was this—a few strands of dead hair. She should have thrown it away. She shouldn't have carried this terrible weakness with her all the days of her life.

Madeleine held back a sob. Her throat burned with the need to let go, to purge her pain. "My daughter's. She's dead."

Bree stared at her, mouth agape. The locket slipped from her hand, as though her fingers had lost their nerves. It fell with a thud on the carpet. Madeleine was thankful that Bree wasn't standing on the stone tile a couple of feet to her left, or it would have broken into pieces. She held the small pouch containing the hair in a fisted grip.

"Dead?" she said hoarsely.

Madeleine rubbed her arms against a shudder. "Yes. They told me she died after I gave birth. I never saw her but they gave me that."

"And you kept this with you?"

Stop this, please. You're killing me.

Madeleine couldn't respond. What reason should she give for holding on to something like that? Should she say outright that she loved her daughter, a person that never was?

"I think we should go back to work. Dinnertime's in a couple of hours."

Flustered, Bree picked up the locket and placed the pouch inside, then handed it back to Madeleine with shaking hands.

Curious, Madeleine looked at her face that seemed drained of blood. Black circles had appeared in front of her eyes. Fear and weariness danced on her face.

"If you're not up to it, we can stop for today."

"No," Bree said, hooking her gaze, blunt emotion in the depths of hers. "I want to stay."

———

EVENING SEEMED a long way away when Emma left. As the hours ticked by, Adam felt like a Titanic survivor on the day of the tragedy, waiting for the Carpathia to come to the rescue and pull him out of the freezing water.

Only, the water he sank in tested for scorching hot. He burned. He couldn't stop thinking about her.

Underneath the strong, guarded veneer was a woman capable of deep passion and empathy. She appeared to be more perceptive and understanding than anyone he knew could ever be. Somehow, astoundingly, she *got* him, and not only because she was like him.

Could this be a biased observation spurred by his primitive attraction to her? His insane desire to take her hard and fast? No, it couldn't be.

On his way to Emma's lodgings, he looked around him from the taxi cab window, his heart lighter than it had been in a long time. Snowflakes dotted the urban landscape that evening and as the street lights and decorations were lit for full effect, they created a picturesque backdrop to one of the most magical seasons of the year. Despite the slippery roads, harried late Christmas shoppers still took to the streets, and rushed to complete their errands so they could go back to their private celebrations.

The pretty picture was so far removed from the image of the tragedies Adam had experienced in Jabala. In that instant, he wondered how the farmer he'd helped the day Abid died was doing. He remembered how he and others had spent eighteen hours scraping and digging until their cut and bloodied fingers turned numb. Their efforts were finally rewarded when the wife and baby came out of their ghastly grave, weak, dehydrated and more than a little traumatized. It was sheer luck—or destiny—that they were still alive.

Seeing those people safe had made him proud. He wanted to feel that way again. The events in India had put a different sort of mark on him. He was blessed to be alive, and he was blessed to now own Abid's treasure. Perhaps one man's curse could eventually become another man's purpose, and what was more important than purpose?

Without purpose, life meant nothing.

He needed it as much as the next person. Without it, his existence would be futile. Going everywhere and nowhere, striving to blend in a sea of families and communities, ensuring he wouldn't stand out and therefore, never meaning anything to anybody. His circumstances forced limitations when it came to building intimate relationships with others, but he didn't want those limitations. Yet, there were times when, God help him, he couldn't live with them.

Somehow, he knew at some deep level that the beautiful creature who often visited his nocturnal dreams—the woman who looked just like Emma—wouldn't want such a fate for him, either.

The thought of the two being so alike shook him to the core. This must be what fascinated him about her. He of all people had reason to believe the power of magic and alchemy. Perhaps his perception of things was becoming twisted. Thrawn, warped, to the point where he couldn't distinguish dreams from reality.

This evening, however, none of that mattered because he had his purpose—to discover Emma. He wanted to know where she came from, how she came to be a Valthrean, what kind of life she lived.

Everything in its own time.

Thrust back into the present when the car hit a pothole, Adam observed the Yuletide activity manifesting around him. He would have been caught up in the milieu, let himself be carried away by the holiday spirit, were it not for the fact that he had lived through so many Christmases he barely gave it much attention any more. For some reason, this time of the year tended to induce him into a strange melancholy. He refused to drag himself in the whole excitement of things, except, perhaps, today.

Something had happened to him today. Emma Deramore was a mystery he wanted to unravel, a whirlwind that put a dent in his routine composure. The acute and varied emotions she provoked in him were absolute proof to a side of himself he thought he didn't possess.

He wasn't yet sure what to make of that, what to make of *her*. Despite the voice of reason that told him he needn't get too attached, he couldn't shrug off the thought that she was different and worth pursuing.

The truth was that since he laid eyes on her, and earlier still, since he first spoke to her, he had been driven by an unconquerable desire to have her. The catch was, he had no excuse to stop it from happening. In fact, a relationship could work between them because she would be able to understand who he was.

What he was.

And if he got too involved, she could destroy him.

His brain was a tangled mess. For this reason, he had to exercise caution. Long ago, he'd promised himself he'd never stick around long enough to see mortal friends and loved ones yield to the ravages of time and then die. He refused to deal with that kind of pain. So he accepted that his life was a curse not to be trifled with, and that he was destined to live it in solitude, with the occasional distraction to keep him from brooding too much about it.

But in Emma's presence, his composure hung by a gossamer thread. He should not underestimate this woman's power over him because he already knew it was going to be damn near impossible to keep away from her. No matter where he went or how much time passed, she'd still be somewhere living her life. And if she wasn't with him, another man would have her.

Never, not while he wanted her with this raw, visceral need that ruled him beyond sound judgment.

What she made him realize was that he'd give up eternity to be with someone he could cherish and love—that was the kind of danger she presented.

Love. What did he know about that?

Unfortunately, he couldn't see a way out, a fork in the road. Perhaps after he slept with her, this baffling obsession, this madness, would end.

The driver pulled to a stop. "We are at your destination, sir."

Adam opened the taxi door. "Wait here, please. I'll be just a minute."

"Yes, sir."

The townhouse was a charming and elegant affair, a small gem in the heart of the opulent Marble Arch area. While he wondered how she'd acquired such enviable lodgings, he went up a few steps to the door and rang the bell.

Moments later, a staggering, olive-skinned vision in a becoming shade of deep red greeted him with a welcoming smile. Emma wore an eye-popping knee-length vermilion sheath and matching suede heels with black trim. A fresh red rose nestled at her nape, above a long, shiny braid of hair. She looked like a ravishing flamenco dancer.

He stood rooted to the spot. "You're beautiful."

"Thank you," she said shyly, blushing.

He reached out to touch her cheek. "Ready to go?"

"Wait inside," she said, motioning him to get out of the cold. "Let me get my coat."

"The taxi is waiting," he said.

He did not trust himself to go beyond the hallway. Should they linger, he wouldn't be held accountable for what happened between them. For pinning her to the wall and kissing her senseless, then tear her clothes off and take her on the carpeted floor. Give her pleasure until she was putty in his arms.

Fortunately, it didn't take her long to join him. She carried a black bundle over her arms.

"Allow me," he said.

He helped her put on her velvet coat and fasten the antique gold buttons. In that garment, which was fitted at the waist and cut wider at the hem, she looked exquisite. Thankfully, the material seemed warm enough for a wintry London evening. She grabbed an embroidered black scarf from a coat stand and loosely twisted it around her neck, then let him usher her outside. He bundled her in the cab and gave the restaurant address to the driver.

Dinner went by in a flash. They talked about their tastes in music and art, discussed their favorite landmarks in the city of London, and Emma regaled him with stories about her experience at the Maastricht fair. They steered clear of any topic that would encourage them to delve into revealing aspects of their past. Emma delighted him with her enthusiastic way of describing things. She was full of life, and he never tired of watching her animated chatter.

After dessert, he caught her stifling a yawn. "Let's skip the club. I can see you're tired."

"No, really. I'm enjoying this."

"We can do dinner again tomorrow. Perhaps we can talk about the interview."

He was an idiot. Now why did he go around and say that?

In an interview, he was supposed to talk about himself, to bare his soul to the world, and that's one thing he wouldn't do.

"I thought you didn't give interviews."

"I'm reconsidering my decision, but I still haven't thought this out."

Damn right.

If nothing else, he got *that* right. Fact was that he'd acted on impulse. He needed an excuse to see her again and he let himself be guided by something other than his brain, put everything on the line to buy more time with her.

"When will you decide, then?"

"I promise you'll be the first to know." He smiled, and drank the last of his wine.

"I hope you'll trust me enough to tell me everything, one day," she said meaningfully. She placed her hand on his and gave him an unflinching look.

His fingers pressed hard on the stem of his glass when a bolt of lightning branched through them from her touch.

She didn't know what she was asking. It would require that he go out on a limb and risk everything for her.

To risk her look of pity or disbelief when he told her the truth about him—that he didn't know who he was.

However, some risks were worth taking. Was this one of them?

He turned his hand to hold hers, palm to palm. Her fingers closed around his, embraced him. That simple act told him things would fall into place.

Something clicked inside him.

A door unlocked, a weight lifted. He was a lost ball in high weeds, but oddly, it didn't feel so bad. For once, he didn't feel alone, and he hadn't realized how much he craved the sensation.

They left the restaurant. After hailing a cab, he saw her home. They spent most of the way in comfortable silence. When they arrived, he bid the driver to wait for them about half a block down the road. Her fingers loosely entwined with his as she matched his footsteps to her door.

She fumbled for the keys and pulled them from her bag.

"So ... thanks for a nice evening," she said.

She hesitated at the door and he looked down at her, saw in her an acknowledgement of something deeper, far-reaching, between them.

The air around them crackled. They locked themselves in a bubble, left the cold outside.

His gaze fell to her softly parted mouth. Slowly, he pulled her close and lowered his head to hers. He stopped a few inches from her lips and felt her warm, steamy breath on his face. She never tried to move away, only returned his stare with naked hunger.

They stood transfixed while his awareness of her grew a thousand fold. Nothing else existed but her. In the hidden part of his mind, he'd already skipped the preliminaries. His animal self was branding her, plundering her lips, claiming her in searing hot passion. The beast wanted out.

He lifted his gloved hand to her cheek and cradled her face. Emma clutched at his shoulders and chest like a lifeline; her eyes misted and brimmed with things left unsaid.

"Please," she gasped. "Kiss me."

What else do you want, mate? A written invitation?

Without a word, he took her lips and she opened to him with startling urgency. Their mouths fed off of each other, while his hands explored, pulled, caressed, fueled the insane passion that consumed him. He tasted her sweetness, and it had him roaring inside.

"Emma," he whispered against her lips.

He caught her lower lip gently between his teeth, extracting a moan from her. He continued his onslaught with a trail of kisses across her jaw line and down to her throat and neck where he lingered to inhale her seductive rose scent.

Greedily, he took more. He caught the tip of her braid, looped it twice around his hand and nuzzled it to his cheek. She pressed her body against his as if craving to be absorbed by him.

And the beast in him wanted to consume her whole because only she could sate his ravenous hunger—a hunger that was so much more than physical. His groin swelled impossibly hard. He ached for her. With a groan, he pressed harder into her belly so she could feel it, too.

"Inside," she gasped. "Come … inside."

Yet, even in the haze of desire, Adam knew this wasn't the right time. Although his body protested to the death, he refused to treat her like a five quid whore with a one-minute fuck on her doorstep. He also needed time to think when his brain wasn't ruled by his cock.

Slowly, reluctantly, he eased away. It took a few moments for his addled senses to float back on solid ground.

Breathlessly, he forced the words from his mouth. "I better go now." He took the keys from her hand and opened the door. "Have a good night's sleep. I'll call you in the morning."

"What's wrong?" she said, a little too harshly.

"I'm just being considerate." Tension fringed his voice. It was hard enough to exercise self-restraint, yet, she was making it even harder.

She flushed, regretful of her outburst. "I … I'm sorry. I didn't mean that. I seem to be apologizing a lot lately," she said dismally.

He cupped her chin between his thumb and forefinger and placed a lingering kiss on her forehead.

"Have patience," he said. "It will be worth it."

CHAPTER 15

EMMA WANTED TO LAUGH HYSTERICALLY AT ADAM'S WORDS TO HER.

Have patience. It will be worth it.

If he could only guess that when she abandoned herself to his sweet embrace, *she* knew it was love. If he felt anything, he probably called it lust.

Emotion rose in a hot mass and burned through the lining in her throat. It took superhuman effort to stop herself from pulling him inside and leaving no doubt in his mind that she was his as he was hers...

He pulled away to drink his fill of her face, uncertainty and bewilderment reflected in his eyes. The leather tips of his gloves sketched the length of her cheeks.

Seconds ticked by. The bells of a nearby church clock tower

started to ring the hour. That rhythmic clang had him blink and release an unsteady breath. After he flicked a loose strand of hair behind her ear, he whispered. "Good night."

Then he turned and left.

She watched his back until she couldn't hear his footsteps any more, then bolted through the door, shut it with a loud bang, and leaned helplessly against it. Only then did she let the floodgates open. Tears of frustration mingled with tears of joy. She cried because she had to hold back from telling him everything, from confiding how much he meant to her.

At the sight of Adam—no, Adrian, to her he'd be always Adrian—that evening, Emma practically went up in flames. She wanted to hold him in her arms, kiss him, caress him, feel him inside her, pulsing with the fire she missed and desired with all her being. After losing everything she knew, everyone she cared for, and headed for the unknown, she had only one reason left to live for.

Now that reason was here, and today he'd called her beautiful.

So are you, Adrian. You're the most beautiful man in the world, and you're mine. Even though you've forgotten...

He had dazed her, so handsome in his long black coat and expensive black suit that fit him to perfection.

For this special night, she had taken care to look her best. She wanted it to be magical and perfect. And she'd succeeded, but there was still much to do. How was she to make him fall in love with her in a short time?

He was attracted to her but held a part of himself back. He'd erected a high wall she couldn't climb, behind a road block longer than the Wall of China. She didn't blame him for being secretive.

Valthreans like them, who lived in isolation, found it hard to belong. It wasn't easy to let oneself be ruled by the gambit of human emotions when, eventually, those emotions would be torn to shreds with the pain of loss. People like her and Adrian had to give up more than they gained, and if one wasn't careful, life would chip away at sanity, one flick at a time.

But what if one were handed a ray of light in a world of darkness? Given a reason to trust in a roomful of sharps?

Perhaps therein lay the key. She set off thinking that Adrian, or the new man he'd become, was the one who had to prove to her she could trust him. He was supposed to fall in love with her. That was the plan —for her to wait until his feelings were engaged, and then she would tell him everything.

But there was another option, one she hadn't considered. What if *she* were the one to lay it all on the line, right here, right now? She'd plant the ball in her court and assume all the risk. This meant one thing—she had to trust fate enough to tell him who she was before she was sure of his feelings. During her first phone conversation with Adam Derringstone, he told her he valued honesty. She had work to do to live up to that expectation.

Fate hadn't given her much reason to trust it, but Adrian always had. He never deliberately deceived her, and had always been trustworthy.

Words mean nothing if they're not supported with actions. She remembered his words to her from so long ago.

Dare she take the plunge?

Dare she let Adrian go and embrace the new man, Adam?

True, life was a knee-jerk test of endurance. But it was a test she wanted to face with dignity.

She made this resolution as she found herself outside the museum the next day. Come hell or high water, she'd brook the consequences of her actions. If she didn't do this, the entire process would take too long and it would mean stretching her deception.

The wise Seneca once said, *It is not because things are difficult that we do not dare; it is because we do not dare that they are difficult.* He was right. Exercising strict prudence was not going to get her out of this muddle.

So there would be no more lies. She'd set fear to the side and take the shot. With *Adam.*

Today.

The sound of the sliding bolt cut through her thoughts. This time, it was the master of the house who opened the door, not his venerable Passepartout. He wore black jeans, a grey sweater, and liquid blue fire in his eyes.

"Hello, Adam."

He pulled her in roughly, a hard gleam in his eyes. Closing the door behind her, he unceremoniously pushed her into the wood and pinned her wrists above her head. His lips swooped down like a vulture honing on its prey and the fiery, bruising kiss he gave her left her breathless and panting.

"Well, good afternoon," she managed between quick, short breaths.

"I missed you," he growled against her lips. "I've come to love the scent of roses."

"But you only met me yesterday." She swallowed, hating herself for that lie and all the others she'd uttered lately.

"Only yesterday?" He smiled into her cheek, then sobered up. "It feels like longer to me."

I wish you knew. I wish you remembered.

He released her but kept one of her hands in his. "Come. I want to show you my office."

They went up a flight of stairs and walked a long corridor to a cozy and masculine room. Not overly large, but there was sufficient space for a desk, a wall-to-wall bookcase, and a compact but well-appointed sitting area. Upholstered in green and gold striped silk, the couch perched on intricately carved, claw-foot legs. A small secretary desk and chair had been set against the wall to the left of a larger, disorderly one. The walls were painted in a subdued mossy green, bringing in nature from the outside as the large terrace leading from this room gave onto a beautiful garden with a path through mature trees and perennial plants in stone pots. It felt more like a comfortable sanctuary than an office.

"This is where I spend most of my day," he said.

"I can see why," she smiled.

He gestured toward the sofa where they both sat. Emma's eyes strayed to his trousers that strained against powerful thighs. He was so close to her. Close enough to smell and touch.

He hooked a finger under her chin and nudged her gaze to his.

"What do you think about an evening picnic in Hyde Park?" he asked. "The weather is mellow tonight and I thought we'd get out and do something different."

"A picnic?" she replied lamely. The memory of their last rendezvous before Madeleine kidnapped him came to the forefront of her mind. "Sounds like fun."

"We don't have to if you don't want to."

"Of course I want to." She grinned.

"I had everything packed a short while ago just in case. We can catch the tube to Hyde Park corner. There is a nice path through the park that leads to Marble Arch. We could have gone straight to that entrance if I'd thought of picking you up, but it was a last minute idea."

"It's all right. I enjoyed the ride here."

"The park's open until midnight so we don't have to rush."

She ran a finger across his knuckles. "You've thought of everything."

"I don't like leaving things to chance," he said.

Sometimes, things just don't happen the way we plan them, she yearned to say. Instead, she gave him a smile of gratitude. "I'm flattered."

His eyes gleamed with mischief. "Don't be. I'm doing this for entirely selfish reasons."

"It doesn't matter."

"But it does." He slid his hand along her jaw to cradle her neck. His thumb strayed to caress her cheek. "I can't stop thinking about you."

He sounded as surprised by his admission as she was. His eyes turned to a stormy blue, dark and dangerous.

Bowled over, she leaned into his touch. "Oh, Adam, I feel the same. You don't know—"

"Please, Emma. I want..." He looked a bit flustered, as if suddenly out of his element. "I know it's early times but before we leave, I'd like to give you this. I brought you a small gift and hope you like it. No pressure."

He presented her with a little black box.

"Why, you shouldn't have!"

The box fit in the palm of one hand.

"Are you going to open it?" he asked when she hesitated.

Heat rushed to her face. She caught herself staring at him and stammered, "Yes, of course."

Quivering from head to toe, she lifted the lid and there, on a bed of black satin, sat the most beautiful brooch she had ever seen. A Rococo-style rendering of a woman in black evening dress holding a long-stemmed red rose. In the heart of the gilt-edged flower was embedded a small sparkling diamond.

Her eyes misted. "I don't know what to say."

"I was passing by an antique store when I saw it in the window and thought of you and your roses. I see you have one again tonight, attached to your bag."

She took a long drawn out breath and let it go. "Yes, I always do."

"Why?"

To remind me of you.

"To remind me of my goals."

"And what are they?" he probed.

"I'd rather talk not about this right now."

She chided herself for being such a chicken, for going back on her decision. But she didn't want to do or say anything to mar the start of a perfect evening. She just wasn't ready yet.

Bloody hell.

His eyes filled with concern. "I didn't mean to upset you."

"It's not your fault. It's just that we have all experienced some loss or regret..." she faltered. "Please, let's forget everything else and enjoy this evening."

He didn't respond, although he kept assessing her.

"Pleaaaaase?" she insisted.

"You're right. This night is for celebrating a new connection."

He leaned toward her, so close his breath warmed her face, and picked up the brooch. "Allow me to put it on you."

Breathless, she indicated the wide lapel of her double-breasted tweed coat. It took him an awfully long time to get the task done. How could it feel so hot in the middle of winter?

Perhaps it was because her eyes were fixed on his, returning his gaze with equal intensity. Or perhaps it was because she'd placed her hand on his as he fastened the brooch to her coat, mouthing a "thank you." Or maybe, just maybe, the temperature soared when he turned his hand around and twined his fingers with hers and brought them to his lips.

Then again, it could have been the magnetic draw that happened as they gradually inched closer until their lips were a hair's breadth apart.

Emma looked into rich cobalt eyes to burn to cinders under their hungry regard. Their kiss was gentle at first yet devastating. She closed her eyes, so wholeheartedly in the moment that she gave a moan of protest when he ended it.

"Better go," he said in a choked voice.

She clutched onto him, resisted as he eased her away.

"I packed an extra blanket." He flicked her nose with his index finger and touched his forehead to hers while he rubbed up and down her arms. "I want to keep you safe and warm."

As long as I have breath in me, I'll always keep you safe, he'd told her in another lifetime.

He stood and offered her his hand. "Basket's in the kitchen."

It was a short train ride to the park on the Piccadilly line. The front of the prestigious Lanesborough Hotel greeted them as they exited the station and entered park grounds. It had been sunny all day but evening was firmly settled in by now, and brought with it slightly crisper currents. It wasn't the biting cold that made your face numb or seeped through your clothes and wrapped a million tentacles around your bones. It was a non-invasive coolness that layered on you like a gossamer mantle.

Being a work night, few visitors frequented the park at this hour. The occasional passerby promenaded past them but it was mostly quiet. The park was lit, and the reach of light illuminated random patches of grass and convoluted tree roots. It was a magical sight.

Emma started to expect forest fairies and elves to pop their little heads around the shrubs and trees and start to dance around them.

Adam drew her close to him and hooked an arm around her shoulders as hers curled naturally around his back. He spotted a large oak on the southern end of the park and nodded toward it.

"That work for you?" he asked casually.

Chuckling, she grabbed the picnic bag strap from his shoulder and sauntered to the private, softly-lit spot. Adam was on her heels, caught her, and pulled her back up to his chest. He slowly slid his hand down her arm and pried the bag from her.

"Let me," he whispered in her ear,

His hard, lean body radiated raw muscle and power into every inch of her back. Goosebumps rose all over her arms and legs.

"Why should I?" she breathed even as she easily relinquished the bag.

"Because I know what you want," he said huskily as he caught her ear lobe between his teeth and gently nipped it.

"And what is that?" she probed as her body shivered and pulsed in delicious, erotic ways.

He pressed his lips to the exposed skin beneath her ear. "You're hungry," he murmured.

"Yes." She leaned back into him and forgot herself, forgot where they were.

"We have sandwiches." His tongue traced her jaw line. "Red wine for the chill." He let go of the picnic bag, and linked his fingers with hers. "Your hands are cold. I hope you brought gloves." His mouth retraced its route to her ear. "Ah, and we also have chocolate muffins…"

"Hmm, chocolate," she panted, her legs going wobbly.

"Let's eat, then," he said, making sure she was steady on her feet before he let her go.

The cheek, he's toying with me.

Annoyed, she turned to shoot daggers at him but his back was to her as he spread a light blanket on the grass and placed a plaid throw above it for her.

"I can't believe all that fit in the small bag," she snapped, supremely annoyed with him.

She heard him make a snorting sound, and when it persisted, she realized it was laughter. He even had the impudence to toss her a mischievous wink.

"Cheek," she grumbled.

When he finished setting up, he pulled her down on the blanket and sat facing her, legs crossed and his face cracked in a broad grin. His eyes sparkled—the first time she'd seen them so buoyant since she reconnected with him. Her mouth felt suddenly dry.

"I haven't laughed so hard in, well, ever."

"Never?" *Not true. You used to laugh like that with me.*

"Honest. Here, have a sandwich. Hope you like chicken."

"I'd rather have the muffin, please."

"Dessert first?"

"Always."

"What the hell," he said, and put the sandwiches down. He opened a box and offered her the contents.

She picked one up and bit into it. "Yum, dark chocolate chip, too. Taste," she said, and brought the muffin to his lips.

He took a healthy bite and chewed.

"Isn't it lovely?"

His eyes delved into hers, went so deep she couldn't look away. "Yes, very lovely."

God, she was automatically recreating the same scene of the past. *Bad, bad idea.* She couldn't stay locked in their history, even if it was her subconscious doing all the work—unless she was using it to let the cat out of the bag. This was a different time and place with a different man, albeit in the same body.

Snap out of it, sister, and end this torture.

Tell him now.

"This reminds me of another place, a rural area close to where I used to live."

"Was it as big as this?"

"Yes, it was big. More untamed, but no less beautiful. It was a long time ago."

He caressed her temple, along the hairline. "Where was that?"

"We had a house in Hertfordshire, near St. Albans."

"Not far from London, then."

"No, but it felt far from all the glitz and glamour. I loved it there."

"Tell me more," he urged. His eyes sparkled under the light of the stars.

Her nerves about to snap, she put down the half eaten muffin and swung herself back on her feet. "At the time, I—I was about to get married." A sudden draft seeped in her bones and she started to pace, while she rubbed her arms up and down.

"Was he Italian? Is that why you moved to Rome?" Thick eyebrows drew together as he followed her with questioning eyes.

Was he jealous?

"No, this was way before then..." Cursing under her breath, she stopped dead in her tracks and wrapped her arms around herself. Her head hung low and her eyes sealed shut.

How would she ever finish this? What a coward she was.

She heard him get up and reach her in two strides. He wrapped the blanket around her and took her in his arms. "Don't force yourself to speak. When the time is right, you will," he soothed.

"Please hold me. Just hold me," she cried.

She buried her face in his coat and let the tears roll from her eyes. "There is so much I have to say. So much..."

"These things take time. We all have secrets," he said, his tone enigmatic.

"You don't understand."

"Yes, I do," he said.

Yes, he did. He knew exactly what it meant to be your own hostage. So why couldn't she speak?

The silence stretched between them. She took advantage to bask in the comfort of his embrace, to savor the peace before the storm. It felt too good to be in this warm bubble with him under the vigilance of the stars.

"I have something to say, too," he said, his voice thick as the night above them.

"What?" she sniffed.

"You're getting in my blood, Emma Deramore. Not sure how or why it's happening. I don't know much about you or where this is going, but it's the truth. I know you feel it, too." He pulled her head into his shoulder. "Perhaps we are meant to be," he added so softly that she doubted he intended her to hear.

A confession, from the depths of his heart. Recognition flared through Emma, remembrances of another confession—sincere, honest, gripping. They had been holding on to each other just like this, while sitting under a tree on an atypically sunny December afternoon.

You are meant to be mine. You are in my blood.

Adrian's declaration of love to her in their old life, that day by the River Ver, had sounded sweet as ripe summer fruit exploding on the taste buds.

Now, Adam was laying his heart bare. He'd found the courage to do it and she should do the same. Swallowing past the lump in her throat, she ran her hand across her eyes to dry up the tears.

It was time to come clean.

Wisps of cold air flowed through her, penned shivers through her in an unsteady hand.

Adam drew her instinctively closer. "You're cold."

She pressed a palm on his chest and took a step back. If she waited longer she'd lose the nerve. "No, Adam, please. I have something—"

"Your money, now."

They both looked in the direction of the voice that came out of nowhere, terse, cutting. A tall man emerged from the shadows of a high shrub and walked cautiously toward them. A flash of metal gleamed in his hand when he stepped into a strip of light.

He had a gun.

"Be quick with it!" He signaled in their direction. He took a few more steps and lifted the gun. "No tricks or you're dead."

———

THE SON of a bitch had gotten close enough so Adam could get a good look at him. A black skullcap covered his head, to frame a square jaw and hard-nosed features. The planes of his face were carved in granite. Grey eyes pierced into them, rigid, sharp, dangerous. This was a man who meant business.

Adam assessed his position. The bloke was large, but he could take him down with a few punches.

The man scoped the area to make sure there weren't any witnesses. He could have saved himself the trouble. Adam hadn't seen a soul in the last fifteen minutes.

"I don't have anything on me," Emma said, while she raised her hands so he'd see she had no jewelry.

"That's a pretty brooch. And what about that bag over there?" He waved his gun behind them where she'd left her sling bag by the bottle of wine. "Bring it here and no sudden moves."

"Okay, I'm going now," she said, and took a few cautious steps. Adam nodded reassuringly when she sent him a silent appeal.

"Your turn, mister. Cough up."

Adam reached into his pocket for his wallet and threw it on the ground by the man's feet.

"Your watch."

Adam removed his Parmigiani watch, one of his few claims to vanity, and flung it next to the wallet.

The man smiled. "Nice taste."

Emma stepped next to Adam, and clutched her purse.

"Don't throw that," the man leered. "Come over here and hand it to me, luv."

Adam's jaw clenched. "If you so much as touch a hair on her head," he warned without equivocation, "they won't be able to tell your face from your arse when I'm done with you."

The man had the good sense to go pale when his gaze met Adam's lethal one. His composure regained in an instant, he shrugged. "All I want is the cash, and to pass on a message."

"A message?" Emma took a couple of steps forward, stretched her arm, and handed over her purse. Her body was stiff, on edge, one hand stuck deep in the pocket of her jacket.

"The brooch. Put it here." He stretched his arm out holding her purse flat. Emma didn't move. "Do you have a hearing problem?"

"Okay." She unpinned it and reluctantly gave it up.

"Much obliged. You can step back now," he instructed.

Emma returned to stand near Adam while the man rifled through the bag and found a few notes. He stuffed them in his pocket and bent quickly to pick Adam's wallet and watch.

"Now, for the actual reason of my visit. A certain gentleman asked me to pass on a proposal."

"Why doesn't he make it in person?" Adam asked. "Who is he?"

"No names. Just a message, for the sweet pea over here." His eyes traveled boldly over Emma's body, stopped on her breasts, then her face. "The gent wants to make an offer of employment. Yea, ain't that nice. I'd take it if I were you. A good job is hard to find in these days and times."

"What are you talking about?"

"Anything you're doing for your friends over at the club, he wants the same thing."

"That's ridiculous. I don't work for anyone," she mocked.

Adam wasn't fooled. Emma was not as collected as she tried to let on.

"Well, it's either that, or your mates are toast." The man made a slicing motion across his throat.

Emma pursed her lips. "Where did you meet this man?"

"Sorry, luv, show's over. But before I leave you guys to your smooching, I think I'll have a last bit of fun. Anything fancy in those pockets, Miss?"

"I gave you everything I had."

"I like to see for myself. Pull the pockets inside out."

Emma started to look like a cornered fox in the hunt.

"Now," he sneered. The man aimed his gun straight at her head and licked his lips as he continued to undress her with his eyes.

Blind rage washed over Adam. All that mattered was Emma's safety, and the slime bag had the guts to threaten her.

Did he know he couldn't kill her with a bullet? It was of no consequence; what mattered was that he *believed* he could.

Taking advantage of the fact that the robber's attention was fixed on Emma, Adam moved with lightning speed to grab his arm and bring it down with force across his upturned knee, taking him completely by surprise. At the cracking sound of his arm breaking, the bastard fell on his knees and screamed in pain, letting the weapon drop in the grass. His hand twisted at an unnatural angle.

Adam kicked the gun far from the stranger's grasp. "Give us our things back," he demanded. His tone brooked no argument.

Still whimpering, his face contorted with a hideous agony, the thief used his good hand to return the items.

"Now go, before I have second thoughts and turn you over to the police."

The man pulled his hulking frame from the ground.

"And tell your employer I'm not interested," Emma supplemented.

He made a face as he grabbed his bad arm. "Can't say you haven't been warned." He scuttled back the way he came, mouthing foul curses.

"You all right?" Adam asked Emma, his gaze glued to the departing figure until it disappeared into the night.

"Yes, I think so," came the hushed reply.

The thought that she could have been hurt today brought him to his knees. It was all his fault. If he hadn't suggested the picnic under the moonlight...

Romantic in theory, but what had he been thinking?

He turned to face her, afraid to look into her eyes. He shouldn't be with her now, with his state of mind. It wasn't safe. Violence was a double-edged sword; it affected the winner as much as the loser in any confrontation. If Emma stayed with him longer, she'd be getting herself in a cage with a restless panther.

"I think it's best to head back." From the corner of his eye, he saw her small figure tremble. While an arm curled protectively around her waist, the other fell inflexible by her side. Her fingers clasped an object in an obstinate hold.

Defenseless and vulnerable.

He knew he should go to her and offer solace but one didn't march in a loaded mine field to prove a point. That mine field was him; one wrong step and she'd be blown to smithereens.

Her feet seemed rooted to the spot as she stared far into the shadows.

"Emma." He took a tentative step toward her.

"I'm fine." Her eyes met his as she frowned. "That man was serious. If I don't do as he says, they may kill my friends."

"How can anyone kill a Valthrean? And who are they?"

"There are ways, trust me," she said vaguely. Emma let loose an unsteady breath. "I must call Max and tell him about this. I have to go to the club."

"Club?"

"The Versus Club, on Clement's Street. It's a research library for Valthreans. Been there forever. Nothing top secret there, but I'm not sure if it's safe anymore," she explained, her brows furrowed in thought.

A place for Valthreans. Not that he'd have heard about it, shut away as he was in the glass case of his world. He wanted to hit something.

"And Max? Who is he?"

Emma slinked her bag over her shoulder and ran the back of her hand across her brow. The wicked, slender blade of a knife flashed when she moved. It looked like some sort of dagger.

His belly churned like it had been sucker-punched. Warning bells pealed loudly in his head.

"What is that?" he asked with deceptive calmness, forgetting his last question.

"What?" she asked distractedly.

He went to her, lowered her hand, and eased her hold on the object so he could have a clear look. His heart started to hammer.

It was a poniard with an elaborate hand-carved ivory handle and pommel. Very unusual and old. The blade was slightly wide at the base and thinned toward the tip.

His fingers closed around her wrist in a ruthless grip. He pried the knife from her hands.

"Where did you get this?" he asked. His words dripped with menace.

Her eyes opened wide in fear; he could see the whites all around. "Please, let me go," she sputtered, and struggled to break free.

It only made him tighten his hold on her. "Tell me first."

"I've had it a long time. It belonged to my father."

"How long?" he demanded. He crowded in on her, forced her to step back.

She yanked her arm. "Why are you doing this?" Several strands of hair pulled free from their fastening and fell onto her face.

Implacable, he urged her backwards until her back hit the tree trunk. At full tilt, he threw the knife into the grass, caught the other wrist and pinned her hands to the rough bark on either side of her to make her his prisoner. She turned her head away, as if that could cut him off, make him relent.

"I won't let you go until you tell me," he rasped, punctuating each word in her ear.

A soft cry escaped her lips.

"Look at me, damn it!" he shouted, enraged that she didn't have the courage to face him.

She had led him on, betrayed him.

Terror-stricken eyes finally searched his face, begged for clemency. "I've had it for over two centuries," she sobbed. Her lips trembled around every syllable. Her chest heaved with every difficult breath.

"That is a very distinctive-looking weapon." He hooked her gaze, gave her no quarter. "It was you, wasn't it? In Leith, that fight outside the tavern. It was you who fought those men by my side. Always you in my dreams." A lump lodged in his throat but he didn't budge an inch.

Resignation clouded her face. She stopped fighting him. "Yes, it was me," she murmured.

His heart shifted inside him. A shock wave cracked it open, bared a deep, dark hole where his feelings should have been. The damage branched through him, irrevocable, wounding, permanent. "Why? Who are you?"

"I had started to tell you that I used to live in Hertfordshire, where my wedding was supposed to take place."

He grunted.

"I was going to marry you. Something horrible happened to us, and now you can't remember me," she continued. The words rolled fast from her lips like hefty bales of hay down a steep hillside.

A pulse ticked in his jaw. "Why should I believe you?"

"Because I'm saying the truth! I've been looking for you all this time."

"If you wanted to be honest, you'd have told me straight away. You wouldn't hide behind stupid excuses."

"I—I had my reasons. You are so different now. I just wanted to try and rebuild what we had from scratch. To be fair to you."

He delivered a humorless laugh. "Nothing's fair about this. What else are you hiding, eh?" He flicked his tongue along her cheek. "Guilt? Shame? Did you find me an undesirable prospect and made a pact with Marie? Huh?" He molded his body to hers, made her feel his hardness. "Did you get her to pack me off to Scotland and hoodwink me with her fantastic tale for ten years?"

"No!"

Was he even making sense?

Don't give a damn.

His teeth nipped roughly at the skin between jaw and neck. "Did you tell her to make love to me, to let me touch her like this?" After he unpinned her wrist, he closed his hand over her breast and kneaded it hard, so brutally it caused her to wince.

"You're not thinking straight. Madeleine did this. That's her real name. It was her fault."

He knew he should stop but the devil in him urged him to get his retribution. To lay all the blame at this woman's feet, measure for measure.

It didn't matter that he didn't have the details yet, that nothing fit where it was supposed to be.

Fact was, she'd lied to him.

"Thank you for that. She was a great fuck."

"Stop it!" she cried. Her body writhed frantically against his.

His hand slid down to explore the curve of her hips, the roundness of her buttocks. He squeezed with rough intimacy. "Don't you like this, cupcake? How about a quick shag, eh? You can have a taste of what I gave to your friend *Madeleine.*"

"Stop! Just stop," she cried louder. Her fist pounded and pushed on his chest.

Finally, her panic-stricken voice slapped some sense into him. He abruptly let her go, as if her body were a flaming pyre that licked his skin then burned through him to punish him for his deplorable actions. While patting the roaring lion inside him and coaxing it to lie back on its haunches, he stood there and stared at this woman he barely knew.

This woman who'd dared to make him want. To make him yearn for what he couldn't have.

The woman who had no qualms about deceiving him.

"Please believe me," Emma tried to convince him. "It was all Madeleine's doing."

Should he believe her? He'd given Marie—or was it Madeleine?— that chance, and she'd shown him she didn't deserve it.

Bottom line was, again, Emma had lied to him, so how could he believe her? Lies, all these lies. They sickened him.

Lies had gotten him where he was now—in limbo, floating in a world he barely connected with. Lies had taken his past, his life. Now, the mockery of all that deceit came full circle, concentrated in his desire for this woman. A desire he shouldn't feel, but push away with scorn.

Emma Deramore, how could you? How could you shatter my hope?

I've been grasping at straws...

"Can't you see?" she said desperately, interrupting his recriminations. "It's why I wear roses every day. You used to give me one, every single day of our betrothal." She showed him the now battered rose attached to the bag strap. "This is to remind me of you, to keep you in my heart each day I wake up without you."

"I don't want to see you again," he said quietly. He refused to process what she'd just told him, choosing instead to voice the first words that made it to his lips.

"If you just hear me out—" she pleaded.

He gave her a quelling glance. "We're done here. If you have any sense of self-preservation, you would just leave now."

"Adrian, I love you," she called to him, her face soaked with fresh tears.

Shocked, he stepped back abruptly, as through she'd shot him point blank. She'd said that name—a name only the woman in his dreams knew. The dark, beautiful vision he cherished.

A coincidence?

I love you.

Adrian. That name.

She had no right to say that. No right to say she loved him, to call him what he wasn't. Anyway, in case she meant it, the man she loved wasn't the man he was. That man had died long ago.

She reached her hand out to him, and kicked his reflexes to take another step back, beyond her grasp.

"Don't touch me," he bit out between gritted teeth.

He turned his back to her, ignored her pleas, locked his heart to the sight of her pitiful form wracked with sobs. All the while, hoping he'd one day be able to blot out the acute anguish he just saw in her eyes.

"Go," he demanded again.

She obeyed him this time. Her boots barely made a sound on the mown glass as swift footsteps took her away. Out of his life.

CHAPTER 16

"I have almost forgot the taste of fears."
[Macbeth, Act V, Scene V]

EMMA DIDN'T KNOW HOW SHE EVER MADE IT TO HER FRONT DOOR, UP the stairs to her bedroom, and onto the bed. After unzipping and kicking off her boots and discarding the jacket with the brooch still on it, she had zoned out from start to end and wished she could stay hypnotized like that forever. She wanted to never wake up, never have to think through a day. Because to wake up meant she'd have to acknowledge the nightmare that her life had become, far worse than anything she'd thought possible.

Before she found Adrian, there was always hope, however slim, that she would be with him once more. Hope that he'd be in her arms again, that they would have a second chance to live the life that was stolen from them. She could live with the past because although the future was a closed book, it offered a fair shake at changing things around.

Not even that glimmer of faith remained after tonight. That closed book was torn to shreds and scattered to the four winds by a mighty squall.

A story over. *All over.*

When she called out to Adam that she loved him, she'd used his old, real name—the name of the man she had always loved. *Adrian.* She needed to hear it reel off her tongue, and she clutched to it, to its memory, like a last, broken straw.

Emma turned on her side and hugged one of the pillows. She'd taken off her coat and shoes but couldn't be bothered to change her clothes. It was pointless.

Everything was pointless, even feeling guilt or recrimination. It wasn't like that would let her turn the clock around.

She was all cried out. Her eyes were dry and she didn't have a drop left to shed. Stretched to exhaustion, her mind shut down to everything except the sound of her breathing in the stillness. The moonlight was banned from the room by heavy lined curtains. Perhaps the pitch black dark would help her sleep.

She'd take care of everything tomorrow.

Pack the bags. Book the flight. Return to the routine. Grieve. Plan a new life.

But all of that could wait until the next day.

Tonight was for forgetting.

Sleep came as a welcome guest, but with restless dreams as its clingy date. Dark shadows darted behind Emma's closed eyelids, while hushed murmurings skirted the veil of her conscious mind, rhythmic and impatient like the hum of voices inside a theater before show time.

She turned on her right side but the sounds didn't stop; they only got closer, more insistent—an echo that kept replaying in the cloudy space of her mind. Arm raised over ear by instinct, she burrowed in the pillow to shut out at once the moving shadows that taunted her.

The blackness sheltered her now, but she struggled to find a comfortable position. She kicked her feet on a moan and angled her head so as not to suffocate herself in the soft, fluffy pillow.

The nape of her neck tingled, the tiny hairs stood on end like tiny needles.

Pricking.

Uncomfortable.

The realization slammed into her then—someone was breathing over her.

Not a ghost, or a vision. An actual person. What kind of dream was this?

No, not a dream.

Coming awake now, she shifted slightly and slogged through her woolly vision to train her eyes ahead. Sure enough, a moth-like shadow flitted at the corner of her left eye. She dared not move much but braced herself in the quiet room.

She focused instead on the breathing that became hotter, heavier.

Slowly, she lowered her arm and tried to prepare herself for the unexplainable.

Bloody hell, I need my knife...

The weapon was in her bag, on the armchair. Too far from the bed. If someone was close to her, they'd get her before she had a chance to make a sprint for it. Either way, she shouldn't panic much. What could happen in a worst case scenario?

Still, this reeked of something foul. Who would want to harm her? Or Max? This was his house, after all.

"Who's there?" she asked aloud as she fisted her hand and hoped that whoever it was, she could tackle barehanded.

A shadow moved again above her.

Then another, and another, in large human shapes.

Three?

"Don't make a fuss and we won't hurt you. Someone wants to meet you," one masculine voice said.

"Who are—"

But she wasn't allowed to finish before sweet and pungent vapors slipped up her mouth and nostrils through a cloth pressed to her face, and finally brought her the oblivion she'd yearned for only moments ago.

———

HER BACK WAS to him as he tried to reach for her in the mist. He shouldn't want this, he shouldn't ache to touch her, to possess her, but he couldn't command his dreams any more than he could control his desire for her.

Long, dark hair moved with a ghostly breeze, but she stood rigid, tense, restrained.

She turned around and Emma's face stared at him—sad, grieving, the gen of loss in her eyes.

"Stop!" she cried. "Stop doing this! Why did you leave me again?"

She looked back away from him, as if she couldn't bear the sight of him anymore.

"No, don't," he said to the fading figure of his angel.

Was she leaving him for good? Was she letting him go?

Then a man rushed in, pointed a gun at her and shot her. She turned around to show Adam a battered face, with streaks of blood streaming past her eyes over her cheeks, neck, and chest. Soon, she was covered in red, and she fell in a heap on the floor, her hand outstretched to him.

A desperate plea for help.

He started to run toward her but she wasn't there.

"Emma! Where are you? Emma!"

She was gone, leaving behind a bright red stain of her blood.

"No!" he shouted.

Adrian cried that single word not in his dream but to the ceiling above his bed.

Because he was awake, panting, frantic. Sweat trickled down his nape, over the tip of his spine.

"No," he whispered to the night. "Come back."

But the night wouldn't listen to him. He was farther from sleep, and from salvation, than he'd ever been.

He sprung out of bed, quickly slid on jeans and a jumper and grabbed his house keys.

The sense of dread bullied him into alarm mode because he couldn't fathom how or why but he knew it in his gut—Emma was in danger.

———

THE KIDNAPPER RELEASED his death hold on Emma's mouth so she could finally breathe freely. Amid the chloroform-induced stupor, she made out they were in a car. She guessed one of the men drove while the other two sat on either side of her at the back like solid columns of marble framing a grand entrance. As she was blindfolded, she could only feel their hulking bodies crowding hers. Wrists bound, it took her some minutes to recover the ability to move her fingers or turn her head.

Should she be flattered that someone considered three burly men would be needed to get her to cooperate?

"What's this all about? Where are you taking me?"

She got no answer, which was more unnerving than being barked at. By the length of the drive, they were going outside London. The vehicle finally stopped and she was dragged from the cool night air into a building, up a flight of steps, and into a room.

After being unceremoniously dumped on a bed, one of the men growled, "You can take the blindfold off now." He untied her wrists and left, locking the door behind him.

Emma didn't have to be told twice. She tore off the blindfold and rushed to the single window that gave onto a small courtyard with a high wall behind it that blocked the view. That meant no chance of deducing where she was by looking at the outside.

She tested the door. Made of solid wood that had likely stood the test of time, it was bolted shut, as was the window. A plan of escape would therefore require creative thinking and most of all, opportunity.

When an hour passed and no one showed up, she decided to lie down and get some rest. Even if she didn't sleep with the adrenalin pumping through her, she would minimize the chances of her system crashing later, when she'd face her kidnappers and need all her wits about her.

Morning came quickly. Surprisingly, she did manage to zone out for a time, although her head pounded with an ungodly ache. She gingerly got off the bed and went to the window. It was well past dusk, but she couldn't know the exact time as she'd taken off her wristwatch last night before bed.

A couple of raps sounded on her door.

"Come in," she called.

A large man—probably one of those who'd paid her the visit last night— entered with a breakfast tray. He placed it on a table by the door.

"You have ten minutes to eat," he said gruffly before disappearing again.

Dying for a pick-me-up, Emma poured some coffee but smelled it and took a hesitant sip to make sure it wasn't laced with something. Satisfied, she uncovered a plate with eggs and buttered toast. She selected a small triangle of toasted bread and nibbled into it after draining a full cup of good, strong brew, heavy with sugar and cream.

Her mind had drained of thoughts, frustration replaced by numbness. A strange sense of calm kept her level-headed, but she wondered if she was just deceiving herself. Without seeing the threat, however, she couldn't form an opinion of what to expect.

As soon as she'd gone through her second cup, the door opened. The same man came in.

"Come with me."

"Whose house is this?"

He grunted but kept mum as he grabbed her by the arm and pulled her into the corridor. Not a big conversationalist, was he?

He took her down the wide corridor and round a corner, which allowed her a quick view of the stairs and the front door below along the way. This was a grand place and whoever owned it had money. The lackey stopped at a door and knocked, then pushed her inside ahead of him.

A young, beautiful woman regarded her with curious eyes.

"So she's the one?" she asked someone who stood behind her.

The young woman moved, giving Emma a better view of an older woman with long red hair and eyes of a vibrant green. Eyes that fixed on her with unconcealed malice.

"Madeleine?" Emma gasped, her throat suddenly scratchy.

"Lady Emmaline Deramore, we meet again. I can't say it's a pleasure."

Emma wanted to scope the room, to weigh her chances of escape, but all she could see was that face—a face she knew well, to her eternal regret.

"What do you want with me? I have nothing else to give you."

"But you're wrong," Madeleine said with a smirk.

"Whatever you say. As for me, I have better things to do, so I'll go now." Emma swiveled boldly and hit a wall of muscle. All three men from last night blocked her from the exit.

"Where are you going so fast? You just got here."

Emma turned back to the hateful figure of Madeleine and crossed her arms. "Why don't you speak up and let me leave?"

Madeleine gave a shrill laugh and waved her off. "See what I told you about, Bree, darling?" she told the other woman.

She sauntered to a large table and picked up a knife. Sighing, she turned it in her hand and tested its point with the tip of a finger.

Emma tried to remain composed although the situation made it increasingly hard. If these people wished her harm, they knew how to inflict it on her in a permanent way. Besides, Madeleine was a witch. Emma caught a glimpse of a chalice sitting in the middle of the table—pretty much similar to the one she'd found in Madeleine's Scottish cottage. That made her wonder, just *who* was protecting Madeleine, and did Emma's involvement with the Council have anything to do with her being forced here? How telling that the same night she and Adrian were accosted in Hyde Park, she ended up in Madeleine's clutches.

But would the Cult have sent a warning and then taken action within hours? That didn't make much sense.

"Did you send that man to threaten us at the park yesterday?" she asked bluntly. The only way to find out was to ask.

"That man?" Madeleine asked, sharing a snide glance with the Bree woman. "Not me, but my superiors thought it necessary. Yet, it clashed with my plans. I intend to serve them well, but before that, I'll have my fun."

Of course, she knew about her and Adrian!

Madeleine's eyes widened like fiery saucers with ghoulish excitement. She made a perfect modern version of Maleficent in her fine black trouser suit with black silk ruching on the high-collared jacket.

"Put her there and tie her up like I instructed," she ordered her minions, pointing to a wooden chair with armrests in the corner.

Tentacles of insanity oozed from every pore, every extremity of Madeleine's being. Emma felt their icy caress throughout her body. The wicked-looking knife flashed in Madeleine's hand. She looked at it and then at Emma with her mouth curved in a knowing smile.

"As I said, I'll have my fun before I reclaim what's mine tomorrow. You know what that is."

"You're mad."

"I did tell you once that you'll never have him for as long as you lived. I meant it."

A chill went through Emma for she knew what Madeleine was capable of.

"Good stroke of luck that you and Adam had a lover's spat last night. So sad," Madeleine said with mock dejection.

She laughed then—a loud cackle—and Emma had no doubt in her mind that whatever thread of sanity Madeleine had left within her was a very frail one.

Emma fought hard when the men grabbed her by the waist and hands. She fought as though it was her last day to live. But that damned cloth was pressed again to her mouth and the dense chloroform did its job as they sat her down and restrained her.

God help her, for this was the end. Madeleine would finish her, and then go after Adrian. She didn't see a way out.

Adrian, how can I die knowing you hate me?

———

MAX'S MORTAL FRIEND, private investigator Jack Steele, switched off the Range Rover Evoque engine about fifty feet up the road from the target. Adam followed Max, Nathan Hart, and Vivian Cross in a stealthy beeline toward the mansion. Jack stayed behind in the vehicle to provide a quick getaway if needed.

A cream and gold Escalade passed them at an unhurried pace. Hardcore rap blasted inside the car, toned down by the rolled-up windows. Although daylight was a disadvantage, the light was weak and the distracting noise aided them to cross a lawn, headed for a side entrance.

With each step, Adam racked his brain over one thing—why did this area seem so familiar? He'd never been here, as far as he could remember. When he'd sought out Max urgently at *The Versus Club*, he never dreamed they'd end up with spot-on clues so fast. Edward Finley, the librarian, didn't waste time when he told him of his hunch that Emma may be in danger. A pang of envy had descended on Adam after that interaction. He experienced burning shame upon considering how much Emma must mean to these people.

And he'd chased her away.

Finley himself looked very worried and contacted Max—the only lead Adam had—at his emergency number. Finley knew the man and nodded at the mention of his name. When Max came within the hour, he said he'd just made it in from Spain a few days before, and he was lodging at a hotel so Emma could use his townhouse.

Max extended his arm for a handshake. "Nice to meet you, mate. I heard a lot about you," he said.

"Same here." Adam took the hand stiffly, feeling like a tightly coiled spring about ready to pounce. Seeing the man up close roused the dragon inside. Max was a handsome man and he was close to Emma. Adam's dormant possessive nature chafed at the thought and he found himself suppressing the urge to plant a swift uppercut to the man's jaw.

Yet, Max was a godsend. Adam related everything—what happened at the park with the hold up and then his gory dream, careful to omit the details of their falling out. Max quickly processed what Adam had to say and took him seriously. He rushed them both to Valthrean headquarters and called in an emergency. Adam had the chance to meet the brothers Waterstone, and Cam gave him a surreal show like he'd never witnessed before.

The Oracle, as they called him, swore him to secrecy, and made it clear he was there at Max's discretion—and for Emma's sake. Adam was privileged to be allowed such a spectacle. In the end, it all boiled down to Emma.

Emma, the woman he loved. Yes, loved and cared for with surprising intensity. It occurred to him that there was no difference between his dream vision and this woman he'd just met. They were one and the same. He didn't care how fast things were going, or that he couldn't explain why he felt this depth of emotion so soon.

And when he found Emma, he vowed to never let her go.

Cam stood over the chalice for a while, eyes closed, his mind shut off from their world. Then, the energy sparked and Cam started to share what he saw. Within minutes of detailed visions that included place names and road signs, they knew where they had to go. At least, Max did.

"The house belongs to the Cult. It's common knowledge in our inner circle," Max explained. "And I know exactly who has Emma now."

His eyes narrowed and darkened to black. Max had some score to settle, and the person he wanted to get must be in that house. Adam was glad he wasn't the brunt of Max's anger because if he were, he'd be in trouble. Max paged Jack and the others who responded immediately despite the ungodly hour, and together, they headed out by early morning.

And now, they'd arrived. Adam looked up at the imposing structure. The grey stone and arched windows had some age on them but had been beautifully restored. Was Emma inside?

Max picked the lock of a side door and let himself into a dim kitchen. All windows were shut. As they progressed, the place was eerily quiet, as though no one was in. However, they'd seen two cars parked on the driveway and some lights were on in the sun-deprived rooms both downstairs and upstairs when they approached.

Not a soul in the wide hallway with a grand staircase to one side, either. Max motioned Viviane and Nathan to check out the downstairs rooms while Adam and Max climbed the stairs, their footsteps muffled by the carpeted portion in the middle.

Shadows played on the walls from the muted lights bleeding from the top floor. Something seemed off. Adam felt like he was walking in a trap and from what Max had told him, he'd learned Cult people shouldn't be trifled with. The same people were targeting Emma, and Adam would never forgive himself if something happened to her today.

Soon, his gut instinct cried victory. At the landing upstairs, a body in motion came out of nowhere and charged at Max like an angry bull. However, size didn't faze his companion. In a clean move, Max hooked an arm around the giant's neck and twisted it. Adam heard the spine snap before the heavyweight fell limply to the floor. An immortal, the man couldn't die, but the sound chilled him, nonetheless.

Before he could pass a comment on Max's dexterity, another man materialized to deliver a knockout punch to Adam's chin, but Adam circumvented the blow that would have surely knocked all his teeth out.

"I'm going in there!" Max shouted to him, and pointed toward an open door. "You can handle this on your own. The other one won't wake up for a good while."

The beast of a man piled his body on Adam's back, bent him forward, and made to push him toward the stairs. Adam kicked up his knee to a meaty thigh, eliciting a pained grunt, and supplied a solid punch to his skull. Adam's attacker looked like he spent more hours per day at the gym than working. Unlike Max's opponent, however, Adam realized this one was a mere human, so he had to be careful not to inflict permanent damage.

Bouncing with renewed energy, he took advantage of the moment of vulnerability by administering a shoulder punch that sent the man flailing backwards on his arse. Adam grabbed an outstretched leg, put pressure in opposing directions, and heard the knee-cap splinter. The man howled like a banshee.

"I'd check into the hospital if I were you," Adam said as he regained his breath. "A couple of months and you'll be as good as new."

He left the man alone with his agony and retraced Max's steps inside a room to the right. His heartbeat ricocheted in his throat at the sight that met him.

Emma sat bound to a chair with Marie—his estranged wife—standing behind her with a knife at her neck.

"Stay right there or I'll kill her," she spat.

He was about to laugh but the look in Emma's eyes gave him pause. Max stopped him with an outstretched arm to his chest.

"She poured poison on the knife. I saw her do it."

"So—"

"It's the kind of poison that kills, man. Easy now."

Adam felt himself blanch. He wanted to be wrong about Emma facing a threat. Being proved right gave him no satisfaction, no validation. Only a flood of despair.

"Go back where you came from and I won't cut this pretty flower." Marie laughed like a madwoman who'd been in Bedlam too long. "Well, well," she said after a pause. "You two know each other as well. How cozy."

Adam stared at Max who, on his part, stared at Marie like a shark studied potential food. His face tense with bloodlust, Max reared for the right opportunity to strike. *What the hell?* He looked about as mad as she was—only the madness hid behind the surface. If he lost it, things could snowball into a catastrophe.

"Don't go and do something hasty, man," Adam found himself whispering to him. "Emma's life is at stake."

A muscle twitched in Max's jaw, but to Adam's relief, he didn't move an inch.

Just then, a clamor outside the room raised up enough noise to wake the dead. It sounded like brass banging on brass.

Marie started and her attention diverted momentarily to the doorway. Things happened in fast motion from then on.

341

Max sprinted and knocked the knife from her hand. Grabbing Marie in a chokehold, he pressed her to the wall and pulled something from his pocket. After he pushed some mechanism, a syringe came out of the unusual object.

"You should remember we have some unfinished business, Madeleine."

Madeleine? Hearing that name brought to mind what Emma had told Adam at the park...

"Let me ... go ... you ... son of a ... bitch!"

"The bitch would be you," he growled. "Your black soul will die here, alone."

After a minimal pause, he said, "This is for Elise."

In one swift, powerful movement, he thrust the needle home above her breast. He placed his thumb on some button and pressed it, hard.

"And this is for my mother. Feel the blade reach into your heart? That's another dose of death for you."

He twisted the object and rammed the needle in, harder.

"My father. A third load of venom." He pressed the button again.

"And here's one for me."

Finally, he pulled back his weapon and jabbed it in her trachea, where it released the last of the poison before she dropped in a heap.

Shaking off the shock of Max's violent reaction, Adam rushed to Emma and dropped to his knees in front of her.

Madeleine exhaled her last breath as Adam released Emma.

Then—that very moment—a new revelation of boundless tranquility washed over him. The storm was over. He gathered her in his arms.

"Emmaline," he whispered to her.

One word. Her full name popped into his mind, taking him off guard.

Memories, blessed memories, rushed forth.

"Lady de Brandeville is an insignificant nuisance. Why do you fear her?"

"I hate being such a ninny," she groaned.

"Tring, Wing, and Ivinghoe. Three churches all in a row," he quoted as he

pressed his cheek in the softness of her hair and inhaled the scent of the fresh red rose—his daily bequest to her for the past two years—nestled atop her head. "Do not be ashamed to turn to me when you feel this way."

It must have been something in his tone, an unmistakable hint of recognition, that made her move. She raised her head sharply to meet his expression of love—because that was what he felt for this woman.

Love. Pure and absolute.

He'd called her name with a sudden, unflinching *certainty*. She was no longer a chimera to him, no longer the inscrutable wraith that haunted his midnight dreams over the years. She was his reality, his past, his present, and his future, and she was his.

He *saw* her.

He *knew* her.

"Don't ever leave me again," she said, blinking back tears.

Like I left you once before. *"Never, I swear on my father's grave." Could he ever erase his foolish past actions that could have destroyed both their lives? "I want to see you carefree and happy."* The way you fill me with joy and excitement each day.

HE HELD her close now as he had then and ... he remembered. Madeleine was dead—he remembered her now, too, and all the pain she'd caused them all—and the spell had died with her.

At last, more memories came. All of them in a jumble, but some stood out.

He recalled that afternoon in St. Albans, the day she became completely his.

"Come sit with me," he called to her without looking back. ...

That had been the last time he'd held her. The last time...

"...I shall take care of you. I shall make you happy," he said against her temple, his tone suddenly serious.

"I have no doubts. ... But please, tell me, anyway ... tell me that we shall always be like this. That nothing will ever change us or drive us apart. Perhaps some would think we are too privileged and marriages of love exist only in books."

"I could tell you whatever you wish, but words mean nothing if they are not supported with actions."

Overwhelmed, he closed his eyes and sighed. Such a strong promise that he never could keep. So many moments to reclaim.

"Emmaline," he repeated, hoarse with emotion. "It's you…"

He'd give anything to encapsulate this moment; he had found his way home.

"Adrian!"

He caressed her back beneath the curtain of silken ebony hair.

"Welcome back, my love," she cried into the crook of his neck. "I was so scared I'd lost you again!"

"Never," he said with conviction. "I came looking for you to tell you that I love you."

At her sob, he buried his face in her hair and inhaled deeply, crushing her against him in the process. And while doing so, he willed the final pieces of the puzzle to fall into place.

Her eyes sought his.

"We lost too much time," he said.

"And we have eternity to make up for that, don't we?" She smiled.

His lips met hers in a chaste kiss. This time, the elemental knowledge, the new awareness, made the touch that much sweeter, that much more pervaded with longing.

But Max intruded into their special moment. "Get a move on, before the loons wake up. You guys can smooch later," he urged.

Adam pulled back and glared at him.

"Let's go!" Max insisted.

Adam stood and pulled Emma up with him.

"Adrian—"

It would take a while to get used to his old name. He hooked a finger under her chin. "Are you okay?" He swallowed when he noticed a few bloody cuts on her forearm. "She hurt you."

Emma—he'd always preferred that to the more formal Emmaline —looked up at him. "I think she just wanted me to suffer at first. When Max barged in, she took out the poison. I—" She licked her dry lips. "I think she was planning to kill me with it, eventually."

Adam gently guided her out of the room, where Viviane and Nathan stood above a broken vase and a couple of silver salvers that had caused the ruckus. They snuck downstairs where a third male body lay unconscious.

"We took care of him," Viviane said matter-of-factly.

In moments, they were back in the car and making a hasty retreat.

———

BREE RUSHED BACK to the parlor from the adjoining room, taking with her a gaping hole in the center of her chest. A terrible void now fermented inside her, because her mother was no more. How helpless she'd felt that there was nothing she could have done to protect her!

She'd just gotten to know her, to build a relationship with her...

Madeleine had sensed them coming. She'd been the first to hear the faint noises coming from downstairs.

"Go and hide!" She had ordered her. "And don't argue with me."

Bree had rolled her eyes but obeyed. Her last communication with her mother hadn't been a word, but an annoyed groan and huff.

Bree sank down to her knees and pulled Madeleine's head on her lap. She caressed her beautiful hair and traced her face. Her mother had likely saved her life. Now she was gone forever and Bree never got a chance to say goodbye.

They would never talk again. Laugh again. Get take-out food or buy stuff online so Madeleine could express her amazement at modern conveniences.

Or work those cool spells...

Never again.

Gently, Bree removed the locket from around Madeleine's neck and held it for a moment, feeling the shapes and ridges of the delicate carving, before she pulled it on slowly, reverently. She'd always keep it there, close to her heart where it belonged.

"Mum," she whispered as tears fell silently down her face.

She mourned a woman she'd never really known, the woman who'd given her life and had never forgotten about her.

345

"Mum," she sobbed, still holding the locket in a trembling grip. "Whatever it takes, I will avenge your death. Whatever it takes…"

And then, she let the dam loose. Allowed herself some moments of weakness before a fresh layer of ice formed around her heart—a wind slab so strong and hard to make her a hazard to all who dared cross her.

"I'll make you proud, Mum. I won't let them use me."

She'd play the game from a better bargaining position. The best position possible. What had happened to Madeleine—being cooped up in that hellish prison for ages—would not happen to her.

And most of all, after she was through with him, her mother's killer would rue the day he was born.

CHAPTER 17

"Memory, the warder of the brain."
[Macbeth, Act I, Scene VII]

JACK DROPPED EMMA AND ADAM AT THE TOWNHOUSE.

Max practically kicked them out of the car. "You two need to get a room," he said, disgusted.

"You know what I told you about you getting your just desserts one day?" Emma countered with a raised eyebrow.

The vehicle zoomed off. Left alone, they walked up the few steps to the entrance. Emma let her hands float to the door handle and opened it.

"I left in a hurry so I didn't lock." She smiled nervously.

"Are you sure I can come in? I don't want to leave you alone tonight," he asked when she just stood there, staring at him like a goldfish daunted by the world outside its bowl.

Now that the ordeal was over, reality came crashing down on them. Beautiful and terrible at the same time—so much to deal with and absorb. So much to come to terms with. But what mattered was that they were together and that Madeleine was out of their lives.

"Are you crazy? I want you with me." She stepped in first and moved aside to let him in.

Adam pulled the door closed behind him. Emma switched the light on in the living room where they sat down and held hands in silence for a while.

"Do you … is there something going on between you and Max?" he surprised her by saying with a frown, before she had a chance to say anything.

Emma noted the telltale pulse in his jaw. "What if there were?" she answered. "What's it to you?" She wasn't going to make this easy for him. Perhaps she was being unreasonable, but she still flinched when she thought of the way he'd treated her at Hyde Park. Even though he'd had some reason to flip out.

"Emma, I," he paused, as if looking for the right term, "over-reacted."

"You said you never wanted to see me again. Now you know how much that hurt me."

"I didn't mean it," he said. "I shouldn't have let you leave the park alone."

"I'm stupid." She groaned, squeezing his hand. "What am I doing? I'm happier than ever. You're here with me…"

"It's what you went through. You're still under shock," he said with a hand on her cheek. "Where's the booze? You need a drink."

"Trust you to think a shot of something can cure everything," she teased.

"It used to be just beer. I've widened my horizons over time." He winked.

On a deep sigh, she leaned her head on his shoulder. "How did you find me?" she asked softly.

"I had a strange dream. It made me think you were in danger. Then they took pity on me at *The Versus Club*. Either that, or I was very persuasive. Max came to meet me and then I saw Cam and—"

"Hang on for a sec." She frowned. "A dream?"

"Yes."

"Like the one I had when you were hurt in India," she whispered. "I felt sick that time."

"What?"

"I think Madeleine's spell was fast eroding. When something happened to either of us, we somehow knew. We were still connected."

He kissed the top of her head. "I missed you, even before I knew who you were. Who I am. I loved you from the start."

His words knocked the wind from her sails because she'd been waiting to hear them so long. "I missed you, too," she said hoarsely.

"Emma, I have been alone so long and life with Marie—as you know that's what Madeleine called herself then—well, let's just say it was a rough ride. It was hard for me to trust, and I've never met anyone who made me want to. Before you."

She hugged herself and he tucked her closer in his arms. "I still have to process what happened."

"You must know Marie always felt like a stranger. Then there was our meeting in Leith... Yes, I know that was you now," he said, smiling. "Then there are the dreams..."

"Did you have them often?"

"I've had these occasional visions when I go to bed. In them, I see a woman who looks just like you. She talks to me as though she knows me. I always thought someone like that may have been a part of my life. The dreams stopped after I met you."

"It's the blood ties," she said. The puzzle started to make sense to her.

"The blood ritual..."

"Exactly."

His eyes bore into hers. "You gave me back my past because you didn't give up on me. Yesterday, I was too foolish to realize that, too afraid of what I'd find out. I still need you to make me whole, Emma."

"Adrian ... how am I ever to call you Adam? I thought it would be easy but since the park, I—" she stopped and smiled through tears welling in her eyes.

"It's just a name." He grinned. "How hard can it be?"

"Oh, bother." She looped her hands around his neck. "I thought I was going to have to spend Christmas alone this year, too." She sniffed.

"We can take a trip for Christmas, or we can stay here. Whatever you like, as long as I have you all to myself. I feel we need to get away, far from here."

"What about the museum?"

"The refurbishment is still in progress. It will be a while before everything is done. All the exhibits are safe in a bank vault for now."

Emma took advantage of his closeness to fill her senses with him, to savor him.

"Emma." Adam caught her head with both hands and turned her face to him. His eyes told her a thousand stories but mostly, they told her how much he needed her. "There is something else."

"What is that?" she said weakly, praying her legs would hold her up.

"I said that I love you even though for years I haven't been sure what love is. But what else could it have been when I couldn't sleep at night, couldn't think of anything but you when you weren't with me? Since you walked into Derringstone, nothing has made sense without you. I found that I need you just to live—I mean me, Adam, not just the old Adrian."

"You sure know how to charm a lady, my love." She smiled. Craving skin contact, she lifted her cheek to his and rubbed it against the slight stubble of half-day-old beard.

She moved her lips to his and demanded a kiss. He groaned, crushed her to him, and readily gave back. Carried away by the moment, she slid the jacket off his shoulders as his hands traveled up and down her back over her soft jumper. She was still wearing her clothes from the day before, anyway grateful that the kidnappers had thought to put some shoes on her that she'd left lying around before spiriting her away. They did, however, leave her without a coat.

His hands left her so she could remove his jacket, and created a void where his touch strayed from her body. But then his mouth became greedier, hungrier, on hers. She let the garment slide to the floor, while he captured her nape and angled her head to deepen the kiss.

Her mind reeled as he drank fully from her, stroke after stroke, in a meticulous seductive ambush of all her senses. *Touch. Smell. Taste. See. Hear.*

He tasted the side of her mouth with the tip of his tongue. But attuned as they were, Emma sensed his restraint and tipped her head back just long enough to say, "Don't hold back. I *want* you to do this."

He lowered his forehead against hers. "Emma, I want you so much. *God*, I want you. I'm afraid of myself."

"It's okay to want me," she said with sass. "Just don't stop touching me. Remember the last time this happened." And she kissed him again.

Soon, they were standing in her bedroom where horizontal strands of light from the closed blinds filtered on the black and white duvet and suffused throughout the room in a muted glow.

Needing to feel skin against skin, she discarded her top and watched him unbutton his shirt, expose his rippling chest inch by glorious inch. She gasped at the sight of his strong, big, muscular nakedness.

Closing the distance between them, she smoothed her fingers over the taut skin smattered by golden hairs. She pressed her face to his chest, loving the feel of it.

"God, I need a shower," she said in the crook of his neck. "I need to get out of these clothes."

"You will in a second or two," he teased. "Shower comes later." He bent down to kiss her neck and shoulders. "I need you now."

"I love you, Adrian. Only love can ignore the immediate need for a shower." She grinned.

"Adam. Might as well get used to it." He straightened and gave her a look, his eyebrow raised.

She made a face. "I will, I promise. I was getting good at it. This is just a glitch."

"Come closer," he whispered to her.

She leaned into him, feeling his hardness. "Closer than this?"

"Yes," he growled in a low voice. A primitive call to her base instincts.

She pressed into him. He brought his arms around her, unhooked her bra and let it slide to the floor, then pushed her jeans and underwear past the curve of her hips. She kicked her shoes and socks off, and left herself naked and vulnerable to his gaze.

"You are as beautiful as I remember. More so," he said. His awed stare held naked desire.

Locked in a kiss, he inched backward to the bed and lay down on the soft duvet. So perfectly numb with elation was she that she could barely protest when he paused to take the rest of his clothes off.

Returning his attention to her, he tenderly placed a leg on each of his shoulders and kissed the back of her knees and her thighs, before running his hands up the full length of her legs. Shy and self-conscious at first, she quickly gave in to his lavish attention.

"God, yes."

He inched forward and leaned above her. Lifting a breast to his mouth, he feasted on it until she became a boneless bundle of taut nerves. Her whole being was slave to his adroit touch, his strokes, his caresses. Nothing else mattered. Nothing outside this room had meaning.

She wanted him to ravish her but understood why he wanted to take it slow. This time was sacred. This time, it needed to be special.

Memories of her first and only time with Adrian at the hunting lodge, of the words of love he spoke to her that day, flooded her mind. She missed that place dearly, not for its own sake but because of what it represented. They had sealed their union there, truly became one in a marriage that was meant to be. He'd worshipped her, treated her with velvet gloves. And after this horrible night, she needed to feel that love. She wanted that feeling back, and he was giving it to her.

His touch swept over her like a sensual breeze and she let herself go. He reached around to twist her ponytail around his fist and tugged on it gently but firmly before freeing it from its binding. Her head instinctively fell backwards, leaving a wide, creamy expanse of neck and shoulder open to his exclusive exploration.

He devoured, tasted, licked, followed the upward and downward trajectory of her delicate veins, and when he found the juncture where neck met shoulder, he nipped lightly on her flesh, then placed a kiss on that sensitized, scented spot.

"Roses," he said huskily. "I smell the roses."

He found her lips again so their tongues could war and dance, one feeding on the other in perfect rhythm. Then she tunneled her fingers inside the thick waves of his hair to tenderly rub on his scalp.

Adam left her lips to travel down her body. He glided down her stomach to her most private place, slowly driving her out of her mind...

"No!" she resisted. "I need to—"

"You're mine," he interrupted. "You smell of roses and woman, my woman. No masks, no pretense, only you."

His words sunk in, forcing her to surrender. "I'm your man. There's nothing to be ashamed of."

I'm your man. That meant no more secrets. No more holding back. No embarrassment between them.

He kept on working her body to the point of no return. Her muscles felt like stretched violin strings, and her pounding heart threatened to beat out of her chest. She crashed headlong into an incandescent whirlpool of emotion from which she never wanted to escape.

"Ah!"

He indulged on her moist flesh, drank her sweet, musky essence, set out to discover her most intimate secrets and brought her to the brink several times, only to stop her upward climb just moments before she reached her peak. She couldn't take any more of this. He'd set her ablaze and the fire spread so far and wide, it'd be impossible to put out.

"Adam!" she gasped. "Please." She writhed wildly, straining against his touch.

"That's my name. Say my name," he stopped long enough to say.

"Adam."

"Again."

"Adam, please."

Taking her plea this time, he lowered his head to his quavering target. As he placed his lips around her clitoris and sucked on the sensitive nub, she throbbed in his mouth, the raw skin pulsed, and she bucked from the oncoming force of her climax.

He increased the tempo of his caresses until the waves washed over her, drawing out a scream. Her hands fisted in his hair, held him tightly against her as her back arched away from the mattress.

He didn't stop until the last tremor racked her body. Then, he slowed his rhythm to ease her back into the real world, gentled her, gave her time to find her bearings.

In the calm that followed, he started to plant tender kisses up her body. First, at the base of her belly, then, up over her belly button, ribs, and in the valley between her breasts.

He settled between her thighs. Instinctively, she opened her legs to welcome him.

His eyes locked with hers as he entered her with a hard thrust. His lips thinned to a fine line as he visibly struggled to get a grip on himself. His head hung over her face. Golden strands of hair fell forward, damp with sweat.

"Emma," he breathed.

He combed back a few wayward wisps of hair from her face and started to move, slowly, gently.

"I love you," he said, hoarsely, his flesh pulsating inside her. "God help me, I love you."

Their bodies moved together, in rhythm. In his passion, Adam's eyes turned almost as dark as her own. His pupils were dilated. In that amazing moment, she drowned in those perfect pools and the flames roared inside her.

They floated, floated.

Soared, soared.

Higher.

His body stiffened as it prepared to take the plunge with her. She witnessed the rapture on his face seconds before he threw his head back with a mighty groan. Simultaneously, the world exploded in her ears. Spasms of ecstasy wracked her, milked her.

"I love you," he repeated, his face buried in her throat.

"And I love you, Adam, Adrian. I love all of you," she said, certain that she meant every word. She loved *this* Adam as much as, or even more than, the Adrian of the past.

Spent, he rolled over and held her body spoon fashion. "You never answered my question," he spoke into the curtain of her hair.

"Hmm, what question?" she asked drowsily.

"Has there ever been anything between you and Max?"

Her mouth curved into the pillow. "Yes, there is. It's called friendship."

"Only that?"

"Only that."

"Good, because otherwise I'd have to kill him."

She laughed throatily. "You men are something else."

"Hmmm. I mean it." He curved a hand possessively over her hip.

A thought struck her then. "Adam, I'm wondering ... did you happen to be in Belgium during the war? I'm thinking somewhere near Vielsalm, around 1944."

His hand tightened. "How did you know? I was with the Americans. One night, my entire unit was blindsided by the Germans. It was a massacre. I managed to get hold of a jeep we'd parked separate from the other two; for some reason, the Germans had left it there. Can you believe the bastards even took some of the dead soldiers' shoes? They'd got me in the chest and the wound didn't heal for days."

"So it was you..."

She told him of her encounter with the Germans, about James and Mary Jane, and the man she'd seen driving the jeep.

The man that she was sure had been Adam.

"Must have been Fate," he said, tightening his hold on her.

"If it were Fate, the car would have stalled and we'd have met that day..."

He shushed her. "Don't do that. It's over now."

Emma snuggled into him.

As his body relaxed behind hers, Emma basked in contentment. She heard only the sound of Adam's even breathing as sleep claimed him.

This reunion was everything her life so far had been about. All she had done, all the places she'd visited or lived in, all the decisions she'd made, all of the situations she experienced, had led to this one moment. She'd done it all for him.

To be with him.

To find him and make him remember what they once had and still had—what they always would have if Fate permitted.

Thanking Fate for this ultimate gift, she joined him in deep, care-free slumber.

———

EMMA'S PERFUME drifted to Adam's nostrils and roused him from sleep. The rich floral tones drilled deep into his memory, too alluring, and her body too supple in his arms, for him to resist shifting closer. He lazily explored her with eager hands, meandered over her ribs, waist, hips, the curve of her back. She stirred and rolled around to face him.

"Hello," she smiled sleepily.

He covered her hand with his between them on the pillow. He had never felt so loved, so cherished, so replete.

"I can't stand that I couldn't remember you," he whispered. "I remembered nothing of our life together, not even a moment."

"Forget the past, Adam," she said, and brought his hand to her lips.

The look in Emma's eyes may have meant that she understood his feelings, but she couldn't, not exactly. Her memories, unlike his own, were as intact and pure and untouched as those entering the mind of a well-loved, newborn baby.

"Thank you for not giving up, for coming back and looking like a vision out of my dreams."

Adam's head reeled. Emma held the answers—she was the key to his universe—and to finally own those answers had shifted his world on its axis. Deep down, his emotions twisted tighter than a Gordian knot.

Adam surrendered to the impulse to caress her face. Her eyes were dark repositories of concentrated emotion. "I wanted to remember, Emma. I just didn't know how to fix it. You sought me out, but I did nothing at all."

She leaned up into his palm that was now cupping her cheek. "You remember those red roses you used to give me?" He nodded. "Each day a fresh one. It taught me that we must look at the here and now, and toward our future. We can't keep mourning what has been, or we'll never change things."

"If Madeleine's magic was so powerful, how did you manage to get close to me?"

"Wait here," Emma said. She switched her bedside lamp and swung off the bed, completely confident in her nakedness. Adam watched, fascinated, as she opened a closet door and slid out a sort of hat box that was stored at the bottom. From it, she pulled an object and brought it to the bed, where she joined him under the sheets.

She placed the object between them, on top of the duvet, and crossed her legs.

Adam sat up to take a closer look. It was a cup that seemed to be chiseled from rock into its concave shape. It looked like...

"How did you get that? Cam has one and Marie—"

"Madeleine, but I understand that for you she's always been Marie. Yes, this was hers. There's more than one and the organization she works for wants them all. Back then, a woman who once knew her helped me come to a decision about where you may have been taken, so I paid a visit to Scotland. However, you were already gone. I've had this ever since."

"I saw it once in Marie's stillroom. She went in a rage because nobody was allowed in her private space, not even I."

Emma clutched the edge of the cup until her knuckles turned white. "Madeleine de Brandeville was a cold, calculating witch, in the true sense of the word. Even I couldn't recall the details for years. My memory loss was Madeleine's doing as well."

NATALIE G. OWENS

She shared what she knew of Madeleine's scheme, including her accomplice Smith's infiltration in the Belvoir household and the forged letter.

"My mother..." Adam said, pain and loss washing over him.

"She was devastated beyond words," Emma said softly. "But she died helping others. You'd have been proud of her."

"Madeleine didn't care how many lives she crushed." Adam closed his eyes briefly to quell the urge to punch a wall.

Emma gripped the counterpane in a crushing vise. "She even *married* you."

He searched her face. "You must know she never meant anything to me," he assured her, aching to take the pain away. "Really and truly, we were only husband and wife on paper. Never for a moment did I feel I belonged with her."

"But at the park—"

"I didn't know what I was saying. I hurt you abominably, and I'll always regret that."

She swallowed hard and nodded.

"Thank you for saying that." Her voice faltered. She moistened her lips, gearing to continue her story—to tell him what she'd been through for his sake.

Adam watched her as she spoke, careful not to betray how unsettled she made him feel with her accounting of those days. He could see that introspection injected her eyes with a melancholic, faraway look, and a river of tears freely streaked her cheeks.

He caught her trembling chin between thumb and forefinger. "Tell me, what's really hurting?"

"It's just that ... it took me ten years to realize the extent of Madeleine's foul play and decide to do something about it. When I got to Scotland, I despaired. You had vanished like a ghost. Then I lost you again at Leith, but I did find this at Madeleine's home, whatever good it did me."

She indicated the chalice.

"Madeleine's magic was too strong at first. The most challenging thing was not knowing what name you went by, not knowing *who* to look for. If it wasn't for the help I received from other Valthreans, I may never have found you."

He trailed his hand down her arm to link their fingers. "One night, I had a heart attack. She had heavily laced my whiskey with one of her potions, to keep me under her thumb." He apprised her of his life with Marie, of the physical and mental challenges he had to face because of her meddling. "I had no reason to stay when I got better. I was ready to seek freedom."

Emma's face registered shock. "You had a heart attack?"

"If I wasn't who I am, I am certain I would have died."

"Wait, when did this happen again?"

"The night Marie left."

Emma's memory stirred. "There was one strange night. I woke up sweating and gasping for breath. And there was this huge pain in my chest. The timing sounds right."

Her face lit up. "That confirms my suspicions, and may explain why I got so close to you in Leith! Madeleine's barrier was only strong as long as we were both alive and well. What happened to you must have affected me, too, and put a crack in the spell."

"Then there's the incident in India," he said thoughtfully.

"The last nail," she agreed, while she remembered her bad spell in Sicily. A strange event that had its place in the scheme of things. "There is so much more I wish to tell you. So much more I want to know," she said in the softest of voices.

Adam was starting to understand why he'd felt what he felt when he was around Emma. This woman had been his once, and he'd sensed that.

You're in my blood, Emma.

Overwhelmed, he pulled her around the chalice and crushed her to him, then kissed her, long and deep. He looked pointedly at the cup, now in front of them. "Let's do it again," he said, looking down at her with boundless love. "Just like we did then but as who we are now … over this chalice."

"Sure?" she asked.

"Filling this gaping hole in my life is all I ever wanted. I can't express how it feels to look at your face and *know* you." He'd never been more determined. "Let's do this now. I lost you once, and I sure as heck won't lose you again. You're mine forever," he said fiercely.

"Forever..."

Emma was beauty personified with her expressive eyes and smooth skin, framed by long, shiny locks. She didn't have to explain the ritual. He remembered every word, every glance they'd shared on that beautiful winter day at the hunting lodge on the Bournemouthe estate. One of the most amazing days of his life that now took a special place in his memory bank.

"Hang on." Reaching over to the nightstand, he picked up a rose from a vase by her bedside.

"Good that you have a supply of these," he said, drawing a smile from her.

Happy beyond belief, Adam lifted the rose over the chalice without breaking eye contact.

"I'll start."

Emma presented her hand to him, palm upwards. "Straight across the palm. Our blood must bathe the rose when it's in the cup."

"Yes," he said, remembering how hesitant he'd been the first time.

You're in my blood.

You're my blood. Mine always.

He made a decisive cut across Emma's yielding flesh before he pierced his own, quickly and efficiently.

Their life source flowed freely as they bonded in the same ritual that had already once united their spirits. Adam placed the rose in the chalice and slightly repositioned their joined hands directly above it to allow the blood to trickle into the waiting crimson petal folds.

Emma spoke first this time around, like an echo of times past. Her voice was like velvet stroking pliant skin.

"Adam Derringstone, from this day forward, as the Universe is my witness, I pledge my heart, body, and soul in eternal love to you. Till the end of time, I shall belong to you as your wife."

Adam spoke his vows next.

Drip. Drip. Drip.

Their mingled lifesource made its way down the crevice between their molded palms, and gravitated toward its final resting place. Energy sparked and flowed through them, around them. The sudden rush that touching her brought him held a cadence of such force and speed, it would beat a parched cheetah in a race to a bubbling stream. It would reach the earth faster than the sun's rays or the coarse gust of a northwest wind.

Adam was the first to feel the pain. It shot through him like a fever, a psychic force that built in his head, a tiny speck of scalding matter burgeoning into a crater riddled with licking, fumigating flames. When its galvanizing heat hit his bloodstream like intense radiation, the world around him seemed to move in slow motion.

He held on tight to her, his grasp steadfast, and sensed a parallel battle raging inside Emma. She emitted a muffled cry against his mouth and clung to him. Her mouth twisted as the sharp voltage of pain injected each sinew of her body.

Within seconds, as suddenly as it had come, the frenzied energy flowing in and around them abated, followed by a new revelation of boundless tranquility. Their flesh was still joined, but the storm was over. The odor of drying blood permeated the air, a not unpleasant herald to the peace that prevailed.

"Emma," he gasped against her lips. "Come closer. Wrap your legs around me." He moved to kneel and rest on his haunches so she could sit across his thighs and cross her legs behind his back. Like the most cherished of lovers, he held her to his heart and rocked her. The tender gesture was both electric and soothing.

Reaching into the cup, he picked up the rose, broke the petals from the stem, and showered them both with a feathery-soft, fragrant rain that peppered her midnight hair with bursts of red.

One petal settled on her shoulder and he blew it away delicately to make space for his lips.

He sensed her moan, more than heard it.

Her arms wound around his neck, he lifted her slightly and settled her on top of him. "I will never let you out of my sight from now on," he rasped as he surged up inside her moist folds.

She moved over him, swallowing him whole. Her pupils dilated more with every sensual gyration of her feminine hips. This joining was soft and slow and earth shattering, inspired by a passion lost and found, a destiny crumbled and rediscovered. Adam caught her waist with firm hands to guide her into a perfect rhythm.

Rising on his knees, he shifted their position and swung her smoothly backwards on the bed where her hair plummeted in a thick bundle onto the mattress. They were still joined, their sex connected, her thighs hugging his waist.

Adam continued measured thrusts inside her, unhurried but unyielding. He wanted to take his time driving them both over the edge. But the best laid plans often go awry. Pushing frantically upward and begging him to go faster, she engulfed him with shameless greed, and that brought him to near breaking point. Finally giving in, he hastened his strokes and she opened further to him, provided him with more welcoming heat.

Too soon, his body strummed the first chords of a mind-blowing orgasm. Her head fell back as a rumble of pleasure rose from her throat. Both teetered at the edge of the precipice.

Waiting to fall.

And finally, they jumped right into the eye of a whirlwind of pleasure and let themselves be swept away, she preceding him by a mere second or two.

His senses plunged into a void; then, peace settled as they both descended from their journey to the stars.

He gathered her in his arms and kissed her tenderly on the forehead.

Later, ensconced in the warmth of the thick blanket and settled comfortably on the pillows, he whispered to her. "Emma Deramore, from this day forward, I promise you an eternity of roses."

A lazy smile tugged at her lips. "I can't wait, love."

An eternity together. An eternity of roses.

A deep, restful sleep claimed them both because all was well.

Everything was as it should be.

362

EPILOGUE

"I bear a charmed life."
[Macbeth, Act V, Scene VIII]

ONE YEAR LATER...

"THIS WAS A FANTASTIC IDEA, DARLING," Emma beamed.

The Demon's Chalice stared back at them from its place of honor inside a glass case in the top secret extension to the Occult Room at the Derringstone Museum of Oddities. The tag said:

"The Demon's Chalice. Reputed to grant its bearer with the gift of immortal life. Legend has it that its powers were used to first separate and then re-unite a pair of lovers within the span of two centuries.

Source: Unknown."

"NICE TOUCH," she added.

Next to the chalice, in a separate case, lay the Book of Magic, which Adam had brought with him from the Kashmir. Below it, on a plate, was inscribed a dedication to his lost colleague, Abid. The translation of the book was taking much longer than anticipated and wasn't yet complete. However, they were expecting it to be finalized in the coming weeks.

This section of the museum would never be open to the general public. The room was to be kept private and secure—accessible only to select Council members. The chalice, after all, belonged to the Council, and it was about time Emma surrendered it to them. Surprisingly, they'd cordially suggested that Adam and Emma keep it here and make Derringstone one of the organization's satellite operation points.

They had, however, worked hard to establish the Occult Room, a permanent exhibit for the general public, which was scheduled to launch in a few days, about a week before Christmas day. In the meantime, they were busy meeting with interested parties, discussing the donation of interesting artifacts that would very soon find a home in this space.

To free up time and focus on growing the business, they hired an Acquisitions Manager to find leads and take care of all the pesky day-to-day tasks. The new recruit, who happened to be Max's friend, Viviane Cross, had an impressive knowledge of history and politics, but her most interesting gift was that she could charm the clothes off of a pauper. A woman with a shady background they never pressed her to share, she had an amazing knack for blending in any crowd, whatever the social standing. Furthermore, a Sandals resort would open doors in Antarctica before anyone managed to fool the resourceful Miss Cross. In short, she had all the requisites for the job and they went along wonderfully.

Emma was so proud of her husband's enterprising spirit—a talent he always had. He was the one who came up with the idea to make this addition to the museum. It would draw lots of visitors this season. Especially because she'd taken charge of the Christmas decorations this year and the place looked so much more attractive, bright and cheerful—with the exception of this room and the Medical Room, where the lights were left dim and dark. There, heavily-paneled walls in an expensive mahogany oak finish added to the overall effect of gloom and foreboding. But all that was part of the intended ambiance, of course.

A thought came to her. "Wouldn't it be something if we had *The Bite of the Cobra* in our private collection? Max's syringe device would make the collection complete, wouldn't you say?"

"Perhaps one day Max will consider leaving it in the private room."

Adam was still jealous of her friendship with Max. He was jealous of anything in her past he was not a part of. However, after he'd ascertained that Max had no designs on her, the two men got decidedly less wary around each other. Emma was overjoyed at how easily their friendship started to blossom; both had in common that they'd lived without a family for far too long.

Standing tall behind her, Adam wrapped his arms around her and dropped a quick kiss on her ear. His fingers toyed delicately with the red rose that she'd pinned to the ruched cream chiffon sash circling her waist. It stood out as the perfect complement to an otherwise simple, retro style black dress.

"How about a nightcap?" he suggested meaningfully.

She turned in his embrace and gave him a peck on the cheek. "Why, do you intend to seduce me?"

"Minx," he murmured, using her favorite endearment. "If I wanted to seduce you, all I'd have to do is this."

He licked her earlobe.

"And this."

He nibbled on it teasingly.

"And perhaps this."

He languidly trailed a path down her neck with his tongue.

"I think ... ah ... you should stop that. Hawkins is on his way to the sitting room with my lemon scones. I swear, those things are irresistible. I tried to bribe Martha for the recipe but she refuses to disclose her family secret," she rambled on.

With his hands, he journeyed to the curve of her bottom and squeezed, pulling her into him. She gasped. "I'm ordering ... a large batch ... for the Christmas party...." He pressed into her, showed her how much he wanted her. "...next week ... oh!"

He traced her spine; his lips moved farther down to her shoulder. "Hmmm, you're the perfect hostess."

"Yes, darling. Keep doing that."

"This?"

He suckled on the exposed skin at the bend with her shoulder.

"Adam..."

"I think you're right, baby. We better stop." With a laugh, he kissed her nose and gave her a playful pat on the bottom when she gave him her most intimidating glare.

"How can you be so cruel?" she objected.

"I'll make it up to you later. I promise," he murmured. Her body shivered in anticipation.

Adam took her hand and looked at her affectionately. Everywhere around them were small but elegant feminine touches. "You've been a busy bee."

"Of course, I must be worthy of the Derringstone name. After all," she lowered her voice conspiratorially, "you *are* a viscount, my love, even though I'm the only one who knows that."

"I think we ought to return to the salon, love." He chuckled. "A warm fire's burning and I think I hear the blokes across the street playing *Chestnuts roasting over the Open Fire*."

It was her favorite Christmas song this year.

"Good that you remind me. I ought to tell Hawkins to return my iPod. I bought him one as a gift, anyway. Perhaps it will encourage him to stop pilfering my stuff," she joked. Indeed, the man hadn't stopped since she'd moved in ten months earlier as Adam's wife.

Her husband threw his head back in laughter. "He can't resist the new technologies, he says. You drive him nuts with your gadgets."

Emma sighed in contentment. The wedding had been such a beautiful ceremony, too. Just them, Max, Martha, and Hawkins in the parlor. Adam had pulled some strings, and the registrar had given special approval to officiate the ceremony there in front of the witnesses and the two hundred and five red roses divided in twenty vases and placed on various surfaces.

The perfect wedding. The joining of two healed hearts.

"By the way," he said as they turned toward the door. "Do you want to ask Max about *The Bite of the Cobra*, or shall I?"

Emma thought of Max and the demons he had to face, the ghosts that haunted him. Life was apt to hold more battles in store for him. She'd always be grateful for his help and vowed to do what she could to support him.

"Now that I think about it, I believe we better let sleeping dogs lie."

At the start of the year, the high ranks of the Council would hold a meeting at the Derringstone Museum. Per Max's suggestion and Adam's consent, the venue would provide adequate camouflage for regular top secret meetings, where new investigative and conflict strategies to counter the growing threat of the Cult of the Snake would be discussed.

At last, she would get to meet the mystery figures whose responsibility it was to ensure the continued survival of the Valthrean race. She couldn't get past that Adam had already made their acquaintance, but she couldn't protest that. She owed a lot to Cam Waterstone and she wanted to thank him in person.

There were many ways in which they could give back to the Valthrean Council. For one, Max had a lot of responsibility coming on his shoulders. Emma and Adam offering their premises as focal point for the organization was only their first contribution.

Unfortunately, Max's theory was proving true. In the past year, there had been four suspicious Valthrean deaths in England alone. Just last week, a British MP—and a Valthrean—was found dead in his home. The man had been instrumental in putting an important drug lord behind bars for life, and just before his murder, he was spearheading an investigation into what could possibly be the largest child pornography ring in British history. The circumstances of his death were kept hidden from the media, and it had been ruled a suicide. But, those in the know knew better.

Furthermore, she'd just found out that although the Council had retrieved the chalice at Madeleine's house, another two of the six Valthrean-owned chalices had been taken over by the Cult ... or perhaps someone else? If the former was the case, the Cult now had three chalices and would clearly aim for the rest. If, on the other hand, the nature of the crime was an opportunistic one by a third party, they were none the wiser. But then, who else would know about the Demon's Chalice? The thought was unnerving. This called for more security as an invisible enemy was the most dangerous kind.

Emma feared for Max's safety.

But that thought flew from her mind when Adam gave her a hard kiss on the lips. Had she ever been this happy?

Yes, you have.

When she had had him first. When they shared the air in a room. Any time he was there to love her.

Yet, she may be happier now because she loved this Adam more. This very Adam, who had saved her life even before he remembered who she was and what she'd meant to him.

She leaned into her husband as they made their way out of the Occult Room in companionable silence. All that she needed was within reach.

All that she wanted—an eternity of Adam's roses.

———

FROM ITS RESTING place in the shadows of its glass case, the Demon's Chalice watched them leave. As silence returned to the room, it glowed and rattled, feeding off the energy field around it.

Because it knew. It saw everything.

The writing was on the wall.

The beginning of the end was starting.

A LIFETIME OF REVENGE: The Valthreans, Book 2

Keeping it simple doesn't always work out so well...

After exacting his longed-for revenge, Massimiliano "Max" Damiani's life is about to get more complicated when he is sent by the Valthrean Council to investigate the mysterious death of one of their Councilmen. Duty bound to protect the victim's daughter and her young brother, the stakes are upped as Max and those around him become targets of a dangerous enemy. The Cult is closing in, threatening the future of their kind.

Fate is a cruel mistress...

Piper Ingram's existence is thrust into turbulent waters. Her father has been murdered in cold blood and she is now sole guardian to her little brother, Charlie. After years of helping others come to terms with their problems and move on to better lives in a domestic violence shelter, she now needs help protecting herself and her kin.

Salvation comes when we face our deepest fears...

Max values his independence above anything. Meanwhile, this case brings him more trouble than he's bargained for, pushing his limits, and testing his fear of commitment. While striving to keep his personal demons at bay and holding on to his set ways, he fights his attraction to Piper, but he fast learns some things are not within his control. Will he save those entrusted in his care this time? And most importantly, will he finally find redemption ... and love?

Get it here: http://www.nataliegowensauthor.com/the-valthreans/

***

MOONLIGHT LOVE MATCH SERIES:

One night. Two perfect strangers. A little happenstance.

Melita Saari-Quinn is living the consequences of a traumatizing psychic event that turned her adolescence upside down. Now, disillusioned with her job as a psychotherapist and desiring a change from her lacklustre existence, she hopes that something out of her ordinary sphere of existence–something totally uninhibited and spontaneous–will renew her zest for life.

Alex Moncado seems to have it all–good looks, a successful business, and a fun life in the "party central" of the Mediterranean: the island of Malta. Except for one day in the year when he can't help but remember a tragedy that never should have been. One day he'd rather forget, because if he doesn't, the guilt will consume him.

Can one passionate night together banish the ghosts of the past and give two lost souls a second chance?

More…

https://www.nataliegowensauthor.com/moonlight-love-match/

ACKNOWLEDGMENTS

To my beloved family, thank you for the support.

To Sadiqullah Khan, a new friend and gifted poet, thank you for allowing me to use your beautiful words. They dance off the page with a special kind of magic.

To my editing, design, and formatting team—Zee Monodee, Monica La Porta—I offer a million thanks and then some. I couldn't do this without you!

Finally, thanks to my beta readers, Dr. Gioconda Schembri and Dr. Sandra Scicluna, who gifted me with their invaluable insight.

ABOUT THE AUTHOR

Natalie is a Harlequin's 'So You Think You Can Write' contest finalist and an Amazon Breakthrough Novel Award quarter-finalist. A USA Today bestselling author, she has always had a thing for Gothic literature, pulse-pounding romances, and exciting stories steeped in mystery, adventure, intrigue, action and suspense. In her stories, fearless heroines and strong heroes find their way in a world sizzling with magic and danger.

When she's not writing, she loves quality time with her family and nurses an unquenchable thirst for reading, traveling, buying bold jewelry, ogling shoe store displays, and exploring different cuisines. She also loves to meet and communicate with other authors and readers.

Keep up with Natalie's latest news here: http://eepurl.com/povjf

Website: www.nataliegowensauthor.com